GAL

# Oi, Ref!

## A Novel About Love, Hate and Football

JOSEPH GALLIVAN

Copyright © 1997 Joseph Gallivan

First published in Great Britain in 1997 by Hodder and Stoughton
A division of Hodder Headline PLC
A Sceptre book

10 9 8 7 6 5 4 3 2 1

British Library Cataloguing in Publication Data

A CIP catalogue record for this book is available
from the British Library

ISBN 0 340 70772 0

Typeset by Palimpsest Book Production Limited,
Polmont, Stirlingshire
Printed and bound in Great Britain by
Mackays of Chatham PLC, Chatham, Kent

Hodder and Stoughton
A division of Hodder Headline PLC
338 Euston Road
London NW1 3BH

# Characters

Tommy Burns – ref & GP
Father Mark O'Mally – priest/mate
Melissa – Tommy's bird, a junior school teacher
Father Kelly – old parish priest
Mrs Dolores O'Connor – housekeeper
Fiona – her friend
Kevin Brownlow – man in wheelchair
Fat Paul – fat cockney bastard
Nick York – Fiona's boyf
Nick Plumage – the Man United Poet
Nick Felcher – radio journalist
Carol – Williams Syndrome girl
Jamie – fuckin' Tretts boy
Darren Coates – dead biker
E. Proctor – linesman
Henry Miller – rated ref
Ian Lockhart – English FA refs' sec
Jim Mitchell – Scottish FA Chief Executive
Dr Aktar – Tommy's colleague
Carol – moaning patient
Mrs Thorpe – old bag in Tommy's basement
Colin Marsh – previous English FA refs' sec
Craig – the personal trainer

# 1

## You Wankah!

'Oi! Ref!' A fat red face with squeezed cockney eyes was looking at Tommy Burns when he turned to see who was calling him. 'You *wankah!*' shouted the cockney, with a mouth full of food. He had his face pushed through the small ventilation window of the train on the opposite track, and his voice cut though the diesel drone of the railway station. 'You facking wankah ref, you *cant*, you facking *cant!*' Tommy moved closer to the window of his own train and looked back at the creature, who was only about fifteen feet away, impassive. He slid his own window open a little further and watched.

'You're gonna die, you *cant*, next time you're down West Ham you're gonna fackin' die!'

The creature in claret and blue was trying to get his whole fat head out of the window, and his body was heaving up against the glass in the excitement. Other faces popped out of windows along the train and the clamour grew. Tommy pushed his own face out of the window and stared as deep into the piggy eyes as the puffy fat allowed. Other Hammers fans had spotted him on the opposite track, and two of them hopped off the train and sprinted towards the bridge that crossed the line. Tommy's heart quickened, knowing they were coming after him. He looked at the angry face a moment longer. Then he finally showed emotion. He smiled and began to sing, loud and resonant across the tracks.

> *'You ate all the pies,*
> *You ate all the pies,*
> *You fat bastard,*

*You fat bastard,*
*You ate all the pies!'*

The tune was 'Knees Up Mother Brown', and it climbed and fell again
in just the right place to get the adrenalin surging through Tommy's
bloodstream. He sang again.

'*You ate all the pies,*
*You ate all the pies,*
*You fat bastard,*
*You fat bastard,*
*You ate all the pies!'*

this time putting more venom in the *fat bastard* and more gaiety into the
rest of it. The lone song rang round the station like a credo in a cathedral,
drowning the cockney in shame and making him hammer all the harder
on the glass. He had finished spraying pie on the tracks and the veins in
his neck were bulging, but Tommy kept on smiling. The two West Ham
fans had only just reached the top of the down steps when both guards'
whistles blew and the trains began to slip smoothly out of the station. As
both trains began to pull away, Tommy mimed a careful last 'Fuck off' at
his adversary, and turned back to face his compartment.

Through the other window, however, Tommy could see the two fans
– a great hulking brute and a sprinting chunk – chasing his train, trying
to get on and sort him out, just as they'd promised as they ran screaming
through the station. A pang of fear ran through Tommy on top of the
juice – *these fuckers could be with me until Crewe*, he thought. As his carriage
picked up speed, the sound of their trainers on the concrete grew faster
and more desperate, and the short one was just feet from the door handle
and running at full pelt, when ... *whack!* he was taken out. He bounced
sideways into the path of the brute, who tripped mightily and sprawled
over him. A middle-aged woman waving her daughter off had caught the
full impact of Shorty in the back, and was herself thrown on her arse on
the ground. The daughter's cries were lost in the open air and the noise
as her carriage left the station. Meanwhile, the fat cockney was carried off
by his own train in the other direction, leaving his fellow soldiers stranded
in a bundle on the wrong side of the tracks.

'Fucking cockneys,' Tommy Burns muttered to himself through a smile.
'Thick bastards.' He was relieved they hadn't got on. Stepping into first

class and sliding the door behind him, he stared back at the man in the suit and tie in his carriage. He had watched the whole incident with wide eyes, but his mouth remained a tight line of disgust, showing no fear.

'I said I'm fucking glad those bastards never made it,' said Tommy, as though he were talking to a deaf old man. 'Otherwise the only thing left of me by Crewe would be a hank of hair and an Adidas bag. Eh, mate?' The businessman ratcheted up his disgusted look, then hid his gaze deeper in his magazine. *That shut you up. What are you doing out on a Saturday evening anyway, businessman?* Tommy wondered, but didn't ask.

He sat down with his bag on the seat next to him and his raincoat on as the train rushed south into the dark. As the thrill dissolved and calm returned to his weary body, Tommy stared at the glass, sometimes at the reflection of his travelling partner and the bleak British Rail fittings, sometimes out at the evening lights of small, nothing towns. After twenty minutes he stirred, getting up to put his bag in the rack but keeping his coat on for warmth. He fished in his pocket for the match programme, which he had bought from some incomprehensible old northerner before the game.

Tommy Burns was a referee. Aged thirty-four, he was the youngest in his field, and, many thought (including himself), one of the best. He was even younger than some of the footballers he now reffed for – the veterans and the journeymen, the centre-halves and midfielders who somehow managed to squeeze another season out of their tired bones. At thirty-four, no footballer with ambitions to be a manager would be anywhere near Premier League level, as he was. He went further. He was FIFA, eligible for European games and internationals. Tommy was proud of himself, and when the fear subsided, was rather pleased that the squeeze-eyed cockney had recognised him. He enjoyed a speculation: *maybe that fat bastard was the Hammers' brains? Their commanding officer? Or maybe he just had a good memory for someone he hated?* Tommy had an idea of what he had done to displease him and his mates – given a late penalty against West Ham in the League Cup four years before, one that might have looked like a close call from the Chicken Run – but since he didn't feel any guilt, he didn't search too hard in his memory. *These fucking London teams,* he thought. *They're always howling for penalties and seeing bad judgment where there is none. Fucking howling cockneys in their poxy half-empty grounds. One thing about fans from everywhere else in the country, they know when to put up and shut up. Fucking cockneys, though. Lippy bastards. And their players.*

He looked over at the businessman, who looked away. 'Going to

London?' he asked. The man said nothing, trying to appear intent on reading his magazine.

'Huh,' went Tommy loudly. *I don't have the energy for this now*, he told himself. *Fucking programme's shit. Match day sponsors – Viking Glass of Leeds. The officials are Dr T. Burns of Birmingham, J. Wood of Macclesfield, and E. Anderson of Liverpool.* The heater had finally started working, blowing hot on his heels, and he put the programme between his head and the cold glass for a minute to doze.

He awoke with a shudder two hundred miles later, his mouth full of sour glue and his contact lenses like cornflakes in his eyes. He watched north London stream by – the drab mixture of container bases and service outlets. Apart from the brief thrill of Wembley stadium, lit up for the dogs, nothing impressive, nothing inspiring. Ranks of dull shops and council houses, then patches of Barratt homes and lethal parks. *Who built this shit?* he wondered for the fiftieth time. *And who are these morons who live here, more to the point.* He saw his first black people for hours – two fly girls walking down a street dressed in hot pants and fur jackets, eating chips. *Funny fashions they have down here. You always know it's London when you see your first funny street fashion. They're up to something, the cockneys. They're always on to something new.*

Even when Tommy had only been away for a few hours he had that feeling. When he came back from holidays and saw it in the suburbs of Slough or Hounslow or Ealing it was almost overwhelming. Then he would vow to treat the cockneys differently, appreciate them more, and it usually lasted until the first evening out, and the first few drinks, and then it would all be back to normal. *You di-rty cock-ney bassssstards.* Tommy's spirits lifted as the train rattled slowly through Camden Town, between the great banks of smutty white flats. He could never shake off the initial thrill of his first visit to London as a kid, that this was the metropolis, and all who lived here were blessed to live there.

At Euston, doors up and down the train opened, letting warm air out into the cool night, and the people who just *had* to be first hit the ground running. Tommy waited, and walked slowly up the platform, just a man in a raincoat with an Adidas bag. He was sore from running, and wanted to get home. The clock on the monitor read 23:43. The trains had been all over the place that day. From Leeds to Euston via Crewe. He didn't bother about the route much any more, so long as it didn't knock him off schedule by hours rather than minutes. *Those West Ham won't be at Euston*, he reassured himself. *Who were they playing again? Some lesser Lancastrians, Bolton or Rochdale. They'll end up at King's Cross, then find their way back to Mile End or Grange*

*Hill or wherever it is they come from. Isle ov Dogs. One thing you can depend on is the blokes who put the trains together. They'll always try and keep the animals apart.*

There were indeed no West Ham, or no anyone else on the platform. Although the programme said he was from Birmingham, it didn't say he had to train it all the way to Leeds from London, and face the wrath of whatever football fans crossed his path. *They don't print that in the fucking programme,* he thought. *I should be getting danger money.* He walked across the concourse and headed down the escalators to the Tube. *What about a load of pie-faced Geordies roaming the station after a piss-up in Soho?* he wondered. *Naw. Geordies go to King's Cross too.* He put his pass through the machine and made his way down to the platform. The only people around were normal people. No one who would want to push him under a train. He stood with his back to the wall anyway.

Sleep came quickly to Melissa, always, whenever she hit the hay, and she barely stirred as Tommy let himself into their flat. He put his bag on a chair and sat down in the living room, with the light off. He switched the telly on and quickly reduced the sound several notches. *The London Match,* as ITV called their football programme, was just wrapping up. Tottenham as usual. The presenter nodded goodnight, and the credits rolled over video of a player rounding the goalie and sliding the ball into the empty net, thus shaking the camera which was rooted in the far corner. The ref was just visible in his black kit, already turning, already whistling, already with his hand in the air. Another camera following up caught the player's nervous look morphing into a giant grin, the scene froze, and the rousing synthesiser music played out. Tommy knocked it off and went into the kitchen, opened the fridge and took a long draught from the carton of milk. He hoped the light wouldn't wake Melissa, and it didn't. He got ready for bed, then slipped his tired limbs under the quilt and fitted in behind her.

There was no moon that night, and no stars. Saturday blended into Sunday, and the only people that saw it happen were the waitresses, bouncers and cab drivers, and the kind of police that have to announce the pulping of young ravers to just-roused and fluffy-haired parents. Tommy Burns slept well, however, with Melissa at his hip.

Nine-thirty the next morning and the phone was going like a bastard. *Who the fuck is this?* thought Tommy, waking, as it warbled. *They're not giving up, are they?* It continued, nag-nag, nag-nag . . .

'Melissa?' he shouted. *Shit*, she was in the shower and couldn't hear anything. He rolled across the bed and let his weight drag him out over the edge, then began crawling through the cool air towards the living room. The phone's nag-nagging was hurting his head, overloading his delicate hearing with bloody surges down his inner ear. This is what he called a ref's hangover. The previous day's exertions – running eight miles, making decisions in front of thirty-five thousand baying men and almost being kicked to fuck by crazed cockneys – had caught up with him. He heard the droning of the shower stop. He hadn't touched a beer all night, but the same weariness and the confusion were there, as though his brain had been bathed too long in the wrong sort of chemical. His eyes were sore, the day was too bright. He heard the bathroom door open and Melissa's bare feet padding on the hardwood floor of the hall. At last the nagging stopped, replaced by Melissa's soft 'Hello?' Pause.

'No, he's still sleeping.' Pause. 'No.' Pause. 'I don't know.' Pause. 'No, I don't.'

Tommy crawled round the corner into the living room and stopped at his girlfriend's feet, looking up at her nakedness. She was dripping water on the carpet, holding her towel by her side instead of trying to cover herself, or dry herself, like every other woman he had known would. Someone on the other end was talking a lot. *Some bastard has a lot to say on a Sunday morning.* The thought exhausted him and he slumped back on the floor, his head on the carpet, near her feet. Without even trying, he could take in the sweeping lines of her thighs as they rose up above him. Her large patch of wet pubic hair. The soft crater of her belly button. The round undersides of her breasts – all the bits so beautiful, so carefully formed, which no one ever got a good look at, even Melissa. The smooth underside of her chin which he loved to stroke, her nostrils, her hairline, then the ceiling. She took all phone calls very seriously. There was a drop of water hanging off one nipple. *God, I'm a lucky bastard*, he thought. *God has been kind to her. And me. He's been off the scene for a long while, but this is one of His enduring works. Why do they have those pubic mounds, women? They're like codpieces. Protection, I suppose. I love them. Last Hard Bone Before The Coccyx, it should say . . .*

'It's Fat Paul,' she whispered with her hand over the phone, looking down, still very serious.

'Reffing?' whispered Tommy back.

'Ten-thirty. You're not going to, are you, Tommy?'

'Ugh. No. Tell him I'm knackered.'

'OK. Paul, he's knackered. Hope you find someone. 'Bye.' She hung up the phone. Then she stretched, making a few water droplets fall on his chest and face.

'Tommy, why do these people phone you at the last minute?' She was smiling down on him, all nostrils and shining eyes. 'Why, eh?' She crouched suddenly, giggling, and pinned his arms to the floor with her knees. Her cunt was on his ribcage, the curve of her bottom in his belly.

Now he was waking up fast. 'Stop!' he shouted, laughing.

'Why? Why?' She wriggled on him. 'Why?'

'Stop! My arms! Ow!' He couldn't stop her, though, and he couldn't stop laughing.

'Do you want it, Tommy boy?' she said with mock menace, coming forward and lowering her cunt until it was a couple of inches from his nose. Her weight was almost completely on his upper arms.

'No! Owww! No! Stop!' He was laughing, he was hurting, his dick had just been jump-started and his heart was full of love for her. *She's my own fucking bra commercial — without the bra. She's my home-grown beauty I don't have to share. She's going to stick that thing in my face and smother me ...*

'Hey, you tella Fat Paul to go take a hike, you hear me?' She was doing her gangster voice, which she did well. She did voices, and instead of making Tommy cringe like his previous girlfriends had, she did them so well he wanted more. 'You tella that liddul fock not to be calling again on a Sunday morning, OK? OK? I like it bloody, OK? Huh?' She pressed forward when she said it, crushing his muscles. 'Huh? Huh? Huh?'

'Yes! OK!'

'Tell him I got a wake-up call for him too, huh? And I won't send the boys round neither, I come personally and boom!' — she crunched into his upper lip with her hard pubic bone, the hair on it soft from the shower — 'Boom! Boom! I rub his fat ass out and no fucking tomorrow. You got dat? Huh?'

'OK, OK,' said Tommy, his eyes wet from pain and laughter together. '*Please* get off my arms. Ow.'

'Ha!' she said, getting up with a lurch to crush him one last time. By now he had a rocket in his shorts. She looked down at him, proud of her work, then turned and walked from the room. Legs, buttocks, back and neck, naked, still holding her towel in one hand.

Tommy rolled on his side and felt the blood return to his shoulders. She had gone back to the bathroom to do her hair. Slowly, he picked himself up, then staggered down the corridor back to their bedroom. He fell back on to the soft warm bed, such a relief after the scratchy carpet. *God, I'm a lucky bastard. Swaggering around the house with her tits out. She is so beautiful and so hard. God, I fancy her.*

She got dressed, then stood there in her jeans and a white shirt, looking warm and healthy.

'Come on, get dressed, you dirty dog. Since you're awake I thought we'd go to Camden Lock. It's really nice out.'

'Er, OK.' The idea of her, in her jeans, driving him in her little hatchback to Camden Market appealed to him.

'I'll buy you breakfast,' Tommy said. He loved the inside of her little car. There was always a pile of marking on the passenger seat, large grey exercise books with first names in infantile handwriting on the covers. There was all that stuff that doesn't belong in a car, unless you've been living out of it for the last two weeks — bags of illicit high-fat foods, the Evian bottle, sweets, change on the floor, religious or superstitious knick-knacks to keep from crashing, magazines, even a hairdryer. If he was really lucky her gym bag would be on the back seat. A quick rifle through it and a lucky car thief would find: sweet little trainers that had never been worn outdoors; stretchy, minimal garments in co-ordinated colours, rich with the scent of effort; a large towel, fluffy, of course; an unbearably sad Walkman made of yellow plastic.

'Don't you mean brunch?' she said, smiling.

'No I fucking don't mean brunch. Breakfast. Or lunch if you're lucky. But not fucking *brunch.*'

'Oh, I fancy a spot of brunch myself. Mmmm, *brunch.*'

'Shut up.'

She started piping in a high voice. 'Brunch, please! For two.'

'You shut the f . . .' Tommy darted towards her, but she was quicker than him and ran squealing to the other room.

'Pah,' he muttered. Then he called out: 'I'm having a quick wash, then I'll be ready.'

'Make it snappy!'

'Hey! Why am I so sexy?' he shouted down the hall.

'Because you're the one who wears the black shorts,' she shouted back on cue.

'Thank you.'

An hour later they were driving around looking for a place to park.

'You know what I hate about Camden?' he asked. 'The crowds. The milling crowds. Look at them. Look in their eyes.'

'What do you mean? Ooh, there's a spot. Missed it. Damn.'

'Look at their faces. They're all in their niches, but they don't know it. They're all trendsetters, aren't they? But they're all looking at each other, terrified that someone knows more than them, that someone is trendier than them, that someone has a better pair of trousers than them.

'Not everyone here's trendy, y'know. They're just people. Is she coming or going? Are you coming or going? Damn.'

'I know that,' said Tommy. 'But the ones who come here to pick up tips, to find out what's new and to see if they can upgrade their dull fucking lives ...'

'Why do you worry about that still, Tom?' she asked. He dropped his head and mumbled. He couldn't explain it, and feared it wasn't even worth explaining. Crowds did it for him. *All those people mingling happily, it doesn't seem right. There must be a way to divide the sheep from the goats.* They parked and walked to the bar. The Prince Albert had inadvertently become their favourite, through over-dependence. They sat together in silence for a few minutes. She read the menu. Slowly he came back into circulation. The bar sold bits of European food, but most people were only there for the beer. And the liquor. And the wine, when they were really desperate. The stone counter swept in a stretched 'S' shape the length of one side of the room. The walls were brown. The lights were low, except for a blast of fluorescent whenever the gents doors opened. A television set burned in a bracket above the bar. Bottles of spirits were lined up against the mirror, from which the barman poured, estimating the amounts. That was the best thing about the place. Even on a Sunday morning – well, half past eleven – just one street away from the hubbub of the market, it was filling up with drunks. That was the second best thing.

Sometimes Tommy and Melissa were silent together like this. They had learned not to step on the cracks, as it were, and were the happier for it. They got a beer each, then their food arrived, brought by a girl with a blond ponytail poking through the gap in the back of her baseball cap. Her face was pretty, from a distance, but was ruined by the scars and pits of extinct acne, powdered over but still unavoidable. *Chocolate and cheese,* thought Tommy. *The twin scourges of the British diet. Too late now.*

'Hey, look! You're on, Tommy!' Melissa had caught sight of a trailer for that afternoon's televised game, which always included a round-up of the previous day's goals. He looked up. They were showing a goal. Leeds v. Man City. There was a silent Tommy, surrounded by players, some covering their faces, or with their hands on their hips. The losers. The ones who had just gone behind. The goalie in his sun cap looking

---

stupid on the floor. There were some of the other team, the goalscorer leaping with delight and coming down into the embrace of two others. More youths rushing to join the group. And there was Tommy in the thick of it, yet ignored by the camera as it tracked the wonder boy and his rush towards goal, then off to the corner flag. Tommy blowing on his silver whistle, in the corner of the picture, turning to the centre spot, saying by his gestures *End of argument*. Tommy briefly checking the number on the lad's back, even though he knew the brat well by reputation.

*Electric Legs*, thought the ref.

'They call him Electric Legs, don't they?' said Melissa.

'Yeah. Foul-Mouthed Fucker would be just as accurate, though. "That was a cocksucking penalty, Ref! Fuck me, Ref, 'e's stamping on me bollocks 'ere! What the fuck was *that*, for cuntin' Ada's sake?" He's only twenty-two. And *Ada*. Where does he get *Ada* from?'

They watched – Tommy the TV, Melissa his face – until the ads came on. He didn't like all this shit in public, especially on a Sunday. He had work tomorrow and wanted a nice day off, not being seen, being recognised, being told to fuck off by total strangers (strangers who had often worked up enough steam in advance to take his head off). But he knew he'd succumb and watch the game. *What else is there to do on a Sunday afternoon in London anyway? All those cunts out shuffling round Ikea or the National Gallery, it's all the same.*

'How's your salad, love?' he asked. Something about Melissa kept him tender, even when there was a storm of hatred in his brain.

'Mmm, it's really *good*,' she said, and flicked some crunchy bits into the radicchio and offered her fork to him.

*A good fuck, a good salad, and Sunday with her sensible boyfriend. That's what she's probably thinking, though she'll never say it. Women are like that. She's still like that. She always will be. Sweet inside. God, she's great.*

'Fiona!' Melissa had spotted a friend, who was smiling a great wide smile of bleached teeth and expensive lipstick as she made her way over to their table.

'Girl, what are you doing here?' asked Fiona.

Melissa had only one fault, and that was that she had a friend called Fiona. She had no shame about using her name, in public, almost as loudly as Fiona used hers. This woman – sunlamp tan, snub nose, brand-new wrinkles – invited herself to sit with them for a few minutes, while she waited for her boyfriend. *Doubtless some fucking jerk I'll get stuck with*, thought Tommy glumly. After paying him the minimum allowable amount of attention (which included offering her warm, damp hand for him to shake), Fiona launched into a breathless, gleeful gossip session with her dear friend, leaving the referee stuck with his food, his second beer and his thoughts.

Tommy looked around the room at the patrons. They were people who thought they had style, people who thought they had taste. A young woman in a black leather biker jacket, only a quarter-century too late. A young man in a beret with a goatee. Gits with stupid glasses. Away to one end of the bar, where, despite the stools which you weren't encouraged to sit on because it ruined the line of the 'zinc', as the staff were obliged to call it, were two old men. Hunched in their horrible threads, they stood out from the fresher faces around them. The bar had previously been a pissy old pub full of unemployed Irishmen who bet everything, all day, every day. Outside in summer the homeless cases from the shelter stood begging between drinks, or petted borderline bag ladies at the wooden tables. In those days there hadn't been much difference between outside and in, especially as the door was permanently open.

That all changed when it went trendy. The new owners ripped out the inside, and then bulldozed the entire front for good measure — asbestos panels, badly etched windows, greasy extractor fan. Everything was replaced with glass. These two old bastards couldn't be arsed looking for a new place to drink, so they kept on coming, sipping dark Mexican beers as though they were the pale ales of their youth. You could still get Guinness, but they got used to the Mexican by accident and stayed with it. They didn't look up when the football came on because there were no horses in it. Everyone else did, though, if they were facing the right way.

Half an hour later, the trailer came on again. Fiona caught her friend's eye as it flicked over her shoulder, and turned to see what it was. It would be unfair to say that this was a woman who didn't normally know her arse from her elbow, because since the wrinkles had arrived, she knew both better than ever. But what did she see on the TV screen? What the colour-blind kid sees at the traffic lights — one blob, two blobs, one blob? What the fly sees with his compound eye — a bank of black-and-white Warhols? Whatever it was, she put the missing pieces together, and guessed that Tommy might well be on the telly, right now.

'Tommy! Ooh, it's you, isn't it?'

He groaned and tried to avert his eyes. He could sense people looking at him. He wished he were a smoker, so he could hide his face with a hand and look semi-natural. She turned to Melissa and got her to laugh, and said what a modest 'fellah' he was. 'Oh, but he loves it really,' she added. That stung him. *How does a moron like Fiona know that?*

Then the moment passed. It was only football, after all, and she wasn't interested in it. Similarly, the others in the room may have clocked him, and filed him away with satisfaction, but no one came up to talk to Tommy. Nobody wanted to chin him while he ate. It wasn't that sort of place. Fiona had resumed talking about herself. That was the thing about being a ref. No one really gave a fuck about you. He'd heard it all his life, from every telly pundit and every gobshite on the radio, about the ref having a good game if you didn't notice him. You were there in the centre of things, but you were invisible in the end. Unless you made some horrible fuck-up, of course. But the better you got, the less you were seen. Not even Melissa wanted to know about being a ref. She was interested in peripheral things, like where he was travelling to that weekend or what he saw there. Meanwhile he was having his greatest year ever. The first half of the year had been one long trail of glory for Tommy. He had only realised how much when the season ended, when he had taken care of a European Cup Semifinal and an FA Cup Final. But she didn't care about the offside rule, or replacing penalty shoot-outs with Sudden Death, or FIFA rankings, or the on-off-on movement towards professional referees. Or even whether he'd been nicked by flying coins or spat at by savage nine-year-olds. She didn't know the latter ever happened, and he never mentioned it, since he didn't like to worry her. But still, no one knew much, and no one much gave a fuck. Except the fans.

Fiona got a call on her flimsy cellphone which she conducted unashamedly in their presence. Tommy gave Melissa the look, the one that said *Let's limit the damage and get the fuck out of here.* However, the boyfriend arrived, all serious forehead, collapsing into crinkly smiles when he affirmed who he was talking to. Someone who might make him seem more interesting. Tommy had met him before, somewhere. All the boyfriends had been recycled by now anyway, and he knew this one would try to talk about football with him. Nick York introduced himself by name. His head dipped gratefully as he shook hands. *Nick York with the crap career,* Tommy reflected glumly. *Welcome, Nick.*

'So, Nick, how's work?' he asked before the man could compose himself. Easily flattered, Nick launched into a monologue about some useless 'art-slash-multimedia-slash-marketing' project, the sort of thing designed to defer the inevitable day when he would admit he was a medioke and should have got a proper job. After about five minutes of nodding in sympathy, Tommy swigged his beer, stood up, and declared that they had to get going. 'We're outta here,' he said, using Nick's lingo, and Melissa rose with him to make speedy goodbyes. 'Yeah, catch you later!' said Nick, turning to track Tommy's passing form. 'Twat,' muttered Tommy, just audibly.

Melissa caught him up at the door. They walked outside together.

'You still don't like them, do you?' she said.

'I just think he's a fucking twat, that's all. He never showed any interest in me until he saw me on the box, now he's all like *leaning* and *focusing* and twitching in his seat while he talks, gives me the creeps. And she ... well, you know what I think of her. She's nice but ...'

'... You wouldn't wanna fuck her,' said Melissa, finishing his sentence with perfect timing. 'Yes, I know.' She laughed at his moodiness, how his face went dark with annoyance just as swiftly and uncontrollably as another person's blushes pink. She caught his eye and after a second his mouth and eyes dissolved into a slight smile. He put his hand in hers as they walked. They went down Camden High Street looking in the shop windows. There was that trailer again on a telly in Grundig's window. That City player running away from his teammates to salute the crowd. Leeds fans stood up and leaned forward flicking the Vs and, in the case of one fan, clearly harking back to the good old days, waving his fist at the player like an angry dad in a comic. Tommy looked at himself again writing down the player's number and the time of the goal. What he saw was his own strength. He marvelled at the way he kept his mind on the game, when really he would have loved to have been over there by the corner flag. Not to be the player, exultant on his knees. But to be in that crowd that was seething with hate, pressing forward to the low, flimsy fence. Contributing to a volley of phlegm. Vowing revenge.

A bloke about forty with a beer gut moved next to them looking at the display. Tommy kept an eye on him. The bloke seemed OK until he saw himself on a monitor, caught by a camcorder the size of a box of kitchen matches, a rumpled, red-faced lump peering off in another direction. Tommy watched his shock and embarrassment turn to steely resolve. The man moved his head slightly, like a falcon judging parallax, pretending hard that he was interested in technical specifications. The picture was shit, that much was true. They left him there at the window and moved on to the next shop.

'Melissa, love – do you think I'm a conceited bastard?'

'Hmm ...' She had to think about it. 'No, not really. Do you?'

'No, not really. But I sometimes wonder what I look like to others. Not on the field, like, I know that, I'm not bothered about that. But, I mean, what do I look like when I'm looking at myself on television?'

'Oh, *then* you look conceited. But so what? You told me that television's full of conceited bastards ...'

'Wankers was the word I used ...'

'Wankers, sorry. So this way you've just joined them. Remember what you said? The thing that annoyed you wasn't how people thought they were seen on telly by the great unwashed, the problem was how they saw themselves when they were off-air. How they expected to be recognised.'

'And I've become that?' asked Tommy, a little hurt.

'You can't help it, love. It comes with the territory.'

Seeing his downcast look, she added, 'Hey, I'm only telling you back what you've told me. Personally, I'd rather be looking at these boots.' She dragged him along one shop. 'What do you think of these?' she asked, pointing to a left boot, thigh-high and kinky.

'I think you'd look fucking great in them. Get them,' he said. *This woman. She makes my knob hard and my heart soar. What more can a man want?*

They were back home by half past one and christened her boots around the house. Melissa tried to drift off to the other room just as the match was coming on. 'I feel like I've seen it already,' she said when he pulled her back and started tickling her.

'Where are you going anyway? I'm on now, have you forgotten? You just going to fuck me and forget me?'

She was writhing and giggling.

'Stop! Stop! OK, OK. What was the score anyway?'

'Man City won three–nil. At Leeds. It was pretty good. But the score doesn't mean much to you, does it, love?'

'You're right, it doesn't.' She put her lips close to his face and breathed, mock-sexy, 'Anything else? Did you give anyone the *red card*, Tommy? Did you send anyone *weeping* to the tunnel?'

'No,' he said, laughing. 'No tears. They don't cry unless it's a really big occasion. Internationals.' He knew she wouldn't sit through more than about ten minutes. 'Ah, go on, off you go and do your stuff.'

She went away and he turned the volume up. The team sheets were projected in white letters over the image of the bristling crowd, caught in the hot August sunshine at Elland Road, the team badge in colour in the corner. Man City's looked disturbingly alien, with its creepy ship and red rose. Tommy had a feeling that would never go away of having strayed into unfamiliar territory. He remembered, age thirteen, getting off a soccer special at Piccadilly Station and seeing his fellow fans dissolve, hiding their scarves, hopping into minicabs and on to buses, and even trying to blend in with passing families. Man City were there to meet them, but even they must have been shocked to see the train pull in with only eighty fans on it. There was no police escort. It was a Saturday afternoon in winter and already dusk was on the way. You don't want to fuck around asking which bus goes to Maine Road and have some fucker send you off to Hulme to get chased around the crescents. Everyone had the same idea – to melt into the mainstream, streaming down the main road, and hope no one starts on you. Maybe Man City had been bemused that day, so surprised that they instinctively followed one of the queer bylaws of football violence and decided to save it till after the game. They probably just wanted to see exactly how many fans there were in the away end before they could get a handle on what they wanted to kick and beat.

Tommy vividly remembered walking down the slope outside the train station, feeling that this must be just the start of a very long and shameful day. Hardly speaking in the street, lest some fleabag Mancunian take it as his cue to introduce himself in that taunting whine they have. Looking nervously around through most of the match, through the near-empty terraces to the home fans squeezed up against the fence. Being genuinely relieved to lose, thinking it might make them more merciful. However, inside the ground the travelling fans were in good form (apart from the wankers in the seats who always came in cars, moaned and disappeared again), taunting Helen the Bell (the old Man City cow behind the goal who always brought a school bell with her), singing long, if not loud, for the lads, going mad at the goal, until it was disallowed. Provoking the home fans on all sides. Telling the home fans each time they scored that they were gonna get their fucking heads kicked in. They seemed to believe their own words, that was the funny thing. Tommy had wanted to shush them. He was thirteen years old so he didn't yet have the kamikaze ethic of the travelling fan. He loved the game, he loved the floodlights, he loved the green turf, the walls of flesh faces behind the goal and sea of denim at a pitch invasion. He loved the flags and scarves and shirts of claret and blue. Most of all he loved the growth of a song from a single shout to a tune that echoed round a ground or up a street and made people bristle with envy and awe, that made shopkeepers come to their doorways and children look up from their games. But nothing happened after the game. Or at least, Tommy didn't see any fighting. He and his mate had scuttled back to Piccadilly with their heads down, guessing the way. On the cold train, a few people reported exactly who had been kicked and jostled and scared, but it was just the dog-end of a long and shameful day. Nothing to brag about.

Blues weren't even waiting when the train pulled into Birmingham New Street that evening. Even they couldn't be bothered. Maybe all the Blues fans were in the bath at eight o'clock, getting ready for a night out up town.

The commentator, John Motson, was talking through the line-ups, imbuing each blokeish name with heroic potency. 'Owen Owen, Welsh international, forty-one goals with Preston last season, and it's his twenty-first birthday. That tan, I'm told, is from the team holiday to Corfu. His mum, as always, is here. She's the one who christened him Electric Legs, so the story goes. You all know about the bicycle rigged up in the Owen family living room when the electricity was cut off. Owen's late father was apparently quite a handyman and the only way they could watch the 1994 World Cup was if Gary pedalled through each game. Hence the name, Electric Legs. So good they named him twice. As they say.' The preamble droned on for a while, then suddenly cut to Tommy, checking his watches, checking his linesmen, raising a hand and blowing up to start the game. 'Referee Thomas Burns, from Birmingham. Voted Referee of the Year last season.' He suddenly became very excited and raised his voice an octave. 'And so the new Microsoft Premier League season begins!'

Leeds kicked off and passed back to their goalie by a circuitous route, and Tommy barely saw himself again in the goalless first half. He savoured the atmosphere once more, though, which was diminished but not destroyed by being on the TV. He loved the first day of the season, the hot sun in fans' eyes at corners, the confusion on the pitch as strange new players tried to make their mark. New managers, young players still living with their mums thrust forward from the reserves, and the sweet, fresh turf like Wembley sward. Yesterday had been good, it had brought back memories from when he was young and went to all the matches. It had felt like a home game to him.

A goalless first half – this was what the new season was all about. Fans looking for some sort of sign in forty-five minutes (plus fifty-one seconds of stoppage time) of play. The statistics sheet still unsullied, while the first news filtered in from the other games. As ever, seemingly incredible news. Sending-off at Chelsea after twelve minutes. Newcastle one down. Everton two up at Liverpool. *Why were those two playing each other on the first day of the season?* Tommy had asked himself at half-time in the dressing room, as he heard the scores on the tannoy. *Couldn't the computer do any better? Maybe like everyone else, the computer wants it all now. No point in waiting till Boxing Day. Get the fans in today. Launch a new strip on Boxing Day instead, that brings in more money. Move the numbers around. Sell a player. It's all fucked up, even outside London.*

Goalless first halves kept up the illusion that all teams were equal, which made it all the more enjoyable when that illusion was shattered. Almost as enjoyable as when that bunch of wankers your workmate supports go thirteen hours without a goal. Or when the newly promoted are dispatched back to hell minus their new fans, with few points, and not a win away from home. The first day of the season was what you waited for all summer long. It was unimaginable to the lads kicking a ball around outside the warehouse at lunchtime in June and July. It was unimaginable as you drove by the silent giant of the stadium, as you sunbathed in Ibiza or Kos, as you got pissed in some pavement café, or even the next morning as you traded muted jibes with opposition fans over lager breakfasts. It all seemed impossible, until the fixture lists came out in the local paper.

Tommy looked at the Sunday paper during the adverts. They'd even printed a league table now, after one game. At one time it felt like you had to be an actuary or a maths geek to get up a table after just one game, and even after the second game of the season, midweek, there was something distasteful about pretending that people could be ranked on so little evidence. But there it was, mostly ones and zeroes, eerily symmetrical, like some brutal little virus written by a crippled hacker. Tommy pored over it, but it didn't make much sense. Except that his team were low instead of high.

The goons were back on the TV, analysing the play. The format had changed for the new season, of course. Jimmy Hill as ever, an unemployed manager and an ex-player tried to make sense of the dull recorded highlights. The BBC was having trouble adapting to showing adverts. 'I thought the young lad Owen looked sharp, but he's rushing his finish. Look at that.' They showed Electric Legs with only the 'keeper to beat, volleying the ball too soon, so that it rolled down his shin before coming weakly off the tip of his boot and looping into the Leeds end, where thousands jeered and cackled to a man, giving him two fingers or the curled-hand wanker sign. Tommy smiled as he remembered the kid's reaction. 'Aw, shite-ing bollocks! Cunt! Cunt!' *They've got cameras in the nets — why aren't the players wearing microphones yet? Maybe nobody was crass enough to think of it yet.*

The second half, Tommy had more of a game. The pace picked up, and he ploughed his course, end to end, in an unwavering diagonal, turning sharply, keeping things moving, making judgments on the run. He sweated, but he held his own. Tommy couldn't match the bursts of speed of the attackers, but he made sure he was always in the right place. He could anticipate the play better than most players, and he could match them all for stamina, even though he was ten years older than most of them. He watched himself. From the sofa, he saw things he had missed. *Look at the way they're circling me*, he thought as four Leeds players gathered while he booked their full-back for chopping someone down. The kid was so thick he could barely spell his own name. Tommy had few words for him. 'One more of them and you're off, sunshine.' He found it helped to talk like a copper.

The second booking was more complicated. Tommy almost never cautioned for dissent. If he had, there would hardly have been anyone left on the pitch by the end of a game, since most players swore. Whether they swore at him or just past him was always the question, and he didn't have time to work out the answer in the heat of a game, so he usually let it go. They all swore, all the time: bollocks this and bastard that, shit cunt and fanny-fuck. They swore at the ball, at themselves, their teammates and their opponents. They probably ordered fucking pints of lager and went to fucking nightclubs after the game. They watched fucking telly and they did fucking charity work 'cos they fucking cared about fucking little kids.

So it wasn't such a quantum leap that it should spill over on to Tommy the referee. 'Aw, Ref, that was never offside, fuckin 'ell.' That was nothing. Players these days said things like ''Koff, Ref! You fuckin' *blind*?' He let that go. It didn't hurt anyone. It didn't hurt him. 'Oi, Ref, you're a fucking wanker!' was pretty normal, as some slighted midfielder walked by towards the tunnel, at half-time or at the end. So what? Everyone knew this about Tommy. All the other refs had heard about it too, and gradually the practice had spread. The law had been stretched, in practice. Twenty-year-olds on their debut in the Premier League listened awestruck as players called referees bastards and blind gits and even motherfuckers. They soon got good at it themselves. But rarely was any time wasted booking them. There was a strange new spirit of co-operation on the pitch, between players and officials, and many people traced it directly back to Tommy and the way he dealt with language.

But when Tommy saw his linesman flag, and pulled up Owen 'Electric Legs' Owen in the middle of his run, something disturbed him about the kid's response. 'Aw, Ref, you cunt!' No player had ever called him a cunt before. It felt very strange. Fans had, but so what? *Cunt.* It ranked alongside *cheat* as one of the things he could not tolerate being called. Here was a cocky little bastard with his forty-one goals and his transfer fee and his new German saloon with the LEX11 number plate and his picture in the fucking papers, *and he's calling me a cunt. To my face.* Tommy was shocked.

'What's your name, sonny?' he asked as he got out his book. 'Eh? Ah, fuckin' 'ell, Ref, what the fuck's all this bollocks?' Tommy never answered him. He could see himself on the telly not answering him. He just walked round the back of him, copied the name and number off his shirt, and walked away. *I could have fucking smacked him one then,* he thought, looking at the evil stare on his own face as he restarted the game. *It's because of little bastards like him that this country's so fucked up. Calling the ref a cunt. Why don't they put that in the papers?*

From then on Tommy didn't like the kid, but he remained fair. He let him have the advantage when he was clipped on the heel as he broke one on one towards the goalie. The little bastard managed to dribble the ball round the goalie, all the time falling sideways, almost horizontal, and slot it in at an acute angle. One–nil and the Man City fans went fucking mad. He protected him when the Leeds centre-half stamped on his ankle while the ball was out of play – Tommy had good peripheral vision. Another booking. And he overruled his linesman when the lad beat the offside trap and flashed a shot against the post. The little bastard had pace, and all afternoon he'd been the proverbial yard quicker than the Leeds defence. Tommy was there and saw it. The linesman wasn't that clearly sighted, he confirmed, after they consulted on the touchline in front of the baying Leeds fans. The ball came off the post and Owen lashed it in at the second attempt, straight through the goalie's flailing arms. A coin hit Tommy on the boot; he ignored it. Gobbets of phlegm flew through the air, all of them missing him (although a streak did land on the linesman's shoulder without him noticing it). Tommy resisted the hatred. After the consultation, he turned, pointed away from the goal, and blew his whistle.

The little bastard scored again. A curler from a free kick just outside the box. '75 min.,' he wrote in his book. *There's going to be some fun at the station tonight. And on the bridges over the M62. I wouldn't like to be a Man City fan.* That's when the lad ran to the corner and gloated at the Leeds fans. It was pure bliss for Man City, beyond their dreams. They bounced up and down on their plastic seats, cracking them and hugging each other. Beating the Yorkshire scum, at their own ground, on the first day of the season, and

Owen getting a hat trick. Stuff like that doesn't happen on the first day of the season. How must it have sounded around the country? Potato-faced Boro fans would gulp for air and retune their transistors. Fair-weather Brighton fans would raise their eyebrows at it as they cruised home in their company cars. In Wales they'd mention it in pubs in towns where they don't even play football. And little boys in Manchester would talk about it at school all week, and remember it for ever.

Tommy waited for the after-match commentary, kidding himself that he wanted to see how they would discuss the controversial offside decision, but he couldn't help his curiosity – any mention of himself would be interesting. 'What about that offside decision, then,' said Des Lynam, the host. 'A bit controversial?'

'Not at all,' answered Jimmy Hill. Such questions always fell to him. 'I think the referee had a first-class game, and if you look at the video, you can just see ... there, Owen makes his move now, the ball comes through, and the Leeds line is just too slow in coming out. I thought it was a marvellous decision.' The player disagreed, as he was paid to do. 'Yes, I wonder how well sighted he was. I mean, the linesman can't see here, but the referee doesn't look much better off. I'd have to say that he's assuming the lad is quicker than the defenders, rather than going by the evidence of his eyes.' *Scottish wanker*, Tommy muttered at his TV set. 'Well, if that's the case, then he's right!' blurted Mr Hill. 'Well, as a defender, I'd say give me the benefit of the doubt,' said the player.

'Still, it didn't affect the result much, I don't think,' said Des, bringing them round. 'Thank you. Great win for Man City. Now to White Hart Lane for our live match.'

'Oh, more cockney wankers. Fuck off,' said Tommy, quietly, and turned the set off. *Jimmy Hill, what a wanker, what a wanker.* That's what they used to sing if they ever saw him at a game. It felt strange having Jimmy Hill, the pointy-faced schoolmaster of English football, on his side. *Jimmy Hill is a bastard, and yet he's sticking up for me on TV.* Tommy pulled his feet up and lay on his back on the couch, thinking about the game. The Sunday afternoon silence sat heavy upon him, the sound of the telly having just been turned off, the sound of the country gearing up for another week of work tomorrow.

*I never liked Jimmy Hill*, he thought. *Hang 'em and flog 'em and, worst, ban 'em from going to games. What sort of ignorant fuck could come up with a plan like that?* SAUNDERS: BIRCH THE BRUTES. *Now that made more sense.* Ron Saunders's plan which periodically popped up on the third from last page of the *Evening Mail*, to thrash convicted hooligans in the centre circle before each game. *That would probably have been good for the gates, especially if you used away fans. 'Where you going, lad?' 'Oh, Mum, the pleece are taking me up to Goodison to be flogged. I'll be home by teatime, 'cos they don't even let you stay an' watch the match.'* But Jimmy Hill, fuck. *Sounding off during the Heysel thing and putting ideas into people's heads about national service, always moaning, always arguing. He's probably a fucking Christian, too, didn't I read that somewhere? Jesus. Yet here he is saying there's room for thought, for subjective judgment, on the pitch, when you're running around. He must know something. Apparently he was quite a good player once, well, at least he was a player once, so he must know something. He's right for once.* Tommy lay in the shady room, then nodded off.

Melissa: Hi, Fiona, what's up? Sorry about earlier.

Fiona: Oh, hey there. What was all that about, then? Going off like that? Was Tommy all right? He seemed a bit moody.

M: Yeah, he was fine. He had to get back and do his paperwork. Doctors, you know.

F: You lucky cow, having a doctor on call day and night. I wish I had one.

M: Oh, Nick's not bad.

F: I s'pose so.

M: Yeah, I suppose you're right. I've never been ill for long since I met Thomas.

F: Unless you count being slightly sick. You perve.

M: Yeah. Me *and* him, both of us. Before he lifted his pen I made sure we broke in my new boots. All over the flat.

F: Ooh, you dirty cow. So you got them, then?

M: Top intercourse – with the accent on the 'into'. I don't think I'll be trading him in just yet.

F: Huh. Where did you get them again?

M: Shop in the High Street ... hang on, it's the other line, I'm expecting a call from my mum, I'll have to call you tomorrow.

F: OK. 'Bye.

Melissa woke him at about 8 p.m. 'Come on, love, or you'll never sleep.'

'What? Oh. What time is it?'

'It's nearly eight.'

'Oh shit. I haven't done a thing. Bollocks. All my paperwork,' he said, trying to rise. '*Ow!* Me neck.'

'What's wrong?' she asked. She held two teas in her hands, waiting for him to take one.

'I've slept on my neck. Ow. Oooh.' He sat up and rubbed it, then took the tea. 'Thanks, love, you're an angel. Ow. It's stiff. Fuck, I remember Des Bremner did this once. It was in the *Mail*. He had a nap on a Friday afternoon, and woke up with a cricked neck. Stupid bastard – he was fit for the game, apart from his neck. He was in agony and had to miss the match.'

'You had a call from someone called Mark,' said Melissa. She sat down beside him. 'Who's he? He sounded like he was from Birmingham.'

'Mark? Mark who? I don't know any Mark. Or at least, I know lots of Marks, but none that I'd call back. Was it Mark with the limp?'

'I didn't see his walk on the phone, you know. No, Mark, he sounded like a Brummie, he sounded like you.'

Tommy thought. 'Was he a patient?'

'No, no, he said you were old friends.' She was almost ready to leave it, since it could have been anyone. His patients were always getting their home number and calling, going on about their chest pains and their blue babies. They were a pain in the arse. Not something he had bargained on when he started out. Tommy got into medical school, like most teenagers, by the Route One method. Since he was good at mental arithmetic, his teachers considered his strength to be maths. Since he did maths, he would have to do science A-levels. And once his parents found out that all doctors had to do science to get into medical school, that was it – he was going to be a doctor. It was as if their prayers had been answered. The Burns work gene had mutated in one generation from pint-necking labourers to white-coated Dr Kildares. Later he found out that it wasn't quite that simple. If you didn't keep up the aspirational momentum with a constant stream of cocktail parties and conferences, you could pretty quickly find yourself all washed up on an estate in Camden.

'Mark ... something Irishy.'

'*Mark?*' Tommy exclaimed. 'You mean Mark? *Mark?*'

'Yes, Maaark,' she said, laughing and pushing her face into his. 'That's right, Mark. Mark who, anyway?'

'Mark O'*Mally?*'

'Yeah, that's it. Sorry, I didn't write it down. He sounded like he knew you. Who is he?'

'Mark? He's a mate from back home. We went to junior school together. We ...' Tommy tried to remember why they had been friends. It was the

'Who do *you* know?' reflex kicking in, on himself. 'We went to the games together. Mark used to be a big mate of mine. What does he want? I haven't seen him for, fuck, over ten years.'

'He left this number. Call him back . . . no, it's too late. He said not after eight. Tomorrow's OK.'

She gave him the piece of paper. It was an 0121 number – Birmingham. It looked strange, but what was next to it struck him as even stranger. SACRED HEART.

'What's this, Sacred Heart? The church?'

'I guess so,' said Melissa. She was curling her arm around his waist and burrowing into him.

'What's he doing at the Sacred Heart? Is he a fucking priest or something?'

'He never said so. Just call him tomorrow. Why, don't you know any priests any more?' She liked to tease him, not for being lapsed, but for ever having been a Catholic in the first place. She was English.

Tommy ignored her because he was thinking. *Mark O'Mally, calling from the Sacred Heart? Mark, a priest?* He couldn't believe it. *Maybe something's happened to him and they've taken him in? Maybe someone's dead? But it doesn't say it's urgent.*

He folded the scrap of paper and put it in his wallet. Melissa was all over him by now like an octopus. Great armloads of hugs were holding him in, so he lay back and let it happen, and soon forgot about everything else. He looked at his soft-skinned lover lying there with him, and felt all the love coming off her, and was grateful. In a minute he'd have to get up and start his paperwork, then do his match report, then get his stuff ready for the morning, then go to bed. *Poor Mark, a priest?* he wondered. *Naw, must be some mistake. He's the last fucker they'd let in.*

# 2

## To Brum; Father Mark O'Mally & Father Kelly (elder); reminisce; the dance

Tommy got off the train at Birmingham New Street. He climbed the steps two at a time without getting out of breath to get ahead of the other passengers. His heart was banging, though, and his eyes were wide. This place he knew so well, with its long white corridor and all the staircases leading down to the trains, hadn't changed in the twenty-five years he'd been coming here, but the feelings it evoked had. At age ten it could have been Heathrow or Newark International Airport for all its promise of new destinations: Bescot, Leicester, Plymouth, London Euston, Glasgow (change at Preston). At sixteen it was a nest of warring forces, where at any time a mob of Blues fans might come round the corner, or a skinhead leave his group and walk over to question him. Or, indeed, where a mob of his own lot could march through, singing, jostling, taking over. In his twenties it was just a node, a jumping-off point at the end of medical school terms or Christmas when he went back to see his family. After they moved away, he didn't go back. *Shit, I haven't been back here properly for ten years*, he told himself as he passed through the ticket barrier on to the concourse. *Look at all those young kids. God. Look at those funny phones.* He passed a pair of the new BT public videophones. *No one's smashed 'em yet. Shame.* He wondered what it would be like trying to vandalise one. *It's all LCD screens now, like trying to smash a bar of toffee still in the wrapper. Wankers BT.* He went up the escalators, past the shops, which now had a bit of upmarketness mixed in with the sad old market tat, and down the Ramp on to New Street.

Mark said he'd pick him up outside the Odeon at 5 p.m. and it was five past. Tommy sat down on his haunches to wait. Birmingham looked odd.

Lots of pretty girls for a start. Lots of teenage kids dressed in fashions he had lost track of. Three dressed-up girls came clattering by on their heels, running for something and screaming. One of them dropped a half-packet of cigarettes a yard from his feet and they were gone so quickly it wasn't worth shouting after them. *I'll save these for some tramp, make his day. Make his fucking weekend*, thought Tommy, putting them in his jacket pocket. *Tramps in Birmingham. I wonder how they do?*

All Tommy knew was, his old mate Mark was now a priest. *A fucking Catholic priest. Yeah, Mark.* The one he used to go to the games with, the one he used to sing and eff and blind with on the terraces, the one he used to run through the streets of strange towns with, terrorising the locals, shouting stuff, chucking stuff, taking stuff. He was a fucking priest. He hadn't seen him for nearly fifteen years. He didn't know what to expect. The last time he'd seen him, Mark was standing in a flowerbed in the middle of a traffic island leading an offensive against some away fans. For a few delicious minutes there had been no police around, and with spontaneous escalation, about fifty of them had ambushed a mob of Albion who were walking to the game. Mark was up there, in the municipal roses, screaming, 'Come aaaaaarn! Gerr'em ... Get the bastards!', and the insults they had been trading across the dual carriageway escalated into action as they went haring across the street and started laying into the West Brom fans. Mark had had on a black raincoat, even though it was a dry day, making him look very sinister amongst all the sportswear and casual threads. It was open all the way down, and his jeans snagged on the thorns as he led the charge. The crown of the roundabout was about four feet higher than the road, and Mark looked like a general, screaming his orders, surveying the field, and handing out punishment.

His hair was jet black but his eyes were blue, and a vein stood up under his ivory skin near the temple. He had a slightly Roman nose and a straight-up forehead. He was always a good-looking bastard – when he was a skinhead for a while, his hairline had perfect natural curves and angles, and the hair looked like black velours, smooth and uninterrupted. When he had a suedehead, the shape of his skull was magnificent, regular, balanced, flawless. When it was growing out, he had soft black spikes like a starburst against the skin of his brow, and jagged edges layered all the way to his crown. A fringe suited him. So did a scouser flick. Tommy was one of the few who'd ever seen him totally bald. He had looked so evil you would instinctively want to cross the street from him, even if you knew him, the hard white skull peppered with black pores. Mark never did that again, shave it. He didn't say anything, but you could tell he felt he'd overdone it.

He was always a good-looking bastard – but he never used it. He always looked like he was thinking about something else, something other than himself.

After Tommy had got that call, after the Leeds–Man City game on the telly a month before, he forgot to call Mark back. He found the bit of paper in his wallet one Saturday night when he was pissed and looking for a minicab number in a phone box at midnight. Being pissed, he didn't see any obstacles to calling there and then that his deep well of bonhomie couldn't overcome. Some old Irish bloke had answered, very ticked off. You could hear him exchanging words with Mark in the hall, and their footsteps overlapping on the bare wood floor, but Tommy decided not to worry about that. Everything would be the better for this call.

Not that things were bad, mind. But something in Tommy, something about his age, and his station in life, couldn't resist the call.

Mark sounded surprisingly alert.

'Tommy? Great to hear from you. Are you OK?'

'A'right!' said Tommy. 'What's going on? How you doing, Mark, old mate? Sorry to get you up. So what, you're a priest, then? A priest? You're not, are you?'

'Yes, a priest. Things are great, Tommy,' said the other cheerfully. He laughed gently. 'You're not doing so bad yourself.' He had a touch of the Irish idiom creeping back in. Mark had had it when he was little, when he knew no different and bore the dark stamp of his parents' culture. He never got it much after about the age of eleven, when he went off to the comprehensive and met more English. 'I saw you on television, and I said, "I can't believe it, Tommy Burns on *Match of the Day*, who'd have thought it?" I don't watch television as a rule. Mrs O'Connor the housekeeper had to come in and confirm it to me. What are you doing with yourself?'

'Hey, where did you get my number?' asked Tommy, without answering. His mind had lurched off down the path of curiosity.

'It's in the book, Tommy. Directory Enquiries.'

'Oh. You're right, it is.' He paused, drunkenly. Mark paused patiently. They started up again when Tommy had found his subject. 'It was never fucking offside, was it? Fucking Leeds, moaning wankers. Oops, sorry about that, swearing an' all. But you know what I mean.'

'Ah, that's all right. I do, no, it was never offside. Mrs O'Connor didn't think so either.'

*Mrs O'Connor, what's all this fucking Mrs O'Connor?* he thought.

Tommy could stand up all night when he was drunk. He had his knee up against the rack that held the directories. They chatted about football for a bit. Not about the old times, but the current league positions, the early sackings, the transfers and the news. Tommy was surprised at how well up on the football his priest friend was, especially for someone who said he didn't watch the box much. This priest thing had thrown him off balance, working deep underground in his mind during that month of forgetting. His brain spun off into a reverie, about all the things he might ask a priest now that he had the chance. But there was enough football to keep him talking sense. *Me old mate Mark. I haven't seen him for years. I want to see the fucker.*

'Do you get up to Brummagem much?' Mark asked him.

*Brummagem. Like an old person would say.* 'Nah. Never. They never give me Birmingham games. Dunno why. I've never asked. Black Country sometimes. And Coventry.'

'I was thinking, Tommy, I do a bit of reffing meself now, for the kids, like.'

'Yeah, mate. It's great, isn't it? Man,' he said joyfully, 'we should get together.'

They made plans for getting together. To Mark, this meant thinking ahead and saying come up one Friday in October. 'I'll pick you up on New Street, outside the Odeon. And you can stay at the house.'

To Tommy, this meant agreeing to it all enthusiastically, then, as he hung up, being caught by that sinking feeling, of guilt mixed up with defeatism, of knowing it was all bull. You don't get to thirty-four in London without talking a lot of shit on the phone.

He forgot about Mark again, until he got the list from the Football Association saying he would be refereeing a Wolves match on Sunday, 12 October. That was the weekend Mark had suggested coming up. He talked to Melissa about going up early and staying Friday and Saturday for the kids' game. She didn't know Mark, but was amused that her boyfriend would be consorting with priests.

'He's not a Born Again, is he?' she mocked. 'I don't want you coming home reconverted or anything. I like you lapsed.'

'Don't be daft. Catholics don't get born again or saved or any of that bollocks. They're just Catholics.'

'So how come this lout, as you called him, is doling out Holy Communion and counselling pregnant women?' She liked winding him up. 'Is he a virgin?'

'I don't know,' said Tommy, uncomfortably. He liked her being one of the lads, but not all of the time. 'That's what I'd like to find out. Why he's a priest, I mean. Man, Mark was such a great bloke. He was one of the greats. We used to go everywhere. I can't see how he could end up like this, though. He said something about how he refs kids' football matches now.'

'Oh. Wants some tips from the master, does he?' She laughed at him, looking him straight in the eyes with her grey-green sparklers. Her cheekbones seemed to lift a little higher when she laughed at him, making him love her more.

'Will you be OK for the weekend, then?' he asked, trying to regain some leverage.

'Me? OK? I'll be fine. I'll be ecstatic. I *am* a big girl, you know.'

'I know, love. But I'll miss you.'

'Thomaaaaaas . . .' She started towards him, and he laughed out loud. It was settled. He was going. They had recently both noticed that over the last few years of their love he had stopped having lads' nights out. He was a solitary soul these days. Just his work, and his hobby, and Melissa.

He never said he was coming in a car — Tommy had to grant him that. The black Vespa rounded the corner on to New Street, an erect figure in a black raincoat perched above the warm curves of the leg guards. Just from his outline Tommy knew him. The scooter pulled up between two bus stops, with the engine puttering in neutral, its back panels all scratched and battered from years of service. Mark smiled at his old friend. The face he hadn't seen for years hadn't changed. He had on a basin-type helmet, the sort not allowed by law, with no visor or chin protection. Like the bike it was scuffed and dull from years of use. Over his arm he had a white full-face lid with no visor for Tommy. They shook hands firmly. It was the first time they had ever had to.

'All right!' said Tommy. 'Nice bike,' he added.

'Hop on!' shouted Mark. Tommy did up the lid without delay, smiling at his old friend. Mark had his dog-collar on, the little white square perched in a wall of dark cloth. Tommy stared at that while he did up the strap, then got on. They scooted up New Street, into Corporation Street, dodging pedestrians and nipping between buses. They passed the white walls of Rackhams and rounded the egg-shaped island without stopping. Tommy was doing his best to lean the right way, but it was so long since he'd been on the back of a bike. He was all over the place.

'Hey, O'Mally, watch it! Whoa, what's the rush!' he shouted as they rounded the huge island at Masshouse Circus. He had assumed the dog-collar would mean Mark would ride like a granny. He remembered something about Mark – he was always surprising you. He'd say the oddest things, turn up in unpredictable places. Like the time in a very tense march down the street to the Annie Road end at Liverpool, when all the scousers had turned out to meet them and there were only about three coppers for miles, Mark suddenly shouted above the eerie silence, 'Zigger Zagger Zigger Zagger, we hate Blues!' No one must have even *thought* that for years, let alone shouted it out loud. It had the scousers nonplussed for a few delicious moments. Or like the time he ran on the pitch at Derby wearing an old-man rubber mask. He did a little dance, then headed for their goalie, as if to take a swing at him, when a copper came at him from the left. He swerved and headed back to the away section on the side, clearing the fence with an almighty leap. He disappeared into the bodies, took off the mask, and no one knew who he was when he re-emerged. Everyone was cheering, but when he popped up with his own face, only a few people knew who he was, or that he'd been the old man. He was just a face in a sea of flesh again.

'I have to get back for the six o'clock Mass. Father Kelly can't make it. Again.' He shouted over his shoulder.

They hared down the slope past Aston University, past the red doors of the fire station, and on to the Aston Expressway. Mark opened the throttle all the way. The Friday traffic was thundering out towards the suburbs and the country, and in between the juggernauts and Range Rovers nipped the two figures on a battered old Vespa. Mark had his head forward, straining to get the 125cc motor over sixty miles an hour. Tommy sat upright, with his hands behind him, his Adidas bag on his lap, and hung on to the back of the seat, hoping his luck would hold. They sailed along, the expressway turning from a sunken motorway into an elevated one, until suddenly Aston Hall and Villa Park hove into view simultaneously on the left. Tommy turned his head to get a better look as they passed, while Mark kept his eyes on the road. For the last six years Tommy had been all over the country to other people's grounds, passing through reception areas full of alien colours, or sometimes squeezing through ancient turnstiles at a tinpot ground before changing in a cupboard in the annexe provided for match officials. He'd been all over the place, but he'd never been sent to Villa. He'd watched them play a few times in London, on night games when he wasn't reffing. But this was Mecca, and it looked so close he could almost touch it.

Aston Hall looked as it always did — rain- and soot-stained brick, laid down in Jacobean times for the use of some nob. It sat on its green hill, oblivious of the times, still taking little tours around its formal gardens, its walking gallery and its baronial hall, even as the crowd roared next door and fans chased each other across the grass, sometimes to slip and fall, and take a good kicking in the face, chest and thighs. It was a big old pile, the original villa that the team took their name from for a laugh, but it looked like a miniature compared to the Villa ground. His stomach flipped as he looked at Villa Park. The Holte End with its back to him. No longer the vast black metal roof angled to the sky over its acres of standing space. It was hard to get used to the new Holte End, even though it was nearly a decade since the decree went out that every ground had to be all-seating. The Holte used to hold twenty-six thousand fans, bigger than the Kop, bigger than the Stretford End, bigger than all the poxy ends in London. So vast that when the FA started using it for cup semifinals, the visiting fans often made a trip to the very back and stood in awe at the view. It was so high that players moved in formations previously only seen on blackboards at training grounds, and a goal at the other end, the Witton End, would be marked by an explosion of moving flesh and colours half a second before the roar arrived.

Now the Holte was a standard shoebox. Slab of seats, little wall thing, another slab of seats. Stands never went back very far because of some old rule that said wankers in the seats shouldn't have to strain their eyes as much as people who stood, so everyone was cooped in. Everyone was a seats wanker now. The old floodlight pylons were gone too, with their AV pattern of lights, visible, whether on or off, from miles away up the M6. And the Witton Lane stand was a new box thing too. *Better than it used to be anyway*, thought Tommy. He glimpsed the green turf between the stands, and shivered. He'd trodden on all the great grounds in England, and on plenty of the shitty ones too. But he had never set foot on the grass at the Villa, and seeing it all again instantly renewed his longing. *That's not true*, he told himself. *I've been on the pitch a few times. With this lout in front of me, in fact. Just never as a referee.*

They sped by, and got off the expressway at Spaghetti. Mark wove past the white tower blocks, along Aston Hall Road and Trinity Road to the Church of the Sacred Heart. The rounded brick building looked so much smaller than Tommy remembered it. And he was surprised by that feeling — at his age he thought it had all been used up. They bounced up the kerb and came to a halt at the front door of the house. They got off, and Mark pulled the battered scooter back on its stand. He let himself in. Tommy followed, immediately taken aback by the strong smell of fatty cooking.

Mark led the way into the humble living room. There was a stiff old sofa, two armchairs, and a sideboard with an ancient radio on it. The TV, which had round knobs and screw-in legs, was partially covered by a lace cloth that protected it from the vase of silk flowers on top. Tommy put his bag down and looked around. *Fuck me, this is a blast from the past.*

'Er, sit down, Tom,' said his friend, as they took their coats off. Mark had on the whole gear – black suit, black shirt, dog-collar, sensible shoes. 'I'll get you some tea.' He stepped out and called to the housekeeper that they would be having tea.

'I have to get off at a quarter to, to Mass.'

'Yeah, you said.'

There was an embarrassed silence. *How am I gonna put up with this all weekend?* Tommy asked himself. *'S fuckin' prison. It's like school again. It's like home.* He looked again at his old friend, who was sitting opposite him. They both broke into grins at the same time.

'I know what you're thinking,' said Mark, laughing. 'You're thinking, "What the f—?" Am I right or what?'

'Fuckin' A, man. I just ... well, all this is a bit much, but it's great to see you again. I hadn't heard a word about you, mainly 'cos I never come back to Brum and I'm not in touch with the old crowd. Do you ever see them? What happened to Trevor, and Hainsey, and the other Mark, and Jimmy Mack, and all that lot? What about Bonce? And Mad Joey? And Kewie?' He started to chuckle at the names, as he hadn't said them out loud for so long. They sounded ridiculous, but they still had some of their magic. These were funny people, or hard people – usually both. People who could make your day with a comment or a gesture, or spoil someone's life with the same.

'Married, kids, inside, unemployed with a few exceptions, *kids* inside in one case ... I don't see much of them. They're not exactly part of my parish. A lot of them have moved out too, past Kingstanding and Sutton. I see the odd face on match days, but then I'm usually busy Saturdays now meself.'

Tommy was thrilled to hear even the most trivial details, and plied Mark with questions. The cast of characters expanded, then included any girlfriends he could remember, then the few fans of other local teams they once knew, then people who worked at the club, then people who worked at the social club. Then the loonies you saw around and never spoke to. In the meantime, Mrs O'Connor, a huge Irishwoman with a fifty-inch bosom and scorched red arms, entered with the tea tray. Tommy recognised her – she'd been a cook at their junior school, and being a widow with her one son away, she had semi-retired to become housekeeper at the Sacred Heart. She wasn't one for smiling.

'This is Tommy, an old friend,' Mark said to her. She sniffed, and put down the things. There were proper cups and saucers, Rich Tea biscuits, and fruit cake.

'I won't be having any cake, Mrs O'Connor. I'm saying the six o'clock. Father Kelly can't make it.'

'That's right, that's right. I'm forgetting. But I'm sure our visitor will have some. What's your name again, laddy?'

'It's Tommy Burns. Remember, we saw him on television. On the football.'

'Ack. Tommy Burns! Sure 'tis you.' She stepped back and looked at him, sizing him up. 'I remember you when you were just a lad. A little face at the hatch! And now you're on the telly. Lord bless us and save us.' And then she turned her great bulk to the door and left them, shaking her head.

Tommy found this all rather amusing, as he remembered her son Sean when he was too young to go to the games. She wouldn't let him go, so he used to collect stones on Saturday mornings and try and put through the windows of the soccer specials coming into Witton Station. Then he'd go down the coach park after the game, and stand around menacingly. Age eleven. He was a bad lot. You could see the evil in him even then.

'And what happened to Sean O'Connor, then, the mad bastard?'

'Oh, he's away somewhere.' Mark shrugged. 'She doesn't like to talk about it, though.'

'I bet.'

They chatted on for a while, then, at a quarter to six, Mark got up to go.

'I'll be finished by half six. We're not expecting a lockout. You can stay here, or ...' He hesitated, and took his eye off Tommy for a moment, dropping his gaze to the carpet. Then he looked him full on, with his pale blue eyes. 'Or you're very welcome to come to Mass.'

'Er, I think I'll stay here,' said Tommy. He hadn't been to Mass for years, and had no intention of starting now. 'You know how it is.'

'Yeah, I know. OK. See you in a jiffy.'

The doors closed and Tommy was alone. *In a jiffy? What do they do to these people to turn 'em into priests? Put the clock back on 'em? Still, he looks well on it. But sidling off to say Mass to a handful of people on a Friday night, what a life. Then again, what would I be doing now at home? Sticking on the telly. Having a beer. Standing around in the kitchen with Melissa. With my hands up her skirt. Dinner out. God, I'll take my life any day.* He rested his hands on his thighs, sighed, and looked around the room again. The old brown-and-purple carpet looked like it should have been threadbare, but hadn't seen enough traffic across its woven fleur-de-lis in the half-century of its existence. The antimacassars were yellow with age rather than Brylcreem. The net curtains were yellow too, the wallpaper was neat but faded, and the old clock ticked with a quiet cluck. The whole place reminded him of the bedroom of a convalescent who wasn't getting any better. A gloom settled over him with every tick of the clock, until after fifteen minutes of getting nowhere, Tommy decided to step outside and have a stroll until it was time.

As he went to open the front door, a figure loomed in the frosted glass, and he waited while it opened the door with its own key. The burly shape came in. It had on a dog-collar too. It was Father Kelly. He grunted as if to say 'Who the hell are you?', and Tommy introduced himself. The priest grunted again, scowled, and walked off up the stairs without looking back.

*Fuck you too, you miserable bastard*, he thought as he let himself out. Long gone were the days when the sight of a dog-collar brought on a mixed fit of fear and respect in Tommy Burns. Just as the sight of a policeman makes some people blush with the guilt of uncommitted crimes, so Tommy had once quaked when this Father or that Father walked by. But now he was beyond that. He looked on them with pity and scorn now, for the wilful waste of life, and for the edifice of superstition they had to promote, at all times and with a straight face.

It was too bad, this life. *Saying prayers in Aston.* In the street five small Asian boys were playing cricket with a scuffed old bat and a tennis ball, using a lamppost as the stumps. They used two slips. A hungry mongrel trotted by on some assignment, stopping to sniff the chip papers in the gutter. It was twilight, the sodium streetlights were making weak pink starts and the red brick of the terraced houses was turning black. Tommy looked around. There was an Indian shop over the road, with jars of sweets in the windows and stickers on the door. He crossed over to it, fully expecting it to be open. *Good old Paki shops, never let you down*, he thought. But it had shut at six. *Shit. What now?* He stood looking up and down the street, then looked at the old church. He was from another parish, a mile to the north, but you always ended up going to other places, just to see what they were like. You'd hear of a priest who did a nineteen-minute Mass on a holy day, or confession at a weird time. You saw other people's statues and candle racks and hymn boards and altar stuff, heard other people's notices and intentions, dipped in their holy water and smelt their church smells of mothballs and damp and floor wax. You saw other people's priests.

There was nowhere to go. *I suppose just a little look won't hurt,* Tommy told himself. He crossed back over and stood in front of the Sacred Heart. It was an all-brick building, with some fake Tuscan trimmings – a square bell-tower, fancy white brickwork round the arches. One of the two wooden doors was ajar. He went up to it and hesitated. The inner doors were closed, and there was no sound. He stepped in and stood in the gloomy porch, where a pile of *Universe*s was bundled on the floor, as yet uncut, and a few notices hung on the green baize board. CAFOD IN THE SUDAN, he read. BINGO – EVERY TUESDAY, THURSDAY, FRIDAY AND SATURDAY. PILGRIMAGE TO KNOCK – CANCELLED. There was a rack of dry Catholic publications, the kind he had always sought to avoid. Things about missions and archdioceses and vocations. The whole atmosphere stifled him as of old, so he went to the inner door. He opened it a crack.

What he saw flooded him again, the ancient image stirring up an old feeling of frustration. The rows of brown wooden pews contained perhaps seven people in all, at least four of them stooped old ladies who kept close to the aisles. A stocky man of about fifty knelt in the front row proper, his eyes closed and his chin thrust out to the heavens. Tommy assumed he was the reader. In contrast to the gloom, the sanctuary was lit with the platinum glow of white strip lights, hidden on the other side of the arch but still easily detectable from the slabs of light they put out. The dome above the altar held an ambitious mosaic of the best of the saints, much of it in dusky gold, and the red sanctuary light hung from a very long chain, all the way from the ceiling down to eye level. The high altar was small, and held the tabernacle, small, pointy, old-fashioned, in its yellowing lace veil. The main altar was plain, with just a white cloth. In front of it sat Mark in his chair, praying. Mass was almost over – into the last leg. Tommy judged this before he had time to think about it. *Jesus. Funny how some things you don't have to think about. They just come. Look at Mark in his gear. Fuckin' 'ell. He looks pretty good.* Suddenly, Mark stood up. The praying was over. *Now the last bit. The relief.*

The little altar girl, her trainers showing beneath her cassock, approached the priest and held the big missal open for him at the prayer. Mark finished reading, his voice filling the church, picked up and relayed round the brick walls by the microphone clipped to his chest.

'The Lord be with you.'

'And also with you,' moaned the seven.

'May Almighty God bless you, the Father, the Son and the Holy Spirit.'

'Amen.'

'The Mass is ended, go in peace.'

'Thanks be to God,' went the congregation in a raggedy murmur.

*Thank God for that*, thought Tommy. *The Mass is ended.* Those were his favourite words once he hit his teenage years and piety became obsolete.

Half the congregation fell to its knees again, to be alone with its thoughts, while the other half stooped for its handbags. Mark had an announcement, though. 'We'll be picking the winner of the raffle after bingo in the club tonight, so if you can't wait to find out whether you've won, come along after bingo and before the dance. Have a great weekend.'

'Thank you, Father,' one of the old ladies incanted. Mark disconnected his microphone with a click that echoed round the room, placed it on the chair, and when his altar server had joined him, they genuflected together, and headed to the sacristy with a squeaking of rubber and a creaking of shoe leather. The main lights went off seconds later, leaving only the glow of some ancient bulbs, and the occasional outcrop of light from the electric candles at the various shrines.

Tommy felt uneasy. He had served Mass once too. Many times. Many times with Mark, when they were younger. But that was just a thing they did to get in the altar servers' football team, which was the best one. Not only did Mark show no signs of having a vocation when he was young (he was often late for Mass), he pretty much stopped going when he was fifteen. *And now look at him.*

Tommy looked around the church. One of the old ladies knelt, saying her rosary. Another whispered loudly to the pious man. After a few minutes, the sacristy door opened and the altar girl came skipping out in her anorak, and left with the woman. Finally, Mark came out. He walked down the side aisle, looking magnificent in his tailored black suit and shirt. He grinned at Tommy as he approached, and they both spoke at the same time.

'Pretty poor gate, eh?'

'How did I do?' asked Mark.

Tommy instantly regretted his remark about the low attendance. Years ago, they needled each other constantly, since they had the buffer of familiarity. Tommy was caught out by his friend's new benign nature. *How did he do? Fuck knows how he did. OK, I s'pose.*

'Er, you were great. Though I wasn't here long. The other priest came home, and I stepped outside to go to the shop and it was shut, so I just sort of wandered in. Come on, let's get the . . . let's get going.'

'Father Kelly's back already?' asked Mark with some surprise. 'When?'

'Yeah, if that's his name. Just after six. So what d'you wanna do tonight? What's your local like?'

'The club's my local.'

By the club, the priest meant the social club a few streets away from the church. This was a hall where everything was held – first Holy Communion breakfasts, pool matches, dances, jumble sales, bingo – and when there was nothing special on, it was the bar, lounge and snug of choice for a legion of ageing parishioners. The renewal rate of worshippers – even the kind who only worshipped the cut-price alcohol – was dropping rapidly. A good half of the core Irish constituency had been caught in the updraught of prosperity and had moved out of Aston into outlying areas, such as Sutton Coldfield, Lichfield and Tamworth, taking their children with them. Others had made a sort of sideways move, to Kingstanding, Nechells, and the unlucky ones to Castle Vale. The next wave of immigrants, in the seventies, had been Asians, who had made their own mosques and temples in Methodist churches and ex-carpet warehouses round the area. A few Vietnamese and people from the Philippines came to the Sacred Heart, but not enough to make much difference. The diocese had cut back the number of priests from three to two, and later, the number of services.

'Let's go over now,' suggested Mark as they left the church. He shut the door behind him, causing Tommy to look at him in surprise. 'Have to lock it. Kids get in and smash it up, or sit around taking drugs.'

'You're kidding. Drugs? Here?'

'We've found needles in the confessional boxes,' said Mark, with an even tone that Tommy couldn't be sure wasn't matter-of-factness. 'And,' he went on, this time lowering his voice, '*condoms.*'

'Huh? Fuck!' laughed Tommy. He didn't know what to say. 'Still, condoms, eh? At least they're taking care of themselves.'

'Yeah, right,' said Mark. Tommy was relieved to hear him laugh a little. 'Let's go straight on over,' he said, changing the subject. So they passed the priests' house and walked on towards the social club. The club was a low building with a flat roof. The first four feet of the walls were brick, the rest was concrete panels. It had been built by the men of the parish who gave their time for free, in the 1960s, when nearly everyone was a joiner, a painter, a carpenter or a subcontractor. The materials had been donated too. Father Kelly hadn't asked where they had come from, and he had restrained his curiosity when they changed halfway though the construction. 'You're doing a grand job, fellahs,' had been his consistent comment as he toured the site twice a week.

Fiona: Hey, Mel.

Melissa: Oh, hi, darling.

F: Are you and Tommy going out tonight? We're going to a party and we wondered if you wanted to come along.

M: No, he's away for the weekend. Gone to Birmingham to see some old friend. Then he's got a football match.

F: So come out with us, then. Perfect! We never see you Friday nights any more . . .

M: Well . . . No, I don't think so. I was going to make the most of it and go to the gym. Then I won't have to go tomorrow.

F: The gym? On a Friday night? Rather you than me. Come on. It's Notting Hill, some plonker of a producer Nick wants to meet. Loads of little girls. I'll need you along for entertainment.

M: No, really, I just want to work out. I was just going out the door. I'm seeing you all tomorrow anyway, aren't I?

F: OK, girl. It's your loss. See you, sweetie.

M: 'Bye, Fi. Call me tomorrow.

They picked their way around the aluminium beer kegs outside the door and went in. The bright strip lighting and the musty smell of beer in carpets brought more memories flooding back to Tommy. He had been here to a disco in his teens which had predictably ended in a nasty fight. He recalled a battle outside the toilets, the sight of young fists flying hard against heads and stomachs. Someone getting their head repeatedly banged into the wall. A full fire extinguisher sailing through the air into the crowd. The dramatic shouts of the peacemakers and the aggressors, as violent as each other. A prone body disappearing into a forest of feet, kicking like little daggers in their best leather shoes. He and Mark walked through into the hall itself, where the fight had started. He could plainly hear again the shrieks of the girls, the smart zzzzip of the stylus as two wrestling bodies crashed into the

DJ's console, the pop and tinkle of beer glasses falling or being converted to weapons for use against some smooth-cheeked youth. They walked out into the centre of the dance-floor, and again Tommy was struck by how small it was. He was used to this shrinking of revisited objects and places, but this one caught him out, since it unspooled an adolescent sensibility he had considered lost for good.

A few patrons were already seated in the curved benches under the huge photo mural of the River Shannon.

'What'll you have, Tommy?' asked his friend.

'Thought you'd never ask,' he replied. 'Lager.'

'Lager top's your drink, isn't it?'

'Top? Fuck. Yeah. Yes! That's right. God, I haven't had that for years. Or even thought about it. Ha! OK, Lager top.'

Mark ordered from the lad who was setting up the bar, a thin boy, no more than sixteen, with a bumfluff moustache, shorn sideburns and a flapping mat of curls down his back.

'And a Coke for me.' He searched in his pocket and found two pounds to put on the counter. 'I'll be back in a minute.' And he went off towards the stage.

Tommy took his pint and sat down alone near the table of elders, nodding to them as he went. He sucked deep on the drink, feeling the hard bite of its cold fizz, then tasting the horrible sweetness of the lemonade. *Eugh. Can't believe I used to drink this shit.* He tried it again. Then waited ninety seconds for the first warm vapours to rise in his brain, staring at the picture. *Ahh,* was all he could think, as the alcohol hit home. The Shannon was still in sharp focus, but he felt a trifle fuzzier. Warmer. The glass was half empty, so a minute later he drained it while walking back to the bar. He had been in there less than five minutes and was ready for another. His legs felt instantly lighter as he walked back to his seat, and his outlook was considerably more optimistic. *Fuck, I should come back here more often. One pound ten a pint, how do they do it?*

Out of neglect, the juke-box suddenly put on a tune on its own. His third pint found him invited over to the table of elders, men with walking sticks, and noses like strawberries, who quizzed him as to who he was, where he was from, and who he knew. When he said he was with Father O'Mally their respect went up a notch instantly. There then followed a long discussion about the lack of priests, and wasn't that a terrible thing, and what would become of the church, and that there was some talk of the Indians taking over the club on Monday nights for whatever they do.

There had already been a visiting Indian darts team, who had won. Pretty soon another record came on and he was tapping his feet and gauging how many mouthfuls were left in his glass.

When they heard he was a doctor – a fact they extracted from him at the third attempt, since they were curious to know what jobs there were for people like him in London – he was obliged to spend the usual five minutes per person diagnosing their maladies. Boils, hernias, bile, gout, earwax, bad back, arthritis . . . all things anyone could suss out for themselves, but which they feel the need to talk about and get a professional opinion on. He repressed the urge to tell them that their cirrhotic livers and clogged hearts were the things that would one day fell them, and that they would know not the day nor the hour, so they had better worry about them instead, but he couldn't be arsed. Why spoil the fun with morbidity?

At last Mark returned from setting up the bingo stuff, and Tommy intercepted him at the bar.

'Lager top and a Coke,' he said with very good cheer to the Kev behind the bar. 'Your other one's gone flat. So tell me, Mark' – he was feeling bolder – 'what's it like, being surrounded by all this now? I mean, don't you wish you could get away from it?'

Mark looked him square in the eye and said, 'This is what I do.'

'Yeah, yeah, I know that. But don't you wanna get away, you know, go somewhere more exciting? Like London, for instance?'

'No. Why should I? These are my people.' He paused, then said much more quietly, but with a seriousness that shocked Tommy, 'There's plenty of the Lord's work to be done here.'

*The Lord's work. Here we go. I'm not getting into this.* 'Like what? Shutting up shop?' he said, but his earnestness came out tagged with sarcasm. 'I don't mean that, but . . . Oh well.' He trailed off.

'It's all right here. Open your eyes and you'll see. It's not like the old days, but it's not all bad either.'

'Yeah. Shit, y'know, I didn't mean to get into all this. Come on, let's have a drink.' He was about to add '. . . and look at the birds', but that was another topic to avoid.

He was already wishing he hadn't set himself up for the whole weekend. Maybe he'd sneak away to a hotel Saturday night. Resurrect some other old friend. But he couldn't think of anyone else. Luckily, the lager took the rough edges off his anxiety, and the more he drank, the more he abandoned himself to his fate. They were now talking about football at least. Mark claimed he didn't go to the games any more, so Tommy had to fill him in on the new developments. The general decline in standards – higher prices, more bullshit razzmatazz, more celebrity chairmen, more spoiled players, better policing, membership schemes, travel restrictions, and of course those acres and acres of new seats ... 'Ah, it's all bollocks now, Mark. It's the same down the Villa. Or so I hear, 'cos they never send me there. All seats, everywhere, can you believe what they did to the Holte? Fucking Taylor Report. They should have made the grounds all standing, that would have stopped people getting crushed.'

They were seated at a table away from the elders, who tried to listen in but were defeated as the noise in the room grew steadily. It was starting to fill up – some lads were playing pool, women and children arrived with their husbands, all gelled and scented and open-collared after work. 'Hello, Father Mark,' they said warmly as they passed, but Tommy noticed from the focus of the priest's eyes and the hunch of his back that he was at last holding his attention. 'I'm telling you, the best place to be now is out there in the middle of the pitch, dressed in black, with a fucking whistle round your neck. It's the last unsullied position. And you know what? I sometimes feel like blowing the whistle on the whole fucking game and ending it.' *No, I don't mean that, that was just being dramatic,* said a voice in his head, trying to catch up with his words.

Aware of their neighbours, Tommy lowered his voice. 'There's more commentary than actual *thing* any more. It's everywhere. And the fucking season goes on for ever. It's not just your daily paper any more, it's TV wankers and hanger-on celebs. All this bollocks about the *beautiful game* – where did that come from?'

'Pele,' said Mark, then snorted a little laugh in sympathy. As Tommy zoomed alcoholically in on his face he thought he saw enthusiasm and agreement in it.

'Yeah, right. It might have been beautiful in Brazil but over here it wasn't. Or isn't. Well, it is sometimes. But who goes for the beauty, eh? I mean, why did we used to go?'

'Because we loved Villa,' replied Mark.

'Yeah, and 'cos we hated everyone else.'

His friend blushed very slightly at this, and confusion in his eyes showed that he thought he had been caught out.

'Well, it's true, innit? You hated Blues so much you had to leave school, didn't you?'

'Shh!' Mark urged him. 'Don't say that round here.' He shifted in his seat.

'Yeah, well, you hated everyone, and so did I. Now you get cunts on telly talking about their fondness for other teams, for second teams. Not Rangers and Celtic but teams they could lose to in the Cup, it's sick, it's really sick. And today, you go to an England game somewhere, like in Holland or Paris, and we start to run them, what happens? You've gone about thirty yards and there's fucking camera crews, and gits with horn-rimmed glasses and notebooks from the *Daily Express* running alongside you, long before the police ever get there, and you might as well turn yourself in on the spot, because they use the pictures to grass you up to the law when you get back.'

'You don't still go for the knock, do you?' asked Mark, incredulously. His eyes widened.

'No, no. Not really. I'm thirty-five now, mate. Thirty-four.' Tommy avoided his eye for a second, took a swill of lager, and continued. 'I think the fans are fucked now, that's the problem. They've let it get out of hand, too thick to organise themselves, so now you pay through the nose to sit in a freezing seat, there's no booze and no aggro unless you're a specialist, and there's no good singing now 'cos you're all spread out and the songs are all shite and no one can remember more than a few words 'cos their attention span's been all fucked up by television and shit schools and instant replays.'

'Know what you mean,' said Mark.

'I'm telling you, it'll be like American football soon. Permanent biased commentary over the tannoy, three hours of breaks and twenty minutes of play, the whole team getting substituted to defend a corner ...'

'Professional refs ...'

'Right, yeah, two or three of 'em just make it impossible to agree on anything, fucking adverts on everything, goalies wearing crash helmets ...'

'Picnics in the carpark ...'

'Franchises! Whole teams being bought by other cities. Liverpool being bought by EMI and made to play in London, ha!'

'A Newcastle and Sunderland merger!'

'Don't joke, it's not far off. I'm telling you, the only thing that's still real, that's not got the fingerprints of the greedy bastards all over it, is the way the younger lads play. Like in the lower divisions, where they're not all somersaulting when they score or getting their hair done funny for the cameras. And when you look at the crowd, you can see some of the old spirit. But there's a lid on it, Mark. It's not what it was. It's like being with a bunch of students.'

Mark looked saddened at the news, and unconsciously matched the scowl of his friend opposite.

Tommy took another swig and was off again at a tangent. 'So whatever happened to Kewie? Oh, I asked you that. Remember when we went with him to Chelsea in his car? And we never knew him very well, except that he had a reputation for being mental? Though he never looked it, did he, 'cos he was just a short bloke with steel-rimmed glasses and a gut? And we stop at that light in Fulham after the game and three big Chelsea fans come up to the car and start banging on it for us all to get out? And Kewie ...' Tommy started to laugh here. 'He gets out on his own, and the rest of us are all telling him to stop, it's not worth it, and he goes up to the biggest one and goes, "Come on, then, you bastard ..." Ha! Then he whips out this hatchet from under his jacket, like from out of nowhere he has a hatchet, and swings at the bloke's face, and it just nicks him on the bridge of the nose, a tiny little cut, and the fucking Chelsea fan goes all white and just looks like he's gonna shit himself and all three of 'em just turn and run!'

Father Mark couldn't help but smirk at this memory.

'The day we ran Chelsea!' said Tommy, laughing even more. They both saw the absurdity of it, and relived the fear too, and felt the warmth of their friendship again. 'Hey, and remember that time Leeds came, and there were a hundred of them that had just arrived at New Street, and a load of Villa chased them all the way down round the Rotunda and back towards the Bull Ring, and the best thing was, they didn't know where they were 'cos we hadn't played 'em for years, so some went into the market, some down the subway, some tried to cross the dual carriageway, and it was like magic, Villa stuck together and finished 'em off, group by group, kicked 'em all over the place, some of 'em even got back on the train according to John's mate, that Bluenose who worked at the ticket barrier. I remember you, you just wouldn't give up, you had your eye on that one with the moustache and chased him all over the market till he got caught between two parked lorries ...'

Mark had stopped smiling. Tommy realised, through the alcoholic heat haze that seemed to rise between them, that he might have gone a bit far, and shouldn't get down to the actual kicking and stamping of the situation. At that moment a middle-aged woman approached Father Mark, greeted him, and thanked him for a Mass said and petitions answered. Tommy sat back a bit, and stared unsteadily at the group next to him. An old man with hair white as an albino's and a red face looked across at him.

'Are ye Tommy Burns?' he asked.

'Yeah,' he said, and grinned a little drunkenly.

'And aren't ye a football referee now, isn't that grand?'

'Yeah, it's great, isn't it?' *What are you grinning at you, you look like a fucking simpleton.* The sentence sprang into Tommy's head without warning, and he found himself grinning too. The old man grinned back even more, so that his wet eyes were almost lost in the folds of soft skin, and raised his pint of stout in a benign, effortless toast. Tommy raised his glass in reply, then extinguished his drink, throwing the last two mouthfuls down as one and putting his plastic glass down a bit more heavily than he intended. He looked around. Mark was now standing talking to another woman, and other parishioners had started coming up to him. A band was setting up on the stage, making irregular thumps on the bass drum and tuning a pedal steel guitar.

'Mark. What are you having?'

'I'm OK, thanks. I'll be doing the bingo in a minute, Tommy, so you'll have to look after yourself.'

Tommy was in such a good mood by now that this seemed to him a most excellent proposition. He went towards the bar. *Must slow down a bit. It's not even eight o'clock yet. Piss call.* He veered off to the toilets. The place smelt of pine. As he stared at the snot-streaked tiles and read the Bobby Sands graffiti, he heard Mark's voice announcing from the stage that the bingo was about to start. He swayed a little, his head coming forward until it almost touched the tiles. *Casino capitalism, casino Catholicism. Who gets into heaven depends on what they're doing in the last few seconds before they die. Shagging your best friend's new wife and you have a heart attack. Stealing supplies from the office and your train goes head on into another on the way home. Slave trader, thief and pederast all your life, and just about to croak when a priest comes in and forgives it all, and ten minutes later St Peter's asking you which way you want your deckchair to face. Off to heaven, seventy-seven. But then there's Purgatory. Forgot about that. Lots of waiting, but you know your name's down, you know you'll get in eventually. Cross the Styx, sixty-six. 1977 — fuck, that was when me and Mark went to our first away game, Wolves. Two kids in bobble hats meet the Subway Army. That fifteen-minute train ride that was like crossing the border into another country. Funny faces, funny voices. But bringing half the population with us. Crammed in and singing. Mark joining in, me following. 'Come and have a go if you think you're 'ard enough!*

He smoothed his hair in the mirror. *I don't wash my hands,* he told himself as he seized the door handle. *I'm a doctor, I wash them fifty times a day. It's Friday night, and I'm off work.* 'Excuse me, love, are you selling raffle tickets?'

he said. There was an old lady sitting in the hallway at a table. She was taking the entrance money and selling bingo cards and raffle tickets. She had her coat on, because of the draught. She could just fit in behind the table, as her breasts were the size of basketballs.

'Fifty p, a book, same for a bingo card,' she said sourly. 'And don't "love" me.'

'One of each, please. What's the prize?' *You fucking bad-breathed old bag.*

'Says on the ticket. Flight to Portugal. Second is glassware. Third is sherry. Are you a member?'

'No. I'm with Father O'Mally.'

'Oh, Father Mark!' The old dragon tried to amend her tone. 'And which parish are you from?' she asked sweetly.

He leant towards her, and said with beery breath, 'I'm from the Vatican. And I know your name already.'

He walked off smartly, leaving her with her old mouth hanging open.

Inside, Mark was up on stage pulling coloured ping-pong balls from the bingo machine. Tommy got a pint of Harp, no lemonade, and sat down by a family to play his game. He couldn't keep up with the speed of the first few games. The grandmother of the party, sitting opposite, took pity on him, and scanned his row upside down after dealing with three cards of her own. 'House,' she yelled, and Tommy thought it was him. It wasn't, though. He won fuck-all while the old lady amassed her points. 'Get the 'lectric blanket, Gran,' her granddaughter kept urging. Tommy supped his pint. Time was starting to accelerate, even though he was only drinking piss-water Harp. *Harp lager is what it is, and what it is is piss. Where did I hear that?* The drink was obliterating itself. As he couldn't feel whether he was any drunker than five minutes ago, he had another mouthful to make it happen. Time was getting jumpy, as if events in the room were moving by at less frames per second. Suddenly he noticed the bingo was over and the juke-box was playing. The lights were much softer, but the mirror ball was now on. The little girl next to him was talking to him, though he couldn't remember the conversation beginning. 'Father Mark's the best. I had my first Holy Communion with him. And he judged the Brownies' competition.'

'Very nice,' he said. 'I hope he was fair.'

'Yes, my friend won and I came second in making tea and sandwiches.'

He couldn't see Mark. Gran came back with a four-inch portable TV set, and the whole family cooed and got it out of its box and fingered it. Time was speeding up. The little girl, Kylie, got all excited. 'Yer tickets, yer tickets,' she kept saying. It was the raffle. He couldn't find his. The sherry and the glasses went, but nobody had claimed the flight to Portugal. He thought it might be him. The whole family egged him on as Tommy turned out his pockets looking for his raffle tickets. People were turning around looking, as though a winner were emerging from its chrysalis. Suddenly, everyone turned the other way, as a frail old lady picked her way to the front with a big smile on her face. She was going to Portugal, not Tommy.

He was still sitting rather slumped and numb, from the lager, not the loss, when the dance started. One couple got to its feet and waltzed stoically round the inner circle of the dance-floor while the band played a cross between country and western music and a polka. Tommy took another piss, carrying his fresh pint to the bog with him, out of sheer mismanagement. *Gotta slow down now.* He drank some cold water from the tap, sensibly trying to stave off a hangover. Then he sucked his freezing lager on the way back to the main room.

It was transformed. The dance-floor thronged with couples. There were old matches and established borrowings, new experiments and boring conventions. A double-chinned girl and her blushing fiancé jived furiously. Children did their own mad dance, the shaking of limbs and childish spasms of joy, and a few of them danced like tiny adults with a loving parent. Kylie asked him where his girlfriend was. 'In London,' he replied. She seemed satisfied with that. He thought she was going to ask him to dance, but she didn't.

The band leader sang 'Coward of the County'. The one about beating the shit out of people. Time was speeding up. The room rolled under his gaze, and the spinning rectangles of light fascinated him, the way they swept the room like elliptical radar, rushing down the straights and taking the ends of the room more carefully. When the world spun his conscience usually kicked in, because it usually meant he was about to throw up. He wished he could rein himself in and slow the flow of lager. He looked at the bright white lights of the bar. Kevin was serving away, a little head coping with the crowds of men. *No, I'll pass on this round.*

'I'm a rockabilly re-bel, from head to toe, I gotta keep a-rocking, everywhere I go ...' sang the band man, a bony face under a cowboy hat. *Fuck, I haven't eaten. Crisps.* He spent five minutes at the bar, getting sloshed with pints that men carried four at a time back to their tables. Just as he was getting his crisps a different singing voice started. Over the sound of accordion and the gentle swishing of the drum brushes, he heard a warm baritone, with a tiny metallic edge from the microphone, singing:

'I just received a letter, from my home in Oi-er-land . . .'

The words went right through Tommy, straight into his memory.

'. . . 'Twas my mother's feeble hand.'

Everyone at the bar turned and looked admiringly. 'Sure doesn't Father have a grand voice.' They were listening to Father Kelly, who crooned in his priestly black suit in the very centre of the stage. Tommy hadn't noticed the old grey head arrive. He held the microphone perpendicular to the ground and sang over the top of its flat head, turning his torso slowly to give his attention to everyone in the room. The sound that came from him was a delight, a rich sound, tender but with a masculine force behind it. But the words themselves had even more effect on Tommy, far more than he expected. He felt a wave of emotion in his chest, nostalgia and pain together, like the double warming of a swig of Scotch. Half the room stood to attention while the other half danced to the slow waltz. Tommy broke free of the crush at the bar and leaned against the wall, so transfixed by the sound that he forgot to eat. The song was about someone in England getting a letter from his old mother in Ireland asking when was he coming back home, to the Wicklow Hills.

> *'As I gaze across those mountains, I relive a moment's joy,*
> *Those same old Wicklow Mountains, where you wandered as a boy.'*

The nostalgia was due simply to the fact that he had heard this song a hundred times before, at dances such as these, in deeply happy times, and then had forgotten it. The pain came from the meaning, the pathos weighing heavy on him and making everything else seem trivial. A mother's love, a wandering son . . . he felt himself getting a bit choked. Father Kelly rendered it to perfection in his deep clear voice, and the couples sailed serenely by. He saw Mark in the arms of a woman, a middle-aged woman in a plain red tent of a dress and some pearls. She danced with her head erect, gravely looking over the shoulder of her priest, as though to accept the acclaim for having made the greatest catch in the room.

> *'Your picture's by my bedside still,*
> *And each night I pray that you'll come back home,*
> *Among the Wicklow Hills.'*

He didn't even put a warble into his voice, since the song carried its own dramatic weight well enough. Everyone clapped and smiled and commented on Father Kelly's beautiful singing, and the old man himself smiled and went to put the mike down. They called for more, though, and after teasing them a little, he agreed to sing just one. Tommy looked at his watch – it was half eleven already. He was starving. He ate his crisps without tasting them. He located his pint on a rail and started in on it. Then he spotted Mark again in the throng, this time accepting a dance from a lady with lacquered hair and pendant earrings, just as fiercely proud as the last. Nobody asked Tommy to dance, and he realised he was slumping against the wall. Though he wanted to enjoy everything, he found himself blotting it all out with his lager. He had a moronic conversation with another old man, this time about the man's old Alsatian, and he stared at the legs of a teenage girl for a few minutes, then took himself outside unsteadily for some air.

He sat down on a beer keg under the sign, SACRED HEART SOCIAL CLUB, and breathed the fresh air, the first cold air of the year. *It's always a degree or two colder up here*, he reminded himself. He found the cigarettes in his pockets. *I haven't had one of these for, God, seven years*, he thought. *Nah, I won't. Oh fuck it, why not? No, don't be stupid.* He took one out, and let it hang from his lip while he searched for a light. He sat there on his keg for a minute, looking rumpled and dazed, until a couple came through the door on their way home.

'You gorra light?' he said to their backs. *God, I sound awful. Gorra. What's happening to me?* They ignored him, like he was a yob or a drunk, and the tab stayed dangling from the wet inside of his lip, until finally it fell, bounced off his knee and landed on the damp ground. He stared at it, feeling the coma creeping up on him. *Too much lager, too much lager.* His face was partly numb, he had lost track of time, and his stomach, which so far had just felt empty and full at the same time, was starting to swirl. *Oh no, gotta get up, gotta get up.* He got to his feet, unsteadily, but the process had already begun. A dizziness swept into his mind like mist. His environment started to swirl a little, and clean saliva began weeping into his mouth from all sides. *Here we go . . .* he thought, and walked a few steps to be out of the light, then leaned his head against the wall, cushioned from the concrete by his hand, ready to throw up. Practice had taught him to lean far out, to minimise the splatter on his shoes and trousers, but as he braced himself, waiting in the dark for the involuntary convulsions from his stomach, he heard a voice.

'Tommy! Too much lager, son?' It was Mark. Tommy turned his head ninety degrees and smiled weakly as he saw his friend standing under the light as though he had just been beamed down from the mother ship.

'I'll only be a minute. I think I had a bad pint.' *Shit. Done it again. Impugned his social club this time. Impugned.* Mark came over to him and rested a hand lightly on Tommy's back. This had the effect of stopping the nausea. Tommy wasn't pleased because he just wanted the lager out of him, and it felt rather like being put off pissing in a public urinal by someone else arriving just before you get started. But then he noticed the nausea stayed away for another thirty seconds. Mark didn't say anything. He lifted his head and took a deep, cool breath.

'Fuck, I feel much better,' he said. 'Did they teach you that at the seminary?'

Mark laughed. 'You still like your beer, don't you?'

'No, I'm much better than in the old days. I hardly drink at all now. Makes you fat for one thing. I guess it was just the excitement of being here.'

Mark spoke. 'Yeah well, remember there's the game tomorrow morning.'

'Oh shit, I forgot about that. What time?'

'Nine-thirty kick-off.' He paused, then offered an explanation. 'The special schools get the worst times.'

'Special? You mean like *handicapped*? It's a handicapped game? I've never done one of them before.'

'Full on. The kids are really excited too, I told them we were having a proper ref off the telly and they went mad. So we better turn in soon. We have to pick half of 'em up too.'

Tommy moved into the light to look at his watch: 12.30 a.m. It was always 12.30 when it felt like 11.30. He felt strangely sober. They went back in, in to the warmth and the lights and the music. He felt the heavy thump of the bass drum as they entered the room. The dancing was still going strong, and as Mark made his goodnights he was detained several times by grateful parishioners. He shook hands and tousled heads and laughed at remarks, and even noted something in a little black book which a curled-up old lady said to him. Tommy had another pint while he was waiting and half-heartedly tried to chat up two sixteen-year-old girls who were sitting near the bar. *This isn't hard*, he thought, as he addressed them fluently, unabashed, *but it's not really working either*.

The fear had gone, he realised, fallen though the generation gap, the old fear he had felt decades before at dances like these. But he may as well have been talking to a couple of aliens for all the comprehension he saw in their eyes. *Just chatting, like,* he told himself as they pushed through the crowd and left him.

*God, this wretched life. Come on, Mark, where the fuck are yah?* He located him and passed him a pleading look. Mark spotted him across the room. He saw Tommy's ruffled hair and skin looking saggy. The eyes red from the day. The tie sadly askew. He broke off his conversation immediately and came across to Tommy, and put his arm around his shoulder.

'Are you ready for home, Tom? I'm sorry, I still have things to deal with here.'

'Yeah, I'm knackered. Love to stay but I'm fucking knackered. Give me the key and I'll see you later.'

'I was just going to say . . . Here it is, the Yale.'

'See ya later.'

'Half nine kick-off, don't forget. I'll wake you anyhows.' Mark smiled his broad, pleasant smile at him, and even through the fog of his drinking Tommy felt the ambient charm. *You dirty cockney bassstards, you dirty cockney bassstards.* It came into his mind how Mark always used to lean extra heavily on the sibilant in *bastards,* to make the sound cut through the air across the pitch and into the other fans' ears. *Now here's this charming man giving me the key to his house so he can stay out later schmoozing for Jesus.*

'Yeah,' was all he could muster by now. He stumbled through the crowd, which was showing no sign of thinning out. A few older couples were leaving, but he passed others still arriving. Out in the cool air he breathed heavily and picked his way though the streets on autopilot, staggering a little.

By rights he should have gone straight to bed – to the couch in the living room. He noticed someone had made it up – probably Mrs O'Connor – with sheets and blankets and a pillow. He should have brushed his teeth and put an end to the night, his dry eyes aching from his lenses, his thoughts passing through his mind as jumpily as a zoetrope. But the lager in him wouldn't let him lie just yet. When he couldn't find the toilet, he went upstairs in search of it, his lens case in one hand, carrying his pasted brush before him like a water diviner. Upstairs were just plain white doors. He didn't want to stumble into anyone's bedroom, but he had to try them. He opened the one furthest away a crack. He saw the foot of a single bed, with a grey counterpane pulled tight, as grim and spartan as in a hotel in Connemara. He pushed the door open a bit more. *They're all out anyway,* he reassured himself. *This must be Mark's room. Jesus.* An eerie shame crept over

him, the trespasser's cowardly fear. Then came the warm buzz of curiosity.
He stepped inside. A bed, narrow as a student's scratcher. An old wooden
wardrobe with a suitcase on top. A plain wooden desk, with two drawers.
An open hearth with a two-bar electric fire in front of it. The floor was
covered in lino, with two rugs, one near the door, the other near the desk.
*He gets out of bed on to the cold lino?* A flicker of a thought followed this one,
an unspoken surprise at himself, at his forensic solicitude for his old friend.
Since he was pissed, however, this feeling swiftly fell away, as a vapour trail
in too-warm air, and he took two more steps into the tiny room. There
was nothing on the walls, except for a crucifix above the bed. This alone
gave the room the feel of a cell, of nuns and monks making infinite space
in their souls. On the desk was a picture of Pope John Paul II in a frame,
and a snapshot of an old lady. Tommy remembered her. Mark's mom. A
small holy woman who had lived lightly on the earth.

There were a few books lined up neatly along the back of the desk:
the New English Bible, a book of biblical commentary, *Crossing the Threshold
of Hope,* by His Holiness Pope John Paul II, *God of Surprises,* Gerard W.
Hughes. There were also some pamphlets at the end with furry spines.
Open on the desk lay an exercise book with a fountain pen on it. Tommy
stood over it, to read it without actually bending down.

> When Jesus fed the five thousand, he didn't magic loaves and fishes
> out of the air like Paul Daniels [crossed out] David Copperfield. No.
> What he did was encourage others to take out their packed lunches,
> which they were all hiding under their cloaks, by taking out his own.
> He made the first move. On that hot day on the hill he broke the
> ice, and that is what we as followers of Christ have to do.

He'd never seen Mark's handwriting before, but there it was, a spiky,
crabbed script, written without haste as though straining against its own
illegibility. *Mark preaching. There's a first.* He turned back a few pages, leaning
closer. There was more. He turned back the pages, browsing.

'At this time of summer holidays let us remember those who are always
with us, the poor.' 'Pentecost means fire, and the fire of the Holy Spirit
should not sit on our heads like a tounge [*sic*] of flame above the apostles,
it should sweep through our hearts every day like an inferno ...' 'New
Covenant ...' 'The Paschal Candle symbolises ...'

Every page was close-written in that squashed script, and every line he
read betrayed an earnestness he had never imagined Mark could possess.

*He's dead serious about this Christ stuff. Jesus.* Tommy swayed and stumbled a little. The only thing within him was the lager. *I had really better get to bed soon. Where's that fucking bathroom?* He looked again around the room and then stepped over to the bed. *The priest's bed. What a life.* Still with his pasted toothbrush in hand, he sat down on the edge of it. It felt like a concrete bench. The cell, the dim light, the spartan surroundings were all getting to him. Mark's struggle with his sermons. He stuck the brush in his mouth. *I'll do a self-cleaning,* he told himself. He brushed away, swallowing the foul minty suds from time to time. Then he kicked off his shoes, and with an expert hand, removed his lenses and put them into their watery case. Tommy lay back, thinking about it all, wondering what he was doing up here, in Birmingham, wondering how so much had changed. A shiver of homesickness ran through him, of missing Melissa. He lay there on his back looking at the lumpy wallpaper and Christ's washboard abs and bare feet above him. *I wonder what position he'd play, if he came down to earth again. If he was picked for England. Or Israel. Eligible for both, I s'pose. Probably fancy himself as a mercurial number ten. Long hair and all that. Maybe he'd just be a glamour centre-forward, a Sniffer Clarke, a goalhanging Lineker. A poacher of souls, and a fisher of men. I'd stick him in midfield, see what he was really made of. Running up and down the field till the only thing he wants is a basin to throw up in. Funny if he turned out to be a hotshot. Peter Lorimer, ripping the net with his free kicks. Bruce Rioch, the King. Or Villa. We'd never have gone down to the Third Division if we'd had him. Wonder what he's like in goal? Jesus saves, but Lockhead gets the rebound. Yeah, right.*

# 3

Tommy wakes up in Mark's bed;
breakfast; to the match, picking up
crips; pixie eyes; second-half Tommy;
rest and review

'Hey, Tommy lad, wake up!'

'*Shit*. What the fuck?'

'Cup of tea for you. It's eight o'clock.' Father Mark put it down on the bedside table and headed out of the bedroom.

Tommy felt like shit. He was jack-knifed across the bed like a hastily stubbed-out cigarette, but the sheer embarrassment of having dropped off in someone else's bed made him raise himself on his elbow, open an eye and ask lamely, 'Uh. Did I fall asleep? Shit, man, I'm sorry. What time is it? Tea, yeah, great.'

'We're leaving in fifteen, got to pick up some of the team. Mrs O's making some breakfast.'

Mark winked at him as he left the room. The priest's wink. One of the lads. But he *was* one of the lads, Mark. No one used to doubt that. He came from left field, with his ambitious raids into other mobs, and his never being a big drinker, but he was definitely a top Villa fan. Not a leader, like some of the other nutters, but not a foot-soldier like Tommy. More of a free agent. A consultant hooligan. Working for himself.

The door was shut and Tommy tried to go back to sleep, but he couldn't. The booze was still coursing through his veins. He was fully clothed, but the blanket was over him. His tongue felt like a pub carpet. His clothes seemed to have shrunk on him. He had a hard-on down one trouser leg.

And his eyes hurt. He opened them and looked up at the crucifix. His mind started racing, as though his sleep had been just a blink. *I fell asleep on the host's bed. What a prick! Oh God, what a prat.* On the bedside table he could see the tea steaming. He hoisted himself up and lifted it over. The cup rattled in the saucer. He could see a couple of tea leaves circling the tan surface like sharks in a pool. He sipped them up. *Mmm. Two sugars. Nice one, Mrs O. You're not such an old boiler after all.*

With a lot of effort he pulled himself up in bed and leaned against the wall. His head was beating. He felt hungry and full at the same time. The slightest sound brought an amplified rustle of blood to his inner ear. The window was streaked with rain, and he could hear the depressing swish of car tyres on the wet street outside. Tommy sipped his hot tea and tried not to think. *I must have worked my way under the covers in my sleep. Haven't done that for a while. Oh God, this game, I feel like total shite.*

Downstairs, Father Mark had rolled up the bedclothes on the couch, packed his sports bag and was sitting down to a fry-up. Mrs O'Connor rattled pans in the kitchen amidst a great hissing of fat. Father Kelly sat opposite him reading the paper. Without lowering it from his face, he suddenly spoke.

'So you're taking the kids up to the field, are ye? Jolly good. You'll be back for the vigil, I hope.'

'Aren't you saying the vigil Mass tonight?' asked Mark, sounding surprised.

Father Kelly lowered the paper and looked at the younger man over the half-moons of his reading glasses. With his white hair and his double chin he looked every bit the stern grandfather. 'Something's come up. I have two weddings to do here, then Mrs Mooney's youngest is getting married in Sutton and they've asked me to do a blessing at the dinner. There's no way I'll be back by six for that. You're taking the car, aren't ye?'

He raised the paper without waiting for a reply. Mark glanced towards Mrs O'Connor, who had her back to them. From behind, her giant bulk seemed to keep mum for the older priest. He often checked her countenance when Father Kelly seemed to be taking advantage, in search of a trace of recognition, if not of support. He had never yet seen it, though. So he put it down to his own lack of trust, and scolded himself. He had even spoken of it in the most direct terms to Father Kelly in confession, for Father Kelly almost always heard his confession. The elder priest had kept his usual silence behind the steel gauze, then gently admonished him in the most general terms and absolved him fully.

The door creaked as Tommy walked stiffly in. He managed a pained 'Mornin'' to the three of them, and stood awkwardly by the table.

'Sit down, Tommy Burns!' cried Mrs O'Connor. She was in bustle overdrive now with another mouth to feed. 'Won't you have a bit of breakfast!' It was an order.

Tommy nodded his assent. He sat down to more tea, four pieces of toast, and a plate of baked beans, sausage, mushrooms, three fried eggs and bacon that had been dipped in scalding water after coming out of the pan. He wasn't able to communicate much at that meal, on account of the grey clouds of depression and uncertainty veiling his mind, but when he noticed Mrs O'Connor retrieving each rasher in turn from a bowl of hot water on the table, and her red hands flipping them on to his plate with a fork like live eels, he raised an eyebrow in Mark's direction.

'It's Father Kelly,' Mark said above the noise of the engine as they bowled along Aston Lane in the elder priest's Morris Minor. 'Mrs O worries about his sodium. She read somewhere that you could reduce your intake by rinsing off your rashers. I don't know. Is that true?'

It was now exactly 8.25 a.m. No sooner was his last mouthful of fried bread down Tommy's throat than Mark had motioned to him that they should get going. Father Kelly had merely grunted from behind the racing page as they left.

'Salt is the least of his problems, given the amount of grease he gets,' replied Tommy, with unconcealed disgust. He was putting in his lenses as they drove. The left one went in OK, but the right was a bastard. It kept folding over and his fingers were so wet his eyelids kept slipping through them and shutting. 'Fuck it,' he muttered, and settled for one lens, for the time being, keeping the other eye shut. 'And you better watch it too. Well, at least you get exercise, I s'pose.'

'Oh, I only eat that stuff on Saturdays. I'm a fruit man in the mornings these days, if I have anything at all.'

'Huh,' muttered Tommy. *Fruit. That's pretty good. I could do with a pint of orange juice right now, and about six Hedex. Jesus, we'll have to stop ... Fucking hell, look what they've done to the Crown, I can't believe it!*

The Crown & Cushion pub had been completely rebuilt since he had last been there. The old brick building had been torn down completely, and replaced with a fake brick structure – brick cladding. The shape was a bit more modern, of course – it was squatter than the old grand building which had a huge ballroom upstairs, but the whole exercise seemed pretty gratuitous; as it was, the bar and lounge looked much the same size as before.

'What happened to the fucking Crown, then?' he asked out loud.

This was the pub they always went to before a home game. It was a definite Villa pub. It was a Villa pub seven days a week, but it was also just far enough from the ground — exactly one mile, or twenty minutes walk — to attract the right kind of people on match days. The locals were supplemented by Villa fans coming in by bus from Sutton, Kingstanding, Great Barr, Walsall, Handsworth and Birchfield, who treated it as their own. The singing was OK, but the best thing was it was situated next to a roundabout at a key intersection, so it made a good lookout post. There was plenty of room to stand outside and sample the atmosphere as the crowd walking to the ground grew towards kick-off time.

Inside on a Saturday it was just full of drinkers. Big men standing around drinking beer and talking about football. Young men cultivating their guts and stories, talking and listening in circles. Sometimes, for a few months at a time, there was a pool table, but pool wasn't much of an attraction. There was no pub shit up on the walls, and no Villa stuff either, not even behind the bar. It was just a drinkers' den, and a lookout. A place to gather at and leave from in a mob.

The other special thing about the Crown was that it was sufficiently far from the ground that it wouldn't be taken by away fans. Pubs on the outskirts of cities, maybe. Places near motorway intersections, when they still have their coach to get to the game. Or pubs right by the ground, so close to the source that the police just let the away fans have them. The Aston Hotel down at the junction of Witton Lane and Witton Road was occasionally like that for a big game. At one o'clock you'd find it surrounded by strange faces and their cheap and nasty colours — dark blues or reds and lots of white — but it was only a two-hundred-yard march from the Witton End, down a wide road full of police. It was within that carnival that builds up around the walls of a football ground before a match, that peculiarly violence-free zone, where, aside from the chants, aggression is still on its leash. But the Crown, the Crown was an inner-city pub, it was territory. You'd have to be mad to try and take it. And get there early.

Chelsea were, and Chelsea did. Tommy remembered how a rogue coachload of them — driven by someone who either approved or didn't care, or even more likely was in there drinking too — had appeared there at half past eleven one Saturday morning. Most Villa were still rolling out of bed or watching *Tiswas*. It wasn't like the barmaids were going to stop them, and they paid for most of their drinks. By the time word got around and the first Villa started arriving to see what they could do, you could hear them inside, singing their Chelsea songs, and see a few mean-looking ones standing outside the main door. On the other side of the street was another pub in a row of shops, in the late-sixties no-effort style of architecture, a mean concrete box with picture windows. It was the New Crown & Cushion. Villa gathered there, until, after an hour of morose drinking, head-scratching, name-calling, dissent and confusion, Mark abandoned his half, split from the pack and set off across the street.

There were already a few mad Villa wandering around the outside of the Crown. Ones and twos of nutters walked by, staring at the pub just as people gather to look at the smouldering remains of a favourite building that has burned down in the night. They were trying to see in through the windows, staring at the Chelsea scum round the door. Mark did a lap of the building too, then, with his nose held high, walked right past the gatekeepers and inside. One of them said something to him – some mock-friendly greeting – and he replied 'All right' back without batting an eyelid.

After he'd been gone for a few moments, and hadn't been thrown out in pieces, another Villa fan walked in. Hainsey, a big skinhead in a combat jacket who couldn't stand to see the Crown being desecrated. A few minutes later, a couple more went in. The Chelsea on the door disappeared inside, and as they did, a steady flow of Villa began crossing the road from the New Crown to the Old, holding the door open for the one behind them as they entered. Tommy was one of them.

Pissed football fans who hate each other don't always go at it straight away – escalation is all part of the experience. They can stand in the same room as each other for up to ten minutes before the lid blows. Villa lurked and murmured at one end of the bar, with growing impatience aimed as much at each other as at the interlopers. These were the days when most people wore no colours except perhaps a round metal badge with the Villa crest on it, so there wasn't yet a formal excuse to start anything, on either side. It was Villa's move, and they didn't have the numbers.

After a few minutes of shameful silence, Hainsey began a song: 'We're the Villa, we're the Villa, we are the Champions!' Not one that was literally true very often, but it always brought out a surge of pride, and everyone joined in. Chelsea cackled and howled, but didn't move; they carried on drinking and replied with some of their own cockney stuff. Everyone knew who everyone else was. If you knew a face, you loved them because they were with you, but if you were looking into the eyes of a stranger across the room, he might as well have been from outer space and you hated the bastard, and wondered what it would be like to kick his head in.

The last thing anyone expected was a singing contest – two lots of fans, away from the law, especially one of them being Chelsea, the cream of the mad bastard crop. For a few minutes, though, as songs were traded back and forth, things threatened to turn pretty. As if these people would end up trading big smiles and good-natured jibes. A few fans on the fault line where the two groups met faced up to each other, unofficially, taunting each other for their accents and calling each other ugly and stupid. Mark was one of them. He was deep in dialogue with a Chelsea fan he had taken an instant dislike to, an overweighter with blond highlights and a gold chain round his neck. Mark had a way of peering down his nose at someone and maintaining a minimal conversation that constantly bordered on the offer of a fight. He couldn't stand this close and not want to hit someone.

Suddenly, possessed by some spirit, either of bravery, shame or just booze, Villa's thirty or so moved forward across the carpet, arms raised, singing as one 'The Villa! The Villa!' At the very same moment, Mark dipped his head and nutted his Chelsea fan, and hell finally broke loose. Half the Chelsea dropped their drinks and waded in, picking their adversaries by proximity, unless they had previously established a match by eye contact. As usual, several of them made a beeline for Black Danny, because he was black, six foot six and fearless, and Hainsey because he was the epitome of an evil skinhead. Tables with wrought-iron legs went tumbling in the scramble to get at each other. Mark was in there on the front line, and fell under several kicks and punches while hanging on to his man by his now-torn Chelsea shirt. Kung fu kicks flew (you had to hand it to Chelsea for introducing the kung fu kick to British football when they invaded the pitch against Leeds in the baggiest days of the mid-1970s), big fists went down on to faces and throats, and as the first fans tripped and staggered over, the boots went in to sides and spleens. The other half of the Chelsea must have thrown their drinks, because for the first few seconds the air was alive with flying glasses. One of the barmaids screamed, people roared their battle cries – 'Viiiiiiilla!', 'Cheeee-elsea!' – and the floor rumbled with urgent footwear.

Tommy now recalled this sound, and remembered doing his favourite thing – hopping up on to one of the benches to see better, whacking Chelsea fans as they struggled in the grip of someone he knew, and picking glasses off the window ledge to hurl into the crowd across the room. The mirror behind the bar shattered, revealing its sad plywood back. Someone on the other side ran forward and threw a stool through a window, just for good measure. *You had to admire that too*, thought Tommy.

At the time it had seemed like great fun, standing on high, screaming and throwing things around, showing the cockneys where they could and couldn't go. Tommy wasn't worried that Mark, although a great mate, was off pursuing his own agenda under a hail of kicks, trying to burst the Chelsea fan's nose. He couldn't have stopped him, anyway. But now he wondered if perhaps he should have been there on the floor with him, helping him. He looked across at Mark driving. He still hadn't answered. His face was concentrated on the road ahead. After a few seconds Mark looked around.

'What?'

'Nothing. Nothing.'

'No, go on, what?'

'Oh, you know, the Crown, I was just thinking about the Crown. Weren't you?'

Mark's eyes flicked back between his passenger and the road. 'No, I was thinking about the game today. These kids are really looking forward to it. They really want to see a real referee, y'know.'

*Jesus. Him and his kids. Ah, maybe he's forgotten all about Chelsea. Maybe he's forgotten lots of stuff — I have. The Church has certainly done a good job on him.*

In big pub fights like these no one wins territory, as ultimately everyone ends up in the street so they can be seen to have been fighting. Most of the Villa were driven out of the door, but in through the other entrance, from the bar into the lounge, came another wave of Villa, bigger, heavier and later, who battled with Chelsea and drove them out. Outside the street was electric — patches of youths fighting in flowerbeds and round parked cars, dedicated individuals racing after their victims like greyhounds after the electric bunny. Confusion reigned, as people jumped off buses to join in and others tried to get on the Chelsea coach for no apparent reason. Some Villa came running up from the direction of the shopping precinct. Chelsea split into fragments but were still making a lot of noise. The last blows were exchanged when a police van screeched round the corner and six coppers jumped out. Spreading in all directions, they took over as the pursuers, rugby-tackling anyone in their way, armlocking necks and losing their helmets. A carload of police arrived too, then a black maria which quickly filled its tiny cells with the arrest quota. Order was restored in minutes.

Chelsea regrouped and went marching down the road to the ground, still singing, high on life, reined in by growing numbers of police. Villa walked ahead and behind, taunting them, but since it was still too early to go to the ground, most turned back halfway and returned to the Crown. Tommy and Mark met up later at the game. Neither had a scratch on him.

*Maybe it's all just ancient history to him.* Squinting out the window, he saw they were heading towards Perry Hall park. More life flashed by. He was glad when the priest started issuing orders.

'OK, Tommy, I'm getting out here to pick up the van. There's two players who live off in the other direction I want you to go and get. Their names are Kevin and little Jamie. Bring 'em over to the park as soon as you can. Pitch fourteen.'

'Oh, and I'm s'posed to remember which is pitch fourteen? It's been a long time, Mark.'

'Oh yeah, sorry. It's the one up in the corner ...'

'On the hill? With the slope? And ...'

'... The mud, yeah, that's the one. It's all coming back now, eh?'

'The pitch we never won on?'

'The scene of your great shame, Tommy Burns – sent off against St Anthony's for dissent.' Mark laughed. 'Hey, that was your only time, wasn't it? What did you learn about reffing from that?' he asked, enjoying his friend's fame and discomfort.

'I learned you don't call the ref a bald-headed cunt. Not to his face anyway. But he was one of their dads. I mean, you could see he was biased from the start.'

Mark was laughing even harder. It made Tommy feel good at last, this slight stirring of the old character he loved.

When he settled down, Mark continued about the players Tommy had to fetch. 'Oh yes, and Kevin's in a wheelchair. I hope the lift's working. He's very independent, though, don't try and help him too much, he hates that. Here's the addresses. Be quick, eh?'

They had pulled up outside a semi-detached house on the Walsall Road. The priest jogged up the drive and rang the bell. Tommy slid over to the driver's seat. *What a piece of shit this is. This gearstick's all over the place.* He saw Mark talking and nodding to a middle-aged man at the door, who gave him some keys, then the priest hopped into a yellow minibus parked in front of the house, backed out smartly and was off.

*Sunshine bus,* thought Tommy. *No seat belts, just weld 'em into place. That's what we used to say.* He looked at the address. Erdington. Watt House.

He stuck the car in first and pulled away, the weedy engine straining to haul a ton of plate steel up the hill. After thirty seconds he got it into second; just as the whinnying indicated it was time for third, he spotted a gap in the central reservation.

Out loud he said, 'Forgive me, Father, for what I am about to do, but hang ... on ...' He pulled the car hard right and began a long arcing U-turn. Halfway round the skinny wheels began squealing, and the car leaned dangerously. Tommy felt slightly sick; the G-force felt all out of proportion to the speed he was travelling at. The St Christopher dangling from the mirror swung and flashed in the fresh sun. The car seemed to move in slow motion as he cut across all three lanes, and he caught sight of the noses of a wave of oncoming traffic dip as they braked to avoid him, headlights pulsing furiously.

The squealing and the lurching and the nausea stopped and he was on his way to Erdington. *Or is it Marsh Hill? Fuck. It's somewhere near the cemetery anyway. This is back the way we came. What were you thinking, Mark? We could have got these two first.*

The car didn't have a radio, so he passed the time looking at the scenery with his one eye. Union Cold Storage, with its big wet patches on its big blank walls. He never did find out what they stored in there. Tucker Fasteners. A classic factory of concrete and glass with a zigzag roof, where hundreds of men worked round the clock to supply the world with ... *press studs*, hadn't someone told him once? *Or zips.* It was closed now anyway. *Maybe someone will buy it and turn it into a dance studio. Tucker Fasteners. Always made me think of Father Tucker at St Teresa's. Nice bloke. White bloke with a natural afro. Years later turned up in a scandal where he ran off to Ireland with a woman who was having his baby. The old devil.*

With the window down and the sun shining he was starting to feel a bit better. The roads were pretty busy with the early shoppers. He took a few side roads out of curiosity and kept coming up against the canal or old industrial sites, but eventually he made it to Marsh Hill and turned into North Park Road.

Cautiously he went over a speed bump. He was in the land of freelance dogs, saplings snapped in two and council maisonettes surrounded by low white railings like pipe cleaners. He followed the curve of the road. *162A, 162A, come on, where are you? 146 ... 150 ... 158 ...* Hardly any of the houses still had numbers on. A few helpful souls had spray-painted or marker-penned theirs on again. *Shit. It ends here.* It was a cul-de-sac, with just a footpath leading away. Five to nine, read his watch. He went back the way he had come, but the numbers on the other side were all low odds. He turned and came back. *158 ... that must be 160. Where the fuck is 162?* There wasn't a soul around. He got out of the car and stood there helpless. He walked part-way down the alley, then changed his mind. *It's not going to be down here. This is just some dogshit path*, he thought, hopscotching round the various coils and mounds.

Back in the road he leaned against the car and waited. *This fucking place, what am I doing here?* This was the sort of place he had given up doing house calls in London to avoid. No more Rottweilers, no more babies wetting him, no more boyfriends threatening to kick his poncy facking head in ... *Fucking dogs, shitting everywhere. Eating babies' faces off.*

He went back and stood by the car. He put his other lens in and felt better. Still no one was around. *Fuck this. Little Jamie can stay in today. Play with his Alsatian.* He got in and drove off, but twenty yards down the way he saw a little girl of about ten.

'Hey, where's 162A?'

'I dunno.'

'Jamie. Little kid, d'you know him? Handicapped.'

'Oh, Jamie, yeah, he's my friend. He's not han-dicapped though,' she said, smiling and amazed. 'Who said he was han-dicapped?'

'I dunno. I'm just taking him to his football match. Where's the house? I can't fuckin' ...'

He stopped himself. He got out of the car, and was relieved to see the girl not run away.

''E lives down 'ere,' she said, and walked ahead of him. She was a little stick girl in pink cycling shorts and a padded coat. She looked like the sort of skinny girl who you see on a beach on a blazing hot day – she's been out of the water half an hour and is still shivering, wrapped up in a huge towel. Then she spends the winter walking round the estate in the frost in a T-shirt and no socks. *We never did this in physiology at medical school,* he thought.

Tommy was a bit nervous about being led down an alley by a ten-year-old. He kept talking, loudly, anything that came into his head, so people wouldn't think he was planning to rip her clothes off, sexually assault her and leave her in a bin bag. She led him all the way down the alley – 'Watch the dog poo!' – past some garages and washing lines, to someone's gate. There was no number on it. She pushed it open and said, ''E lives in 'ere with 'is mum.'

'Hey, thanks,' said Tommy, vastly relieved. He was so grateful he wanted to give her some sweets or something, some money to reward her kindness, so she'd do it again someday. But he didn't want to risk it. *Paying little girls in back alleys. Nah. I'd have a tattooed fist down my throat in minutes. I'd be lynched. The whole street would roll out of bed for that. Probably a lot of Villa fans round here too.*

She gave him a big smile, said ''Bye', and skipped off the way she'd come, obviously very pleased with herself. Tommy pushed the gate and gingerly stepped up the path. There was no 'Beware of the Dog' sign, but there was a great skid of tan faeces on the concrete in front of him, like a serving of butterscotch mousse.

'Er, Jamie? Does Jamie live here?' he called out. He didn't want to sound like a poncy doctor, but he knew he wasn't calling on some mate his own age. A three-year-old wearing just a nappy came out of the back door and stared at him with big brown eyes. She had a pale blue dummy in her mouth that hid half her expression. She looked at him as he approached, then ran silently back into the flat. He advanced and tapped on the open door, looking into the gloom. It led into a hall, with the kitchen off to one side, so he stepped in. He saw the little girl silhouetted in the hall, looking back at him, then she turned and ran shouting, 'Mummy!' Then he heard the scuttling of claws on lino and a white bulldog came running at him. It stopped a foot away, its ears back, growling very softly, but not showing its teeth.

'Hey, boy, easy, easy. Friend!' he said pathetically. It was nearly his turn to make a coil on the carpet. His heart was hammering. He took a quarter-step forward, and the dog adjusted its volume upward. *Fucking hell, let me out of here.* 'Hello? Is anyone home?' Tommy shouted. The dog barked. *Fuck. Oh fuck. No more dogs, please. God get me out of this mess.* Then a woman emerged into the corridor.

'Who the bleedin' 'ell are you?' she asked. She was a fatso of the highest order. Even with the light behind her, Tommy could make out the tractor tyres of flab stuffed into the front of her cheap yellow leggings. Huge plates of puckered fat showed on her thighs through the fabric. She put the light on and he now saw her in three full dimensions. Her face was a round puddle of puffy fat, with hard eyes and a mean mouth almost lost among the reams of dull skin. Her long hair was flecked with grey and hung in a vague fringe that looked like she'd cut it herself with nail scissors. She wore a tent of a T-shirt, the huge neck of which had been puckered and stretched by many a tiny hand. Her giant breasts were flat and smooth like two lava flows, widely divided at the top and still dividing when they finished hanging low on her belly. Between the fat digits of her right hand was a cigarette burning. *Only years of childbirth and chips could do this to a human body*, thought Tommy. *Oh I wish this dog would fuck off.*

'I'm Tommy. Father O'Mally sent me to pick up Jamie for the game today.' A face peeped out from the same door behind her, then another. Two little boys, their bullet heads identically crewcut, jostled and whispered. The near-naked girl reappeared, this time carrying an infant in her arms, leaning back to take the strain.

'Gerrin, you lot! Gerrin that fooking bedroom!' She looked at Tommy with her mean spot-like eyes.

'Hey, could you call the dog off, please. He's making me nervous,' said Tommy.

''E's all right!' piped one of the boys. 'Sketch is a good dog, he wouldn't fuckin' 'urt no one! Look! Sketch! Sketchy!' The lad, who was aged about nine, rushed forward past his mother to get to the dog. She lurched to try and stop him, and shouted, 'Gerrin, you likkle bugger! Come back 'ere!' but he got past her.

She looked at Tommy. ''Ow do I know you're who you say you are? 'Ow do I know you're not some pervert?'

'Er, well, I don't know. I've got Father Kelly's car outside. How do I know this is 162A? Someone told me, that's all. It's not written on the gate.'

'Are you from the fookin' council?' Her mouth was a tiny slit of fear and suspicion.

'No, I'm with Father O'Mally from the Sacred Heart. Father Mark,' said Tommy. As he had got older he had developed an impatient tone, purely pragmatic, which had proved quite effective in getting through to bureaucrats and the many time-wasters who cluttered his day. It had no currency here, though.

'Huh. Father Mark,' she said. A hint of recognition passed like a ripple across the sea of fat on her face. Then, 'I fookin' don't go to Mass no more,' she said with a snarl.

'Look, 's all right! Sketch wouldn't hurt no one.' The two boys, who couldn't have been more than a year apart, had fallen to their knees at Tommy's feet and seized the dog's attention. Under its wrinkled face Tommy could almost see a dog-like smile as the boys wrestled with him, kissed him and paddled his paws. The dog caught his eye for a moment and stopped smiling, but Tommy was able to step forward into safety.

''E's good at football, our Jamie. Best in 'is class but they won't let 'im play in 'is team.' Jamie's mother seemed to have resolved the perversity question on her own. 'Yeah, take 'im off me fookin' hands for a few hours, I've got the babby to deal with, an' likkle madam 'ere,' she said, yanking the nappied one's head back as she too advanced down the hall towards the excitement. 'Then there's 'im.' She gestured to the other boy, who looked up proudly at the man. "E's gooing with his fookin' dad today. Gooing to the Blues with Daddy today, aintcha? Yeeees. I don't fookin' follow fookin' football meself but 'is dad always takes 'im down the Blues when 'e can. Nice break for the likkle bugger. Hey, you! Get back in that fookin' bedroom, you. And take the babby with ya.' The mother turned to Tommy again. 'She's a bloomin' pest from the moment she gets up. She's a real likkle madam. Shurrup!'

'Pet him! Pet him!' Jamie was shouting to Tommy. 'He's never 'urt fuckin' no one! Play dead, Sketch!'

The dog rolled on to its back and lay in the hall displaying its hard belly and swollen bollocks. Tommy put out a toe and touched its stomach. Sketch looked at him through half-closed eyes, then up at the boys. He kept quiet.

"E's a brilliant fuckin' dog,' said Jamie.

'Er, yes. But he's not coming with us.'

'Awwww!'

'Come on, get your things,' said Tommy as patiently as he could.

Jamie's mother produced a plastic bag with the boy's football kit in it. Nothing had been washed. She held it up to her nose and sniffed the muddy shirt, then handed the bag to him.

"Ere. Haven't fuckin' 'ad time to wash it, with the babby an' all. Maybe the fookin' priest can wash it. Well, off yer fookin' goo then,' she said to them both.

'Er, there's one thing, Mrs, Mrs . . .'

Tommy was surprised by how alien the speech and gestures that he had brought with him from his doctor's life in London were. Jamie's mom made no attempt to supply her missing last name.

'Well, isn't this supposed to be a . . . handicapped sort of team, you know.' She looked at him blankly. 'There doesn't seem to be anything wrong with Jamie. He seems pretty able . . . You know, the kids are supposed to have special needs, I thought . . .'

'Oh! Special needs.' The light came on in her mind, and the word came out with practised ease. 'Tretts! 'E's got fookin' Tretts Syndrome, the doctor said at school.'

'Fuckin' Tretts!' echoed Jamie proudly. 'Fuckin' Tretts!'

*Jesus Christ, get me out of here,* thought Tommy. He stepped over Sketch and left, Jamie hurrying behind him, his mother shouting down the path after them, 'Tara, petal, tara, love.'

At the car, he let the little boy into the back and watched him clamber all over the seats and Father Kelly's umbrella with his little trainers, but he didn't have time to admonish him. It was already ten past nine and he had another address to find. He sped out of the cul-de-sac and went looking for the flats.

'Fucking Watt House, where is it?' he muttered. 'I'm sure I know that name.' He checked the signs above the entryways of each block. 'Cowper House, Boundary House ... It must be round here somewhere.'

'Bollocks!' a hard little voice in the back piped up.

'Hey, you, do you know where this effing Watt House is?'

'No,' he said, meek as a lamb. Then followed it with an acid outburst: 'Cunt! Bollocks!'

'OK, son, settle down. We're not going to be late,' he lied.

'Are you the referee from London? Cunt! Shit! Cunt!'

'That I am,' said Tommy, and despite his hangover, and his being late, and the dog shit he thought he was getting wafts of in the car, he started to smile. 'Hey, fucking stinks in here, doesn't it, Jamie?'

'Fuckin' stinks!' repeated the boy in his angelic voice. 'Shit!' he piped in an involuntary squeak.

They circled the estate another time. There was one block completely unnamed. 'I bet this is it, I bet this is fuckin' it,' he muttered. It was 9.20 a.m., ten minutes to kick-off. Finally Tommy saw the word 'WATT', spray-painted in white on the galvanised steel bins under the refuse chute, in a dim cubby-hole round the back of the tower.

'This is it. What a fucking shithole, eh? Who'd ever want to live here?'

'Shithole,' said Jamie, spontaneously. Then, in his softer tone, the sentence open-ended with innocence, 'Our dad lives here.'

'Oh, sorry,' said Tommy, and he checked the mirror. The kid was looking out of the window again. *Tough little bleeders, nine-year-olds. He'll be OK.* He paused a moment.

'Hey, what d'you think of the Blues?'

'Bollocks!' shouted Jamie.

Tommy got out of the car chuckling. 'I like you, my new little friend. Come on, let's go find this cripple bloke.'

The flats had entryphones, a hard steel box punctured minimally for the speaker and the mike, with tough industrial buttons. The idea was to make it harder for non-resident rapists, muggers and milk-stealers. Now they had to wait until someone came in or out before they could slip in. The milkman had stopped coming in the early nineties after the dairy was sued when a baby was flattened by a pint travelling downwards at its terminal velocity.

'Sixty-two,' said Tommy. The kid stood on tiptoes and pressed the button.

'Yeah?' said a voice that sounded like it was coming through a hiking sock.

'Come to take Kevin to the football match. Is he there?'

''S me. Come up. Lift's bust.'

'Shit!' said Tommy after taking his finger off the button.

'Shit!' said Jamie. 'It's always bastard broken.'

Tommy stopped and took a closer look at him as they went in. 'Are you sure you've got Tourette's Syndrome? The doctor told you that, right?'

'Fuckin' Tretts!' said the boy proudly, and beamed up at him.

'Come on.' Tommy went up the stairs two at a time. Since he had stopped doing house calls the only tower blocks he had been in were posh offices and big hotels. Now he remembered that sixty-two wouldn't necessarily be on the sixth floor. And it wasn't. The number signs in the sparse stairwells were mostly gone, but people had replaced them with a kind of graffiti. 'FLATS 12–16,' he read. 'Sharon is a FUCKING SLAG.' Tommy hurried ahead, the little boy scrambling up the stairs behind him. He looked behind him at the figure. 'Stick with me, kiddo, I'm used to all this. I have friends in high places.'

'FLATS 22–26,' he read. A few floors later: '33–37'. He could hear his own breath coming a little heavier, so he breathed noisily in the athletic fashion. Jamie was doing OK behind him, not panting at all. The city was starting to take shape below him. Through the reinforced glass of the stairwell he could see the low, flat roofs of the maisonettes, with their TV aerials and empty washing lines.

42, 43, 44, 45, 45A, he saw, taped to the wall. They both heard the sound of an ice-cream van and stopped to watch it, on their separate landings, as it crept along and turned the corner. *Ooh, I could handle an ice lolly now. Something a bit juicy. An orange crush, or whatever they're called. Or one of those raspberry ones with the white stuff in the middle. What were they called? A split. Always loved them. Wonder what Jamie would have?*

'Shit! Fuck! Fuck!' he heard the little lad shouting below. Tommy slowed down a little for him. 'Flats 52–57,' he read, written hundreds of time in Biro on the cream gloss paint. The smell of piss wasn't as bad up here.

'Here it is,' he shouted. The kid came bounding up, his eyes wild with excitement. 'Cunt! Bastard! Cunt!'

'Steady on, Jamie. We'll be in and out in a second, then we'll be off to the game.'

The smell of cooking fat mixed with sour municipal mustiness hit Tommy as they entered a hall where the front doors were ranged in a dogleg formation. Each door had a reinforced glass window with a little curtain behind it, and was set back a foot, adding to the gloom. Tommy finally made out number sixty-two, and rang the clockwork doorbell. It was like a handshake buzzer from a joke shop, only it was already wound down and made just a brief raspberry.

He heard slippered feet slowly coming to the door, which opened on a chain. One wrinkly eye and a section of puckered lips appeared, but said nothing.

'I've come to take Kevin to the game. Father Mark sent me.'

'Ooh, yes, come on in, luv, we've been expecting you.'

'I'm Tommy Burns.' He put out his hand to shake. The tiny lady in front of him was as slight as a thirteen-year-old. She looked at him with surprise and pleasure, and extended her own hand as though she were greeting a dignitary. Tommy squeezed the feeble, soft thing as gently as he could.

'About fuggin time, eh?' came a voice from the yellowy gloom. Tommy was surprised that the old lady showed neither her generation's disgust nor a mother's angry shame at his language. She merely pressed herself against the wall to allow her son's wheelchair to come forward. The character in the old grey frame must have been at least thirty years old. He had long black hair and a wispy beard, and his chunky torso was crammed into a black cap-sleeved T-shirt. As he came under the yellow light bulb, Tommy could just make out the word Metallica in black-on-black writing.

Tommy nodded. The cripple sniffed at him, then craned his neck backwards. 'Mum, where's me jacket? We're off. At last. At least I fuggin think so. Oh, and me other stuff, don't forget them this time,' he added rather sorely. The old lady disappeared down the passageway. Kevin eyed the man and the little boy, waiting for an explanation.

*Cheeky fucking wanker*, thought Tommy. *I'll fucking roll you down those steps as fast as . . . shit, the steps.*

'What do we do about getting down, then?' was all Tommy said.

'Oh, don't worry, I'll walk.'

'Let's go, then,' said Tommy to all three of them. Kevin's mother was handing her son his jacket, and a plastic bag. He pulled it roughly from her, embarrassed at the attention.

'Well, fuggin hurry up, then! I wanna gerra kick around, you know.'

Tommy backed out of the door, followed by a wide-eyed Jamie, Kevin the wheelie pumping hard with his powerful arms to get through the shag pile carpet, and the old frail mother in her housecoat who had followed them out.

She looked up at Tommy with the moist eyes of a worn woman, and laid her bony hand on his arm.

'Look after my boy, please. He doesn't get out much.'

'I will,' he said firmly. If there was one useful thing being a doctor had taught him, it was how to reassure people of something without having a clue about the outcome. In case after case, saying he would do his best was always taken as a guarantee that things would be fine.

He left her at the door, and headed towards the commotion that had broken out at the stairs.

'Bollocks yourself, you little git. Leave the cowin' door to me.'

'Cunt! Shit! Shit!' Jamie was shouting. Both had their hands locked on the door handle that led to the stairwell.

'Hey, come on, he's only trying to help,' said Tommy, intervening.

'I don't need no fuggin help. I know how to open a fuggin door by now, you know.'

Kevin gave the door a great heave with his arms and it swung open, sending the little boy flying forward. Once they were all three through, Tommy waited to see how they would get down the thirteen flights of stairs.

'Here we go, then. You 'ave to carry me this bit.'

'Carry? What do you mean, carry?' *You've got to be fucking joking, mate.* He looked at Kevin, a brawny chunk wedged into a chopped-down NHS wheelchair. The man's chicken legs protruded as an afterthought from under his torso. Tommy felt immense pity.

'Yeah, I was only joking when I said I would walk,' sneered the cripple. His years cooped up inside had given him time to hone his sarcasm until, entirely drained of humour, it was as useless as a scythe without a handle.

'What do you weigh?' asked Tommy.

'Eight stone. Come on, I thought you referees were s'posed to be fit.'

Tommy eyed him. Kick-off time had already passed, but he was determined to get there. His head still ached, a creeping sleep slime was taking over his mouth, and he still felt hungry and bloated at once. *Right, you moaning spaz, this is it.* Tommy bent down two steps below the man and, with all his might, pulled the chair forward and on to his back, so that man and chair were attached to him like some jet-age crustacean of soft flesh and steel.

'This won't last,' said Kevin, with a nasty smile in his voice. 'I'll give yow three fuggin floors and yow'll be knackered.' Tommy took a step down. His foot hit the ground heavily, and his thigh muscles instantly heated up. The next step, the same with the other leg.

'Oh, very good, nearly there,' the voice said in his ear. 'Hey, great view from up here. Is that the Rotunda? I haven't been to town for three years. 'Course, it was better from me old flat. I used to be up on the twenty-first in Boulton, but the council said I should be lower down because of the lifts, in case they break, like. There's some real bright sparks working for the council, y'know. Hey, what yow bring this weird kid with yow for, then?' he continued merrily. 'I know he's a great player and everything. Not.' He left the nasty smile in his voice hanging in the air. Having found someone he could bait, his spirits were raised.

'Shut the fuck up, will ya?' grunted Tommy. 'Big Fat Ron's Claret and Blue Army,' he read out of the corner of his eye. His legs felt unsteady.

'Fuck up!' chimed in Jamie.

'Oh, very nice. I'll tell ya something, there wouldn't even *be* a team if it wasn't for fuggin me.'

Tommy laboured on. Kevin marked every new floor they reached with a cheer. Tommy struggled, occasionally scraping the chair against the wall. 'Hey, watch me fuggin wheels, mate!' Kevin shouted every time. As Tommy tottered around some old rubbish bags, he yelled in his Wild West voice, 'Whoa, slow down, Silver, me hair's nearly blowing off!'

'Look ... shut ... the fuck ... up,' Tommy gasped. 'Or you'll be going down in the fucking chute.'

'Oh, I was wondering when that old one was coming! Very original.' Tommy was sweating even more. 'So you're matey with the priest, then?' he surmised out loud. 'I'm not religious meself, I think it's all a load of bollocks.'

Then followed Kevin's disquisition on Christianity and Satanism, in which he quoted liberally from the work of some of his favourite bands – Alice In Chains, Death, White Zombie, and, of course, 'Sabbath'.

At the seventh floor, they rested. Tommy dropped the chair on a step behind him and sprawled forward on the piss-stained concrete. He listened to the relentless whining of the cripple, the odd snatch of swearing from the little boy, his own breath racing through his mouth and the blood pounding painfully in his head. He looked out over the grey cityscape towards the tallest building, the Post Office tower with its abstract sculpture of shields, dishes and antennae, and asked himself with an earnestness and despair that he didn't like, *What the fuck am I doing here?* Miserably, he looked at his watch and saw that the game was well under way by now, then felt a surge of determination to make it.

'Onward and downward!' jibed Kevin. 'Come on, time to get on yer fuggin bike, Ref, you've got a game to take charge of, and me an' the nipper have got goals to score.'

Tommy didn't look his charge in the eye before he hauled him on to his back again. He felt the man's strong arms holding on to his shoulder. He peered down the centre of the stairwell, where there was a narrow gap that went all the way to the basement.

'No gobbing!' warned Kevin. 'Residents only.'

'Shit on the City tonight,' he saw scrawled on the wall a few floors down.

Tommy was feeling very weary by now, counting each step as he went. His legs burned even more. 'Sharon is a FUCKING SLAG.' *Good old Sharon, nearly there.* Kevin droned on, in sarcastic praise of the unknown architects of the building. The last two floors were agony for Tommy: sweat stung his eyes, a sharp piece of metal seemed to be twisting itself into his back, and his legs, from the balls of his feet to his calves to his thighs to his buttocks, were on fire. The last few steps were just numbness. With tremendous strength Tommy didn't know he had, he laid the man and the wheelchair down gently on the flat concrete. He sat a moment, staring dazed at the ground. He heard the strong springs of the door out to the lift area give and the door flap back, and saw meaty elbows propelling the chair forward. Jamie looked back at him, then followed.

*These poor bastards really do want to get to their football game.* He found it hard to believe, but he found it even harder to raise himself off his haunches on to his wobbly legs. But he did it. By the time he reached the car, they were both already inside, Kevin recumbent in the back, his long hair up against the side window, Jamie's little bullet head showing over the dashboard.

'Where's the chair?' asked Tommy, leaning in.

''Kin' stashed it. I'm norra fuggin invalid, you know.'

Tommy wasn't ready for debate. He gunned the engine and took off.
The car bowled round each corner like a 2 CV, almost on two wheels.
Tommy waited for no man, slipping through Give Ways and amber lights,
pulling out in front of speeding cars and even trying to overtake on a
roundabout. He looked at his watch. Ten o'clock. 'Shit!'

'Fuck!'

'Bollocks!'

'We'll make it, you'll get a game.' *Come on, you bugger, where's yer power?*
They sped on, past the Crown again – 'Why yow gooing this fuggin
way?' moaned Kevin – past the old Poly and the new dog track and on
up the Walsall Road, straight as a die up the hill at a fixed forty-five
miles per hour. Tommy relaxed a little, and called back over the whine
of the engine.

'So, Kev . . .'

'Kevin.'

'So, Kevin. How d'you do your back in?'

''S not me back, me back's foine,' he snarled. 'Me back's probably twice
as strong as yours. 'S me legs.'

'Sorry.' He paused. 'But how'd you do it?'

'Wiped out on me bike.'

'Ah. What was it?'

For the first time he heard Kevin hesitate. 'CX500. 'Onda.'

Tommy let out a little phatic sound, 'Pah!', then immediately cursed
himself. *Shit. Wonder if he heard that. Crap bike, though. Not to be seen on, let alone
lose your legs over.* 'Were you a dispatcher?'

'No.' He heard the sullenness he'd feared, and checked the mirror.
Kevin's eyes were lowered in shame. 'Don't 'ave them up 'ere.'

'Honda have been making some pretty good bikes for the last ten
years, haven't they?' *Fuck, that sounded even worse.* 'I mean, the Fireblade and
the VFR.

It was silent in the car. *Shit.*

'We're here,' declared Tommy, mightily relieved. He pulled through
the gates into Perry Hall park, went past the paddling pool and tea shop,
ignored the carpark and took off across the grass. The ground felt soft
under them. Jamie bounced in his seat excitedly, and grinned at him.

'A man's gotta do what a man's gotta do, kiddo,' he said to Jamie. He
could see pitch fourteen from three hundred yards away – it was the only
one with a game already started. He saw the bright yellow sunshine bus
too, then Mark in the middle of a tangle of kids, all ages, trying to referee.

The whole game suddenly stopped and the teams faced the car. Then the
players started cheering and making their way towards them. Tommy was
getting the wheelchair out of the boot when the first of the mob reached
him, chanting, 'Tom-my! Tom-my!'

'Hey, steady on, kids, you're in the middle of a match!' he tried, but
more kept coming. They gathered round and wanted to touch him. Little
kids with calipers tugged at his jacket, girls in orthopaedic boots tried to
catch his hand, a great strapping lad with bushy eyebrows clapped him on
the back and honked incomprehensibly though his giant grin. 'Tom-my,
Tom-my!' they were chanting, as best they could. Some of them went
'MMM-nnnnn, MMMM-nnnn', but the effect was much the same.

*Jesus, what a bunch!* he thought. He heard wheelchairs clicking and crutches
clacking, there were shrieks and moans, thick old Coke-bottle glasses stared
up at him ... even the blind came, towed by friends. 'Whoa, kids, hold
up!' He saw Jamie smiling at his side, shouting 'Shit! Cunt! Bollocks!
Bastard!' through his joy, like someone in a sneezing fit. Mark walked
across the pitch beaming. Tommy had never seen him so happy. Or
rather, he had, but never beaming. Going over the gruesome details of
the kicking he'd given some away fan that he'd hunted down, perhaps, or
outlining a strategic success in the back street of some obscure industrial
town. But he had never beamed, he had rather gritted his teeth with
pleasure.

'Told you they were excited!' he called above the throng.

'I can't f ... I can't believe this, Mark, I've never seen anything like it.
And they're all different ages. You've got one of those balls with a bell in
it. You've got blindies here too?'

'The blind, yes, Tommy. Keep your voice down.'

'So that's the opposition, then?' He was looking at a bunch of kids in
red who hadn't joined in the commotion, and a row of adults down one
side of the pitch.

'Yep. That's St Philips, the opposition.'

'They've got a decent kit.'

'Yeah,' replied Mark, 'and some pretty good players too. Are you ready
to ref? There's twenty minutes to go in the first half. They're all over us.
It's nil–nil, but only just. We started late, of course. It was pandemonium
getting them off the bus and into their gear.' Mark found all this rather
amusing, smiling as he talked.

*Mark O'Mally, sunshine bus driver, friend of the crippled and the crazy, and referee.
I don't believe it.* Tommy's whole body was still hurting. Although it galled

him to stand on the sidelines and watch Mark in control, he needed a few minutes to rest.

'Nah, I'm not changed or anything. I'll do the second half.'

'Sure?'

'Yeah. Go ahead. Restart the game. Drop ball.'

Mark raised his arms and addressed the crowd.

'Come on, kids, back in position.' One by one they reluctantly peeled themselves away from Tommy.

'Oh yeah, can you look after this little one? She's called Carol,' he said, pointing to a small girl on the touchline. 'She looks fine but she can't do a thing for herself. I mean, some of this lot are bad, but she can't even dress herself. Williams Syndrome. She likes to watch, though. And talk. Hold on to her hand.' He flashed Tommy a look of sudden seriousness. 'Don't let her wander off. If anything happens to her they'll crucify me.'

After a split second, they laughed together at his choice of words.

'Well, you know what I mean.'

*Williams Syndrome? What the fuck is that?* He looked at the girl. She looked like a pixie. She had one of the strangest faces he had ever seen, pure white and heart-shaped, a big forehead, no nasal bridge, full lips and a pointy chin, all framed with ringlets like a little Victorian. She had on a purple anorak and yellow trousers, and walked up and down the touchline hesitantly, without the healthy spring of a normal girl. When he looked closely at her eyes Tommy noticed star-shaped patterns in her irises.

'Hello, Carol,' he ventured.

She was too shy to speak, but put her little hand in his. They both turned to watch the game.

The drop ball had been more like a rugby scrum. The ball was lost as a dozen players battled it out in a patch of mud, letting out howls of pain, incomprehension and excitement.

'Blow up, ref,' Tommy immediately shouted, but Mark turned and just shrugged his shoulders at him. The muddy ball popped out of the scrum and was immediately intercepted by Jamie, in his stained yellow shirt. Most of his team had some sort of yellow shirt on, though there were a few odd T-shirts, white, green, Spiderman. The other side had proper kit, all red. Those whose feet weren't clubbed or numb or amputated even had proper boots. Like a weatherman with a satellite photo, Tommy saw the money holding them together, just as he could see the lack of money hovering over his friend's team. St Philips had their mums and dads there, busy-looking people in well-made coats and shoes too good for park grass.

Their children had natty, customised wheelchairs, made of lightweight alloy tubing, often further chopped down for speed, with mountain bike tyres and foam handgrips in colours like neon yellow and hot pink. Their crutches came in fun tints too, brushed metal in gold and green and rose. One glance at the Sacred Heart and he could sense the four-hour waits in clinics and the endless fittings for used prostheses. He recognised the shades of grey steel and the waxy whiteness of the plastic arm cuffs and neck braces. In his mind's eye he saw hospital orderlies in their duster coats sorting through rooms piled high with artificial limbs, aluminium canes and zimmer frames. He gave a sigh. *This wasn't what I wanted to come back for.* He suddenly missed his flat in London, and his weekends insulated from all this appalling sadness.

The ball popped out of the scrum and fell to Jamie. He put his head down and tried to dribble forward, but after beating one man – a girl with a cane – he was easily dispossessed by a boy twice his size with the small eyes and page-boy haircut of a Down's Syndromee. The parents cheered and he launched forth on a run. Crutches rattled, the blind hurled themselves at him and wheels spun in the mud. He beat seven players, including two from his own side, before threading a beautifully weighted pass through to his forward. The lad, however, a small boy with a twisty foot, dithered in the box too long. The hulk with the eyebrows, looking like a mad werewolf in his banana-yellow shirt, came charging forward and hoofed the ball back into the other half. Except for the goalies – a wheelie for Sacred Heart and another Down's Syndrome kid for St Philips – everyone on both teams turned and chased the ball, until the pack had grouped in the centre of the pitch again.

Tommy watched. Mark didn't have much to do, as he strode around in his black Fred Perry and shorts. *Looks pretty fit these days, the handsome bastard.* Tommy noticed he was giving free kicks when someone in a wheelchair was tackled by someone not in a wheelchair, but not when someone in calipers or on crutches was tackled. *Must remember that one,* he thought. After fifteen minutes, Tommy conceded that aside from the healthy-looking Down's kid, both teams were utterly appalling. Yet he had never seen so much strain or effort written into young faces. Even the blind were frowning. The teams clashed like two medieval armies in the night, toing and froing without sense of time or place.

Out on the wing near where Tommy and Carol stood was a paraplegic with some sort of added mental disability. In his work – and in his life – he had always steered clear of the disabled, especially the mentally disabled.

The young man was a teenager with the nerdy look of the true gimp: Dad's glasses, short back and sides, pale face with bumfluff. When the ball was over on the other side of the pitch and he was all alone on the wing, in the quietness, even the whirring of hydraulic pumps and motors ceased, and the locomotion stopped. He had a sheepskin-covered buffer on which his head rested, when he wasn't writhing and grimacing under the influence of God knew what screaming mental feedback. Tommy stared. *What can you do with a person like that? What instrument can you insert into their cranium, or what drug into the back of their hands, to make them better? What would be the procedure?* Love was the only answer he could come up with. He had to wrench his eyes away to catch up with the game.

The ball with the tinkling bell kept gravitating towards Mark, who kept jumping out of the way. The rest of the time the priest trotted around shouting out elements of the play to help the blind on both sides.

'What a shambles, eh?' Tommy said to Carol, who still clung to his hand.

'A shambles?' she said, looking at him wide-eyed.

'Yeah, y'know, a mess.'

'It's disorganised, disorganised is lack of organisation. Order is missing.'

Tommy stared down at her in disbelief. He said nothing, so she resumed.

'I have been to four matches this year, and, what it is, all four were disorganised in the extreme. What it is, the ball is your friend, and what the ball is, is a spherical object under pressure, with an outer casing of leather or some other approved material. Other shapes could be a rhomboid, a trapezoid or a cube, which are all shapes but do not roll. There is another game with an egg-shaped ball, perhaps that would be a good shape today, an ellipsis, and there are other games, played with a puck, a shuttlecock, which is a hemisphere with feathers, and darts, or arrows, for archery . . .'

Tommy looked at her in amazement while she chattered on. *Did I hear all that or what? Hemisphere? Puck?* He listened on for a minute, waiting for a break in her spiel.

'So,' he heard himself saying, 'what happens when our friend the spherical object goes over the line?'

'If it is a touchline, or a sideline, a throw-in shall be awarded against the team that touched the ball last, and if it is the goal line, a goal kick shall be awarded to the team that is defending, providing that one of their players was not the last to touch it, and a corner if it was, and if the whole of the ball has passed over the goal line, between the goalposts and under the crossbar, provided it has not been thrown, carried or intentionally propelled by hand or arm, by a player of the attacking side, except in the case of the goalkeeper, who is within his own penalty area, a goal is awarded. What it is, a goal is a point awarded to one side or the other.'

'Hey, you're good.' Tommy was impressed. So he thought of a question for this little fount of answers. 'Is Father Mark a good referee, then?'

'The referee is empowered to terminate the match in the event of grave disorder, but, what it is, he has not done it, despite the disorder, so he is good. I like him.'

Her little pixie face looked up at him, and her ringlets rustled slightly in the breeze. When the whistle sounded for half-time, the parents came on to the pitch to stop their kids endlessly chasing the ball. A dad in a sheepskin coat produced a bag of orange quarters from the back of his Range Rover. The Reds gathered in a rough huddle to collect theirs, but when he saw the motley Yellows milling around with nothing, he halved the ration so that everyone would have something. Father Mark thanked the man warmly, and the two chatted for a moment. All was quiet as the kids sucked and chewed. Some ate hungrily, some were fed, some let the fruit fall from their faces, some rocked and moaned and stared at it on the ground in front of them. The parents from St Philips moved among their kids giving advice, rubbing tired legs and squeezing cold hands. Tommy secured a quarter for the little girl.

'I bet you like all kinds of citrus fruits, don't you?' he asked, then with a grin, 'How many of them can you name?' He pulled the little girl along with him – 'Tangelo, tangerine, mandarin, lime, lemon, grapefruit . . .' – as he approached Wheelchair Kevin, who had had a quiet game so far. He felt an urge to get back into Kevin's good books, although he didn't understand why, as he prided himself on living beyond casual guilt. 'Hey, what's this rule then, about tackling and people in wheelchairs?'

'Bollocks to that. I'm not having no special rule. I can run rings round these spazzes, I don't need no special protection.'

'Well, rules are rules when I'm reffing,' said Tommy. He looked at the stewing chunk of arrogance, who stared back at him competitively.

Tommy went and changed behind the sunshine bus. As he pulled his spare black referee shirt over his head, he felt the same tingle of pride and importance he had always felt, whether it was marching out on to the sweet turf of Wembley or some bankrupt Third Division scumpatch for an end-of-season formality. He felt the power and the seriousness begin in him. He put on his second watch, in case the first one should fail him. He checked that his notebook, biro and cards were in his breast pocket. He hung his silver whistle around his neck. He straightened his hair in the wing mirror. Then he marched out on to the pitch and was mobbed again.

Mark laughed even harder this time. 'Super Tommy, eh?' he half chanted. 'Not quite what you're used to, is it?'

'She's a one, that Carol,' he shouted above the racket. 'Bloomin' spherical objects, where'd she learn all that lot?'

'I told you, Williams Syndrome. That's what they do. Language.'

'Mental. Can she count cards at blackjack too? You should take her to Blackpool, to the casino.'

'Nah, none of that stuff. She can't do the pools either. Or Spot the Ball. She's just a little girl lost in her own world.'

Father Mark walked over to the sideline and took up the little girl's hand. She resumed her chatter instantly.

'OK, second half. Yellow to kick off,' shouted the new referee. He blew his whistle with a sharp peep that echoed off the fence by the railway cutting. Kevin had made himself centre-forward for this half. He collected the ball and pushed powerfully against the slippery ground, making some headway. Some of the opposition left him alone, on account of the rules, but there were others who tried to catch him up. Kevin battled on, swivelling round and shielding the ball whenever someone got close.

'Come on, you bastards, come on,' he muttered. To Tommy's surprise he made it twenty yards down the field, although the crowd around him was growing all the time. A blind girl launched herself at him but only kicked the hard steel of his chair, fell to the ground in tears.

'Play on, play on,' Tommy shouted. He'd never seen a blind person cry. He was tempted to linger to see the tears, but snapped his attention back to the game. Kevin had proceeded another five yards – he seemed to be dribbling with the ball locked between the footrests of his wheelchair. He was sweating and his teeth were showing. Then, from the side, the Down's kid came jogging over, rolled the ball out with his sole, rounded Kevin and set off on a run towards the other goal.

'Ref!' shouted Kevin. 'Refer-ee! What the fuck? Foul! He can't do that!'

Remembering the rule, Tommy blew up. All the Reds' parents complained and shouted from the touchline, and some of the players ran towards him murmuring. Tommy back-pedalled away from them, and ordered a free kick for the Yellows. Kevin wanted to take it, but he wanted to score too, so when the whistle blew he began dribbling. Tommy had to blow up again, because the free kick should have been indirect, and awarded one the other way. Both sets of players milled around, confused, and the parents shuffled and gestured, asking each other what was going on.

'What you fuggin doing, Ref? What are you playing at?' bellowed Kevin.

'Hey, watch that language. Any more of that and you're booked.' *Bastard. Where's his respect on the pitch?*

'I don't fuggin believe this,' said Kevin, exasperated. He hung his head down, his long hair in his face, then stiffened his back and worked his wheels madly in disgust.

The free kick was eventually taken, and the seesaw pattern resumed. The ball bounced around like a pinball, crashing off crutches and cheekbones without distinction. Tommy too found that wherever he stood – and there wasn't much running to be done – the play came towards him. The pitch had an unnatural camber, skewed off towards one corner flag where there was a permanent marsh, which drew the ball a little too. For Tommy there was no ploughing the usual diagonal path – this game consisted of trotting one way, then another, and occasionally crouching a little to try and spot the ball hidden in a cluster of thrashing limbs.

There were tears. There were howls. There were shrieks. Tommy found himself with a teenage girl lying on the grass at his feet. Something had happened to her in the scrum and she was wailing. He stopped the game, deciding that a drop ball would have to be in order.

'What's wrong, love?'

'Nerrrrr, werrrrrr!' was all the reply he got.

'She's deaf, Ref!' piped up a ten-year-old. 'She can't speak neither.' The boy who gave him this information looked up at him, a little rodent face, sharp as a hatchet and beset with three rows of yellow teeth. Apart from his limp he seemed OK to Tommy. *Compos mentis, I hope*, he thought, looking from the girl to the boy.

'What's she saying?'

The rodent child translated. 'Someone touched her bum. And her tits.'

*Jesus. Aggravated sexual assault. What's the ruling on that?*

'Well ... Are you OK, love?' he asked in a loud, slow voice.

'What's up?' He heard Mark's voice behind him, and turned to see the priest on the field of play. *Hey, I didn't signal you on*, he thought with indignation. *Oh well, exceptional circumstances, I s'pose.* 'I don't know. I think she was ... y'know, someone grabbed her, I think.'

'Ah, that again, it's always happening. Just give a free kick. And let her take it, she'll be OK.'

'I can't give a free kick for that!' *Telling me how to officiate now? Jesus. Stick to ...* Then Tommy stopped his train of thought. He was silent for a moment, then raised his arm and pointed in the direction of the Reds' goal. The braying around him got louder. Someone was tugging at his shirt, and a little boy in dark glasses tried to insert a cold hand into his. He looked down. 'Not now, sonny!' The child burst into tears and ran off.

'He'll be OK.' Mark rolled the ball to the wailing girl. She was crying like a six-year-old, but as soon as she spotted the ball she smiled through her tears. She clambered to her feet.

'Back ten yards!' shouted Tommy. He kept shouting it, and when it had no effect, he ran forward himself. *OK, kids, follow me.* As a body, the cluster moved, trying to keep up with him. The deaf girl took one step back and with a meaty leg pumped the ball upfield. She stood back, wreathed in proud smiles.

To Tommy's satisfaction, Mark stayed off the pitch for the next fifteen minutes, but before the half-hour mark he had to come on to sort out a pair of tangled wheelchairs and a mild epileptic fit. The score remained the same, nil–nil. The parents kept up their cheering, and the kids their frantic running. Time and again the Down's Syndromee in red made strong runs from the back through midfield, set one of his forwards free, only to see the attack frustrated by the Sacred Heart goalie. This was a young blond boy, no more than twelve, who despite a chair a few sizes too big for him had an uncanny knack for coming off his line and closing down all angles without the assistance of his defenders, one of whom stood very still, stared at the ground and pretended to be invisible whenever the ball approached.

'We have some substitutions!' Mark called from the touchline. He held the hands of two fresh Yellows, a black girl with a distracted look and a pink plastic leg, and a fat boy with what looked like flippers for arms. *Jeez, I thought all the flids were in their forties by now. Where did he come from?* The silent defender, and an obese boy with no expression who had done nothing all game, struggled off the pitch together. Mark could see his friend's curious look, so he filled him in after checking the subs' footwear and sending them on to the pitch. 'Birth defects,' said Mark. 'No one understands it.'

*I s'pose you tell 'em it's the way God made you, eh?* thought Tommy, and he felt a wavelet of resignation. A drop of bitterness came mixed in with the pathos. *Yeah, I s'pose he does. And maybe they like that. Special needs: limbs. That's one way of feeling special.*

All this unexpected emotion was wearing him out. To Tommy, a football match was about feeling passion – passionate hate for the other side, passionate joy at scoring – and if you were lucky enough to be involved, the thrill of physical exertion. If you were even luckier and were involved at Tommy's level, you also got the sober enjoyment of the exercise of power. There was something he loved about free, young spirits running wild until they came up against the limits of the law, and in the last four years of his life, since he hit the big time, Tommy had grown keenly appreciative of his position, like a politician intoxicated by the democratic process, or a policeman who loves his lot. But the clanking prostheses and the streaming eyes were getting to him.

His body soldiered on, however, and his strong legs took him from one end of the pitch to the other – which he found opened up the game a little. The sun came out every now and then, for a few seconds at a time, as the white clouds tumbled across the sky. The players charged back and forth in larger patterns, becoming more excited and energetic as the game went on. The play got better too. The Down's boy made another strong run from deep and chipped the blond goalie perfectly, who floundered in his seat, unable to reach higher than five feet. The parents went mad. One grown man in a body-warmer and glasses hissed 'Yesssss!' on the touchline as though his offspring had been selected to go up in the space shuttle. Tommy disallowed the goal for offside. A lanky teenager in red had been caught out by the Sacred Heart's accidental offside trap. Tommy felt the decision was a little harsh – the boy was blind, after all. But he also felt fairness had prevailed – there was no way he could say the boy was not interfering with play, since he had spent the entire game trotting around with his ear cocked in the direction of the tinkling bell.

*Blind. Or should that be 'visually impaired'?* He realised something. *Shit. I don't have to write a report on this one. What am I thinking of?* While he waited for the free kick to be taken, Tommy's mind, still echoing from the night before's drinking, had jumped ahead to the match report that a referee has to file within two working days of a game. He always wrote his the evening after the game, or early the next morning, to get it down fresh. Who said what and who did what to whom. He had seen referees get up to their armpits in shit for a misremembered fact, when the papers got hold of it. The wrong accomplice named in a punch-up. An own goal misattributed. Then he remembered that this was a nothing game, in the great scheme of things. A bunch of kids chasing a ball around in the park.

He noticed that Mark was getting pretty excited now on the touchline. Mark did the substitutions, Mark fixed the bumped shins and rubbed the sore thighs, Mark came up with the tactics. He was the lone voice cheering on the Sacred Heart. Tommy noticed that whenever their attack broke down he was disappointed, but not abusive in his old style. There was no 'Oh, you useless fucker!' or 'Christ, you cunt, what the fuck was that, you dozy git?' He just chopped his hands in the air and smiled out his disappointment, and never failed to flash the unlucky player, who was usually a child sprawled in the dirt or a teenage tangle of bendy limbs and steel rims, a look of warm acknowledgment and a word of encouragement.

*Mr Fucking Nice Guy*, thought Tommy. *Where will it all end?*

Cries of 'Penalty!' went up all round him. There were six minutes to go. If he had been paying attention to the game while he was thinking instead of watching his friend's noble profile, Tommy would have seen Kevin holding the ball on the edge of the other side's box, and just as he propelled himself forward, receiving a hard blow to the face from the elbow of a St Philips defender. But all he knew when he flicked his gaze that way was that he had not seen what happened. He knew the dangerous reflex, that of trying to convince yourself by hard deduction that you had seen something, and he knew he had to resist it. There was nothing more mortifying to him in the game of football than to miss a controversial incident, but experience had taught him to come clean and to consult his linesman. Only in this case he didn't really have any.

'Fuggin 'ell, Ref, you daydreaming or what? He hit me in the fuggin nose!' screamed Kevin. He was holding his nose, and his eyes were watering. That was usually enough evidence for Tommy – that and a tall, guilty defender trotting backwards and trying to keep an extremely straight face. But he had to go by someone who had seen the incident. Through the tumult, he marched to the parents on the touchline, on the other side of the pitch from Mark and the little girl. They were jumping up and down in the excitement.

'I'm afraid I was unsighted,' said Tommy to one of the mothers. 'Did you see that?' Before she could answer, the man at her side jumped in. 'No one touched him, Ref. He's faking it. And he was outside the box anyway.' Tommy could see the venom in the man's eyes. As the man spoke he saw the desperate dilation of the pupils meant to show innocence and stoic candour, which to Tommy just signalled one thing. *Fat whopper. Penalty it is.*

He thanked the man, turned, ran to the penalty area and pointed to the spot, blowing a long peep on the whistle. Sacred Heart went mad. Mark and the girl cheered and waved. The parents cursed and turned round in disgust, and waved their hands upward in clear-off gestures. For that moment at least, everyone was convinced they were right.

Tommy had to stop the watch for five minutes while the Yellows congratulated each other and cleared out of the penalty area for the kick. Then they had to select a kicker. Kevin protested loudly that it should be him, and being the oldest player on the pitch, his teammates deferred to him. But Mark knew that he didn't have enough power in his shot, since he couldn't do a run-up. He couldn't dribble it over the line. Mark was on the pitch again, giving the ball to the rat-faced boy with the yellow teeth, telling him what to do, ignoring the barrage of complaints, effing and blinding from Kevin, who cursed him out until his vocabulary was spent. Exasperated, the man in the wheelchair spun round and propelled himself with furious bursts back into his own half. He would not watch any more.

After much shooing and shushing, Rat Face was ready to take the penalty. Eighteen players were lined up along the rim of the goal area to watch. Tommy blew. Rat Face ran forward in a loping arc, like a spin bowler coming up to the mark. He reached the ball, closed his eyes and swung his boot as hard as he could.

Loud cackles of laughter and cheers exploded from the St Philips support as the child's boot skimmed the top of the ball and sent it rolling along the ground towards the goalie, who had not moved. Only an extreme optimist would have thought it could have the energy to go in, and that the goalkeeper would miraculously step out of the way. As it was, the ball met a pool of water and stopped dead three feet from the line. The goalie waddled forward and collected it, Rat Face hung his head, distraught, and the Reds went thoroughly mad.

'Play on, play on,' shouted Tommy. His task on the pitch, as he had always defined it, was not to wallow in sentiment but to keep the game flowing in the confines of the rules. He looked at Mark, who shrugged his shoulders on the sideline. Carol was no longer holding his hand. Tommy looked round and noticed she had wandered off to the other end of the pitch.

The final few minutes passed in a whirlwind of flying limbs and wild ball play. Tommy had noted the passing of the ninetieth minute, and calculated he had to play six minutes of stoppage time. The ball toed and froed. The parents shouted louder than ever. It felt like a cup tie to Tommy, the all-or-nothing atmosphere pushing the players to new levels of effort. But just as it looked like it was going to stay all square, St Philips made a swift break. It was the Down's sweeper again. Seemingly frustrated with his role at the back, he collected the ball, as usual, in his own penalty area. He began running, easily avoiding this player's metal foot here, and that player's flailing arms there. He made it into the other half. A shoulder charge from the black girl made no impression on him. Two more tiny kids tried to tackle him, but their nips and kicks bounced off his hard legs and feet. Rat Face couldn't catch him, he was so exhausted. When he was five yards from the edge of the Sacred Heart goal area, he passed Kevin, who sat still in his wheelchair, in a thunderous sulk, conspicuously letting him go unchallenged. *You little bastard*, thought Tommy.

He had no trouble keeping up with the action. If fact he enjoyed the player's agility, his balance and his elegant dribbling. *He must be one of those like Carol*, he thought, *only she's got language and he's got football. Go for it, mate, see if you can go all the way.* The Down's kid was now inside the box, his supporters' roaring growing louder with every twist and turn he made. It was a beautiful run, and when it came to the point where he would lay the ball off for one of his forwards, he looked up, saw no one, and decided to go it alone. The goalie was wheeling himself off his line to narrow the angle. He only had one defender to beat – the Wolf Man, who came charging at him like a steam train. The attacker looked up again, flicked the ball to his left and ran round his right side, meeting up with the ball a second later and facing off with the goalie.

To Tommy, this was all so lovely to watch that it appeared to happen in slow motion. He saw the lad's stocky legs bring him to a sudden slow-down. He saw his feet thinking. He saw the player dribble precariously close to the 'keeper's wheelchair, dance round him, line up his shot at an angle from ten yards out, and place the ball along the ground towards the empty goal. The crowd on the touchline roared, as if the ball were already in. The player even turned to run away in triumph. Then something caught his eye and he strained his neck to follow what happened. The little girl was on the pitch, running across the empty goalmouth to the rolling ball.

*Oh no*, thought Tommy. 'Carol, no!' he shouted, with the tragic helplessness of an adult watching a child running into a busy road. 'No!' The little girl toe-poked the ball away, and it ran down the slope and off the pitch.

When he didn't give a goal but indicated another drop ball, Tommy went through it all again. The uproar from the parents. The man with the body-warmer, in his face, threatening him if he didn't give a goal. The Down's kid shouting at him in whole sentences – 'It's a goal! She's not playing! One–nil, Ref!' Everyone joined in around him, including the Yellows, many of whom didn't understand what was happening but were compelled to throng round Tommy. Mark had the girl in hand, and was quietly telling her not to do it again. No one fetched the ball. The man with the body-warmer was really annoying Tommy. 'Get off the field of play,' he shouted back at him. 'Drop ball.'

This sort of thing didn't happen very often. But Tommy knew that he could never award a goal if the ball hadn't crossed the line. The rules were clear. Football was strict like that. And that was what he liked about the game. There were no half-goals or part-goals, just goals or no goals in their pure binary splendour. He'd even seen it on TV once about twenty years before – a Scottish ballboy coming round the posts at some midweek cup match (maybe it had even been at Parkhead? It looked like one of those grounds with a running track) and side-footing the ball away as it rolled towards his team's open net.

'If you don't get off the pitch I'll call the game off,' he shouted to all the parents.

'It's all over now anyway!' shouted one of them back. 'We've won.'

'Clear the pitch, please,' bellowed Tommy. *Man, I didn't come up here for this shit. These fucking people don't understand football.* 'Get off the fucking pitch!' he shouted at Body-Warmer. 'Or I'll throw you off.'

'Load of rubbish you are,' grumbled the man. 'Bloody biased ref, I knew this would happen, letting him bring his mate.'

When Tommy heard the word 'biased' his heart leapt. He wanted to tear across the pitch and place a hard, studded kung fu kick in the back of the man's body-warmer, but he controlled himself. *Cunt.*

'Drop ball. On the edge of the penalty area.' Tommy knew he would probably have to explain this to some interfering adult too – that you don't give a drop ball in the box, it has to be on the edge, in line with where the infringement took place. Jamie eventually went to get the ball, but Tommy looked at his watches, and saw time was up. There was barely time for the ball to hit the ground. He blew three long blasts on his whistle with his hand in the air, waited for the kid to give him the ball, and began his ritual lonely walk to the sideline. Boos rose up from the parents and more verbal abuse came from the direction of Kevin. The players drifted off the pitch, while Tommy marched with his head up. *Perhaps I am a conceited bastard*, he thought, as he caught himself trying to brave their anger and hang on to his sense of right.

Mark caught him up, and walked by his side. 'Good decision, Ref!'

'Yeah, well, it's the last one you'll see me do up here, I've had enough.' He turned on Mark. 'I've had enough of your Mongs and their fucked-up parents. If they want a proper referee they should fucking abide by the rules. And my decisions.'

'Come on, Tommy, you were great. The kids had a great time. And nil–nil was a fair result in the event.' Mark being so nice still distracted Tommy.

'Aw, fuck off.' He paused, and they looked at each other, both wondering where he would go next. 'I've never heard such shit.'

Tommy hadn't told Mark to fuck off before. And he had never told a priest to fuck off either. It didn't go down too well. Mark said nothing, just shrugged, and led his charge away to the players. The little girl looked back over her shoulder at him in wonderment. In a minute, Tommy could hear him pep-talking them back down to earth. As he rested on the footplate of the sunshine bus, he even watched the priest shaking hands with the man in the sheepskin coat. *Fucking priests. Fucking robots*. He got his tracksuit from the bottom of his bag and began pulling it on. When he looked up, he saw Carol coming towards him. He wasn't in the mood for any more vocabulary.

'Hey, naughty girl!' he said, and laughed bitterly. 'How's that for disorder?'

'Tangelos are a cross between tangerines and another fruit, I forget which . . .'

'If,' said Tommy, loudly and sternly interrupting her, 'when the ball is going into goal, a spectator enters the field before it passes wholly over the goal line, and tries to prevent a score, a goal shall be allowed if the ball goes into goal, unless the spectator has made contact with the ball or has interfered with play, in which case the referee shall stop the game and restart it by dropping the ball at the place where the contact or interference occurred, unless it was within the goal area at that time, in which case it shall be dropped on that part of the goal-area line which runs parallel to the goal line, at the point nearest to where the ball was when play stopped. You knew that, didn't you, love?'

She said nothing, only looked down dumbly at the zip of her anorak.

'OK, little girl. I'm off now. Have a nice life.'

'I'll have a nice life,' she said.

Tommy made his way back to the car. His head wasn't hurting any more, but he still felt old and cloudy. Most of the Sacred Heart team were standing around in their kit looking lost, while the Reds were being packed successfully into their cars and vans. He saw Kevin sitting in a sulk to one side. *I'm not getting you up those fucking stairs, mate, no way. You can stay down at ground level till the lifts are fixed, far as I'm concerned. Let's get out of this fucking place.* He looked across the park, with its acres of wet grass, and its tree-lined river cranking its way through the middle. The pitches were beginning to fill up with other games. Some beerboys, just like Fat Paul's team in London but with less jewellery, were warming up thirty yards to the right, and twenty spindly schoolboys were chasing an over-inflated caser about to his left.

'Yeah, anyway, I'm going back now, I'm knackered,' he shouted to Mark. 'Who d'you want me to take?'

'We're OK, thanks,' said Mark. 'And thanks for refereeing, Tommy, the kids loved it. Really they did.' He was being nice again, the moment's moodiness seemingly past.

*Mark thanking me. Another first.* 'Yeah, well.' Tommy looked at his watch. It was gone eleven-thirty. 'I'll be going back, then. I'll probably have a sleep, don't feel too good. There's the match tomorrow.'

'Of course,' said Mark, to show he hadn't forgotten his higher purpose.

'Right. See you later.'

Tommy set off across the grass in the Morris, weaving between the pitches. Once on the open grass, he saw the white changing rooms in the centre of the park, with their square metal drainpipes and flat roofs. He remembered when he and Mark were both fourteen, pegging it across the park, pursued by the park keeper on his fixed-wheel bicycle. The bastard in his prison warder's uniform, bottle green. Tommy running faster, and having to persuade Mark to keep up, because Mark was changing his mind about running, and wanted to stand. After years of fear and persecution, he wanted to have the parkie. He was getting big enough. They'd only been throwing stones up on to the roof of the changing room – hardly a capital offence in Tommy's eyes, then or now. *Not like burning holes in the hockey nets with cigarettes, or smashing bottles in the goalmouth. Fucking mad Mark tired of running, saying he wanted to have him, the parkie bastard. I only just convinced him, maybe just by carrying on running. He must have looked back, then looked forward at me, and decided which way to run. A year later he would definitely have stayed. Today, what would he do? Probably intervene and give everyone a good talking-to. God, it's sick.*

As he had the car, he was tempted to go into town to have a good look at all the changes, but fatigue got to him. He wanted to call Melissa too. He drove back to Aston. Saturday lunch-time and it seemed rather quiet. He went by the Villa ground and remembered they were playing away that afternoon. *At that god-forsaken hellhole the Dell. What a fucking shithole.* He pulled up next to the Vespa and went inside. All was quiet. *Must be Mrs O's day off.* He considered having a snoop around, but didn't feel like it. He'd never snooped on anyone before moving to London. It was a cockney thing to do, a London thing that seemed to come with the territory of rented houses and neighbours you never got to know. *I couldn't snoop on Mark.*

He put the TV on and sat on the sofa. *Football Focus. Oh, here we go. Bob fucking Wilson again. He called one of my decisions 'questionable' once, the useless Arsenal fumbler. Still, he has a bit of humility. Not as much as me but enough.*

Tommy liked the midweek action, that sense of catching up, but he fell asleep during the Motherwell goals. He slept until four-thirty, dreaming of ice hockey and horse-racing, when the scores came in on the teleprinter. Villa won, three–one. *Yessss.* That was all he wanted to know. *Those cunts at the top of the table can fuck off*, he thought, as he switched off the old set and replaced the lace mantilla.

*Now what?* He went outside, thinking he would take a walk and kill some time until Mark got back. He got some chewing gum at the corner shop, then strolled on down to Villa Park. He marvelled at the high walls of the new stands. Things had changed since he'd been away – grown instead of fallen to pieces as he had expected. *The Doug Ellis Stand – what a joke. Why not the Ron Saunders Stand – the man who got us out of the Second and took us to the championship? That's the thing to do, name the infrastructure after yourself. The bastard, with his travel agency and his Travellers' Club coach trips. And he used to be on the board at Blues.* He walked behind the Holte End, so close to the walls that an old chant rang in his mind:

> 'We are the 'Olte, we are the 'Olte,
> We are we are we are the 'Olte . . .'

It was almost his favourite song, ever. Hundreds, thousands of people jumping up and down on the spot. He reached the Trinity Road side, the only relic of the old days. The thing was closed, but he did see the reserves drifting out – fresh faces and wet hair. They played at Walsall for a bit, which was stupid, to save the pitch. Now they were back where they belonged. Things changed so often now, nothing felt stable any more.

He pondered this as he walked back. He ran into Mark on the way in, and found he was pleased to see him again. He was rushing to make the vigil Mass and couldn't talk, but made Tommy welcome. He even directed the doctor to a four-pack of Skol in the fridge, much to Tommy's delight.

Alone in the house, he made a start on them, and watched TV. The lottery was on. Tommy chuckled and slapped the arm of his chair as the plea went out for some dreadful old toff, a duke they said, who had won 2.1 million pounds, but hadn't yet claimed it. When Mark eventually came in, it was near half seven.

'Hey, ministering to the needy, eh? Where were you?'

'Marriage instruction, a young couple, straight after Mass. They're nice but she's having a baby.'

'No time to lose, then?'

'Right.' Mark flopped down in one of the armchairs, put his head back and sighed heavily, as though he hadn't rested for a long time.

And slowly, they began to talk again. Mark had nothing to do, nowhere to go until Sunday. Nor did Tommy. Plus he had a can of Skol in his hand. As he popped the third top he was feeling great about the world. He felt great about the good he had done that day, great to be back in the shadow of the stadium, great to be back with his old mate Mark. Gradually he revived some of the old warmth in his friend. He even managed to press a drink on him. They talked about old friends again, and old connections between their schools and families. They caught up on each other's trainings – seven years at the seminary, seven years at medical school. Mark stretched his long legs in front of him, and looked pleased to have company. He looked at the door a couple of times, as though expecting to be interrupted, but eventually he relaxed. When Tommy walked down to the corner for some more beers, he was extremely pleased to come back and find him in exactly the same place. He had feared the priest would move and break the spell.

*Kevin!* Tommy suddenly remembered the obnoxious man in the wheelchair. 'So what happened to old Kevin, then? How did he get home?'

'Oh. I took him,' said Mark, as nonchalantly as he could.

Tommy stared in disbelief. 'Yeah, but how did he get up to his flat?' He waited. 'You didn't carry the bastard, did you? Oh no. Who helped you? Oh no.'

Mark looked away, then down at the carpet. He hadn't yet perfected the priestly knack of holding someone's eye without making them feel uncomfortable. He still looked away from others' guilt, and he still downplayed his own good works.

*Aw, fuck,* thought Tommy. He looked away now. He stared at the black hole in his beer can. *He was a bastard to get down — how could someone carry him all the way up again? Alone? Jesus, that must be where he was all afternoon.* Returning the handicapped to their homes. And me sleeping like a sod on his couch.

This depressing mood passed over him like a cloud in front of the sun on a windy day, and just as easily passed on. *Fuck it,* he thought, *it's done now,* and he felt great about the world again.

The subject of the disallowed goal came up.

'That Down's Syndrome kid, he was pretty good, wasn't he?' asked Tommy.

'Oh yeah, I think his name's Terry.' Mark paused, guiltily. 'He's a bit of a ringer really, though.'

'What do you mean?' asked Tommy, surprised. He didn't like the thought of the rules of engagement being further undermined.

'Oh, he's not proper Down's Syndrome, he's Down's Mosaic. You know what that is?'

'The bastard! Down's Mosaic, I never even suspected it. Yeah, I know what it is — well, I've read about it, never seen one. They have the gene that makes them look like Down's but they're perfectly normal.'

'Yeah. So technically, he shouldn't really have been in the team.'

'Bollocks. If I'd have known I'd have . . .' *Well, what would I have done?* The booze was tripping up Tommy's thinking again. 'Yeah, well, I hope they fix the parents' gene soon too.'

'What gene is that, then?'

'The gene that makes the parents always give 'em the same awful basin haircut. Jesus, I hate that.'

Mark had to laugh. At ten o'clock he placed his second can gently on the carpet and declared he was going up to bed.

'Big day tomorrow, son?' asked Tommy.

'Eh?' said Mark.

'I mean, Sunday.'

'Oh yeah. 'Course, Sunday.' He laughed, caught out by the obviousness of the comment. 'Tommy, you heathen, when will we make a Catholic of you again?'

'Eh, don't start that. Melissa said . . . shit, I forgot to call her again. Bollocks. Oh, I'll do it tomorrow.'

They parted on the landing, Tommy heading for the bathroom with his washbag in hand. 'Big day you and all tomorrow, eh?' Mark asked him. 'Wolves–Man U?'

'Yeah. Tell Mrs O to get the beers in, it'll be on the fucking telly. Man U always are.'

Fiona: Mel, are you still on for tonight, then?

Melissa: Absolutely. What time is it?

F: It's six. We're all meeting at eight in the Ahh Bar.

M: OK. What was that thing like last night anyway?

F: Oh, you know, telly people. I got talking to this bloke from Radio Four who says he knows Tommy. Nick something or other. You know him?

M: No. Tommy doesn't know anyone. What did he look like?

F: Nothing special. He told me he had a great face for radio. Like I was supposed to say. 'Oh no, you're lovely!' He was a bit of a prat. How was your workout anyway, you old gym rat?

M: Great.

F: Hmm. I think I might just check it out some time, your gym. Are there any hot men there?

M: They're all right. Depends what you mean. A lot of yuppies.

F: I like yuppies! You've got me interested now. Come on, what's it like?

M: Girlfriend, I've got to go. The bath's running and I'm still waiting for Tommy to call.

F: Oh, where's he, then?

M: He's in Birmingham, I told you yesterday. And he's probably trying to get through right now.

F: OK. OK. I'll let you off. For now. But I expect to hear more later.

M: Yeah, yeah. See you later. You old slapper.

F: Cow. Seeya at eight.

4

# Doctor work; Wolves retrospect, Plumage, & the decline

There are two kinds of football fan. The one, when he hears that a fan of another team has been killed, feels the initial thrill immediately tempered by the thought that perhaps someone, somewhere, may have overstepped the mark. What prompts this downward adjustment of feeling is the quiet belief that football violence isn't really about making other people die. It is about facing off, about standing, about not shitting out. It's about putting on a good show. It's about battering enemies in a saga that goes on through the seasons, year after year, with the added pleasure of chance meetings in the cups and at service stations. It's about turning up in a strange town and immediately knowing where you are by instinct, or by your leader's memory, or simply by the trail of colours and faces leading through other people's streets to other people's pubs and other people's grounds. It's about making a lot of noise, charging and scuffling. Scattering ugly people from other horrible cities. Being able to hold your head up, at home and away. But it's not about killing. Death ups the stakes a bit too high. If killing was the point, then everyone would carry weapons.

The other kind of football fan is the Mark kind. The nutter. No one ever knows what he's going to do, or what's going on in his head.

Tommy had grown to admit that he was the former kind of football fan. As his active participation had dwindled to nothing when he took off for medical school, hindsight revealed that he had been a pack animal — noisy, of medium courage, good-humoured, and dedicated in his hatred of all things not Villa. But he had kept alive the pilot light of hate, and he had unconsciously assumed for all the intervening years that Mark had too.

He pondered this now, as he sat on the edge of the bath at seven o'clock on the Monday morning after his West Midlands weekend. Mark had changed a lot. But had Tommy? He was looking at the ring finger of his right hand, at a short, deep laceration below the middle knuckle. He had just taken the tape off it. It had been produced by the canine tooth of a Man United fan, whom Tommy had punched during a scuffle before the Wolves–United game the day before. Although he knew he could stitch the cut in a few minutes once he got to work, he was bothered because it looked out of place on his hands. These were the cool, smooth hands of a doctor. Hands that could ease a patient's pain just by the probing of a gland, or read an illness by a finger's gentle insertion into an orifice. He knew how it felt when he tapped different areas of a patient's back in search of the hollow sound of shadows. He knew that they felt 'on the mend', immediately, because they smiled and looked relieved, and happier as they put their shirts back on. So the toothmark on his hand seemed odd, after all these years of trying to be good. He replayed the moment in his mind again. A one-eyebrowed Mancunian with a drawn face and sunken cheeks, tall and thin, perhaps not even twenty-five years old, had come at him as two rivers of fans met near the ground. Nothing much had happened, it was just a bit of pre-match posturing. The fan had swung at him and stung his ear. Tommy swung back, fired up by the double venom of long-term hatred and instant revenge. He was lucky and got the fellow hard in the open mouth, sending his head flapping backwards. One punch was all he got. Still surprised but excited, Tommy watched as two policemen charged straight past him and arrested the stunned United fan and one of his scowling mates. Then he stepped into the Wolves crowd and faded away before anyone could try to involve him.

'So. How was your lost weekend?' Melissa came into the bathroom. He hadn't spoken to her since the previous Friday morning.

'Oh, it was OK. Did you watch the game?' he asked innocently. He was sitting like someone waiting for a bus, leaning forward slightly, spreading his weight with his hands. He only had to avert his gaze from the cut to draw attention away from it, and then keep it hidden. He could explain it later in the day.

'Some of it. Why didn't you call back? I left a message for you.' She looked like she was cross and controlling it.

Tommy groaned internally. He had forgotten, several times. There was no excuse for that, and he knew it.

'I'm sorry, I just kept . . . forgetting. There was a lot going on up there. Y'know.'

'Don't worry about me,' she said. Bitterness was vying with indignation in her voice. 'You had a call from the Football Association. I was only trying to pass it on. It's not like I was craving the famous Tommy Burns or anything.'

'I'm sorry,' he said again, more meekly.

*She's a loyal bugger,* he thought admiringly. She was one of those women who even at seven in the morning can drum up, and successfully employ, an attitude. Once she was awake, she was fully awake, with a crisp sanity he could only emulate. Tommy liked to think he was the same sort of person, and that this was one more reason why he loved her, but more and more as he aged he found he kept his Attitude to himself until the appropriate time. He was awake too, but he didn't want to get into anything until he had more time to talk. He had to be at the surgery at a quarter to eight. She didn't have to be at school till eight-thirty.

Gloom swept over him on hearing her tone, and doubt upon hearing that the FA wanted something. They never telephoned. They always wrote. The FA had meetings of its Premiership referees three times a season in hotels around the country, often at the Friendly Hotel in Walsall, just off the M6. They avoided Birmingham – Tommy was used to that. They looked at videos of key decisions and discussed them. People might chuckle in the dark over a split decision or a lip-legible obscenity, but the atmosphere was far from the laddish rowdiness of a football team trying to get its head round tactics and the rules.

There was a sense of solidarity among the referees, born of knowing they were ultimately on their own. He wasn't matey enough with any of them to get a lift up from London, but he felt strongly that he would back any one of his colleagues to the hilt if he had to. No poxy manager, or agent or pundit would ever bring one of them down.

A few of the Referees Committee always turned up too. Tommy liked the fact that the chairman of the committee could be someone from a shitty club – the chairman of Lincoln City, perhaps, or some old codger from Bramhall Lane who had seen it all. It wasn't all sewn up by the fat cats and the big-money loudmouths yet. He enjoyed the meetings, because there was a feeling that this was a refs' bash, and representation by the FA was merely symbolic. Tommy took the train there, changing to the local line at New Street without venturing beyond the ticket barrier. As he passed through the familiar old stations – Witton, Aston, Perry Barr

— he caught glimpses of the old territory but couldn't bring himself to get out and explore. He always made sure he had too little time for that.

He contributed at the meetings, and he had been discussed too, more often commended than questioned. The clubs gave the referee a mark after each game depending on his performance. There was B: Below Expectation, G: Good, I: Impressive, and E: Exceptional. You were expected to get at least nine out of ten Goods to remain on the Premiership list. Tommy had never had anything less. He'd had a handful of Impressives, and the previous season three Es.

Everything else to do with the FA came in the mail, sent out on their behalf by the Football League in Lytham St Anne's. He never went to the FA's headquarters at Lancaster Gate. No business of his ever took him down W2 way, because no one had ever had cause to fault him.

He fought his instinct to ask Melissa about this phone call first.

'Yeah, it was great. Met all Mark's kids and that, the handicapped team he looks after. Saw where he lives. Did the game Sunday.' He looked up at her, trying to forget about the spot of trouble he had been in. She wouldn't like that at all. 'What about you, love? What did you do?'

Her only answer was to bend over the sink to drink from the tap, exposing herself to him as her T-shirt rode up. He smiled.

*She loves me.* 'So I'm not totally in the dog-house, then?'

She straightened up, and spoke with her toothbrush fully in her mouth. He was able to interpret her muffled words at once. 'Not this time, but if you mess me around like that again . . .'

He smiled, and got up saying he'd get the tea on, hoping she wouldn't notice he was cutting short getting ready so as to avoid her seeing the cut on his finger. He managed to keep things covered up while they had a cup of tea together, then kissed her goodbye and set off for work. That Monday morning was lighter than the previous Friday as the clocks had gone back over the weekend, and although he appreciated the extra daylight, he headed to the clinic with foreboding in his heart, as though he were afraid of being caught out.

The clinic was a small box at the base of a pair of tower blocks in Camden Town, and seemed to serve only occupants of the nearby council flats. He always checked the patients' addresses on their medical cards, and it was always some kind of Tower or House. It seemed to Tommy as though anyone that could afford to avoided him.

'Happy Monday, Marge,' he said to the receptionist he shared with Dr Aktar. He had always made a point of saying hello to staff before they could say it to him, and they unfailingly took it as a sign that he cared about them. This was a great dividend on a small investment. And he found with practice he had grown to mean it.

After a minute she brought him his mail and a cup of tea, just as he was setting up to sew his finger. Busted, he came clean.

'Er, could you give me a hand here, please, Marge?' he asked. 'I need to suture this . . .' He showed her the cut.

'Ooh, Doctor, are you all right?' she asked, with deep sympathy. She jumped to his aid immediately. She didn't ask how it had happened, but put three perfect stitches into his already healing knuckle, pulling the dry edges of skin together. *Good old Marge*, he thought. *She fields the phone calls, operates the computer, and can stitch up the locals before their seat is even warm. I bet if she was allowed to write prescriptions she could run this place on her own.*

'Thanks, Margie.'

Under pressure from above, Tommy had seen his clinic turn into a mini-hospital over the last few years. It was cheaper, he was told, to deal with small amounts of surgery — mainly stuff to the limbs, but lately also ear, nose and throat problems — on the spot, using his initiative. As he had fewer specialists to refer people to, he found himself faced with increasingly complex problems. He found himself pulverising gallstones and lasering tonsils in his ten-by-twelve office. *Eyes will be next*, he thought. *I s'pose if they can whip out a beggar's cataracts in a tent in India, there's no reason why it can't be done in Camden. I wonder if Marge will be able to handle the tonsils kids then? She's done OK with the sutures I've given her so far.* He heard the door handle rustle. *Uh-oh, here they come.*

Then followed Monday's regular stream of misanthropes and malaprops, the self-specialists and the hypochondriacs, the moaners and the mad, the great hacking, spluttering, groaning procession. Plus the merely ill, pale as daisies and silenced by their ignorance. Tommy was pretty confused himself. He had been taught that his patients could best be sorted out by whatever was new or powerful from the drug companies, whose reps traipsed through his office three times a week, with their gee-whizz folding briefcases full of sponsored endoscopes, hand-held ultrasound scanners, and personal organisers. The latter were typical of the drug companies' gifts. Tommy took a pen from one of them once, to hang around the neck, which said 'Zantac, Glaxo' and had a yellow smiley face on the top through which the string ran, and ever since he had wished he hadn't. He told them to keep their spiels under three minutes each, which they did, because they were good. Tommy wished they would all go away, but Aktar had taken him aside one day after he had been publicly offhand with a boy from Wellcome, and explained, very gravely, that he liked the free stuff. And that he'd been there twenty years longer than Tommy.

Not wanting any trouble, Tommy had capitulated to Aktar's wishes. But as an experiment, he would sometimes try to go a whole session without prescribing any drugs. Doing this on a Monday morning was a challenge because some of the patients knew more about their medicine than he did. But Tommy was feeling a bit odd this morning. In the back of his mind he was distracted by his friend Mark's new career, and he was bothered too about the call he had missed from the FA.

He thought he'd give it a go anyway, the drug-free zone. He spent the morning dealing with a man with shingles, an old lady with a hip that wouldn't heal ('Wear a cricket box on each hip so you don't bash them again,' he told her loudly), twins with measles, and a woman who wanted an abortion because she didn't think she'd be able to give up smoking. He referred the latter to Dr Aktar – he was good with smokers. Tommy dealt with them by listening earnestly and, like a chess player who sits on his hands, refusing to take his pen to his pad.

Around ten-thirty a chronically unemployed young woman called Carol came in to see him, big-boned and plain as a Rich Tea biscuit. She had a vague south-east accent that had been filed down by three years' attendance at a technical college and by a lot of TV watching. Carol talked about her job hunt for a bit, then gave him the latest about the bad things her sister had told her mother and her stepfather about her, etc., etc. She waited for him to renew her Amitriptylene prescription, which she took for her depression.

Tommy paused. Just for a laugh, he brought up some familiar names: Premarin, Zoloft, Prozac – all drugs for unhappy people. He told her about the effects of each one, using the words the reps had used on him. He couldn't be sure any of it was true, since he had never actually tried Prozac or any of that stuff, but he carried on deliberately. From her face – she had a suspicious look that threatened to break into a scowl at any moment – she seemed to be wondering what was going on, while following the familiar names, until he mentioned one new to her, Trazadom, whereupon she assumed he was going to start her on a new drug. This cheered her up. But Tommy changed tack and began asking her more about her week, her family and her feelings. This wasn't what she wanted to hear, but she went along with it, dredging her store of complaints, still expecting her reward.

Next thing she knew, he was telling her she should try going without the 'Ami', as she called it, and come back and talk to him in a week. She didn't even have time to get nasty, or tearful, because the phone went and Tommy gestured her out of his office. When the door was shut, he laughed to himself as he considered his hustle, and picked up the phone. It was Marge with a man from the FA.

*Oh shit. The FA.* 'Go ahead, Margie.' He inhaled nervously. 'Dr Burns speaking,' he said.

'Mr Burns. So glad I could reach you, at last,' said the male voice. *Fuck. These people never phone. It must be bad.*

'Mr Burns, I would like to have a word with you,' said the voice. Tommy imagined that everyone at the FA spoke in flat suburban accents, like so many of the accountants and tradesmen who refereed. 'This is Ian Lockhart, the Referees' Secretary.'

Tommy knew the name, as it had just that season begun showing up as the signature at the bottom of all correspondence from the Football Association to referees. He could see the spidery loop of the handwriting, and the carefully placed possessive apostrophe at the end of the title typed below. The blood was draining out of his head. Lockhart had come from nowhere over the summer to replace the previous secretary, Colin Marsh, who had been a great favourite with the officials. The word was that Marsh had been forcibly retired to make way for the new man, who was younger, at forty, but had no real record as a referee. It was said he had made Class One, but that meant nothing. There were five thousand Class One refs in England. That was just the bottom rung of a very long ladder. Tommy had asked around, but nobody knew much about him. No one had been formally introduced to him, as there had been no meetings in Walsall yet. He was just a laser-printed signature, not even a voice on the phone. His own secretary had been handling the day-to-day queries of the officials, telling them of last-minute changes and taking their calls.

'We'd like to make an appointment to see you, Mr Burns. A matter has come up for discussion.'

*Fuck.* Tommy couldn't think.

'Er ... what? Er ... when? When do you want it?'

'Well, as soon as possible. Let's say ... Thursday? Can you make it that early?' The voice showed no friendliness. It wasn't allowing itself any warmth. It had something on its mind, something it was having to hold off on.

'Yes I can. I have surgery in the morning. I can be there at, say, three o'clock?'

'Four o'clock would be better. Lancaster Gate – do you need directions?'

'No. I know where it is. I ... I'll see you Thursday.' He paused. He
heard the other man signing off with a neutral 'Goodbye.'

Tommy went into a contortion of grief and guilt. Just the implied threat
to his hobby had his mind reeling and his life unravelling. He felt he was in
trouble. It never occurred to him that he might be being called in to receive
a commendation. That didn't seem to be the way it worked with the FA.
He sat back in his chair and looked at the miserable ceiling above him,
with its sickly white tiles, pockmarked in the same places by supposedly
random air bubbles. *They know about yesterday. They know about it all. There must
have been cameras. Or someone in the crowd recognised me. Oh shit. Oh no.*

There was no time to mourn, however, as Marge buzzed him, ready
with the next patient. She knew he was off the phone when his light went
out on her console, and she wanted to get the next one through the door.
The traffic light above his door was showing green too.

*I can't go through a whole afternoon of this*, he thought. *Fuck 'em.* He got up,
grabbed his coat off the hook and marched out.

'Marge, I've got to dash. Something's cropped up. Sorry.'

Marge looked worried, and made a curious gesture with her mouth,
but Tommy knew she was too professional to question him in front
of the patients. He turned as if he were about to address them: a
roomful of young mums, writhing pre-schoolers and decaying old folk.
They had become alert, wondering what the doctor was doing out of his
box so soon, and with his coat too. He changed his mind and hurried
out the door.

Once out in the street he didn't quite know which way to turn: north,
home, or south, to the West End? He didn't fancy central London much,
as in all the years he had never found a good place there to sit that wasn't
a pub, but he fancied going home even less. He joined a queue and got
the bus into town.

London was looking really shit. Monday lunch-time, and the streets
were full of office people dashing out to buy sandwiches and cold medicine,
nasty-looking kids who should have been in school, delivery drivers and
motorcycle messengers loafing around their vehicles and tourists putting
brave faces on it. Tommy got off at Centre Point, not sure where the bus
would go next. He had often wondered why he lived just off-centre of
one of the greatest cities on earth yet availed himself of so few of its
pleasures that he could go years between visiting the same place twice.

What did he need the centre of the city for? He didn't go out much at night any more. Melissa had once asked him to think globally and act locally, and he took her up on it. Six years later and they were still working their way through the vast number of restaurants in their own little sector of north London. 'What do you feel like eating this Friday?' she'd ask. He'd always smile first, like a big joke was coming, and reply, 'Ethnic.'

He found himself caught behind a couple of dawdlers out window-shopping. A young couple. *Jesus, don't these people have jobs to go to? Where do they get their money from for all this purchasing? Maybe they're a shift-work couple, get ready for breakfast when everyone else's having their dinner? Maybe it's their day off. Fucking hurry up. Make up your minds!*

''Scuse me,' he muttered, as he squeezed between them. He continued down the street, annoyed by the pedestrians, taking offence at the traffic, and bothered by the stuff for sale in the shops. He turned down by Oxford Circus Tube and soon found himself on Carnaby Street. Whatever it had been in the fabled sixties, Carnaby Street was now an embarrassing mess, a collection of shops catering to the tourists who themselves came to see the tourists. The shops were like a museum of street fashion, trying to encompass everything. Each one started at the officially sanctioned beginning of it all – Teddy boy drape coats – and went through all the Mod and Rude Boy revivals and ended up with a jumble of fetish wear, film star posters and shirts from the biggest football teams in the League. A group of young Scandinavian punks and skinheads sat in a doorway, passing round a family-sized bottle of beer, waiting for something to happen. Tommy felt a wave of pity for them, a bunch of schoolkids waiting around for history to start up and include them. Too disgusting for girls and too poor for power. *At least they have lager,* he thought. He winked at the one who was just putting the bottle to his lips. The kid stopped the bottle in its path, glared at him, waited for him to pass, then shouted, 'Fuck off, you fucker!' in rigid Teutonic tones.

*You little bastard,* thought Tommy. He was about to turn and at least stare back at the boy when he caught himself. *What am I thinking? Why am I worrying about these little punks when I have to face the fucking FA this Thursday? The whole fucking lot of it could come tumbling down.* He passed another shop selling football kits and his eye quickly picked out the Villa one. The shirts were arranged in alphabetical order, presumably to avoid the dilemma of who to offend when it came to sorting the sheep from the goats. Tommy remembered his surprise at ever seeing a Villa shirt for sale in London, except on days when

Villa were in town. The old cockney bastards who sold them outside the ground would probably have gone down to some warehouse in Battersea or Epping on a Friday night and picked up a bin-liner of Villa scarves and shirts to go with the Spurs rosettes and all that cockney clobber. In shop windows in later years he had seen Villa stuck in with the purely provincial teams such as Southampton and Ipswich, pushed up against the erratic internationals, such as Leeds and Newcastle, and even once or twice lumped in with the corporations – Man U, Liverpool, Tottenham. It didn't seem to matter how these teams played – if enough daughters of politicians or sons of Arab sheikhs supported them, that was good enough for inclusion. Sometimes Villa were up, sometimes Villa were down, according to the people who ran these things. In Carnaby Street they were mostly down.

Something caught his eye in the bottom of the display – a linesman's flag for sale, in dazzling orange-and-yellow checks, the dayglo colours recommended by FIFA. He was pleased by this sign of recognition for his craft, but then the fear came to him. *This could be what's ahead for me, back to running the line. Back to being overruled and covered in flob. Oh God, why didn't I just keep my head down and stay out of trouble?*

He tried to banish the thought, and stood at the cross-road wondering where to go. He was hungry by now, and really wanted a cup of coffee, but most of all just wanted to sit down. He walked hopefully down towards Piccadilly Circus, another place he hadn't been in over a year, stood outside a shop and looked around the intersection. He noticed a new sign, next to the Criterion Brasserie. The Soccer Museum. *Ah, that place. It's open now, then?* There was a huge blown-up photo of Pele about to head against Gordon Banks in the Mexico World Cup. Banks was grimacing. He still had two good eyes then. It must have been taken with a zoom lens from the other end because the net and the faces crammed in behind it were in focus too. He saw other names: Planet Hollywood, the Hard Rock Café, Sticky Fingers ... Everything was archiving itself and charging admission. Football was just next in line. *I wonder if this soccer place has a café? Probably not.* There was an admission fee of eight quid. He looked around him again, and crossed back to the corner of Regent Street by Boots. He saw nothing, and, hating himself, he stepped into a doughnut shop.

What brought on the crisis of faith? Tommy had risen the morning before, in Birmingham, in a good mood. He wasn't hung over from the few Skols he had had on the Saturday night, and he hadn't made a fool of himself in conversation with Mark. He wasn't too hungry or too cold, too horny or in pain. He knew he was going to Wolverhampton to referee the game with Man United in the afternoon. He rolled off the couch feeling fairly good about himself. The clock said 7.30 a.m. He could hear Mark in the kitchen, so he dressed quickly and went in to get a cup of tea.

'Hey, Tommy Burns, how are you?' asked Mark. Tommy didn't have an equivalent greeting ready. Something like *Mornin', Father Mark* might have worked, but he was still adjusting to the possibility of irony and mockery between himself and his old friend.

'All right,' he said. He sat down and Mark poured him some tea. They drank in silence and looked at the *Sunday Mercury* for a bit.

'What have you got this morning, then?' asked Tommy.

'Eight o'clock Mass for starters. Then eleven, then benediction at six.'

'Those are funny times. It's like the football. Wolves, twelve o'clock. Stupid. For the television of course.'

'I know. They changed them again.'

'Oh yeah,' said Tommy half knowingly. 'To fit in with people's lifestyles?'

'You're right!' said Mark, surprised. 'That's exactly what the pastoral letter said. "People's changing lifestyles ..."'

'People are just too lazy to get out of fucking bed, that's all it is. Rather arse around all weekend watching sport on telly and playing with their cars. Or shopping.'

'You might have a point there,' said Mark, lowering his eyes for a split second. They grew quiet. Both knew it was nearly time to part. Mark stood up. 'I'd better be going, then.' Then he fixed Tommy with a clear, unembarrassed look and said, 'It's been a real pleasure to see you again, Tom. I've often thought of you, wondered where you were, but you seem to be doing better than I imagined.'

Tommy was on his feet by now, and seized the firm hand that was offered him. He in his turn looked the other man in the eye.

'It's great to see you too, man. Thanks for the hospitality – thank Mrs O for me too.'

'I will.'

'And come and see me in London some time. You should meet Melissa.'

'I will.'

They both paused, their half-smiles fading at the proper rate, like parachutes coming down in a green field. Tommy glanced around the

room. 'I might as well be off now too, since I'm up.' He picked up his
bag and they left.

'Out in the street they approached the gates of the church. There wasn't
a soul around. No close-parked cars, no old men talking on the steps.

Mark's attention was consumed by the sight.

'Bit quiet, isn't it?' Tommy remarked. He was ready to get going, but
felt himself lingering. He watched Mark walk slowly but more deliberately,
as though he had just rounded the corner on a very strange spectacle. The
church doors were closed. Mark tried them – they were locked. He looked
back at Tommy.

'This is a bit weird,' he said. 'What time do you make it?'

They looked at their watches.

'Seven forty-six,' said Tommy.

'That's what I make it. Where the heck is everyone?' The priest stood
with his mouth open. Tommy was about to make light and ask him if
he had lost his flock, but thought better of it. *It does feel strangely quiet*, he
thought. They stood there in silence for a whole minute.

Then Tommy got it. 'Aw, fuck, it's the clocks, the clocks went back
an hour last night! Fuck, I completely forgot. Fancy getting caught out
by that old one.'

Mark gave a huge sigh of relief, then smiled. 'And here was me thinking
it was all over!' he said.

*Oh, you of little faith*, thought Tommy, but he controlled himself again.

'What are we going to do now, then?' he asked. He'd said his goodbyes
and didn't want to go back inside the priests' house, but neither did he
fancy setting off for Wolverhampton an hour early. The many places in
which he could waste an hour flashed through his mind. He could walk
round Villa Park again. *Nah, all the magic's gone on a Sunday, especially this
time of morning*. He could walk round town. *Nah, it's just depressing when the
shops are closed*. A rummage through the magazines at New Street? *Possible*.
Wander round Wolverhampton town centre? *No thanks*. He sighed silently.
He went back to the house with Mark.

There are many ways to waste an hour, and the number of ways grows
as you get older and have fewer hours to waste. A cup of tea alone can
be stretched out to twenty-five minutes, from cupboard to sink. An
unnecessary phone call – five minutes. Fiddling with baggage, another
five. The two men sat at the kitchen table, prepared to try all these things.
Tommy especially was unsettled. But a short time into the tea they found
themselves deep in conversation. Mark had read in the *Express* and *Star*

that the famous English referee Jack Taylor was ill. Tommy had heard this, and admitted it would be good to meet him before he finally checked out. From there Mark asked what he thought he could do for him, and when he heard that Tommy just wanted to ask him a few questions, he said that this was very similar to what he did.

Seeing his chance, Tommy broached the question of how he had made the transition from being what he was to being a priest, and the priest replied that he had had a job putting the holes in washers in a factory in Hockley, and was beginning to wonder if this was it for his life, or could he become a toolmaker somehow, when Father Kelly had visited the factory one day, to see some old fellow whom he had known for years, and remembered Mark, mainly from seeing him around as a kid, and later seeing his name in the paper for football-related incidents. Standing at his drill, Father Kelly had trotted out his standard vocations speech, about how the Church desperately needed young men to keep it alive, to administer the sacraments, to visit the needy, to organise the parish, to counsel converts and newlyweds, 'and so on,' as he put it. An ingrained respect that hadn't come into play for a long time, Mark said, had kept him from telling the lonely parish priest where to get off, especially in front of all those atheists at work, and that afternoon, as he put the holes in a few thousand more washers, the bit about administering the sacraments – baptising babies, doling out communion, confirming kids, marrying people, hearing confessions, anointing the sick and burying the dead – began to make him think.

Tommy again had the odd feeling that things had been going on without him. He had fucked off to London, but against all odds life had gone on for those left behind. Mark looked calm as he spoke so casually about his change of job. 'I just kept thinking about it in the strangest places. I was at Forest a week later,' he said, then lowered his voice, 'and I was laying into this Forest fan curled up on the pavement, just kicking him, y'know, as much as possible before the law came, and I thought of something – like, who is this bloke? Where are his mates? That sort of thing. Which was odd, because I never used to think about anything when I was doing it, other than the task in hand ...'

'Yeah,' cut in Tommy, chuckling. 'Amen to that.'

'Then a few weeks later Tottenham came up for the knock, and just before I nutted this copper, a split second it must have been, I got the same thing.'

'Sort of humanising them?' Tommy felt relieved it was something he could understand. 'And it was all downhill from there, I suppose?'

'Looking back, it seems like it all, y'know, went from there. Some of the lads thought it was too weird for them. But a lot of other stuff happened around the same time – Billy went inside and came out queer, or gay rather, Trevor stopped going to games altogether, and Barnie and one of his mates both joined the police. So it wasn't that odd. Father Kelly told me later I should read St Augustine and St Paul to understand it, but I can't really get my head round it.'

They talked more, and the hour was soon done. Tommy left feeling a little better informed, and a little more envious. They shook hands again, and finally parted. The referee walked down the road and got his number seven into town.

Mulling all this over in the doughnut shop, he dropped his cigarette butt into the coffee cup with a satisfying sizzle, and exhaled against the plate-glass window. His eyes followed some late lunchers going about their business. Three men with grey suits and shiny faces emerged from a nearby bar, the one he should have gone to, screwing their eyes up in the daylight. They moved clumsily. He could see the effort in their mouths and throats as they spoke loudly. *London wankers*, he thought. *You fuckin' failed barrow-boys. Probably not from London either. Surrey, or Middlesex. Agents. Reps. Managers*. One of them had a sauce stain on his white shirt. *Wankers*. Tommy caught the eye of the leader, who immediately looked away. The three men seemed to exist in a private world of ease, even luxury. Getting pissed in the day at someone else's expense when everyone else is back at work. Wearing suits. *And looking at the ground*.

*It's not like the rest of the country, this place*. He heard himself rehearsing this as though he would have to testify on the subject soon. He thought of Wolves again. At New Street he had got the train to Wolverhampton, a journey of only twenty minutes. It was a London-to-Manchester train, but too early for fans. Cockney Reds, Hampstead Reds, neither were there yet. The only people on board seemed to be train-spotters – styleless, sexless men and boys with locomotive number books and lunch bags who were constantly meeting up and parting during their cross-country day excursions. Britain must have been a tiny place to them. Breakfast in Exeter, lunch in Glossop, tea in York, home to mum.

Two sat down across from Tommy. The general public, so far as Tommy could tell, didn't mind them. Fans were different, however – or 'mindless morons' as he had heard train-spotters put it. He had seen football fans torment them several times, usually name-calling and throwing all their possessions out of the window, but also cruel, one-sided gang beatings when one of them had fought back in a flailing-fists, glasses-flying-off sort of way.

'Do you lot thrive on mockery?' he had asked them, out of the blue.

'Pardon?' asked the elder of the two, interrupting their conference.

'I said does this stop at the Wolves ground?' replied Tommy.

'I believe it does,' he said, holding on to his dignity, ready for a rough ride.

'Thank you.' Tommy let it go. He knew he was too old for this nonsense. He thought he probably got almost as big a kick out of being on a train as they did, only not from what he saw out of the window, but from who he might run into on board. He merely tousled the unsuspecting man's hair as he got off. He twitched and reeled and stood up, and muttered 'Moron! Bloody lunatic!', but did nothing.

Wolves–Man United had always had a bit of magic about it on paper since the day over twenty years before when Tommy had read an account of some trouble at that fixture in the newspaper. It was the *Sun*, and the reporter was describing the effects of putting a fence down the middle – or rather, two-thirds of the way across – the South Bank, so the away fans could share it. Later in the season they put a net up too, before abandoning the experiment entirely, but at this game the air was thick with missiles being traded and recycled. The reporter wrote that the police had found metal discs with specially sharpened edges and handwritten messages taped to them, such as 'I HOPE THIS CUTS YOUR F—ING HEADS OFF YOU DIRTY MANCHESTER B——S'. What a testimony it had seemed to the old crafts, men taking the time at their lathes to carve out death stars and sharp discs for the visitors due that weekend! And the sticking-on of personalised labels! The story had had the right effect on Tommy, filling him with awe. The paper's delicacy with rude words worked well on him, rousing in him wonder. *And 'handwritten' too*. And so it was that the twin virtues of dedication and pride always came to mind whenever this fixture came around. To be asked to referee it was a special honour.

Things had changed a bit since then, he had noted as he had walked out of the station. He wanted to revisit the famous subway near the station. He had heard that the Subway Army, who used to line the concrete tunnel and wait for visiting fans in the eerie light, leaving them with nowhere to run, had been policed out of existence, but now they were back. Fifteen years ago Wolves had fallen headlong into the underworld of the Fourth Division from the First, losing several thousand fans on the way. *What kind of fans were they anyway? Just the wankers in the seats*. Huge tracts of yellow seating he had seen on the telly. *The people who drove to the ground from their detatched homes in Cannock and Wombourne and Studley. Mind you ... the North Bank emptied out a bit too. But that was their other end. Then again, the South Bank's been pretty sparse since the days of The Doog. And John Richards.*

Tommy was having trouble with the idea that real fans would stop going to games too. Real fans – the kind who sing and stand and fight, the kind who put up with shit from other fans all week at work and live for those sweet days that follow winning a local derby; the kind who get to the ground late not because they couldn't find a parking space close by, but because they got to the pub early; the kind who take pride in sticking with the team through thick and thin, through the shit nights at Wimbledon, as well as the glory days on packed trains and in captured streets when promotion is assured and one more point will take the title. He found it hard to imagine explosive seventeen-year-olds fresh out of school or borstal choosing to go shopping on a Saturday, or thirty-five-year-olds covered in Wolves tattoos cutting the grass. He couldn't imagine it for any club, in fact. From self-aggrandising Millwall to fickle Palace, everyone had their hard core. But the figures showed that it went on. Everyone's hard core could lapse.

There was nobody in the subway. He went back to the railway station, bought a coffee from the Upper Crust, and headed towards the ground.

From his stool in the doughnut shop, Tommy could see only a slice of sky, but he could tell from its thick whiteness that it was going to go down in the record books as a standard-issue cloudy London day. He watched a young builder on some scaffolding dropping lumps of plaster into a skip in the street thirty feet below. *Cockney bastard.* The words just crept up on him before he knew what was going on. It was like being pissed sometimes, being surrounded by all this life. When the builder wasn't concentrating on his job he seemed quite cheerful, stopping to scan the women and trying to attract their attention by yelps and lip-flapping fingerless whistles. *You half-friendly cockney bastard. I know how you get on Saturdays. But I'm always like Saturday for you.* Tommy's mind spun off into an elaborate fighting fantasy, in which he acquitted himself well. A hard and savage punch to the throat. A many-horsepowered kicking to the internal organs. A final flourish of gratuitous grinding of the evil pug face into the pavement. *Want some more, you fucker?* When he got up for a second cup of coffee the girl serving him suggested a set of doughnut holes with cinnamon. Dollops of dough deep-frozen in a factory in another country deep-fried before his eyes. She was friendly, in a genuine way, full of the optimism of a new arrival at the bottom of the food chain. Tommy barely noticed. He was still wrapped up in the previous day's proceedings.

Back at the ring road near the Wolves ground there were a lot of fans milling around. Wolves lads, teenagers, young men in their twenties, men with beer guts in their thirties, just hanging around. There was a quietness about them that Tommy recognised at once, a palpable self-control that always thrilled him. This wasn't quite the moment before it went off, it was the moment when it still *might* go off. Or nothing at all might happen. This not knowing, Tommy had come to realise in his years out of the game, was one of the details he loved. Being out of the game, though, had given him an odd sense of invulnerability. He felt he could glide through the fans untouched. Instead of being at a game where he had two sets of fans to fear, he feared none. That wasn't to say that Wolves weren't impressive, with their distrustful eyes, mutant fashions and bad skin. They had come out of their council houses by the thousand to look for trouble. It was just that Tommy thought they would instinctively leave him alone. That they would give him the benefit of the doubt. And they did.

Although he was in a hurry, he couldn't help but slow down as he mingled with them. He didn't want to look too conspicuous, but he didn't want to miss anything either. A ripple of awareness went through the crowd, three or four hundred strong. Some of them crossed the road, jaywalking fearlessly, the rest marched through the subway, joining another hundred already on the other side, outside the station. He went through the subway.

A train was coming in. United were coming. The fans around him moved slightly closer together, including him in their fold. They were still far enough apart to be able to see a good way ahead, and to convince themselves that they didn't look like a mob. Seven or eight coppers were spaced around the edge. Tommy loved the way they restrained themselves too. Maybe the law made them do it. The sensible thing would have been to send in the horses now, and the dogs, and swing those heavy hickory nightsticks. But they stayed on the fringes.

The first United started coming out of the station, craning their necks to see what sort of a reception they were getting. Wolves jeered at them. They sang back, 'United! United!' A dozen police led them down towards the subway and the stadium. The Wolves fans, including Tommy, moved towards them. The coppers still did nothing, except keep up with the situation. They all had the same look: between the chinstrap and the low brim of their helmets, a solid, patient look. Looking for trouble.

Tommy stayed with the group. United were coming down the path, led by police with shaggy Alsatians, and began funnelling into the subway, singing louder when they felt the concrete around them. They emerged, unscathed, as expected. They knew about the Subway Army, and its demise. The coppers still kept their positions, but the Wolves fans began moving forward, then alongside the procession, until several hundred of them were on the move together, doubling the size of the march towards the ground. Tommy found himself in the thick of them. They were shouting things at the strange lads only a few yards away: 'Wankers!', 'Glory-Glory-hunters, Glory-Glory-hunters' and 'Do you come from Manchest-er?' The United fans laughed and jeered back, and a pocket of them broke into a chant of 'Manchester, La La La', which caught on rapidly. Wolves responded with a thundering chant of 'Wanderers! Wanderers!', which had a manic urgency in its hard sound. Tommy felt the power of several hundred people with their arms raised, only feet from the people they hated, chanting the thing they knew best. He almost joined in, but he couldn't. He had to remain impartial.

After walking a couple of hundred yards, the front of the crowd had got so far ahead that the police presence was stretched thin. Suddenly a roar went up at the front, and though the people around Tommy couldn't see it, they all knew what was happening. Everyone on each side turned and faced the other, and the shouting grew and spread. The first lad went over the line, throwing his fat pink arms at a particularly verbose United fan, his beer gut jiggling in an old gold shirt. He was kicked to the ground in seconds, but then United scattered, many backing up against the wall, when a policeman came wading in. This pattern was repeated, and then it was Tommy's turn. The bony United fan swung at him, clipped his ear, and then got more than he bargained for.

It was great fun being back in the mob even if it was somebody else's. Tommy had had his share of scrapes during his reffing years, simply because, no doubt inspired by reports from places like Peru and Lesotho, some wags had occasionally waited after the game and tried to kick shit out of him. Help was never far away, however. There was always some beefy steward around who saw everything building, and even if it was the steward's own fans carrying the grudge, he and a mate would nobly do their duty and hustle him out of a side exit. Tommy never really understood why the stewards did it. He felt sure that if the Villa had been wronged, he would happily have thrown the ref to the pack.

It was great fun being back in the mob, but Tommy had a job to do.

He melted back into the Wolves crowd, and away from them. *Wonder if they'll recognise me? They'll never recognise me. They won't think to look here.* He looked at his watch. *Jesus, I'm fucking late.* He jogged towards the ground.

Outside the main entrance, it was a little less busy. He went through the main gate and made his way to the players' entrance. He had never reffed at Wolves before, and didn't know where to go. Tommy figured that this would be where most of the officious people would be hanging around. He was mildly surprised to see that Manchester United had brought their own stewards. They were standing around in their new rainproof jackets (they had a fresh design each season), chatting with the Wolves stewards. An old man in a yellow anorak with a large cartoon wolf face on the back sent him round the corner. He made his way through a yellow door and down a concrete tunnel. At a T-junction he saw a sign saying PLAYERS ENTRANCE to the right, STANDS to the left.

*Now what?* He opted right. Carpeting began. A row of doors ran along one side, like in a hotel, entrances to the executive boxes. He heard laughter and voices, and passing a door that was open, saw eight or nine men in suits standing round, each with a glass or a beer can in one hand, the other thrust nervously into a pocket. Behind them he caught a flash of the brilliant green of the turf, in contrast to the dull suit colours of the salarymen, and his stomach tightened a little. He had already passed them, but he heard the conversation level drop, and felt himself being incorporated into their shabby bonding ritual. Then there was a new burst of laughter.

This was next to nothing, less than a drop in the ocean, compared to what he suffered in the name of football. The phlegm that flew his way (and that he always dodged). The kicks to doors of whatever car he was in and the hammerings on car windows. The evaporating upmarket hospitality of clubs who had just lost at home. And the hot, unholy blast of abuse from the fans who ran down the front just to make sure he knew he was a blind, biased, cheating slag of a man whose mother was probably sucking cocks in hell. And that he was a nonce, a ponce, a queer shit-fucking botty bandit and a friend of Jimmy Hill.

It was next to nothing, and yet he duly noted it, and recalled the feeling that next day while eating his doughnut holes, and filed it away, to be picked up at a future date, his reaction to this little drop of opposition from the group of businessmen. Another turn and he could smell the mixed Ralgex and mildew smells of the changing rooms. HOME. VISITORS. He walked on further, past an unmarked gold-and-black door, round another corner and found himself at the plush reception room where the players and VIPs entered. *Fucking hell. Where the fuck do they put us here?* Tommy hated these last-minute obstacles to his progress.

'Young man!' he called to a jug-eared fellow in a blazer with the Wolves fox on it. 'Where do the match officials change?'

The man blushed to be in the presence of someone who went on the pitch, even though he was not an entertainer. 'Er, er ... just back there on the left, through the black-and-yellow door.'

'Thank you.' *Another great transfer from McDonald's.* The dressing room for referees and linesmen was average by Premier League standards. A ten-by-ten cube with three lockers, a slatted bench, one shower and a small table. Wolves had laid out some albino cheese sandwiches under clingfilm, some crisps and three tins of Wolves Cola. Tommy sat down and ate his share, then took up his copy of the match programme. Under the teams on the back he read: Referee: Thomas Burns, London. Linesmen: E. Proctor, Swanage, T. Crawford, Derby. *Proctor. I like Proctor.*

Proctor walked in, already in his kit. He was a punctual man. He had been in the Army.

'Tommy Burns, good to see you,' he said cheerfully. 'I've not known you to be late before.'

'It's been a terrible morning for traffic. I made a miscalculation and got caught up in it. Has there been a problem?'

'No, everything is fine. I took the liberty of going through the team colours on your behalf. Old gold and red shirts, full home kit for both sides. I'll alert the managers that you're here.'

Tommy liked this linesman because he kept in good cheer despite the troubles that had befallen him the previous season. He had fallen off the Premier League's list of nineteen preferred referees, in the annual performance review by the committee, for getting low marks. No one had been particularly explicit, other than to remind him of the two controversial decisions he had made that year, which had been forgiven at the time but still tipped the balance against him. There were no rankings published. Referees were left to compare marks amongst themselves, and Proctor was convinced there were worse around than him. But he was replaced by a younger man. It was suggested that a season or two in the First Division might help him 'regain his confidence', but everyone knew that in a season or two he'd be forty-eight and retiring. Then he injured his hand sailing and decided to volunteer for linesman duties. They took him up on it, because there had been a shortage of linesmen, or assistant referees as they were now called, at the start of the season. Someone had forgotten to post a pile of application forms.

Tommy liked him because he didn't complain. He accepted his new status with the equanimity of one who loves football at every level, not just at the top. He was happy just to be out there, and he was happy to be running the line.

He was a bank manager, like his father had been. He didn't care much for 'the young men of today', as he called them, and he dealt with them all the time. They came in with their half-baked ideas for businesses, asking for loans, showing off their over-optimistic spreadsheets and talking their hollow marketing-speak. He didn't like the way they had the accessories of the successful businessman – the silver business card-holders, the electronic personal organisers – before they had done any work. But he liked Tommy. When he was out on the pitch, Tommy was Army too.

Then the third man arrived, accompanied by the reserve official. Tommy listened to their excuses, then explained that he had had traffic trouble too, and that everything was in order. Then he pored over the programme again, until he was taken by a small paragraph in the middle. He read it out.

'"The Manchester United poet Nick Plumage will read from his collection entitled *Own Goals* before today's game." What the hell's that all about?'

'Pre-match entertainment,' said Proctor, and he sniffed contemptuously.

Tommy shook his head. They didn't speak much more. He began changing, hanging up each piece of his clothing with care on the folding hangers he brought with him, balling his socks into his neatly paired shoes. He laid out his clean uniform – he thought of it more as a uniform than a kit – on the bench before him. He pulled on the black shorts that tied at the waist. Then the black socks with the white band at the top. He put on his extra watch, a digital one – 11.14 a.m., it read. He watched the second hand of his Swiss analogue approach the twelve, and saw that the minute hand was in place at exactly that time. His eyes flashed two inches to the side and caught the tail-end of the liquid crystal minute changing too. 11.15. *Beautiful.* Then he smoothed out the black shirt with the English FA crest, and pulled it on, feeling the coolness of the fabric and, as ever, a shiver of pride. He smelled the smell of home and of laundry. *I must call Melissa, straight after the game.* He buttoned it three times up to the neck, then sat down to put new laces in his special refereeing boots, which had a raised chevron pattern on the sole instead of studs.

The door opened and the Wolves club secretary came in, letting in the sound of players' voices in the corridor, and the distant white noise of the crowd. He was wearing the same fox-faced blazer as the jug-eared boy. He was bursting to say something. After the helloes and the handing over of the team sheets for both teams, he exclaimed, 'Did you hear? Jack Taylor's dead! Died this morning.'

'Jack Taylor?' chorused the linesmen. They looked shocked, and turned to look at Tommy.

'Dead?' he said. For a second or two he felt like he had been plunged underwater. He couldn't hear anyone else's words, though their mouths were going. Then he burst back up to the surface. The Wolves man was gabbling. 'Didn't even know he was poorly. I just heard it on the car radio.'

'What was the cause of death?' Tommy was instantly relieved to hear himself. Being a doctor gave him access to a different angle on death.

The other officials went into their 'Oh no, not Jack Taylor, he was one of the greats, remember the World Cup Final when he gave that penalty in the second minute.' routine, and the secretary answered only that he didn't know, he didn't know, but he was one of the greats.

The dressing room then became silent, and all five men looked at each other, then at the floor, and shook their heads to varying degrees.

Tommy had an idea. 'Is it too late in the day to organise a minute's silence for him, today?'

The secretary looked nonplussed. He wasn't used to making decisions, let alone rapid ones, but the referee before him had an urgent authority that he instinctively deferred to.

'I ... I could ask ... Yeah, I'm sure ... I don't see why not.' He looked very doubtful.

'It's 11.36. Have the announcer announce it at five to twelve, so as many people hear it as possible. Then give them a minute or two to digest it, the teams will come out, we'll come out, all stand in position for sixty seconds, then I'll give the signal and they can get on with the warm-up, and the game.'

The others began nodding and murmuring their assent.

'Roight, I'll get off and find the announcer roight away!' And the Wolves man scuttled off.

They finished getting ready, checking their notebooks, the linesmen their flags, Tommy his cards, his Biros and his watches again. They all stepped out together into the corridor and walked down to the players'

changing rooms. A man in a Wolves tracksuit handed Tommy the match
ball. By squeezing it with his thumbs he could tell whether it was up
to pressure or not. Then he bounced it and listened. Then he threw
it in the air, spinning it to check its shape. He passed the ball to his
colleagues, as he always did, to get their opinion, but was distracted by
the sound coming from the stadium. It was six minutes to twelve and
Tommy was curious to hear how the announcement would go. He made
his way to the tunnel, cocking an ear to the noise. What he heard wasn't
the usual buzz of anticipation – the sound of real fans answering each
other's taunts in full voice, underscored by the murmur of seats wankers
reading aloud from their programmes or standing up to talk to people
in the row behind about their golf game or their kids. He heard the
frantic screech of prolonged whistling, punctuated by a highly nervous
voice speaking through a microphone. Tommy hastened up the slope of
the tunnel, which was darkened at its mouth by the usual cluster of bobbies,
stewards, ballboys, photographers, freeloaders and handicapped. His heart
beat more quickly as the noise grew louder – the searing whistles, the high,
nervous voice on the tannoy, and now the individual bellowing coming from
the stand above his head. He pushed his way on to the pitch, and saw the
rich green of the chequered turf all before him. His heart leapt at the
sensory deluge – the tang of cigarette smoke and fresh-cut grass, the loud
drone of the crowd, the acres of faces spread around the stadium. Then
he saw what the fuss was about. A man wearing a Barbour who looked to
be in his thirties stood in the centre circle at a lectern, reading aloud in the
high, quavery voice that was blasting round the ground. Two giant video
boards showed his face – sandy eyebrows, John Lennon glasses, oily nose,
a chinless English profile, with his wet, cherubic bottom lip quivering as
he tried to concentrate on his words.

> '. . . And so it goes.
> Each miss, each kiss,
> It was the same to me,
> And I was not a man,
> Until I found Man U.'

The crowd was incensed even more by these last detectable words. Booing
was coming from all sides. 'Booo, boooo, fuck off! Fuck *arf!* You fucking
wanker!'
    'Who's this?' Tommy asked a steward.

'No frigging oi-dea, mate,' said the man, clearly amused. 'Pre-match entertainment.'

*Oh yeah*, remembered Tommy. *Nick Plumage. The Man United poet. Cunt. Get off the pitch.*

'Well, he's not got much longer,' snapped Tommy.

'The next one is the title poem from my book *Own Goals*.' He picked a book off the lectern and waved it in the air, sharing an ironic grin at his own vulgar commerciality with the crowd. Nobody grinned back. The whistling sounded like the last minute of a relegation battle when the home side are hanging on to an advantage under merciless pressure. At the halfway line a huge fan leaned over the advertising hoardings, jeering, over and over, as loud as he could, 'Yow big ponce, yow big fooking ponce! Yow big ponce, yow big fooking ponce!'

Tommy was only interested in getting the pitch clear for the game and the tannoy for the announcement. But he became transfixed by the spectacle.

> 'There they stood, just four feet high.
> The nets were orange, Euro-style.
> The posts were white, and rang like bells,
> Whenever people like my brother just missed.
>
> We played till dark . . .'

'You're just a fucking WANKER, you're just a fucking WANKER, you're just a fucking WANKER,' the crowd chimed in.

The poet paused a moment as he made out their words, swallowed, then went on, raising the volume of his voice a little more . . .

> 'That birthday of mine,
> When I was nine.
>
> My father said to me,
> His last words before he left the house:'

'You're gonna get your fooking head kicked in,' went the crowd, the singular 'head' sounding especially rich and correct on the lips of the fans. The reader could hear them, but ploughed onward with his poem.

*'Nicholas, your mother and I,*
*No longer see eye to eye.*
*I've got a job in Saudi.'*

Changing to the tune of 'On Ilkla Moor Baht 'At' the crowd chanted, 'Get off the fuckin' pitch, get off the fuckin' pitch, get OFF the FUCKin' PITCH.'

Their emphases were starting to bite. The poet wavered for a second. His fleshy bottom lip trembled on the big screen. Some of the United fans were out of their seats, trying to look supportive, trying to look disgusted, waving their arms at the Wolves fans and telling them to be quiet. Tommy could tell at a glance these were the massed ranks of glory-hunters, the part-time supporters who had found themselves become full-time due to United's extraordinary success. They were a breed of fan that had come to football through televised finals and colour supplements, from round-table chitchat and invitations to executive boxes. All around them, however, were clumps of Mancunians, some jeering and laughing at the man in the middle, some still embarrassed by his presence, all of them wanting to get on with the game.

Tommy walked further up the touchline. He was almost at the halfway line. He didn't care who saw him now. The poet continued:

*'So it was Audi.*
*And since then I have had*
*No dad to speak of.*
*But I have always found my way ...'*

The crowd continued with an old favourite: 'You're gonna get your fuckin' head kicked in! You're gonna get your fuckin' head kicked in!'

*'Thanks to ...'*

He paused again, caught up by a dryness in his throat, and swallowed nervously.

*'Thanks to my own goals.'*

'Booo! Boooooooo! Fuck off! Get off the pitch. Gerrim off.'

Tommy was now at the halfway line. He spotted a young woman who looked completely out of place and went up to her. She was small and pretty, and wore a tight black miniskirt that looked like a bandage around her bum. She had a matching tailored jacket, heels with tiny mud stains where she had been walking on the pitch, a clipboard, and the clean, fine-grained skin of the well fed, the well educated, and the well paid: She looked like a boarding-school girl.

'What is this person still doing on the pitch at two minutes to kick-off?' snapped Tommy.

She turned and looked at him, with no idea who he was, and treated him accordingly. 'My author has one more *piece* to perform,' she said sniffily. 'Our contract with Microsoft ...' Before she could continue, Tommy leaned close to her and said, 'Get that little worm off the fucking pitch *now*, or I'll drag him off myself,' and he stared hard into her eyes. She turned pale and looked around, as though fearing assault.

The poet shuffled his papers and began speaking again.

'Er, this is the last one,' he said apologetically. Then he glanced across at Tommy and the girl. Seeing the referee with the girl from his publishing house, he seemed confused, and paused again. It was 11:59 by the stadium clock. Then it dawned on him that even the referee had come out to hear him, and he beamed, glanced at the camera and announced: 'This one's called "Cover Me in Glory". Ahem.

*Glory, Glory Man United ...'*

The girl edged away from Tommy, still looking horrified. 'I *rarely* don't think ...' was all she managed. Tommy turned away and stepped on to the pitch, just as a roar went up in the South Bank.

He stopped and turned to see what had happened. Three fans had gone over the fence and made it on to the pitch. They started running. A desperate steward managed to rugby-tackle one of them to the floor, and a policeman joined in, writhing in the penalty box, mud and grass sticking to their clothes. The other two fans were away, though, sprinting toward the centre circle. Plumage heard the crowd and looked up, startled. To his left he saw the advancing fans. His mouth fell open in surprise, and he stopped speaking. For a split second he thought they must be coming on to pat him on the back, or ... what did people do? Drape him with scarves? They were about thirty yards from him, their eyes fixed upon him.

'Shi ...' was the last thing the mike picked up as he turned and ran, his papers lifting off in the breeze like disturbed doves. He only had a twenty-yard lead by now, and lost some of this by altering his path to head for the tunnel, and by casting a terrified glance over his shoulder. They were almost upon him, the crowd hollering like it was the home straight of the Gold Cup. Then they were upon him. He was dragged down on the corner of the penalty box by the first of the two Wolves fans, who caught the tail of his coat, then stumbled. The second fan barely slowed, aiming a brutal kick at the vulnerable hip before him, like a rugby player making a conversion. The poet writhed in agony, and the crowd erupted into an outburst of joy. It sounded more like a goal had gone in than the usual 'Goowaaarn!' egging-on of a crowd having to watch a fight from a distance. Stewards and police were homing in from all corners of the ground, not so much to protect the poet, who was now curled up and foetal under a rainstorm of kicks, as to attack the two fans. In the final few seconds the bigger of the two dropped to his knees, the better to aim his punches at the bits of lip and nose that were still uncovered. Then he was bowled over sideways by fifteen stone of charging policeman. A steward arrived and sat on his chest as he lashed out with his feet, while the other fan got in a few last kicks before turning, and swerving past one copper straight into the arms of another. The crowd was clapping and cheering, then broke into a spirited chant of: 'Wanderers! Wanderers! Wanderers! Wanderers! Wanderers!', as if to rubber-stamp what had just taken place.

Tommy felt a thrill run through him as though he had touched a live wire, and his scalp bristled at the pantomime. The guest reader remained in the fetal position. The girl behind him was screaming, 'Oh my God! Oh my God!' But she would not go on to the pitch.

*Ha!* he thought. *Ha!* Once the two fans had been subdued with batons and arm-wrenching, a St John Ambulance man came jogging up to the poet, who flinched again, uncovered his face, and finally managed to sit up. He began sobbing uncontrollably, and the camera caught the full glory of his screwed-up face on the giant screens. Tommy's relief was short-lived when he noticed the time: it was gone noon. He was furious, and marched back along the running track to the tunnel. Police had materialised from nowhere and were lining the pitch in an ominous midnight-blue cordon. Some leaned into the crowd, so easy ever since the high fences of the seventies and eighties were taken down, and took swings at the more excitable fans. Each of the three men on the pitch was escorted off by a phalanx of coppers. Tommy reached the tunnel at the same time as Nick Plumage, pushing his way through the overexcited men who thronged its mouth. He gave him a very black look as he passed, being too angry to speak.

'What was all that about?' asked Proctor the linesman back outside the dressing rooms.

'Fucking pre-match fucking entertainment dickhead running over time. Got a good fucking kicking. Or not good enough. I'd like to . . .' Tommy trailed off, biting his lip. Proctor was all right. He could pretty much say what he liked in front of him. But now he had to concentrate on getting his act, and everyone else's, back together. Both sets of players were standing in the tunnel by now, like it was Wembley, chomping gum and bouncing balls off the breeze blocks, impatient but professional. None of them asked him what was going on. Tommy saw the United manager, a Scot, approaching from the back, so he raised his hand to signal silence and spoke. 'Gentlemen, sorry about the undue delay. The playing area has now been cleared, and we will commence forthwith.'

They walked down the tunnel, past Plumage who was sitting in a daze, having the blood dabbed off his nose by the old ambulanceman. The young woman from the publishers was hunched over her tiny black cellphone. Tommy led both teams out on to the pitch to resounding applause. It was five past twelve. *Fuck! Fuck!* he kept telling himself. *And now there'll be no Jack Taylor announcement. That dickhead, that stupid dickhead!*

And so it was. By now the Wolves theme tune was playing on the tannoy. Tommy felt a loss of control as the event began to take its course: the players fanned out and began kicking practice balls around and stretching; the linesmen moved to their respective sides; the managers and subs filled up the dugout; and the fans began baying at those in front of them to sit down so they could see.

*No tribute, then. I wonder if the announcer will still mention it? No, there's no time.* With a heavy heart, undetectable in his face, Tommy gathered the captains together for the toss. He warned them, as was his custom, to keep it clean, and that he would hold them partly responsible for any unsporting behaviour by their teammates. He heard his voice as though from outside himself, as he went through his peculiar ritual.

'What do points mean?'

'Prizes,' chorused the two young men in front of him, like robots.

Then he took them through the drill, telling them how they could avoid trouble. This was a fixture he had been looking forward to, but he already felt it had been soiled. The next thing he knew, he had blown his whistle, the ball had assumed its Brownian motion,

and he was swimming in a sea of his own highly tuned conscious-
ness.

This was how it always was. Like a player, he ran with fear in his
stomach, fear of making a mistake; but unlike a player his senses were
heightened by the adrenalin, making him see better, allowing him better
to calculate time and distance, letting him hear the spin of the ball or the
tick of it brushing a defender's thumb above the noise of any crowd. His
breath rushed like cold mountain air through his throat and lungs, and
he accelerated with the play with painless changes of gear that he could
never recapture during his training runs.

Three cups of coffee were apparently the limit for loafers in the doughnut
shop. The girl who had served him came and hovered at his shoulder as
he sat in the window going over his thoughts, to encourage him to leave.
Tommy was pissed off, and left slamming the door behind him.

'What are you looking at, cunt?' muttered Tommy to a studenty-looking
kid almost blocking the way. The youth stepped quickly out of his path. He
marched off up Regent Street to look for a bus. He was still cross when he
got to a crowded bus stop. He leaned back against a shop window and lit
a cigarette, hoping it would calm his nerves. Immediately his bus came, so
he crushed it against the glass and joined the clump of people preventing
others getting off the bus by trying to get on themselves. There was no
order, so he positioned himself on the flank of the wedge, prepared to
insert himself and be drawn on to the bus by the inevitable pressure of
the crowd. Halfway through, the conductress declared the bus full and
rang the bell. The crowd swore and got back out of the gutter. Tommy
went back to the window.

There wasn't another bus for forty minutes. His anger was replaced by
a dull, fatalistic frustration that he noticed actually lessened the longer
he lived in the city. Finally, one came, and ensconced upstairs, he gave
himself over to the bus's unsteady progress. *Maybe I didn't play enough injury
time?* he wondered. He knew about Man United's reputation for getting
extra injury time when they weren't winning, and made a conscious effort
to be absolutely scrupulous when dealing with the clock in their games.
*So they lost. Big deal. A lot of people would pay extra for a five-goal classic like that.*

After fifty minutes, the game was tight but scoreless. Wolves took the
lead with a bullet header from veteran Tipton lad Steve Bull. United
came back immediately, and their own shaven-headed midfielder scored
direct from a corner. They won the ball back from the kick-off, swarmed

forward and scored again. As the goal went in their fans screamed with the
hysterical edge to their glee that comes with a sudden reversal of fortune.
Two–one United. Tommy wasn't that bothered. Partly because he was
busy – calculating angles, rerunning the play in his head several times a
second till it made sense, checking with his linesman. Partly because he
had a feeling Wolves were going to win, and he trusted his instincts. It
was no great mystery: Wolves hadn't won for eleven games, United had
won six on the trot. It was the sort of feeling any fan might have on a
Friday, looking at the weekend's fixture list. Anyone who did the pools
would be especially attuned to such hunches, ready to convert them into
fantastic amounts of cash. As for Tommy, he could sense a small fall coming
after a good deal of pride. But the sharpened steel discs flying through the
air in the South Bank were what gave him his real insight into the score.
So much hatred, so recently in history – even though the industrial age
now seemed such a long time ago – had to amount to something good.

*The pools! Maybe that's it. Someone out there thinks I'm doing the pools. Bending
games my way. How ridiculous.* Tommy thought disgustedly of the few
pitiful attempts to rig the English game he had known. Revie's bunch
paying opposing defenders to crock their forwards in the box in the
final minute, the year they won the League. And who knew when else?
Malaysian 'businessmen' offering money to referees and players to keep
everyone happy. Like all refs he was, of course, forbidden to do the pools.
How he was supposed to swing twenty-four points his way while working
on one game was beyond him. It wasn't like doing a quiz on a crisp packet
and seeing if your auntie at Walkers could get the Disneyworld holiday
for you. A whole syndicate of refs, or friends of refs, would have to be in
on it to get anywhere.

Wolves were not playing very well – their slump had taken them to
twelfth in the table after a bold start – so it wouldn't be fair to say they
*waited* until the eighty-fifth minute for the equaliser. Rather, that is when
the ball ballooned off their centre-half's knee and set Bull running free. He
smashed the ball into the top left-hand corner and the stand behind the goal
erupted like a badly poured pint. So in the last minute, when the ball came
off a United defender's arm on the goal line, you could understand why
they were even happier. It was an accident, of course, in so far as the player
didn't have enough brainpower devoted to his upper arm to consciously
stick it in the way of the ball, but Tommy knew there were no accidents
on the goal line, and when it came to handball unconscious crimes were
as punishable as elegantly planned ones.

The penalty was missed, but the goalkeeper moved two steps before it was taken, so Tommy ordered it to be retaken. Much to the chagrin of the United fans, who sang to the tune of 'O My Darlin' Clementine',

*'You're a bastard, you're a bastard, you're a BASTARD referee,*
*You're a bastard, you're a bastard, you're a BASTARD referee.'*

With the sound ringing in everyone's ears, and the Wolves fans behind the goal trying to stand as still as possible so as not to distract their penalty-taker, Bull stepped up again, put it the other way, and missed again. Tommy ordered it to be retaken, because the goalie had moved his feet again.

'Listen, son, I do have eyes in my head, you know. And you know the rules,' he told the furious goalkeeper who was screaming in his face. He booked him. 'Remember to wait until he kicks the ball before launching yourself this time.'

It took a minute to clear the box. Tommy was in no doubt that he would do it again if the goalie moved his feet again. He blew his whistle, watching for encroachment in the box, then for unfair hesitation by the kicker, then for early movement by the goalie. The fellow stood helplessly rooted to the spot as Bull cannoned the ball off the base of the post. It ran straight out to him, but remembering the rules, he lifted his foot and let it past him, only for a surprised Wolves player behind him to side-foot it into the opposite corner. End of game.

'You're a BASTARD referee' was ringing round the ground again as Tommy collected the match ball. *At least they can still sing when they're away,* he thought. The Wolves players were still rolling around on the grass as though they had won the European Cup. Most of the United players came over to Tommy to abuse him, but he only had to book one of them for calling him a cunt. He booked the manager too. He didn't like this trend of managers coming on to the pitch, for whatever reason. They should stick to the cinders. He heard a coin pass his ear with a thrilling sound, a metallic whizz that reminded him of the old days. Only, when he and Mark used to throw them, they usually hit someone. It always seemed good and proper to see a fan being helped down a gangway with a surface wound to the head. If it was an old man, even better. It showed everyone you meant business. You didn't see it so much at the end of a game, though, as all heads would turn in the direction of the post-match entertainment: the streets around the ground. A sea of brown and mouse hair heading towards the exits. Not the time to be throwing things then. *You don't get that with this seats business*, Tommy thought, and he got off the bus.

Walking through the cool October air soothed him. He was approaching home. Two more turns and he would be in his street. His north London street, where his home now was. A row of damp houses knocked into flats for nurses, students and quiet men who always paid their bills. Young couples who seemed to magically get pregnant soon after marrying but never stayed long enough for you to see the baby. You could always find a room with black walls and some zodiac stuff painted on the floor in red, or a view of some shed roofs and the screeching freight trains.

Tommy counted the sets of stone steps that led up to the communal front doors, stretched up the street ahead of him. *Eighteen, seventeen, sixteen.* You could see into most of the downstairs living rooms, as Londoners didn't seem bothered about net curtains. Mostly all you'd see were bare bulbs, murky posters, decorated mirrors, and the tops of people's heads turned towards the faint light of the television, if there was anyone in at all. Every now and then, though, you'd see the properly built-in white bookshelves of the real middle classes, the home of a professional who had decided to stay put. There wasn't much badness to screen out in Tommy's area, he was relieved to tell himself. Just car alarms and the odd rape. They were too far from any of the London grounds to get mixed up in any cockney aggro: Arsenal was away across the tracks, and Tottenham a lot further up. Culturally, it was a bit of a wasteland, unless you really liked pub culture: big-nosed cockneys playing darts, bragging about their cars and trying to sell each other things. Insoluble falafel and baklava vomit piles outside the newsagent. And always the big wide pavements and the big grey sky. It would have depressed the fuck out of him, if he thought he had anywhere else to go.

He thought when he rounded the last corner he might get a glimpse of Melissa, coming home from school, and there she was, unloading her books from her car, deliciously unaware of his gaze. She finally caught him out of the corner of her eyes as she straightened up and shut the door with her hip. She smiled, pleased to see him.

'What are you doing home so early? Did you get fired?'

'Took the afternoon off. And most of the morning.'

'Are you OK?' She cocked her head to the side.

'Yeahhh ...' he trailed off, self-pityingly. They went up the steps in silence. Tommy let her in and sorted the mail. 'Postcard from your sister. Letter from the FA. Looks like the List. Pizza offer ... Can I clean your gutters, fuck off ... YOU MAY HAVE ALREADY WON ... Fuck off. And I'm pre-approved for another platinum card,' he said, tossing the junk back on the ledge. They went up the stairs and let themselves into their own flat. Tommy lay on the couch, and Melissa came and planted herself next to him.

'What's your Rebecca got to say, then?' he asked.

'She's having a blast hitching round Italy. Meeting lots of fabulous *ragazzi.*'

'Oh yeah? Gotta watch those devious Italian lads. They run the streets but they live with their mums. No place to shag.'

'Thomas! That's my little sister you're talking about!'

'Yeah, well. What's the List say?'

The List was the referees' booklet from the FA, saying who was doing which games for the month ahead. Games were allotted depending on recent performance. A ref having a shit time of it naturally got given all the mid-table clashes. Hotshots like Tommy got the cream of the crop. A bad game for him was a bunch of no-hopers entertaining one of the in-form clubs, or one of the rich clubs. Melissa tore open the envelope and shook out the small black-and-white booklet. They always liked getting the List in the mail. Except for now. Tommy had a feeling it might already be obsolete.

'Manchester City–Manchester United in two weeks. Newcastle–Sunderland. European Champions League Madrid–Ajax. Aston Villa ... Ooh, Tommy, Villa! League Cup four, Aston Villa–Birmingham City.'

'Jesus! That's a fucking royal flush. Let me see ...'

'FA Cup two, Torquay United–Arsenal. Hey, what happened to your hand?' She tried to grab it but he pulled it away. 'Tommy?' She said it sternly. He was still reeling from the information, the dream month that was supposed to lie ahead. All those local derbies, all those hate matches. *Villa–Blues, for Christ's sake.* In the light of which, his hand felt neither painful nor important. He felt like answering her question straight.

'Ah, I cracked this United fan in the mouth. I had to, he came at me.'

'What? Where was this?' She was shocked.

'Outside the ground. It's not hurt. Minor laceration, three stitches. They'll be out in a week. Keep it clean ...' He trailed off. Then paused. She looked pissed off. 'Do you want to see?'

'No thanks. Tommy, why were you *fighting?* You're the bloody referee. What do you think ... Oh.' Now she was unable to finish, too disgusted and confused.

'I wasn't *fighting*,' he protested. 'Just one whack doesn't count as fighting. Anyway it was self-defence. They came at me.'

'*They?*'

'You wouldn't want me going down under a load of United fans, would you?' He was guilting her round.

'That's not the point.'

'Yes it is.'

She threw his hand back at him, to hurt his feelings. Then she spoke one last time, glaring.

'Listen, I spend all day getting kids to be nice to each other, to stop the boys from beating the crap out of each other and the girls from torturing each other, then I come home and hear this. It's not very impressive.'

He let her words hang in the air for a while. He didn't like to argue with Melissa, since they were almost everything to each other and arguing usually had the net effect of making them both feel bad. They weren't very big on making-up sex, like other couples seemed to be. Tommy spoke, to reassure her that she had been heard, and to let her go and be apart from him for a while.

'I'm sorry, love. It was just a circumstance, but I won't let it happen again. I was on the wrong side of the ground. I should have got there earlier. But I was late.'

She sniffed, not really satisfied, and got up.

'I'll be in here sewing,' she said, going into the tiny second bedroom, with its bunnies and balloon-patterned paper. She stopped on the threshold. 'How was your priest friend?'

'Oh, he's great. Great. Really . . . *priestly*. Black suit, dog-collar, the works. Not the lad I used to know.'

'The Pope's really been to work on him, eh? Has he got a girlfriend?'

''Course not!' Tommy shot back. *These non-Catholics, they read* The Thorn Birds *and they think they know the score.* He would have said that to her, had not the situation been so delicate.

'Oh. Good. I didn't know what you were up to up there. Could have been all sorts going on.'

'Melissa!'

But she had shut the door.

Tommy relaxed on the couch for a long time. *Local derbies. Villa at last! And yet it was all going down the drain.* He felt sure of it. The blues weren't fading, so he decided to have a nap, but just as he was getting off to sleep, he had a fragment of a dream in which he was falling. His body jerked violently and his head lolled off its cushion. He was left with the blood pounding in his ears, far more awake than before. The room was dark. He heard the irregular whirring and straining of Melissa's machine.

*A run. That's all there is to it. I'm not so old and knackered I can't train on a Monday.* Tommy went into the bedroom and got a vest and some socks. He found his running shorts in the laundry basket, and put them on. He put his door key in his sock and went down to the street.

British Summer Time was over. This was winter, the new regime. Dark by five and getting worse all the time. Residents hunkered down in their flats. The street was always quieter in the dark. All down the street, in fact all over the city, and all over the nation, people were hunkering down, for their teas and dinners, their Kids TV and their local news, their quiz shows and their soaps. On a Monday night you couldn't even expect the pub people in their bomber jackets and tracksuits to appear for another few hours. Tommy pounded the concrete, heading for the main road and the route up to the park. He looked like a runner, not a jogger, with his shorts with the divided side hem and his light blue nylon vest. He had the sinewy physique of a fell runner, legs as lean as a willow tree, pectorals visibly linked to his arms. And when he ran like this, not chasing anything, not having to worry about anyone, he was swift and elegant, upright and noiseless but for the swish of his clothes and the chomp of his trainers. His running shoes were his only indulgence, three-figure Puma monsters covered in hieroglyphs and gel cells and windows. The bloke in the shop had sold him on the need to look after his feet, without seeming to know that he was a first-class official. Tommy liked that. Their soles were light and hard like polystyrene, the uppers a net of information-age fibres.

Melissa: ... Go down the gym any weekday night and if I'm not there mention my name and get Craig to show you round. He's all right.

Fiona: So what's he like, then?

M: Built like a tank. Buff.

F: Sounds nice.

M: He's got a ratty ponytail, though.

F: There's nothing wrong with ponytails.

M: Anyway, tell him you're thinking of joining. Just say you know me.

F: Are you OK? You sound a bit pissed off.

M: Yeah, I'm fine. It's just Tommy. He's just being a dick.

F: What's he done?

M: Aw, nothing. I mean he's out running now. He didn't phone all weekend, and I didn't know what was going on up there with that Catholic priest bloke.

F: Who?

M: His friend. Mark. He's just popped up out of nowhere and now he's a priest.

F: Weird. Is this in Manchester?

M: Birmingham.

F: Birmingham, sorry.

M: Whatever. Anyway … ah, it's nothing. I just don't think he tells me everything, that's all.

F: Hmm, well, I don't want to know everything Nick does.

M: Yeah, but we've been together a long time, yet he still surprises me. Ah, never mind. Look, you ring me when you've talked to Craig.

F: Sure. And I'll let you know if Mr Ponytail tries anything.

M: Ha. In your dreams, girl.

F: We'll see. 'Bye, sweetie.

M: 'Bye.


Tommy ran on the outside of the pavement, by the kerb, as no one in London ever made way for joggers. As he made his way up the hill, he felt a slight lightening of the blues. He didn't run for relaxation, or for endorphins, he ran to make sure he remained the best ref in the land. He approached a pile of cardboard boxes placed by some shopkeeper, and swerved around them. Twenty yards up the road was another cardboard box, all alone. As he came up to it, he overcame his usual mental injunctions against kicking the box — *there might be an abandoned baby in it, how would that look flying in the path of a taxi? It might be full of concrete, or stones, or nuts and bolts, or bags of offal, or wet newspaper. What would people think of a thirty-four-year-old doing that anyway? Kicking stuff in the street. Men would want to kick shit out of me — too happy; women would think I'm a weirdo; middle-class people would veer out of the way. Kids would like it. Probably copy. Not worth it.* Stretching his stride to accelerate and to find the sweetest spot in his run-up, he swung for the box with his left foot, sending it high into the air in front of him, with a loud empty bang, its flat sides deadening its path through the air so it fell short, once again in his way. Without changing pace he reapproached it, and gave it a harder, sweeter kick with his right, sending it spinning off into the busy road, where it fell beneath the wheels of an oncoming bus. Tommy ran on full of satisfaction.

# 5

# Meeting; London, exile, back to Mark; time starts to pass

From his seat in the wood-panelled reception area at Lancaster Gate, Tommy heard the thump-thump of car doors closing in swift succession, a sound with the sweetness and solidity of a half-volley. It might as well have been a rifle volley over his grave. *That's them.* He held his copy of *Shoot!* still before him and listened. They would be coming up the steps now, and through the reception at any moment. He slowly returned the magazine to the table, not wanting to seem ruffled, but not also wanting to be caught holding something with Nick Plumage's unbattered face spread over the cover, and Taggart all over the back. Silence. He sat still. The receptionist was doing something with her computer. She hadn't looked up for over a minute.

It was the dreaded Thursday. The Thursday after the originally intended Thursday, because Tommy had been phoned by the secretary's secretary and told the meeting would have to be put off. The secretary would be going to a funeral at the time they were due to meet. And was it possible that they could rearrange for the following week? Tommy said it was. There was an England game coming up, and all Premier League matches were off that weekend, to protect the stars, so he passed an extra ten days in sustained and miserable anticipation, gameless.

He guessed the funeral in question was Jack Taylor's. The papers had been full of his obituaries. The timing of the famous Dutch penalty had varied from sixty-six seconds to 101 seconds. They even showed it on the news – Cruyff's long hair swishing, the orange shirts and the green grass dull on the decaying videotape, as though seen through a bromine fog.

Tommy called Proctor just to check the funeral was on that Thursday, and Proctor, ever obliging and efficient, made a few calls and confirmed. He wasn't going either. Wrong part of the country for him. Long way from Swanage.

Tommy rather liked funerals. That is, he liked the prospect of them. Whenever he heard about one he would have to attend, or would like to attend (you were never invited, the social bullshit being all over by then), he thought of afternoon drinking and not having to go back to work. He relished the mood wherein the men would tackle their melancholy in public, with much shuffling around, and the women would pick from a set of roles for the day – the brave but tragic widow, the hanky-eating hysterical sister, the mysterious beauty in black, the dumbfounded daughter, the marginal relation or acquaintance struggling to appear concerned but relieved when the private gossiping starts. And of course the bustling organiser. They were all brought to silence at some point in the proceedings. Tommy had scanned bonny fetuses *in utero* and he had held the twig-thin hands of dying maids, but he had to admit that the interring of a fresh corpse-in-a-box had a solidity to it that none could argue with. Being a doctor didn't count for much in the face of death. The mourners gathered round the hole in the soil and peered in, looking very worried, and everyone was equal, for a while. Plus everyone dressed smart for a change – no disgusting tennis shoes or jeans allowed, just sharp black suits and coats or you were nobody. He liked this, and the drinking and the gossiping afterwards, and the not being at work in the afternoon. But he had no desire to go to Jack Taylor's funeral. He had already mentally seen him off. He would honour his memory by refereeing even better. Going up there and bumping into all those others, the family and the hangers-on, wouldn't help anyone. *Don't want to see that lot more often than I have to. I'd be a hanger-on too.*

He heard an approach – footsteps and the automatic muting of final words – then two men entered the room. They were both of medium height, brown-haired, in their forties, wearing nondescript office gear – cheap off-the-peg suits, black shoes chosen from the left foot on the rails of suburban shopping centres, white shirts. They pretended Tommy wasn't there and went upstairs, and he pretended he hadn't seen them and stared down at the cover of *Shoot!*

After seven minutes by his watch the secretary received a buzz, looked at Tommy as though she were holding him with tongs, and spoke:

'Mr Burns, Mr Lockhart will see you now. Take the lift to the second floor.'

He thanked her, and noticed that she returned to poring over her machine without saying anything else. This was a moderately bad thing.

He knocked on Lockhart's door and was called in, like a kid going to see the headmaster. Once inside, it was all downhill. Tommy sat down opposite the Secretary, the grand wooden desk between them. The second man was nowhere to be seen. There was another door off this room, the only one the stranger could have gone through. *So he must have been his superior. They're pals enough to have lunch together, but this is not so grave that he needs to be here. Or I'm not so important. Stop thinking. Concentrate.*

'Mr Burns. Thank you for coming.'

*Yeah, right, get on with it.*

'Er, you're welcome.'

'Terrible shame about Jack Taylor, wasn't it? I thought I might even see you at the obsequies.'

*Obsequies? Get a fucking life, mate.*

'No, I wasn't invited.'

'Oh!' Lockhart looked at him over his spectacles.

'With all due respect, I have to get back to work this afternoon. What is this meeting about?' *Shit, that sounded too impatient.*

Mr Lockhart looked taken aback. He had not even got as far as leaning forward on his elbows and rolling the two ends of his pencil between finger and thumb.

He straightened up to make himself look bigger, sighed, and spoke. 'Mr Burns. It has come to the attention of some of us here at the Football Association . . .'

The words seemed to race ahead in Tommy's mind, so that for a microsecond he thought the man was going to say '. . . that not only do you have a long personal history of football hooliganism, but that even now, while you hold the privileged position of referee, you have continued to mix with known hooligans and even engage in acts of violence.'

What he actually heard jerked his mind back and sent it spinning in uncertainty.

'. . . that your behaviour has become somewhat, well, *erratic.*'

*Erratic? Erratic? I'm not fucking erratic! I'm anything but, I'm the model of . . .*

Tommy sat with his mouth open, still trying to erase the previous fantasy and focus on the words used about him. He was unable to speak.

Mr Lockhart pretended to be uncomfortable, in the practised English manner, and that this discomfort was the most important thing in the room. He sighed theatrically.

'Controversy seems to follow you around.'

*Where, you bastard, where? Show me.*

He had to go on.

'It really is a rather delicate situation. We can't really quantify the harm it does to the game.' He plucked at a final straw. 'Some people here are very concerned about you.'

When he tried to speak, Tommy couldn't. His throat had constricted to a narrow slit and he felt like he had lockjaw. His mouth ached. His first instinct, when the verbal dust settled, was to take the man's head in his two hands and smash it over and over on the hardwood surface of his desk. He sat as still as he could, however, anxious for the pain in his throat to pass so he could ask a question. *Show me, show me, come on, show me, you bastard, where I've been at all inconsistent, where I haven't done my utmost to be fair, where I've given less than 110 per cent in a game. You bastards. What is this?*

Lockhart looked at him as the seconds ticked by without a reply. He began to wonder whether the referee was all right, which in turn only strengthened his suspicions.

Finally Tommy got out a respectable sentence.

*What the fuck do you know about refereeing, you fucking desk clerk?*

'I'm sorry, I don't quite know what you're referring to.' His throat felt like someone had shoved a hammer handle down it.

'Ah well,' said the secretary, relieved to have something to go on at last. 'You see, take for example the first game of the season, Leeds versus Manchester City. This business of juggling the *ball*. You've done it several times since, I might add.'

It was partly true. Twice that season Tommy had found himself waiting in the middle of a game for something time-consuming to finish. Situations where he could not restart the game. If a player went down, he could have them stretchered off. If the ball went out of the ground, some weasel in a tracksuit would roll a new one out to him in seconds. At Leeds it was one of the goal nets, which came undone at the foot of the post. A groundsman had to be brought on, out of the stands, to reattach the netting to the post. While he laboured away on his knees there was nothing for anyone to do. A Leeds player took the opportunity to get some treatment on his ankle. Tommy stood on the edge of the box, ready for the subsequent corner.

The work was taking minutes, but there was no question that it would be done. Both sets of fans were at that point, twenty minutes into the game, of having vented their spleen on each other, but as it was still nil–nil they had nothing new to taunt each other with. A slow handclap began in the expensive seats, and spread down the sides to both ends. A couple of Leeds players near him had the ball. One of them, bored, scooped it with his foot and lobbed it to his teammate, who trapped it on the loose muscle of his thigh, caught it in the crook of his foot, then began juggling it. He did it with an ease that showed he had been doing it for years. It was no effort for him to keep the ball off the ground, and his head bobbed mechanically as he worked. The fans noticed and began cheering. Without warning he passed the ball back to the first player, who headed it gently on to his own foot, and took over the juggling. The crowd cheered more loudly, the happy, infantile cheer of the innocently pleased, like the sound of a Mexican wave. Even the main Leeds end, normally a slab of malevolence, joined in. Man City stayed silent, unsure how to react. The beady eyes in their drawn Mancunian faces watched the spectacle. It wasn't their men, but it was quite entertaining. More players turned to look at them. The pair passed the ball back and forth more frequently – one touch, then pass, one touch, then pass – all the while keeping it off the ground. The crowd got a little louder. Then one of the players lost control and, lunging for the ball, sent it five yards through the air towards Tommy. He had his hands on his hips. Without removing them, he trapped the ball in the air, juggled it for a count of three, and passed it right back on to the toe of the player who had lost it. The crowd doubled their volume at once, and applause rippled through the ground, surprising everyone still further.

Both players grinned at the intervention. Each pass of theirs now got its own cry of 'Ole!' They began heading it between them, with such accuracy that their feet stayed planted on the ground while only their heads moved, like birds of prey lining up distant objects. One of them suddenly switched the ball back to Tommy. It was an invitation to play he could not resist, especially as the ball was falling in a sweet arc to his head. He nodded it back, this time to the other player. Suddenly they were a triangle. Within seconds the ball came back to him again. He passed it on.

As he sat there in front of the Referees' Secretary trying to understand his crime, Tommy remembered thinking at the time that he had to do something to show the players and fans that he was still not one of them. But he also remembered his own pride, and vanity, at having been included. He wanted to get serious but he wanted a laugh.

The next time the ball came to him he headed it straight up, three feet above his own head, let it fall and caught it in the crook of his foot. This was a first for the crowd, and they went wild. For a couple of seconds he held the ball still. By now the other two were itching to get hold of it.

Tommy flipped it with a pointed, outstretched toe, sending it back to the player who had given it to him. The crowd became even louder, even more pleased. He was trying to fight it, but his thirsty ego was drinking in the applause. Then Tommy noticed out of the corner of his eye that the groundsman had finished his work, and the linesman was checking it, tugging at the white string. It was time. The next time the ball came to him – a flash back-heel on the volley – he caught it with both hands. Then he tossed it to the player waiting to take the corner. The cheering climaxed. In the last few seconds before the corner was taken he heard a faint chorus of 'Referee for England! Referee for England!' from the Leeds end. And he smiled down at his feet. The thing was, he could have caught it on the back of his neck and made himself look *really* good.

Tommy answered his interrogator slowly.

'Twice. And the second time I really didn't want to. At the time it was just a bit of fun, for the crowd. I had a suspicion that it wouldn't go down all that well with everyone . . .'

'Meaning who?'

'Meaning you, the FA, so I don't do it any more.' He paused and held his gaze. 'What else, though? Is that it?'

The man stared back, then moved on to point two.

'No. There is a lot of talk of increased dissent among players. Much of it vulgar.'

'These are vulgar people,' said Tommy, getting heated. 'I suppose I'm to blame for that, am I?' His throat was loosening up.

'Your name has been mentioned amongst your colleagues, when the subject is brought up . . .'

'So what? Jesus!'

Mr Lockhart raised his eyebrows.

*You cunt. I can't believe this.*

'This is the Premier League, Mr Burns. We have standards to maintain. This is not Hackney Marshes.'

'You really think I'm responsible for a few kids swearing? Show me how? Isn't each referee responsible for his own game? And if I am, so what? Have you ever thought it might help the game flow a little, to be not always stopping to book people for language? They can't talk the ball over the line. I book them when they kick lumps out of each other. Why don't you talk to some of my so-called colleagues about that? And it's Dr Burns, actually, since you're such a stickler.'

'Dr Burns, there's no need to raise your voice.' The Secretary showed his first sign of agitation. Tommy saw the man's eyes flashing with anger, which sat uncomfortably with his attempt to play cool.

'So what else?' Tommy's voice was back, and he was feeling pissed off.

'Judgment calls.'

'When? Where? Who's complaining?'

'Offside, four weeks ago, Liverpool–Blackburn . . .'

'There are proper channels for dealing with this. What about the meetings where we discuss these things? With other referees present. And video. And four weeks is too recent. Just so you know,' said Tommy sarcastically.

Lockhart grimaced. 'The incident concerned an offside that you over-ruled. In the . . .'

'Seventieth minute, yes, I know. It took a slight deflection off the defender.'

'Why didn't you mention this in your report?'

'Do I have to justify everything I do, just because the TV cameras didn't catch it? It's my job to make the calls. What's yours?'

'There's really no need to be impertinent, Dr Burns.'

'I'm not being fucking impertinent!' Tommy could feel the argument slipping away from both of them. While he was relieved that they weren't trying to pin any hooligan accusations on him, he was still confused as to what they might have up their sleeve. 'I want to know – I demand to know now – what I have been brought in for. As far as I can see it's nothing that couldn't be dealt with through normal channels. At our regular meetings.'

'Well, your general *attitude*. Some people are not prepared to put up with it much longer. I'm sorry, Mr Burns . . .'

'Doctor.'

'Doctor, but there are more than a few people around the country, both in and out of the Association, who feel you think you are, well, let's say bigger than the game.'

'What!' Tommy exploded. He stood up. 'Bigger than the fucking game? I don't believe this. I'm out there weekend after weekend, and a lot of midweeks too, getting trains all over the fucking shop, changing in piss-poor changing rooms, taking charge of twenty-two lads most of who don't know the rules, plus their idiot managers . . . I'm the one trying to stop players and managers and coaches from cheating, helped with only a very few exceptions by surly linesmen who want my job and think that making me look foolish is the quick route to getting it . . .'

'Dr Burns, please sit down!'

'... I file my reports on time, I attend every meeting I'm ever asked to, including that boring FIFA jaunt to bloody Switzerland last year about the new shirts, which turned out to be a complete fucking waste of time ...'

'Sit down!'

'And I was the only one who had to stay in a pensione because you were too tight for the Holiday Inn ...'

'Be quiet!' shouted the secretary. 'None of this is relevant to your case.'

'Oh, I'm a case now, am I? And what are the charges?'

'There are no charges against you.' He tried going softly-softly. 'Tommy. No one here is attacking you. We just have some concerns about how you're behaving on the pitch. We just wanted to find out what was going on. You are a very good referee. One of our best.'

*If not the best.*

Tommy sat down. He thought it was time for the man to become reasonable again. 'Well, then. Treat me like you mean it.' He was breathing heavily. Both men sat listening to it. The secretary's eyes flicked to the clock on his desk and back.

*This is it, he's going to get rid of me now.*

'Look, Mr Lockhart,' he said, looking straight into his eyes. 'I'm doing the best I can out there, to give people a good game of football. I've seen what it's like at Hackney, when there's no ref, or a stand-in, and I've been through all the lower divisions, just like you, where there's a lot of bad refereeing. I do *everything* I can to keep our League as high above all that as possible. But there are some things about football that you can't destroy, you can only control, and that's where the real difficulty lies. And that's where I think *I*, if I may say so, do a good job.'

'Well, Dr Burns, I appreciate your input.' The softness had been replaced by bureaucratic neutrality. 'I can't say we've solved as much as we'd hoped to today, but ...' He extended his hand to shake, instead of finishing the sentence.

*But what?* thought Tommy. *It must be OK, then? It doesn't seem like it.* But his courage deserted him, and he stood up too.

'Er, thank you.' Tommy didn't know what else to say. He felt the apathy in the man's hand. Mr Lockhart looked down at his shoes as soon as the handshake had fizzled out. He came round from behind the desk and led Tommy to the door.

'Thank you for coming,' he said again.

'Yes. No bother.' *Fuck.* ''Bye.'

And he found himself back in the lift, then walking past the giant trophy cabinets to the reception. The secretary smiled a saccharine smile to encourage him to be on his way. He got his coat from the peg and, looking around once, headed for the front door.

Out in the street it was almost twilight. His heart was still thumping. He didn't yet feel like going home. As he walked up the street towards the Tube station a vehicle passed him, then violently pulled over. Tommy saw a typical London van – dirty white paint with finger writing in it, rust around the wheel arches like herpes sores, and a deep score mark down one side. The window wound down rapidly and a face like a pig's popped out. It was Fat Paul.

'Oi, Ref! Wot you doin' round 'ere, ven?' Tommy was in a black mood after his meeting, but the fat face seemed genuinely pleased to see him. He caught up with the van.

'Tommy Burns, fack me, collar an' tie. Been in court?'

Tommy grunted. He ran his eyes over the van like a man meeting a woman. Fat Paul decided to overlook this effrontery.

'Which way you garn', ven?' he asked charitably. He still had a bit of a grin left.

'Home. N7. Tube,' replied Tommy.

''Ere, 'op in, ven, I'm garn ap ver Edgware Road. Norf Circular.'

Tommy thought about it. *Cockney bastard, all the way home, some nutter with a vanload of tools?*

'Nah, I'm all right. Fancy the walk.'

'Faaaack me. Ge' in the vaaaan!' He said it with such unexpected warmth and sincerity that Tommy changed his mind on the spot. *Fuck it, I've got nothing better to do.*

He shrugged and opened the passenger door. He felt the traffic flashing by on the other side as the lorries, vans, motorcycles and buses were supplemented by shoppers and commuters abandoning the West End for the suburbs. The headlights were coming on and people kept their speed up, no one wanting to get caught at a light or, worse, have to slow for pedestrians at a zebra. Fat Paul had sliding doors and what felt like bucket seats but were really normal seats whose springs had been destroyed by years of obese passengers. Tommy hunted for a seat belt as they pulled out into the traffic and sped away.

'Nice van,' he said sarcastically. Inside it was raw metal – the vinyl panels had been ripped off the doors and the ceiling, and a small pool of rusty rainwater lapped around Tommy's shoes.

Fat Paul turned his whole face to him, his eyebrows arched as high as they would go, his mouth round with surprise.

'Fanks! Used to be my ole man's, bless 'is soul. We used to do ver runs togevver. You're sittin' in wot used to be my old seat. We 'ad a lo' o' 'appy times together in vis van, me an' ver ole man.'

The engine had just hit the screaming point of third gear when they came up behind a Mercedes that was letting an old woman in a fur coat cross the road on a zimmer frame. She was exactly halfway across their lane.

'Cam on, darlin', fer fack's sake, 'arry ap,' Fat Paul muttered. She proceeded at a snail's pace. Tommy was still feeling around under his seat for his seat belt. The trees, thinned of leaves, waved their black filigree against the pale blue sky over Hyde Park.

'Wot you doin' round 'ere anyway, Ref?' Before waiting for an answer he leaned out of the window and hollered, 'Cam on, darlin', speed it ap! You can go, you can *go!*' The little old lady was clear of the Mercedes' bumper, but the silver-haired head behind the wheel of the car refused to budge. 'Wot, you seein' a specialist, then? One of them fancy doctors? Trabble wiv the ole wa'erworks, is it? Ass wot my ole man 'ad, bless 'is soul. Bleedin' prostrate. Bleedin' cancer. Bleedin' killed 'im. Cam on, lav, you can go now, you can *go!*'

'I *am* a doctor,' said Tommy. He didn't normally go on about it to people like Paul – or any people except other doctors – since they always wanted free and instant treatment, but he felt the prick of pride at the suggestion that he should need to see a specialist for anything. *I'm fucking fit as a fiddle. Unlike you, you fat bastard.*

'At last. Fank YOU!' Now that the pedestrian was well on to the pavement, heading up the slope, the car ahead pulled away. Fat Paul stamped on the accelerator and, with his piggy bare arm just inches from Tommy's knee, wrenched the spindly gearstick into second, then third without letting it go.

'Oh yeah, ass right, 'eard that somewhere already. Ain't got one.'

'Eh?'

'Seat belt. Ain't got one on that side.'

'Oh,' said Tommy.

The driver stuck it in fourth and with the engine whinnying, pulled the van into the imaginary middle lane astride the white lines, and leaned out of the window as they passed the Benz. 'Get back in yer 'ome, you rich ole tart!' he hollered, giving her the imported American sign so fashionable amongst van drivers, the single-digit 'Up yours'.

*Whatever happened to the good old British two fingers?* wondered Tommy. The silver-haired woman dared to glance at the roaring rust heap as it passed, without moving her serene-looking head, but quickly looked away. Fat Paul was delighted that he had caught her eye even for a split second. It meant she was weak, and that she would kick herself for giving him all the time he needed to download his vicious hatred on to her. Fat Paul gurgled with glee.

They slowed to an immediate halt, stuck behind traffic going round Marble Arch.

'What runs?' asked Tommy.

'Eh?'

'You and your dad. Said you used to make runs in this van with him.'

'Oh, vat!' said Paul, like he had just been told something that had been eluding him all day. 'Paper runs. Vijoes. Gaming products.'

As they crept up the Edgware Road, Fat Paul began a detailed account of his business dealings coupled with an extended eulogy of his father. Fat Paul Senior was 'one of ver biggest men on the scene', they used to go out to a nightclub together, then drive to Harwich at three in the morning to meet the night boat from Amsterdam. 'He still 'ad his gold belt buckle on. From the club. Everyone knew him by it. 'E used to swing it when fings got 'eavy.' He paused soulfully. 'Break a few heads.'

Fat Paul went quiet. He was choked up. Tommy looked across, but it was too dark in the van, and the pale western sky was behind him, so all he could see was the sculpture of the piggy eye sockets and the flattened cockney nose, running down neckless into the huge bulk at the wheel.

He felt a twinge of sympathy for Fat Paul, for the first time.

'So, what was it, then, import-export?' *God, I sound like a patronising cunt.* He had forgotten how to talk to people like Fat Paul. This wasn't a case of 'How are your piles/fibroids/blisters/cultures and seeya'. This was harder than work.

'Oh no!' Paul explained, turning in horror to look him full in the face again. 'Strickly import. No export!' He looked like he could have been offended if he hadn't already decided that Tommy was probably a bit *fick*, being from up north, and didn't know how fings worked. He turned back to his driving.

'Is there much call for Dutch videos? . . . Oh, I suppose there is,' said Tommy.

'We did *everyfink*,' said Paul proudly. 'Kiddies' toys, stereos, Sony Walkmans ...'

'Fake Rolexes?'

'No, real Rolexes, made by Rolex. Pit bull puppies. Computer chips. S'curity equipment. Handbags for rich tarts. Perfume ...'

He went on like this well beyond the Westway. Tommy could see a long night opening up before him. He considered the etiquette involved in bailing out and getting a cab. But Paul was on too round of a roll. By the time they got to the edge of Little Venice he was actually warming to him.

'Jus' gotta make a drop-off 'ere,' he said suddenly, and crashed up the pavement into a pub carpark.

'Yeah, OK,' assented Tommy feebly. Fat Paul struggled out, pulling his T-shirt down over his mammoth beer gut, and headed for the back of the van. Tommy looked back for the first time. There were about twenty orange crates scattered in the back. No tools, so far as he could see. Paul hefted one up noisily, kicked the door shut and went inside.

After ten minutes Tommy looked round for something to read. There was nothing on the dash. Nothing in the back. Nothing under his seat, not even a shred of a tabloid. Not even a delivery notice or receipt. *Come on, you fat bastard, what are you up to in there? Talking your fat gob off. What's this?*

In the glove compartment he found the manual of the van – 'P. Vincent, 1976' – and began to read that. Where the brake fluid goes. How to service the throttle cable. Modifying the air intake manifold for cold-weather operation.

*Jesus, twenty minutes, that's it.* He jumped out of the van and strode into the pub. Fat Paul was sitting at the bar with a pint in front of him, talking to the barmaid. They were chuckling away, but before Tommy could get his first complaint in, Fat Paul had stood up and ordered a pint for him. He looked at his watch. It was just after six. The news was on the telly above the bar. He thought of home, and why he hadn't just gone there. But the news was on. If he waited till the end, there might be something on the sports bit. You never knew. He was mightily pissed off. And that, he felt, could best be remedied with a pint of strong lager.

He sat down next to Fat Paul – one stool away, to accommodate his huge girth – and drank. Paul was introducing him to the barmaid, who was quite sexy in a somebody-else's-wife kind of way. Mid-thirties women all had that about them. Before the divorces started raining down anyway. Paul was saying what a great ref he was, that he was on telly all the time, went all round the world, and still had time for his old mates down the park. Tommy watched the fat little mouth speaking its rosy version of things. He wouldn't have used the word 'mate' in this context. He had met Fat Paul by chance, when he was first training to be a referee. That was when he was hungry for games. The Fat One's team were in the Essex County Cup Final – he was the player-manager, though as a left-half he was largely carried by his teammates – and Tommy was the referee. They won, fair and square, with two goals in the last ten minutes. Fat Paul was so chuffed he invited Tommy into their dressing room after the game, where there was champagne, and girlfriends who looked like they might be car dealership secretaries and/or glamour models, and Tommy, like a fool, said yes. And the other team got wind of this, and thought it unfair, and there was a bit of a ruckus, as Paul put it at the time. A lot of a ruckus, really, because when the shoving started one of the 'page-free' girls got slammed against the wall, and someone said she was pregnant, and then someone from the other team had his head split open with a corner flag, and when the police car arrived it was stoned, and turned over, and set on fire, and then some people from another team joined in, because they knew some of the other lot, and then the fans of course joined in – the mums and dads and aunties and sisters and even some of the little kids, the hard knocks, and all this time Tommy was shut in a storeroom, a bit worried, partly about his safety – he could smell the smoke – but more so about his reputation as a referee. But mainly, this was just a fight amongst a bunch of loudmouthed cockneys, nothing to do with him, though he did wish that there had been a few Villa there, just a few of the old lads, from Kingstanding, Perry Barr, Great Barr, Aston, Lozells, Castle Bromwich, Castle Vale. And Mark, of course. They could have carved their way through the crowd, shown them a fing or two on their home turf. That was the first time he had really missed Mark, since they had drifted apart. Looking at Paul's swollen face and listening to him, he found it odd to be reminded of Mark.

'Same again, doll.'

'Lager.' Tommy enjoyed it. It went down quickly, but not as fast as Fat Paul's pints. He drank as though they were thimblefuls.

Five minutes later – 'Same again, doll.'

Tommy got his wallet out, but Paul put out a fat forbidding arm. 'Nah, mate. You get ver next.' So Tommy got the next pair, glugging the last third each time to keep up with him. They were chatting about travel. Fat Paul didn't go to Amsterdam any more, except on occasional business. 'Too many wankers,' he said. Tommy picked up the word football on the telly and saw the camera go to a fresh stuffed shirt who presented the sport.

The screen filled with the vivid green of a pitch. It was QPR's ground, a nasty little matchbox of a place. Then they showed their new manager jogging with the team at the training ground. The lager had him feeling fine, which was soon transformed into passion.

'Fucking Queens Park Rangers, eh? There's a team I hate. What a bunch of wankers,' he said to the TV.

'Yeah,' said Paul, staring up too.

'Poxy team, never won anything but act like they have, media always licking their arses. What a bench of tossers. Poxy ground, though, that was the worst thing. You could *count* their whole mob, it was so pathetic, looked like about forty people jostling each other. Then the seats would get going: "Wain-gers, Wain-gers, Wain-gers!" Fuck off.'

Paul was laughing at this outburst. 'Tommy, you bleeder, I hope vey never get you in the Cup.'

Tommy scowled at him, then got back to his pint. He loved the sound of the glass clacking on the wooden bar. Rangers came and went. Tommy was enjoying himself. His body was melting away. All that was left was the warmth and fullness in his stomach, and the lightness in his brain.

He had never found out who Paul supported – his Sunday team was a mixture of north and east London, a catchment area that included a lot of clubs. He looked at the tattoos on his arms. Union Jack. Paws of a bulldog sticking out from under his T-shirt sleeve. Long dagger on the inside of a forearm – tasteful, though, well done. Swallow on the back of one hand. Blurred naked lady. And on his hands, some fuzzy Indian ink letters. He could just make them out now as the fat paw held the glass. SUFC. *Sheffield United? Swind ... no. I'll just ask him, then. He's not a QPR fan anyway.*

'So who d'you support anyway, Paul?'

Paul muttered without turning round. 'Sarfend.'

*Southend United? Course. Poor bastard.* 'Southend?'

'Yeah.'

Tommy waited for an explanation, in vain. They punctuated with another mouthful each.

'How come? You're from London, aren't you?' One thing Tommy had noticed over the years was the way people from way east of London sounded more cockney than the cockneys. There was a desperate, exaggerated sound to the way they spoke. Paul sounded a bit more centred than that.

'Well, it was me ole man, 'e was evacuated to the country in the war, to Sarfend, and he just got attached to the place.' He was sounding a little touched. Then he put on his stiff upper lip. 'They let ver kids play in the ground, 'cos there were no matches. They dug up the metal bars and used them in the war effort. Guns and tanks and suchlike.' He sighed heavily. 'So when I was a nipper he took me to their games.'

*You poor bastard*, thought Tommy.

'Then I stopped garn when I was about sixteen. Wanted to be a Spurs fan.' He sighed again, and tried to laugh through it. 'So he made sure we always worked Saturday afternoons. He never forgave me for vat. Well, I was just a kid, wasn't I? Rebellious yoof an' all that. Rebel wivout a cause. James Dean an' all that.'

Tommy took a swig of lager to stop himself laughing.

''Course, I'm going straight now. Free nippers of me own to support, ain't I?' He paused. 'Same again,' said Fat Paul.

'How can you have the same again?'

'You wot?'

'Same again. How can you have the same again?'

Fat Paul stared at him. 'You're maaaaad, you are. 'E's mad, doll, look a' 'im.'

Tommy just laughed. He remembered the van. 'Here, Paul, are you sure you can drive after all this? I mean, I want to get home ...'

'You'll get 'ome,' he said, looking slightly put out.

'... in one piece.'

'Vis is *naffink. Naffink, mate.* You should see wot my ole man, God rest 'is soul, could put away and still do a night's work. You Norverners ... Doll, make that a pint of Ben Jonson's. For bofe of us. I prefer it to Carriage, anyway. Vis is real *Landan* ale. If 'e could 'ave lived to taste this ...'

Fat Paul got prouder the more he drank, and Tommy enjoyed his company more. He started telling him about all the great things about London. Why no navy could invade because of the Thames Barrier. The A10 at dawn in the mist. The limousines pulling up at Stringfellows. Seeing stars coming out of the TV studios in Docklands when he used to deliver breakfasts there – George Michael, Naomi Campbell, Paul Daniels, the lot.

'This one, then we have to go,' asserted Tommy. The barmaid was starting to look like Grace Kelly.

'Yeah, OK. Gotta get you home. 'Ow's your old lady anyway? You still wiv 'er?' Without waiting for an answer he drained his pint, stood up, arranged his gut and bade Grace Kelly goodnight. Tommy followed.

They stumbled to the van in the dark. Tommy sat in the passenger seat, numb and pleased. He liked that effect of going into pubs on a whim and coming out, not much later, with the world changed. Changed utterly. In one and a half hours he had found something new. Here was a seemingly ordinary cockney – ugly, brutish and dedicated to his own greatness – but he wasn't mad for some football team. He wasn't some figure from the past whom he might have seen, or taunted, or chased, or even run from. He didn't have to hate him. And for that, he rather liked him.

Fat Paul looked serious once he got behind the wheel, almost sober. Tommy let himself lurch as they pulled out into the traffic, his body its own buffer. He listened to Paul's friendly voice getting more excited and proud. The Ford plant at Dagenham and their record productivity. London's parks, which he admitted he never went to. The hundred-odd pitches at Hackney Marshes. Tommy let it all wash over him. Then they turned right to St John's Wood.

'What about the North Circular?' asked Tommy, puzzled, but without the requisite energy to care. Time was skipping, jump-cutting like an old film, thanks to the strong lager and the Ben Jonson.

'No worries, I can go fru norf Landon, 's quiet now.' Then with real awe in his voice, 'Look at vese houses. Worf millions. Where else on earf can you see houses like vat?'

'Nowhere,' chimed in Tommy. It was true. At least, it was true when he was this pissed.

Paul was hunched over the wheel, peering up at the huge brick homes with their fully grown trees out front and their double garages. He sped up a little. Tommy lurched. They turned the corner sharply into Abbey Road. Paul had sensed something. He sped off down the road. 'And vis, look, you know what vis is?' Somewhere up ahead in the darkness Tommy knew there was the zebra crossing the Beatles had posed on, the same one all the tourists constantly stopped the traffic for with posing of their own.

'Uurrp.' Tommy let out a long and rolling belch. The next thing he knew they were heading for the zebra at thirty miles an hour. Paul was singing at the top of his voice, 'When I was younger, so much younger van to-da-ay . . .' Tommy saw something dark and box-like by the side of the road. He heard himself shouting, 'Watch the fucking skip, Paul!' He heard a metallic bang as the van clipped the unilluminated corner of a steel skip filled with two tons of rubble. Then he saw the road spin and the lights streak like an overexposed night photo. His whole body felt abandoned and in peril, and it was as delicious as a fairground ride. One more clang as they hit something else and they came to a bruising halt.

All the noise stopped. Fat Paul looked like he was just waking up. Tommy was cold sober. *Not dead. I'm not dead. He's not dead. How are my legs? Shit. They move. Fuck, they move. My hand stings. It's broken.* He looked at it, expecting it to be all twisted. It looked OK. The little scar was still there. It reminded him that he had a life. A past. A girlfriend at home waiting for him. Paul was groaning. The steering wheel had buckled under his flying weight. *He couldn't have moved much, with that gut protecting him*, thought Tommy. Using both hands, he slid the door open. It was bent and stiff, and he had to squeeze through a small opening.

Standing back in the middle of the road he could see where the van had clipped the skip, ripping the wing off the passenger side without moving the metal box an inch. It had spun three-sixty, crossed the road, flattened the right-hand Belisha beacon and come to a stop against someone's front wall. One headlight, the one on Tommy's side, had survived. The road was strangely quiet, so quiet he could hear the cooling tick of the engine, and even Fat Paul's moans. The world started jumping again – sobriety was wearing off. He was leaning in, asking Paul if he was OK. The only answer he could get was 'Faaaack' and 'Jesus'. Tommy took this for a good sign. In a moment of lucidity, he remembered that Paul was drunk too, so he probably wouldn't be that bad.

He stepped back again. No one had come out to help. The wall had a nasty crack in it. A car came up behind them, slowed down, then sped up and drove on.

'I'll go and get help,' he shouted in to Paul. 'I'll go and look for a phone. You'll be all right, mate.' Tommy set off down the road at a gentle jog, looking for a pay-phone. The wobbliness soon left him. He felt quite good as he ran, nicely balanced, his feet pushing the ground away effortlessly, his breath coming smoothly. After a hundred yards he looked back. *Good*, he thought, *someone's helping*. Without stopping, he watched, back-pedalling along the centre of the road. He saw a pair of headlights nestling next to the one bulb of the white van. He turned and jogged onwards. At last he saw the lights of a pay-phone, and approached it. He still had perfect breath, but as he hit 999 something caught him up inside.

'Which service do you require?' asked a sensible female voice.

'Uh, ambulance,' he replied, using the first disguise that popped into his head, his generic Scottish accent. 'Helloo,' he trilled, then, realising he sounded like Miss Jean Brodie in her prime, switched down an octave.

He tried to think of Bill Shankly, Bob Paisley, even Taggart. Coalminers kicking a super-saturated caser around on a Sunday afternoon. 'There's bin an accident. Aye, a white van. Abbey Rood. Aye, right at the crossing. No, no one hurt, well, one maybe.' They wanted to know who he was. 'Och, I was just passing. I must be off now. Aye. No . . .' He hung up. *Fuck*. He looked back up the road, but couldn't make out the scene. He dithered on the pavement for a moment. *Paul'll be all right. He doesn't need me any more. Probably be a doctor out to him any moment. He looked OK. All that padding. This wouldn't look good down at the FA. Just the sort of thing they'd jump on.* He dithered a moment longer. Duty was telling him to go back and make sure Paul was OK. Another duty, to himself, his hobby, and – if he pushed it – to football itself, told him to get the fuck out. He saw the amber light of a vacant taxi streaking up the road towards him. *Fuck it.* He stuck his arm up, and the cab came to a sudden stop, its brake shoes emitting a high-pitched hissing. He jumped in and slumped back on the seat. 'N7. No, go the other way, will you?' The cabbie, uncomplaining, did a U-turn and they headed back down Abbey Road in the direction of Lord's.

The night city streaked by through his drunken haze. All the delicious central London stuff first – he saw Harley Street types getting into their cars, the bright yellow signs of Europa Foods, darkened ancient churches. It wasn't long before he was in his own territory of fast foods and shuttered shops.

'Down here. Thanks.' He let the cabbie keep a twenty, for not being nosey. When it had pulled away and vanished, he realised Melissa wasn't home. *Parents' evening. Shit, I forgot.*

He let himself into the flat, which was like an oven. Melissa liked to keep it way up in the winter, and it was beginning to feel like it. He stood over the box for a few minutes, expecting there to be a news flash any second. That the famous Fat Paul had died of internal injuries in the arms of a paramedic, and that top Premiership referee Dr Thomas Burns had been seen fleeing the scene. But it was just the usual weeknight drivel. *This Is Your Life*, for some fucker who didn't even have one. This time it was the fat bird out of *EastEnders*. *Miss Brahms*.

Tommy knocked it off. He took off his tie, then hung up his suit. It was so hot he took off his shirt, then decided it was but a small step to pad around the flat in his underpants. He threw all the laundry in the machine, and suddenly, realising he was starving, went to the fridge. Rummaging around at the back, beyond all the smoked turkey and falafel balls and extra-thick yoghurts, he found two cans of Red Stripe, and went and stood in the lounge with the light off. The first can tasted very good. He decided to have them both and count them as a pint, or two units.

The best thing about their flat was the view south. He could see the lights spread before him all the way to Crystal Palace. This reminded him. One of the referees' board members was the chairman of Palace. Then the whole horrible afternoon meeting came back to him. The accusations and insinuations, and his wobbly self-defence. He resolved to write a letter to the FA's Referee Committee at once. He took some of the headed notepaper Melissa's mother had given them for Christmas and sat down on the sofa using a *Vogue* on his knees as his desk.

Dear Sirs . . .

   *I could resign. Dear Sirs . . .*

   Further to our meeting of this afternoon . . . *fuck, that's crap. But I can't go crossing it out now* . . . I, er, would like to point out that I hold your accusations and insinuations in extreme . . . *extreme, extreme what? –* ly low *esteem* regard. *That'll have to do.* I utterly reject the in . . . *sinuation? –* implication that I am less than professional, in either my judgment or my conduct, either *fuck* on or off the field. *Of play. No. Full stop. So if you bunch of jug-eared bureaucrats don't want me to resign . . . nah. So if . . . so if what?* He read it back to himself. *Bollocks. That'll do. The shorter the better.* I suggest we say no more on this matter and resolve to do our duty with renewed commitment.

   *Yours faith . . . no.* I remain Yours sincerely, Thomas Burns. *There. Fuckers.*


He looked with some admiration at his writing, the deliciously controlled script as clean and steady as any printed font, and waved the sheet of thick white paper for a few seconds, making the fresh ink dry thoroughly. He folded it, put it into a stiff white envelope and fetched a stamp from the tin. 'First Class,' he read. *Good. Might as well post it now. I always forget.*

He opened the flat door and looked out. What difference would it make if he trotted out to the postbox in his Tommy H. Y-fronts, so long as nobody saw him? It was right opposite the house. The street would be dead now anyway. Without putting the light on, he stepped lightly down the flights of stairs, feeling the temperature gradient as he descended, until the final blast of cold air as he opened the front door. 'Brrrrrr, fuck,' he muttered as his skin shrunk. Pulling the front door almost closed behind him so that it couldn't get up the momentum to slam shut, he hurried down the steps on to the pavement. Immediately a draught eased the door open and slammed it shut, producing the dreaded clunk that he heard once every two years or so. *Shit.* 'Shit!' He stood on the kerb, unbelieving, looking back, unsure of what to do. There was no one around. 'Bollocks!' he whispered. He wanted to get rid of the letter, so he ran across the crown of the road, rogue pieces of grit under his bare feet making him hop. The kerb on the other side felt hard and dirty as he hesitated on it and whacked the letter over the edge of the slot.

The letter was forgotten in a moment. A man in a red van collected it around 9.30 a.m. on Friday morning, took it to the depot, where it was sorted into a plastic crate for W2, then lay around until Monday morning, whence it was delivered, businesslike, bright and early with a bundle of other stuff for the FA, only to lie around again until the afternoon, when the Secretary's secretary got around to opening it. The Secretary himself was out of the office until Tuesday.

Tommy rattled the front door, as though just this once the heavy lock would amicably yield. He looked up at the darkened building, and rang a few of the bells. They were a weird lot in there, in that they went out a lot in the evening. The fresh-faced young temp girl went out a lot with her temporary friends straight from her temporary job; the stripey-shirted bastard on the first floor went out a lot with his sour Sloane of a girlfriend, eating in restaurants and falling asleep in crap movies; and the forty-year-old schoolteacher with the biggest flat stayed out a lot, leaning against the wall in windowless bars and nightclubs or hanging around the park toilets after dark.

So there wasn't much hope for Tommy. There was no loose window catch, no spare key in a magnetic box behind the drainpipe. The possibilities ran through his mind. *Mel gets home early. Call the AA. Call the cops — no. Call Marge out in Enfield. Hypothermia. Exposure. Arrested for exposure. Sit in the car — no, no keys. And Mel's got it. Fuck, I need a piss.* Standing under the stars in his underpants, in the empty street in the darkness, he felt intensely vulnerable. He stumbled to the side of the steps that led to the front door and pressed himself into the corner, in amongst the bins where he was hidden from the streetlight. *It's an emergency, after all*, he thought, as he felt the heat rearranging itself inside him and the pressure leaving his bladder. The hot river ran past his bare feet along the paving slabs. After thirty seconds — he was still only a third done — it found its course, turned ninety degrees and streaked across the path to collect in a pool in front of the basement flat.

*The basement lady. Of course.* Her door was right there. In a moment he was peering through the chink in her thick curtains.

He could see the telly. The cold was now getting to him, shooting up his thighs and across the small of his back. He rapped with his knuckles on the feeble plywood door. After a few moments it opened a crack, and a worried eye peered out at him, waiting for him to speak. As he did, it flicked downwards, saw his nudity, and the door abruptly shut.

'Mrs ... wait a minute! It's Tommy Burns from upstairs, I'm locked out. Please. I need help. My girlfriend will be home in a bit. I'm freezing.' He went on like this for another minute, until the curtain was drawn back a little. He made his case all over again to the silhouetted head. After another minute of begging, she opened up the door again, and made him state his case more fully. He was locked out. He had gone to post a letter. Melissa would be home soon. He was freezing. Could she let him in the main door so he could get back to his flat?

Eventually she relented, having weighed the risk of being raped by a neighbour against the fact that she lived alone and didn't get many visitors. Plus, if he was legitimate, for helping him she would be repaid in gratitude and gossip kudos for many years to come. And so the man in the underpants entered her hot little studio flat, and stood behind the sofa trying to hide his shame. Mrs Thorpe, a small, earnest woman in her fifties with bug eyes and drooping jowls, her dyed red hair contrasting with her powder-blue jogging suit, and her bright white scalp contrasting with her dyed red hair, rummaged in her handbag for her keys.

'Thanks, thank you,' he grovelled, as she pushed open the door ahead of him. He stepped into the slightly warmer air, and turned to take his leave. She tossed her head back slightly as though he were a weirdo, and disappeared.

Once back in the flat, Tommy warmed himself by the radiator. After a few minutes he saw Melissa's headlights in the street.

When she got in she wanted to know what was going on. Mrs Thorpe had stopped her on the path and told her something about him hanging around in his pants. She dropped her bag, stood there and looked him squarely in the eye. She could be intimidating when she wanted, although at times like this it had the opposite effect on Tommy, making him dissolve with desire.

'So?'

'I've had a terrible day.' He played the self-pity card first, to get it out of the way. 'Hey, come on, love. I got locked out.'

'In your pants?'

'I just popped out to post a letter.'

'In your *pants*?'

'There was no one around. I got locked out. It was freezing.'

She glared at him. 'So you sat down there in someone's living room in your pants? What kind of a nutter am I going out with? What are people going to think when they hear about this?'

*Fuck, so that's what she's worried about.* Purely from relief he let out a laugh, but this made her even more annoyed.

'I'm serious.'

He straightened his face. 'I know. I didn't *sit* down there with her. You weren't jealous of me being with . . . you know, down there with a strange woman, in my pants, were you?'

She looked at him incredulously, and shook her head. 'You stupid berk,' was all she said. Seeing her standing there with her dark bob curled against the clear olive skin of her cheeks, her tits sticking out, her hands on her hips, Tommy suddenly felt very foolish. She was too gorgeous for jealousy. He felt the old gulf open between them, the incomprehension, and wanted to make it good.

'Aren't you going to ask me how my meeting at the FA went?' he tried, sounding more aggressive than he intended.

'No. When I'm at work all day, and all evening, I don't have much time to worry about your hobby. And when I get home I don't expect to find you pissed and annoying the neighbours in your underpants.'

To Tommy, this was clearly meant to make him cross. 'Yeah, well, you might not have to worry about my hobby much longer. 'Cos I might just be doing it professionally.' He had to lie to win this one.

She looked at him, hiding her curiosity, gauging the moment at which to turn away from him. Tommy continued, raising his voice as he went.

'It might just be goodbye yeast infections, attention deficit disorder and anal prolapses, and hello . . .'

She turned away and headed for the bedroom.

'. . . three games a week, proper hotels, and proper fucking pay!'

It wasn't working.

'Sponsorship deals. They'll pay me to wear my boots. Do you know what that means?'

Her voice was cold. 'I'm off to bed. You're on the sofa. Don't wake me up.'

*Fuck. This again. And out of nowhere.* A great heaviness settled on Tommy's chest, the misery of failure. He'd let her down. He didn't know how, or rather, he was too slow in finding out. She was often a step ahead of him when they argued, and always two steps when he argued pissed. And yet it could have been even worse. The alcohol was like a thick lens over his thoughts, stretching them so they bulged in places, blurring them at the edges. He could see now that he should have asked her about her day, her long and tiring day dealing with the shellsuited delinquents and their similarly dressed parents. She was just mad at him for being pissed, so how much worse would it have been — would it be, because he could still see the light on under the bedroom door — if he told her he'd been out D&D-ing with Fat Paul, then fucked off and left him by the side of the road? Or that the FA actually thought he wasn't such a golden boy and wanted to clip his wings? Or that his job had lost all meaning and that if it wasn't for Dr Aktar making him look good he might well soon be out on his ear? Or that every few hours he fantasised about coming across that United fan whose teeth were marked upon his fingers and not letting up until he had given him the rest of the battering he deserved, some lumpy cuts, some fractures and internal ruptures to take back to his sorry Stockport maisonette?

And so in his misery, Tommy got the scratchy blanket from the hall closet, and knocked off the light, and curled up on the settee, and remembered the glass of water he should have got, but was too melancholy to get up and fetch. He lay there and covered himself, and looked up at the streetlight's yellow glow upon the ceiling, and closed his eyes, and let the room spin harmlessly a few times, and sank into a deep sleep.

There was a cup of tea in front of him on the coffee table. After a minute he remembered seeing water vapour coming off it, but now it was dead. He reached out and touched the mug. Stone cold. *Melissa. Marge.* Tommy didn't want another day of words, but the ticker tape in his head was already off and running. He could drown it out by getting up, or he could lie there for another hour, which might pass in seconds. *Fuck. Whatever the time is, I can still make it to work.*

Throwing the blanket back, he limped to the shower as fast as he could. The tea was from Melissa, he knew, a curious gift. Not so much a peace offering as a love offering. She had, after all, left him to sleep in. Once out of the shower, though, he noticed a dark red lipstick kiss on his cheek. Melissa's colour. He melted inside. *She loves me still.* Through a porthole of steam in the mirror, faced with his wretched stubbly mouth and bloodshot eyes, Tommy was overcome with shame, the shame of someone soaking up more love than he gives. He leaned on the taps to rest his sorry self, and looking down, spotted a slight sagging of his belly, a small tyre of flab. *Fucking beer. I'm letting myself fucking go. I've got a match tomorrow. I'll go on a run. I'll go to work. I'll run to work. I'll skip the shave.* He dressed himself to run, then packed his doctor gear – his white Fred Perry, his black trousers and shoes – in a small backpack, grabbed an apple, and went downstairs. *Yes, this is it, what have I been thinking, how could I let myself get so down ... QPR tomorrow, nice dinner tonight at the El Al, I'll surprise her ...*

The good mood only lasted as far as the front door. He stooped to pick up a single letter from the mat. It was addressed to him, in an FA envelope, with 'By Hand' written where the stamp should have been. Tommy's stomach convulsed as he opened it. *Oh God. It's short. Bad.*

'Dear Dr Burns.' *Bad.*

'At an extraordinary meeting of the Referees' ...' *Oh no, that's Lockhart* ... his eyes flicked down to the signature and confirmed it ... 'Committee last night it was voted unanimously that your officiating duties be suspended forthwith pending further discussion.'

His stomach sank to his arsehole.

'Your attendance at Saturday's fixture at Queens Park Rangers is not now required.' *Cunts.* 'I shall be in touch with you in the near future to discuss your future as a referee in the English Premier League.' *Bastards.*

'Bastards! Bastards!' Tommy started shouting and punching the wall. There was a spot of blood on the paint where his finger had opened up. He kicked the door and watched it wobble on its hinges, all the time cursing, then slammed it shut, raced upstairs and dialled the number on the letterhead.

'Mr Lockhart's in a meeting, I'm afraid,' said the Secretary's secretary.

'Well, tell him to call Tommy Burns at home. It's urgent. Thank you.'

Half an hour later, Mr Lockhart was at lunch. Half an hour after that he was out of the office for the rest of the afternoon.

Tommy sat brooding on the edge of the couch, staring at the tea, waiting for the phone to ring. He couldn't believe it. No referee was ever dropped in the middle of a season. The worst that happened was their marks were tallied up in May and they were asked to apply to referee in a lower division next season. It was the most humiliating thing that could happen to a man. And there were other ways the FA could have told him. A phone call. A telegram. They could even have had the weasel who brought the letter

round come up and tell him in person. They could have invited him back
to Lancaster Gate. They probably could have told him yesterday when he
was there. They could at least have let him do his game this weekend.
What really got him was the way they were unable to wait for the real
mail, and just dropped the letter off like a stalker's Valentine. Then he
remembered his own letter to them, with its conciliatory tone, its offer
to put the matter behind him, and he groaned.

*What to do? Call Colin Marsh, who was the Referees' Secretary for years until last
season? What would he say?* For a rash moment he thought of calling Mark
to tell him about his rotten luck. Then he thought of turning up for an
afternoon of work. Then he thought of the pub. Then he considered going
for that run, since he was dressed for it.

The sunshine was already wintry, pale and low as it shot though the
thick glass of the Spread Eagle windows that Friday lunch-time, on to the
puckered, pocked and life-scorched faces of the regulars. Tommy didn't
want to talk about anything to anyone, he just thought of the pub as a
warm alternative to getting four tall cans at the supermarket and drinking
them in the street. But the local pub – he would not stoop to calling it
*his* local pub, when he had a rare visitor to entertain – was filled with
all the daytime cockney lowlife that he normally steered so clear of.
Fat bloke at the bar with jewellery. Big-boned security guard off duty
playing pool with his mate. Alcoholic woman clutching her bag, talking
to two alcoholic men. Self-employed man at the bar, talking bollocks, not
business, to anyone in earshot. Unemployed girls in ten-quid tracksuits.
Rotting old lady, with rotting old man. Nasty youth, joshing, cackling,
swallowing hard and thinking ahead.

After the first few hundred yards of his run, Tommy passed the Spread
Eagle and decided to go in and slake his hangover thirst. There wasn't much
he could do about the misery. He sat in his running shorts, knapsack on
the bench next to him, and thought about his options. They seemed to
be narrowing. Kick the fuck out of Lockhart on his doorstep. Take
Melissa away for the weekend. Go and see Mark in Brum. Spend some
money (which they didn't have to spare). Have another drink (increasingly
likely). He thought about telling the press. He only knew one journalist,
Nick Felcher, a sly, dishonest reporter at Radio Four with whom he had
once fallen out over a badly chopped interview conducted outside the
Bournemouth ground. That was when Tommy was on the way up and he
foolishly had thought the gentleman from the press wanted to know about
refereeing. The Blow-Wave Bastard was how Tommy always thought of

him now. *Maybe he has some lingering regrets? Maybe he'll want to try again with me?* He got up and called from the pub phone, easily penetrating the layers of BBC desk-fillers and secretaries until faltering at the last hurdle. On his voicemail Felcher's fake London accent – which he always used in connection with sport – declared he was out of the office. 'Tips and messages welcome after the beep.' Tommy faltered, then left only his name and home number, asking him to call back, giving no reason, and no reintroduction.

Tommy drank slowly and with waning appetite. From time to time he caught someone's eye, returning the malevolent stare and the openly nosey gaze in kind. He could feel himself slipping into the position he despised and feared. *Home every single weekend. Media talking about me. Fans learning my name and using it. A whole lot of fuss distracting from the football.* When it came to his second pint, he made a decision. *Mark won't be doing anything. I can make the same train to Brum as last time. Melissa . . .* he didn't want to think of her. It was too shameful to admit that he had been booted off the roster, too hard to explain, and too at odds with the drunken nonsense he had come out with the night before. The hotels. The pay. The glory. It made him feel sick. *I'm going to Mark's.*

Euston had a holiday feel to it on a Friday afternoon as thousands streamed out of the capital back to their rightful place. Student nurses abandoned their hutches and headed for Mother. Itinerant construction teams tore open their pay packets, left their caravans and sleeping bags, had a few swift ones in the Rail Bar and hit the north. Day-trippers and interviewees made their way home, in more leisurely fashion than the hordes of hard-core commuters around them, who were off to the lost cities of St Albans, Leighton Buzzard, even Leamington and Daventry. He tried phoning Mark but there was no answer. Otherwise, Tommy's timing was perfect. Time enough to queue up for his ticket, purchase a sandwich and a magazine from the shop, and settle into his seat just as the doors began · slamming. As the train slid out of the station, smooth and silent as an ice cube in its own meltwater, the regulars rustled their papers while Tommy, the interviewees and the day-trippers stared out at the dimming city.

Father Mark sat down in the front row, resting from having prepared the church for the funeral. A little-known, little-missed but devout old lady would be buried the next morning. Her little stick body would be arriving soon, in its five-foot coffin. He would have to help her out of the hearse, as he knew Killingworth & Son, Funeral Directors, operated without the

Son on Friday evenings, because the son was a horny and pustulent teenager who liked to go up town on the piss. According to her last wishes, her body would lie one last night in the church where she had worshipped for the last thirty years, before the funeral at Witton Cemetery.

The fact that there were three weddings scheduled for the next day meant that her funeral had to fit in around them. Weddings were long planned, but death came like a thief in the night. She had been dead for five days now. It had taken four of those to trace a relative, and he turned out to be a surly and irresponsible middle-aged son in Bury, Lancashire. He had been very evasive on the phone on the matter of where Killingworth's bill should be sent, but Mark managed to talk him round. He impressed upon the son the old lady's pitiful isolation, which no one had realised was so extreme, and, in his mild and plain manner, that as a mother she had been there for him in the beginning, and didn't he see the rightness in his being there for her at the very end? The son was turning up tomorrow.

Death did not make Father Mark melancholy. From what he had been taught at the seminary, he believed it to be the gateway to a better world. After a brief spell in a holding pattern, Justice would be administered. All the extreme bastards would be packed off to Hell, which would be something like a cold desert, a high plain in February with no promise of society, just the endless whirring of one's own thoughts. This was the updated version of the lake-of-fire-and-the-pitchforks scenario. Heaven, he imagined, would be well lit, geographically infinite and, best of all, would lead to the complete cessation of all longing, all desire. It would be like permanently kicking back in front of the TV on Christmas Day after lunch. The entertainment would be good – the communion of saints meant that you could meet any saint you liked and ask them about themselves, and they would treat you like an equal. For example, St Anthony, how do you manage to find all those keys? Or St Christopher – how do you decide which aeroplanes go up in a ball of fire on the runway and which make it there safe?

It wasn't a very adequate picture, he suspected, and so he preferred to spend more time on the other aspect of his ministry – making life on earth a little more bearable for the living. The funeral would be a very early affair, then, since the first of three sets of lapsed Catholics would be arriving with their lilies and their compact cameras at half past nine on Saturday morning. He hoped the grooms would remember to tip the altar servers. They didn't seem to know this any more. He often had to do it himself from his own pocket.

Melissa: Fi? Oh, thank God you're in. Listen, you haven't heard from Tommy, have you?

Fiona: Tommy? No. Why should I? What's wrong, babe?

M: I've been home for a couple of hours now and there's no sign of him. I called the clinic but everyone's gone. I called Fat Paul ...

F: Who's Fat Paul?

M: Oh, some fellah he knows. Not very well, though. But his brother says he's in hospital or something.

F: Calm down, love, he'll be back soon. It's Friday, right, you're going out, you always do. He can't forget.

M: I know. We always go out to dinner. Well ...

F: What? Did you have a row?

M: We had a bit of a row last night. I was so angry I just let him sleep in. But I knew it was just a silly thing.

F: What did he do?

M: He was ... he got locked out last night. It's a long story. And he was drunk. But anyway. I don't know what to do. I don't know who else to phone. He doesn't really know anybody. I just thought, perhaps he talks to Nick or something ...?

F: No, I don't think he's *ever* phoned here. Listen, hon, erm, we're just going out to eat ourselves.

M: Oh.

F: It's our anniversary. Two years.

M: It's two years already? Wow.

F: Trust me, it feels like it. Sweetie, I'd ask you to come, but ...

M: Of course not, of course not. But anyway, I'm sure he'll be home soon.

F: He probably just went to get you a little something after work. I'm sure it's nothing.

M: Yeah. Probably. He's been acting strange lately, though. I don't know what's getting into him. I'm really mad at him. I hope he's OK, though.

F: I'm sure he's OK. And when he comes home you can throttle him.

M: You're dead right I will. I'm sorry, love, for making a fuss.

F: Hey, it's nothing. I'll call you when we get in, just to make sure you're OK. And if I get the answermachine – I'll just assume you're making up.

M: OK. You're right. He's probably on his way right now. Thanks, love, you're an angel.

F: 'Bye, Mel.

Tommy opened his copy of *Cosmopolitan* on the train and turned to the article on cervical cancer. For a while there he had fancied himself as a gynaecologist. It seemed like a fascinating speciality, until he met one, a man who told him it was like working in a chocolate factory and he was now off it for life. Tommy had stalled and missed his chance to specialise, so he decided he would be a general practitioner for a while, serving the community with a humble invisibility. He read a couple of sentences, then reread them. He read on a bit, and began to feel sleepy. The page blurred a little. *Hmm. A nap should do it.* He could see the lights of a suburb out of the window – an underpass lit with sodium yellow, an Astroturf playground under bluey-white halogen lamps on poles. It felt like somewhere like Luton. *Luton. An hour or so to go. Mmm.* He felt his head against the soft canvas of his backpack muffling the cold and noise of the glass, and his head swam with warm waves that disorientated him.

Back in the shadow of Villa Park, Mark remained on the front pew for a long time, thinking about the church. The cleaner had gone in for an operation a week before, and it had fallen to him to clean the building. He rose from his place, genuflecting as he crossed in front of the tabernacle, and took the broom from the cupboard. Sweeping the whole church took a long time, but he worked systematically, leaving little piles at the end of each pew for gathering later. A man in a suit with a broom.

Tommy was dreaming on the train.

He had in his hands a newspaper, and he was reading the front page. The headline was *THE MC AT THE FINAL. A CHAT WITH JOHN LEWIS (By 'THE VILLAN').* He noticed that the paper was really old, and had no photos, only pen-and-ink drawings in the ads. The masthead read *The Birmingham Daily Gazette*, and the date was obscure, except for the year, *1897*.

*J.L. is never too busy to spare half an hour in chatting about football. Allude to the ancient aspect of the game, and he is ready. Mention the modern, and he is willing. He has a close acquaintance with both, and will tell you more about their strengths and failings in five minutes than can most men. If you lead him on he will spend an hour in discussing the principles and ramifications of his pet pastime.*

*As you all know, Mr Lewis was, in a non-combatant sense, the central figure on the Crystal Palace playground on Saturday afternoon, directing the ceremonies of Aston Villa v. Everton for the English Cup. A few days after his appointment as referee for the Final was notified I sought him out, and invited him to be formally interviewed.*

*'What do you want to know?' he enquired. I strapped him securely in the confessional chair, and said he couldn't be released until he had given me the material for an article one column in length, and entitled 'Reminiscences of a Referee'. Then I told him to collect his thoughts and relate some of his most amusing experiences — 'mobbing', for instance, and pleasant little incidents of that sort.*

He read on excitedly, feeling his mind making up the text as he read it, like a frantic hand scribbling with a pen, always a few words ahead.

*'Yes, I've been mobbed,' said J.L.; 'and like many another referee who has experienced that distinction, I didn't deserve it. The first time was at Bury. Accrington were the visitors, and were winning easily. Bury never scored, nor did they dispute any of Accrington's goals; but the spectators kept shouting to the Accrington umpire (it was in the old umpire days) to come off the playground outside the touch-line. He wouldn't go, and then they shouted to me to make him: but I had no power to send him off, so he stayed where he was.'*

*'Well?'*

*'Well, the crowd waited until the game was over. The umpire got away somewhere, but they took it out of me. Not very badly. There was a bit of rough hustling, but I managed to get off without a broken head. On another occasion Accrington were playing Darwen at Darwen. I forget what match it was, but I remember the bother arose over a goal I disallowed Darwen for offside. Well, "after the ball" the crowd corrected my ruling. You had to pass right through the spectators in those days to get to the dressing-rooms. They made a lane for the players and officials, and as I went through they hacked and punched me right and left a good one. No; I've never been ducked that I remember. If I had, I should probably recollect it, so you can put down "No" to that question.'*

*Harking back a bit, Mr Lewis said it was sixteen or seventeen years since he first wielded the whistle. He began in small matches, and gradually got into the better ones and since then he had controlled the proceedings at some scores of matches — League games, Cup ties, 'friendlies', and encounters which were anything but friendly, and which needed prompt and punitive measures to keep the players under control.*

*Several months ago, when the clubs of the League had revealed a fair proof of their 'form', I asked Mr Lewis what was his 'tip' for the League championship. 'Aston Villa,' he replied, without hesitation; and then he added, 'And if they get the League championship they'll win the Cup — now mark my words.'*

*'And how does it feel to referee in a final with a little crowd of fifty or sixty thousand people looking on?'*

*'No different to any other match, that I know of. You don't need to bother with the fifty or sixty thousand. Just keep your eyes on the ball and the twenty-two players, and you're right enough. With a knowledge of the game and its rules, and the little tricks sometimes adopted by players to cover their transgressions, you cannot go far wrong. Referees should administer the spirit while observing the strict letter of the rules.'*

*Mr Lewis has the reputation of being known as a 'strong' referee — prompt to penalise where he considers it necessary, and one of the sort to stand no nonsense from players. I questioned him on this point, and he said he was seldom bothered by refractory players. Now and again, when his ruling does not suit a peppery Scot or Englishman, he receives a 'back answer' of a sarcastic character; but a discreet silence turns away wrath in such cases. On referees and refereeing in general, J.L. expresses himself with engaging frankness.*

Tommy was struggling to get to the end without waking up, or without the writing machine in his head giving out. It felt as though time were running out. He could see where the article ended, just a few column inches away, and in his dream his pulse rose anxiously.

*'There are lots of referees who have a perfect theoretical knowledge of the rules and how they should be administered, yet who are rank failures at enforcing them when they step on the field. It is simply a constitutional inability to grasp a situation which suddenly occurs in the progress of play and decide promptly there and then whether it is right or wrong.'*

*'Just one more question, and then I'll let you off. What are the Football Association to do to get good referees?'*

The print was dancing before his eyes. He pulled the paper up to his face, so not a word would be lost, and he cursed that his mind was splitting three ways — one part reading, one part writing, the third watching over it all and doing the cursing.

*'Suspend all those who do not see the game played according to the laws,' said the referee of the Final, as he rose from the confessional chair; 'and in that case there will be a rare lot of 'em out of work.'*

*John Lewis has all the characteristics of a good referee. Quick to see, prompt to act, decisive in his rulings, he is one of the strongest referees on the roll. Being mortal, he sometimes makes mistakes, but he has the merit of being able to stick to them, and this virtue he commends to all who aspire to become 'strong men' in the ranks of the referees.*

The text ended with a jolt and Tommy awoke. The train was half empty. *It must have been a stopper*, he thought. He shielded his eyes to see through the glass, but it looked like countryside, pitch black. *Whew. What a dream!* He felt immense pride at having made it to the end of the text without missing a word. He felt he had to get some of it down on paper before it evaporated. *All of it.* He knew the half-life of his dreams. Nothing in them was sacred, every second of them, every pixel, was subject to decay.

He stood up and limped to the gap between the carriages, still needing to know whether he had missed his stop. It was late, well past the arrival time for Brum. Opening the window and sticking his head out, he was hit by the roar of the engines and the icy blast of the accelerated October air, and the inky darkness all around him. The horizon was flat. *This can't be the Black Country. This feels like way after, or way before.* He tried to remember whether the horizon of Staffordshire was flat, or rolling, or peaky, but he found he didn't care enough to go and ask. *No one knows where I am anyway.* He was loving the bracing air in his face and the pale brown light cast by his own train's carriages on to the steel rails. The noise was the suffocating clatter of engines and air, like the sound of generators around the backs of fairgrounds where it was traditional to get kicked to fuck without anyone seeing or hearing. It was the train sound, with the gravel and the sleepers rushing by at cheese grater speeds, where innocents might be bunged off, or suicides leap, without a sound being heard by the world they left behind. And he was loving his dream.

*Birmingham Daily Gazette? Never heard of it. Not the* Post, *was it? John Lewis, John Lewis, John Lewis ... maybe it's just the name of the department store. Maybe I was just looking forward to going to Rackhams?* It all sounded deliciously real to him. He knew Villa hadn't done the double since the last century. Maybe he could look it up. *'Just keep your eyes on the ball and the twenty-two players, and you're right enough.'*

Tommy laughed out loud into the dark. 'Referees should administer the spirit while observing the strict letter of the rules. I agree, Johnny boy.'

He pulled in his head and searched for his pen. Back in his seat he made notes of every noun and every quote he could remember.

'Where are we, love?' he asked the young woman sitting next to him. He could see city lights emerging ahead.

'This should be Coventry.'

'Coventry. Great.' He smiled at her, and she looked down shyly. It was the way he said it. The surprise and the pleasure in his voice. It was her home town. She was a lawyer who worked weekdays in London. But she just preferred living in Coventry and taking the train to what she told her colleagues was 'all that *City Limits* crap' in London. They thought that made her an oddball – the whole pay-off for working in London was the bit where you turned up at other people's houses clutching a bottle of Shiraz and talked bollocks about yourself all night – but she was good at her job. She looked all right to Tommy. *The old white silk blouse. The old A-line skirt. Nice pair. Nice waist.* He imagined them locked in coitus in some disused BR office round the back of a station somewhere, and gave her another warm smile, which she returned.

*Coventry.* He was pleased to hear its name. Not just because it meant he was back on track, but because of the happy memories it brought. A shithole ground in a shithole town, it was a place Villa took over once a year, effortlessly. As they pulled into the station, which still looked modern with its optimistic concrete and glass, he remembered the noise a fresh wave of five hundred fans could make on the clean, shiny concourse. He remembered one time, being quite young, not tall enough to see over the backs and necks all around, hustling along with Mark while the police dogs snapped at them and the Villa fans laughed back. And the sound of the singing, which seemed to make the building vibrate. The coppers held them back, getting ready for the escort, and all the voices chanted together:

> *'Mortimer is magic, Mortimer is magic,*
> *La la la la, la la la la!'*

Villa had just won the League Cup a few days before, on a Wednesday night, so it was no surprise that everyone had turned out. Some stray civilians pressed themselves to the wall to keep away. A young woman in a sari put her hands over her little boy's ears. People who never went to away games braved the seventeen-minute train journey from New Street, and marched, awe-struck, through a foreign town. Admittedly, it looked a lot like Birmingham, with its cold concrete centre and its high-rise flats. The Coventry ground was a fair old walk, at least half an hour, from the station, and inevitably small mobs broke off, crossing dual carriageways or turning off suddenly down side roads. There was a big park to pass at one point, and Tommy recalled how proud he was that, despite the party atmosphere, some people were still bent on battering some locals, chasing them through their own park or hammering on their cars. Coventry were a soft target, but they did have their tiny grain of disaffected youth, their few hard pubs and their warriors. And while most Villa fans thought they were a joke, they cultivated a special hatred of Villa since they had no other close rivals. They were like an even sadder version of Blues, and that was funny.

Tommy had a vague soft spot for Coventry – one-way hatred was always flattering. He remembered that Mark used to take it all a bit too seriously, especially as they got older. Once someone told him that Coventry cared enough to shadow the escort or pick off the early arrivals, so he started making a point of going really early, in a car or a van, driving around the city centre looking for strange faces who looked like trouble. Tommy usually went along, impressed by his friend's devotion to a cause. Mark was the sort who'd leave the ground early – at half-time, even – with a few other madmen, to hunt down people in side streets and carparks. Tommy sighed. He really had admired his commitment.

After he had swept the church and tidied up the kneelers, hymn books and missals, Mark sat down again to pray in the front bench. He prayed for a congregation, that the Lord would supply him with one. Then he prayed for the fifty or so souls he did have. Then he prayed for the soul of Mrs Coombes, the little old lady who had died. Then he prayed for the poor, the ill, and for those in prison. He was interrupted by the screeching noise of the church doors being fully opened. The funeral director called in to him.

'Father O'Mally, she's here.'

'Righty-o, I'm coming.'

Outside, as they were loading her on to their shoulders, Mr Killingworth at the front, Mark bringing up the rear, Tommy rounded the corner and waved.

'Hey, just in time. Give us a hand here, Tommy boy.'

Tommy was a little nonplussed. He hadn't expected to be expected. But he went along with it.

'Who's this, some kid?' he asked, feeling his thirty-pound share on his shoulder.

'No. Mrs Coombes. English lady. Thirty years in the parish and no one's come to claim her.'

'Ugh. That's terrible.'

'It is,' said Mark softly.

The undertaker took his leave noiselessly, an art he had perfected over forty years. He knew, and Mark knew, and Tommy knew for that matter, that the dead weren't going anywhere. He'd be back the next day to transport her to her plot.

The two friends sat down in the front row, six feet from the pale ash coffin. It sat on a chrome trolley with zigzagged, expandable sides that locked into place.

'So, Tommy, what brings you back to Brum so soon?'

His troubles flooded back to him. 'Ah, man, you wouldn't believe it. You wouldn't fucking believe it.'

# 6

## Time passes; no games, Melissa's sister, Xmas; Brum, aggro at Blues, arrest

'Hey, get the fuck off me, you City tossers . . . Oof!' Tommy bent almost double under the blows of three Birmingham City fans who had come across him in the Bull Ring. They were at the top of the other ramp, which leads from the outdoor market up to a covered row of shops. He was up against the glass pane of a clothing store. The shoppers scattered as the shouts went up against Tommy and the fists and feet began to flail. He covered his ears and temples as best he could, which left him a view of a small patch of pavement, on which various shoes and training shoes scuffled eagerly and flashed back and forth.

'You cunts!' he shouted, though it was muffled by his arm.

'Villa bastid! Fookin' Villa bastid!' someone was shouting, breathlessly. It was a young, high voice full of razor-wire hatred. Tommy felt the soft sole of a trainer shove his upper arm, and then he was toppling over. Sprawled on the floor, with his head down by the stone skirting board of the shop where the dogs pissed, he felt the blows raining down on his stomach, head and thighs. Someone tried to get at his bollocks but he pulled his thighs up close to his stomach. The shouts and the thumps went on for longer than he expected. In the thirtieth second he became very worried. Taking a chance, he took a quick look. One of the Blues fans was standing over Tommy's feet, looking down at him without tilting his head, with just his eyes. His chest was stuck out and his arms were straight down by his side – the exact same stance he had taken when they first started arguing. He had bleached blond hair and wore a green flying jacket, like he was some hard knock. A leather shoe came shooting towards Tommy's unprotected face and caught him a stinging blow, right on the eyebrow. That pissed him off.

'You fuckers,' he roared, protecting his face for the next few kicks. He made a grab for the foot the next time it came in, knowing that concentrating on one of them would cause the other blows to seem harder. The shoe was too fast and slipped through his hands. *If I could just get that bastard I could topple him* ... Tommy's breath was coming in pants, his eye stung, his stomach he knew was already bruised. He knew if he could get a hold he wouldn't let go until the bastard was on the floor with him. Then they could do what they wanted. The foot slipped through his grasp again, just as he heard the shout 'Old Bill!' There was a scrambling sound as they ran off. Tommy took a peek, and saw Blondie stop, turn and give a last couple of stamps to his thigh that hurt with a sickening depth. Even to an old hand like Tommy, the hate in the kid's face was just as hurtful.

A few seconds later he heard the rubbery soles of a copper's Docs sprinting past him after the City fans. Looking up, he saw the bright blond thatch weaving through the crowd below as he followed his mates in the direction of the Rag Market.

*Bastards! City bastards.* Tommy's body hurt, but he smarted far worse inside at the humiliation of having been jumped by three City fans, in the middle of the Saturday shopping. Into the empty space around him came an old man and his wife, both looking dignified in their warm camel coats. Everyone who saw the fight from the beginning was hanging back, unsure whether to pity Tommy, as the odds had seemed against him, or to shun him for being a hooligan. The elderly couple had only just rounded the corner, however, and had missed everything. All they saw was a thirty-five-year-old man on the ground, trying to gather his limbs together and get his breath back. He looked quite respectable, from the cut of his clothes, and from the fact that he was wearing shoes, not trainers or bovver boots.

'Are you all right, young man?'

*Young man?* thought Tommy, looking up at them. In between gasps, he managed a laugh. 'Yeah. Yeah, I'm OK. I just got ... mugged, I think.'

'Oh *dear*,' clucked the lady, with a concerned frown on her face. Tommy looked up and saw the quality of the powder on her face, then the evenness and richness of the lipstick on her neatly puckered lips. Her skin was fine-grained, still, from a lifetime of good care. He saw her small gold earrings, and her soft perfume arrived. Looking up at her, he found himself relieved to see such kindly people, and slightly guilty at their misprision.

'George, find a policeman.'

'No, it's OK,' said Tommy hurriedly. 'They didn't get anything.'

'Oh, are you sure? Oh, George, his head is cut.'

The two strangers saw Tommy trying to get to his feet, and both leaned down to help. Their light old touch brought him to his feet.

'Bloomin' hooligans,' George was grumbling. 'You can't even go shopping on Saturday morning . . .'

As he pulled level with him, Tommy noticed he had a silver fish sign in his coat lapel. He felt stiff and sore, and his eye hurt. The lady gave him a tissue to dab at the graze, and they stood protectively beside him while he sorted himself out, not understanding Tommy's worried glances over their shoulders for the return of the copper. The gawkers had started to speed up and turn corners by now, passing information back and forth as they went. Apart from the man dabbing his brow and being talked to by a wealthy-looking old couple who stood extraordinarily close to him, the shopping centre had returned to normal.

'Thanks, thanks for your help. I'm OK now, really. I'll just go and sit down somewhere and take it easy. No, I'll be OK. Thanks for your help. Thank you, really.'

They mumbled and fussed a little more, sensing that their job was not really done, but Tommy wasn't about to wait around. He pulled himself away and, with a little wave, rounded the corner out of sight.

'Ow. City bastards,' he muttered. Limping from the pain in his thigh, he walked as quickly as he could through the crowd to the steps at the bottom of the Rotunda that led up to New Street. He saw no coppers, and he knew he'd be in the clear once he got back up to street level.

It was January. Tommy was in Birmingham for the second local derby of the season with Blues. This time it was the FA Cup fourth round. The draw had been sweet to Villa that year. But he was there to watch, not to officiate. He had not refereed a game since Wolves in October. Letters had been exchanged – Tommy's impatient, and then sarcastic; the Football Association's stony and infuriatingly vague. The official position was that the FA and the Referees' Committee were 'reconsidering Tommy's record'. They were going over his match reports, and the reports of observers – the ex-referees who are paid thirty pounds and a meal to sit in the directors' box and study how a referee handles a game. They were talking to other referees and 'assistants' – Proctor hadn't been called, but he knew someone who had been and was asked his opinion of Tommy's general refereeing. Proctor didn't know the answer. Unable to get anywhere with the hierarchy at the FA, Tommy had put out feelers amongst his colleagues. He telephoned several Premier League referees, but no one seemed to know anything about his case. He floated the idea of a petition, but there were no real takers. Contrary to what he had expected, nobody wanted to put their name to anything, unless everyone else was. It was just too risky. The new Referees' Secretary had a reputation as a hard man to please. Everyone ummed and ahhed and worried about their future. Each time Tommy replaced the receiver, he sank a little deeper into gloom.

January was patchy in Birmingham – sun and clouds, cold sun and cold clouds. On the morning he was jumped, Tommy took himself across town once more in the direction of Aston and his friend Father Mark. He limped up New Street until he found the number seven bus. From the top deck he could see out over the Saturday shoppers. There were patches of kids on street corners. Some Villa outside a record shop, eight of them muttering and looking around. Some Blues walking along in a huddle, looking for more of their own. A lot of standing around and checking each other out. Tommy thought about the three bastards who had just jumped on him. They had come up to him out of the blue and challenged him – What the fook was he looking at? sort of thing. He pushed past them when they tried to block his way. They walked along with him until Blondie decided he was the enemy. 'Whoja support, mate? Cuz if it's Villa I'm gunna batter ya!'

Tommy turned, unable to resist. 'Fuck off, you City fleabag.' He had never been able to get over that aspect of his aversion for Blues fans. To Tommy they seemed like urchins who emerged from the rubble of the de-industrialised eastern side a few times a year. The blond-haired one had the City crest tattooed on his throat – two balls with what looked like a piece of toilet paper running round them. None of them could have been born at the time he went to his first-ever game – Villa against Blues, 1975, when Villa had just returned to the First after an odyssey that had taken them as low as the Third Division.

'Gerrim!' he shouted, and all three set to work on the man ten maybe fifteen years their senior at the top of the ramp. He had to admit he envied their spirit. Roving through the market hours before the game, picking off the enemy ... it was just the sort of thing Mark used to do.

November was a black month for Tommy Burns. It seemed like every time he switched on the telly there was football on. And it was always some dazzling goal being disallowed, or some hot-headed hotshot getting himself sent off. He caught the goons laying into a new referee, Graham Barber, fresh out of the First Division and having a bad season. Bad calls and human error were part of the game, but this fellow had been spotted by the media and they were turning him into Mr Wrong. 'Och, noo way, noo way was that offside!' muttered the ex-player. 'It took a deflection off the defender!' said the sacked manager, who had by now been installed at a failing tinpot club but had a watertight BBC contract. 'He's straight out of the First Division and into the Premier League … it's out of the frying pan and into the fire for Mr Barber,' he said, then sat back, pleased with his poetry. Jimmy Hill preferred to take a wait-and-see attitude, which surprised Tommy. All the same, he just wanted to get out there himself and show them how it should be done. He was certain the cameras were spending more time on the referees, and the commentators were finding more to comment on.

Nick Felcher never rang back from the BBC.

November was a black month for Tommy Burns, because Melissa gave him a hard time when he eventually phoned her from Birmingham.

'What the hell are you doing up there? We're supposed to be going out to dinner tonight. Why didn't you call?' She was at home in the empty flat.

'I tried to call. From the train,' he lied, nervously. 'I borrowed someone's mobile. You weren't in.'

'Oh, a likely story! I get one chance, then you can't be bothered to call me again until eight o'fucking clock? Thank you very much.'

He didn't like her saying 'Eight o'fucking'.

'I'm sorry, love, but I went straight to the church. I had to help Mark carry in some old girl in her coffin.'

'Oh, please. Spare me.'

She hung up, and wouldn't answer again. She wouldn't all weekend. He tried calling her again on Saturday but got no answer. He came back on Sunday to a frosty reception. She wouldn't speak all Monday or Tuesday. Wednesday they had a nasty row in the bathroom before work. She was so upset she skipped school. Tommy found out in the evening when he got home and she was watching some crap teatime talk show on telly, *My Boyfriend Cheats But I Still Love Him*, *My Guy Is a Skinflint*, *My Best Friend Is a Man-Eater* … that sort of thing; he didn't catch it.

Melissa said she was sick of his neglect. She didn't think she could take much more of it. Tommy panicked and blabbed, telling the whole story of the interview, the letter that came by hand, and the outlook for the season. The local derbies were gone, the European game was gone, the London night games, where he could just come home from work, have dinner, then get the Tube to the ground, were gone. He was off the List.

Her frown evaporated. Her lips softened with a new feeling, the deepest of sympathies, and turning her frustration around she took his head in her hands and soothed him with gentle words and mild self-reproaches. Tommy wondered if he could tell her about Fat Paul and the van at this point, but decided not to push his luck. He was also rather touched by the strength of her feeling, and the depth of her love. So he was right all along to be upset. *The fucking FA. Look at all the trouble they've caused.*

But even after this warm rapprochement, things were not quite as good as before. Tommy now had his weekends free, but he found that his girlfriend had her own routine that she didn't want to give up just like that. She had her friends to see, her shops to go to. He found out that far from sitting in and watching the old film and switching over for *Final Score* on a Saturday afternoon, she stepped into her beautiful Speedo swimsuit and took herself off to the pool for some lengths, then she met up with friends and went for lunch, or coffee, or dinner, in places like Kensington and Islington. After a couple of tries, they realised they didn't really want Tommy around after all. He thought about finding a Saturday or a Sunday league that needed referees, just to keep his hand in. But all the leagues were tied up with the county associations, and the county associations couldn't afford to annoy the FA.

Fat Paul was coming out of hospital in good time for Christmas. Tommy was surprised to hear this. He heard it from Melissa, who got a nasty call from Fat Paul's little brother Phil at the end of November. Apparently the punctured lung – caused by the sharp ends of a fractured rib – had taken a lot longer than normal to heal, thanks to an infection. Tommy found it hard to take the blame for this infection. He found it hard to take the blame for the fracture either, since Fat Paul had been the one pissed out of his head driving and singing in the dark in that shit old van. He replayed the scene in his mind, but the pissed mind records as badly as a 50p cassette from the Rag Market, and he couldn't make out much from the imagery it supplied. He even noticed steam coming from the radiator, and couldn't be sure whether this was just an embellishment on his part, or something he had really seen.

'Fat Paul is a piss artist!' he exclaimed when Melissa confronted him. 'He was loaded.' She was shocked. She was white. She had to sit down.

'A punctured *lung*? You left him there with his lung punctured? Was he breathing? Was he *conscious*?'

'I didn't know it was punctured! You can't tell stuff like that. Anyway, I'm the one who called the fucking ambulance. I didn't see any of the rich tossers round there coming out to help us.'

'Jesus, Thomas!' She looked at him with the did-I-marry-a-monster? look.

'And of course he was breathing. He had another lung.'

'Oh, great. Terrific. I hope *I'm* never in a crash with you.'

'I wouldn't have left him if he wasn't breathing. But being unconscious isn't such a bad thing. It was the best thing for him at the time.'

'Yes. Well. I think Fat Paul returns the sentiment. His obnoxious little brother said you weren't to come near north-east London again for a long, long time.'

'Is that what he said?'

'Yes. "A long, long time."'

They looked at each other. Melissa's beauty shone – her cool olive face showed she hadn't lost the ability to be amazed by him, and that she secretly rather enjoyed that. She liked him for his surprises, and she liked herself for that. It didn't take long, after the facts about Paul had been established between them, for the emphasis to fall back upon themselves.

Tommy held his own in this exchange. In his civilian clothes he might not have the authority and presence he had when he walked upon the green turf of great grounds in the black kit of football's élite, but the way he carried his body still spoke for him. He stood erect and unflinching when he heard of Paul's threat, and in between marvelling at his girlfriend's beauty, his eyes gave the faintest of smiles at the thought of Fat Paul issuing threats from his hospital bed. Still, although he wasn't particularly attached to north-east London (it was a shithole) he didn't like the idea of a bunch of cockneys jumping out of a van and chasing him up the street with iron bars.

December was a black month for Tommy Burns. The leaves had finished falling and lay in piles for a week, curled and dry, until it began to rain, whereupon they became a rusty sludge that stuck to his shoes, staining the leather and gumming up the stitching. The sun went down shortly after lunch. The numbers of patients claiming to suffer from Seasonal Affective Disorder – when you get depressed because the days are so short – went up steadily, by the day as well as by the year. They had this new thing where they heard they could get special light bulbs, paid for by the Social. Over the month this turned into free tanning sessions, and then grants for holidays – somewhere sunny, of course. Malta. The Azores. Florida. Tommy's favourite was South Africa.

But still there was no football for him. The days dragged, the endless stream of patients with their endless streaming colds began to get him down. He even caught a cold himself – something which never usually happened. He prided himself on his immunity. He could hold the itchy little boy with eczema and show the head lice to his mother without a single bug landing on him. He took hundreds of samples of blood from his shrinking Aids patients, without flinching, without spilling a drop, and without unconsciously mixing up the vials. Melissa came home from school full of stories of her kids, how hyped they were about Christmas, how they were starting to bring in presents for her and put them under the tree, and how their reading was coming on in great leaps. Even the hopeless cases had proved her wrong. Tommy's lot, on the other hand, were inching towards their graves, coughing and spluttering as they went.

The inky streets were lit for the festivities by now – plastic Santa moulds and irrelevant cartoon characters hung from wires across the shopping streets and waggled in the wind on lampposts. The chilled rain fell in gold streaks past the headlights of taxis at four-thirty when he got off work. It was the season of goodwill, and he went to Oxford Street to look for a present for Melissa. It was all shit, but he saw a wonderful umbrella that was stout as an ash-plant, double-strutted and covered with a thick black nylon. He thought Mark would dig it. He could even share it with Father Kelly if he wanted. They could leave it in the hall.

One of his patients, an old bus driver with a giant gut, gave him a bottle of tequila as a seasonal thank-you for fixing his piles. Tommy had used a new gadget that a gorgeous rep, Denise, had given him, a cauteriser that looked like a one-cup travelling heating element. The bus driver swore by it. Tommy stopped in at a pub on the way home, by way of getting into the Christmas spirit. He hung on to the umbrella but left the tequila in its plastic bag under his seat while he went to the toilet. By the time he got back someone had nicked it. *Bastards*. No one in the pub knew what he was on about when he asked, of course. He wasn't a regular.

Taking a second scotch and lemon for his cold, he spied a pay-phone and decided to make some calls. Melissa was home. She was pleased to hear from him. She had just heard from her sister, who was heading home from Europe for Christmas. Then he called Mark. Long mournful rings again. He imagined the metallic after-tone in the cold hall. Mark answered, and seemed glad to hear from him again. The coolness that came with separation, and with being a holy man, was breaking down. Tommy wanted to revive their old ways and their old dialogue. It was December and he was hurting from the lack of football.

'What's up, Mark?'

'Hey, Tommy Burns! How are you?'

'Shit, mate. Still on the bench. I hate it.'

'That's terrible.'

'It's the fuckin' refs' Christmas dinner next week. Not going, of course. After what they've done to me.'

'Right, right,' said the priest soothingly.

'Fucking bastards. What about you? How's business at the old Sacred Heart?'

'Oh, it's hotting up. I've got a few parties to do. Where are you?'

'Parties?' *Parties?* Tommy's ears pricked up at the word. He realised he didn't have many ... didn't have *any* parties to go to this year. Except through Melissa. Teachers' stuff, and her other friends. Fiona might invite them again this year to one of her dreaded mixers. He'd get to talk to her boyfriend Nick again.

'What sort of parties?' he asked eagerly. To Tommy, the best thing about London was rolling round the streets drunk in the week before Christmas, the secretaries brushing past with their tinsel headbands on, singing bastardised carols, the motorbike dispatchers with their twelve-volt fairy lights draped around their windscreens. That was how it should be, this city. There was room for a lot more peace and love.

'Oh, y'know, old people's homes and stuff. Orphans.'

'Oh.' Tommy was embarrassed. 'Yeah. Hey, you know what? I got you a prezzy today. No shit.'

'A present? You shouldn't have.'

'Don't you want to know what it is?'

'Er, go on, then.'

'It's an umbrella. A fucking smart one.'

'Great. We need one. It's pouring down here. The last one got mangled somehow.'

'So how d'you want it? In the post?'

'I was going to call you anyway, I have to go to London soon, you could give it me then.'

'London? Yeah, smart. Great!' Tommy was exceptionally pleased. It

wasn't like his old mate hadn't ever been to London before – he had,
and they had, lots of times. Wembley for that boring League Cup Final
when Everton passed the ball back to the goalie eighty-two times. Mark
didn't get the curious Wembley vibe, the live-and-let-live thing, since he
had never been before. He thought fifty thousand each of both types of fan
meant a significantly higher chance of aggro. He had gone down wanting
to slice up some scousers, as he was convinced they all carried Stanley
knives. His big dream at the time was to get one off some wedge-headed
scally and use it back on him. The game was so depressing, though, they
just went straight home on someone else's coach. It didn't even stop at
the services. Then there had been countless Arsenals and Tottenhams
and West Hams and Chelseas, plus a few shitty clubs like Palace and
Wimbledon and QPR, when they were up. Mark never liked to hang
around after a London game, and since he didn't, Tommy didn't either.
The geography of London confused him – the way the suburbs all looked
the same, and you never knew who owned the city centre. You couldn't
really walk anywhere, so you often just emerged from a hole in the ground
to another damp high street. Plus there were all those places glimpsed
from the coach that didn't have any football, the St John's Woods and
the Claphams. It didn't make much sense. Tommy had sort of got the
hang of it during his medical school days, but only passively, as he had
largely lost interest in going to games by then.

'You're staying with *us*! You're definitely staying with us! Great. Melissa
really wants to meet you. She keeps asking me why I keep going up to see
you. I tell her you're an old mate, but she has to meet you, I s'pose. Hey,
Mark – you know we live in sin, right? You won't get in trouble for that,
will you?'

Mark laughed. 'No. The Church has come a long way, you know.' He
paused. 'So you're in Camden, then?'

'Yeah. Not really, actually. Tufnell Park, sort of. Where do you
have to go?'

'Oh, I have to see the top brass. Westminster Cathedral. You know.
They call us in from time to time. Is there a bus?'

''Course there's a bus! This is great. Can you make a day of it?'

And so they made plans. Tommy finished his whisky and walked out
into the rain, full of bonhomie. The tequila didn't hurt so much. The dull
ache of the refereeing shame even faded away, for a while, while he lolled
in the back of a taxi.

December was a black month for Tommy Burns. One of his Aids

patients checked into a hospice. He loaded up his plastic bag of medicines, all of which had 'Dr T. Burns' typed on them, and stopped at the clinic to say goodbye. Tommy didn't have much time for him, as there was an epidemic of Chinese flu going on that Londoners seemed particularly susceptible to. The waiting room was standing room only. The man was only thirty-two, and came in with a blanket round his shoulders. He looked fifty-two, lined and drawn. Bronchitis was the latest ailment, and they both feared for his life. He was being driven out to Barnet by his mother, who had loaded the car with his effects — hardly enough to cover the back seat. Tommy came out into the cold to wave him goodbye.

*Poor bastard. Ill, but well enough to drag himself to his grave and topple in. And his poor mother! What does she make of all this? Nursing him, again, when he should be nursing her.* The whole thing made Tommy feel sick. As he walked back in through the crowd waiting for him he just wanted to get out. He was powerless in the face of entropy, and having his face rubbed in this fact every day he suddenly felt very self-destructive. *Be nice,* he thought, *to go on the rampage. To really smash things up. With Mark.* He sat down at his desk and paused before buzzing in the next mother-and-child unit. *Mark was good at that.*

Tommy was starting to itch for a match to referee, the way a pianist itches for the piano at the end of a holiday. He longed for the scrunch of turf under his feet, for the vibration of the whistle in his mouth, for the baying of fans who wanted to see a dirty player sent off. His mind spontaneously called up scenarios of delight: the precious second when the wall is straight and far enough back, and both teams and the crowd await the whistle; explaining a decision to the curious hordes with a mime, like a throw-in or a handball. He could feel the gestures queued up in his nervous system, just waiting, the way an amputee feels action in a phantom limb, then feels ridiculous. His hand twitched at one point, as though getting ready to point at the penalty spot. *Christ. This is withdrawal.*

December was shit, and Christmas was shit, and Mark's visit was a disaster, and Melissa's sister annoyed him, and it seemed every time he turned on the box there was live football. Six games in two weeks — that was what most teams had to get through. Six games in two weeks was Tommy's idea of service and commitment. While there were roughly two refs for every Premiership game played, the previous Christmas Tommy had been asked to take six games over the holiday, because of his fitness, because of his availability, and because he was one of the best. His judgment was unclouded, his positioning was superb, his rapport with the players was so good it had a measurable effect on the teams. This was in part his own opinion, but it was formed from scraps he overheard from his colleagues, and even from the powers at the FA. Colin Marsh, the old Referees' Secretary, was always nice to him. Dissent was low, bookings were low, Tommy was practically invisible. Except to Jimmy Hill, who never failed to point him out and praise him.

But that was the beginning of the year, and now it was the end. *Maybe I shouldn't have kicked the ball around at Leeds? Bastards. I was late to Wolves, but that was the first time.* He stared at the screen. It was New Year's Day. He was feeling rather delicate – unsteady on his feet, wobbly within. Tommy poured the rest of his can into the glass. It foamed up and over and made a crescent on the carpet. *Fuck.* The year hadn't started well for him. At Fiona's big party the night before he had made an arse of himself in front of Melissa. Paralytically drunk, he had been approached by Fiona's Nick in a friendly manner. Tommy remained slumped against the pillar, studying the man through half-closed eyes. The music was beautiful, washing over him, an unflinching house rhythm with mad trumpets and sampled choirs. When Nick got round to the subject of football, he felt pissed off and straightened himself up. The film-maker played his trump card: he wanted to make a documentary for the cinema about football referees, and he wanted to use Tommy as the central figure. *This cunt doesn't even know I haven't reffed for two months.*

'Aw, why don't you just fuck off.'

Nick stared at him, unable to tell if he was joking.

'The proposal's *practically* been accepted. They've all heard of you.'

He looked at Melissa for support, but she turned away and left them.

'Go on. I said fuck off. I don't want to be in your poxy fucking programme.' He stood staring at him.

'Hey, no sweat, no sweat,' said the perplexed, then indignant Nick. 'I can find someone else. Happy New Year to you too,' he said, ironically.

'Go fuck yourself. Twat,' shouted Tommy, scowling.

Melissa heard the rest of the conversation third hand a few minutes after it happened. That was all she needed. She grabbed Tommy and drove them both home in silence, he with his head against the window, catching glimpses of the revellers in the street, she a smouldering pyre of inexpressible rage.

He watched the live game all the way through with increasing bitterness. Liverpool v. Man U, the perfect hate-fest to start the year. You couldn't say Anfield was packed any more, but it was full. The Annie Road End, where

Tommy had once stood, gobsmacked and terrified, in a hail of bangers and sparklers one November twenty years before, was smoothed and spread and regulated, like everywhere else, into rows of weedy seats. In the corner, Mancunians traded phlegm and insults with the Liverpudlians, but because there was no standing they couldn't do their party piece any more – press their faces up against the fence and bleat in mock pain, in memory of the scousers crushed to death at Hillsborough a decade before.

If he were reffing, Tommy mused, he would be wide awake and in control, instead of glued to the sofa in a fog of Red Stripe, with his better half sulking in the sewing room. And if he were a fan still he would be at some ground like this, chewing on a turkey leg and taking nips from a bottle of horrible Bells, hollering abuse and encouragement. Now he looked with envy at the referee who had been given this big fixture. His name was Henry Miller. *What a poncy name. Sounds like a rugby union official.* Tommy didn't know him very well, they were always at opposite ends of the country. But he knew of him. They shared international duties; that is, they alternated games as FIFA wished, Tommy off to Turkey, Miller off to Poland, Tommy Spain, Miller Germany, and so on. He was OK, according to Tommy. *No flair, though.* His games were always ordinary. And he didn't look that quick. Word was he spoke two foreign languages, though, as against Tommy's ropy French.

He caught a glimpse of Proctor – a black blob, a flash of neon yellow. *Bank holiday.* Tommy's mind was slow and detached, thanks to the lager, and the lager of the night before. *Good work, son.*

The game was great. There was a fight in the centre circle, three players were sent off, and Liverpool hung on to their lead for eighty-four minutes. The referee played less than a minute of injury time, much to Tommy's approval, and Taggart's chagrin. This served to catapult the referee into the limelight, however, and the goons spent a good proportion of their time discussing the brawl and the 'excellent' handling of Henry Miller from London. *How could he be from London? No one's from London.* Melissa sewed all afternoon, and went out in the evening without saying where, slamming the door behind her.

Christmas was shit. In the way that only Christmas can be: a huge anticlimax, unsuccessfully compensated for by a campaign of destructive self-indulgence. It was like a crowd of thousands being herded through a single turnstile, the way the whole country counted down to the twenty-fifth, then spewed out, dazed, on the other side. And Tommy was drawn along with them, jostled by people he had no wish to go near. He couldn't take his mind off his misery for very long.

As was their wont, they had a very adult Christmas on their own, only this time Melissa's sister Rebecca joined them. Tommy came home from work one afternoon to find her sitting on the steps smoking an MS cigarette. He smiled and greeted her warmly, ever conscious that only the great barn dance of fate had thrown them together. He took her modest rucksack and let her in. He checked out her bottom as she went up the stairs ahead of him, and saw that it was good. It was winter, but she was wearing cut-off jeans, and her legs were still tanned from her endless summer. In the time he had known the sister she had gone from being a nubile, go-straight-to-jail early teenager, to this mini-version of his girlfriend. She didn't have Melissa's tits-out Amazonian quality, the sleek hard body and the long, well-proportioned bones. She had the same nice bottom, but the rest of her was softer and rounder. Her face was rounder, although she had the same nose. Melissa had the first lines of experience around her mouth and eyes, a delicate filigree that marked her apart from all his previous girlfriends, in that he could see written on her face the years they had spent together. It was easy to trust her. He could see why he could trust her.

Rebecca made herself at home on the sofa in the lotus position. She chatted a little about the places she had been, the family with the beach house near where the Pontine Marshes used to be, the other family in Florence. Rome was the best, she declared, and as she spoke she dropped the names of Italian boys . . . Carlo and his Moto Guzzi, Segundo who took her to see *Phantom* in Verona, Fabrizio and his bar in Livorno. Tommy sat upright in his chair, listening politely. When she took her bright eyes off his to look down at the joint she was rolling, he glanced at her crotch and wondered. Being completely hypothetical, it didn't bring him much of a boner. He had a stronger, contrary feeling of being very responsible, and very old, which had a pleasant novelty about it.

*So, being twenty-one hasn't changed much.* He had a flash of when he was a teenager — a time when he assumed he would one day grow up to be a leader at the Villa, along with Mark. Then he remembered twenty-one, and how different it all was by then — textbooks, mail-order paper skeletons and brown-nosing old professors at sherry parties who wouldn't recognise an ill person if one threw up all over them. Mark too, he calculated, was out of the game by twenty-one. Tommy would have been on his own.

'Hey, I've been to Marseilles,' he interjected at one point. 'Did a

European Champions League game there last year. What did you think of it? I thought it was a fucking dump. Like Liverpool, only sunny.'

Rebecca had fallen in with a band of roving thespians on the Côte d'Azur, and one of their parents had a big house in Marseilles that wasn't being used. She couldn't act, but she could fake a noisy climax and that was enough to get her accepted as one of them.

'I hated it too, except for the Moroccan quarter. That was cool.'

There was silence for a few seconds.

'So are you still refereeing the football matches?'

Tommy felt a sting in his heart. *What does she know? She's been away so long, surely Melissa hasn't said anything? She calls them 'football matches' like she's never had to say the words before, so she probably doesn't know anything. Does she care, though? Does she give a fuck? Probably, now that I've made a bollocks of it all.*

'Er, no. Not at the moment, anyway.'

'Oh, Well, I guess the season's over now, isn't it, Christmas and all that. What are we doing for Christmas Eve, then?'

'Er, yeah, I think Melissa's got some party to go to.' It always amazed Tommy how little people knew about him and his world. They could have done so much better.

'Cool. Hey, put this on.' She gave Tommy a metal cassette. He put it on and a rumbling dub reggae bass began. Followed by some strange twisted sound effects – plastic bands being twanged, bottles being opened – but all polished and well organised. Then a very croaky voice came over the top, an old Jamaican man. He seemed to be talking about lavatory attendants and aliens.

'What's this?'

'I dunno. I was hitching in the Swiss Alps and this old black guy in a BMW stopped for me. He gave me this as I got out. Jamaican.'

'Great.' *Life's so fucking simple for these people,* thought Tommy, enviously. Rebecca was still bubbling.

'Hey, I got some great clothes in Italy. Look at this.'

She reached into her bag and pulled out a full-length dress made of a thin, stretchy nylon, which balled up to the size of an apple. It was translucent, but there was a faint pattern printed on it, repeated images in soft blues and silver. He could see her hand through both layers of the material as she held it up for him to see, and imagined the weight of her breasts making the fabric conform to their shape. He took a deep breath. *Next thing she's gonna want to try it on, and ask me what I think. The cheek of her.* But he envied her too, and admired her. Just as an eighteen-stone prison warden with thirty-inch femurs throws his weight around on the night shift; or as a crinkly executive with a brand-new Cosworth lays rubber at the lights in small country towns, and takes blind corners with his lips set tight and only the G-forces of the leaning vehicle making any difference to his expression; so young Rebecca threw her beauty around.

She threw the dress on the carpet and rummaged for the next item. *What next — a ra-ra skirt made of chain mail? A miniskirt made of inflated johnnies?* She pulled out some pink angora undies.

'These are all the rage at parties in Milano.'

'Really.' Tommy was worrying about Melissa coming home and catching them there, admiring her pants, when he heard the muffled drumming of her step coming up the stairs and the scratch of her key in the door. She entered, smiled to see her sister, dumped her books and her keys on the table, and as the youngster squealed, then laid her unlit joint down and jumped into her arms, Melissa took the whole weight of the girl on her arms and thighs.

They spun round a few times, then came apart, while Tommy watched from his armchair. Melissa sat them both down and declared that she wanted to hear everything.

'Look how brown you are, it's sickening!' she said. The hairs on Rebecca's legs were still sun-bleached fair. A bit later, Melissa groaned theatrically as the girl described a party she had attended in a cathedral in Rome, for the opening of some gym. They had just hired it, like that.

'Why couldn't they have had it in the gym?' asked Tommy, trying to hide his irritation as the women ignored him and talked on about the differences between Italian men and British. Tommy listened for a while longer, thinking he could hear his girlfriend hint that she thought her life could be better. *She'd probably rather be out getting fucked by some Vespa-riding coffee-sipper who nibbles her ear and talks the same bollocks to every girl he meets.* The thought made him gloomy, so he got up and went to start the dinner.

Rebecca stayed for five days. Her effervescence vanished in a haze of reefer smoke, and she spent most of her time sitting on the couch watching soaps and talk shows wearing his ratty old dressing gown that was rescued from the jumble pile. She was distinctly uncharming. Tommy knew it was abortion time when she got up early on the fourth day, put on her boots and her serious face, and set off for the main road just ahead of him. He saw her getting on a bus across the road, heading away from the city centre. And there were the puffy eyes when she got home in the evening. Two meetings with her sister in the bedroom. An hour on the phone long distance, again in the bedroom. She left a warm spot on the bed where she had talked, and half a box of balled-up Scotties in the waste basket. Tommy had to move into the bedroom because suddenly the women wanted to be in the lounge together.

He leaned back against the bedstead, wondering how long he would be in there. He had brought in nothing to read, though he knew he had two new pamphlets in the other room – *Guidelines for the Medical Care of Football Players* (Sw. Frs. 5.–) and *Technical Recommendations and Requirements for the Construction or Modernisation of Football Stadia* (Sw. Frs. 20.–). He had nothing to read and being a GP he had no homework. He had had his fill of homework at medical school, and now he made sure he dealt with people in the here-and-now only. If he had to look something up – the name of a drug, a peculiar collection of symptoms – he did it at work, and made the patients wait. He was not doing any research. The problems he treated were the ancient problems, the small downward adjustments of ordinary entropy: a sniffle, stiff joints, shortness of breath, a scaly ear. Any other time, stranded in the bedroom like this, he could have found something to do. If his match report was done, he would consult the FIFA *Handbook for Officials*, go through the newsletter, or reply to letters he had received pertaining to his hobby. There was always some earnest Scander with perfect idiomatic English wanting to know about the structure of the Premier League, or an army captain in Senegal who had seen him on telly and wanted to know the supplier of black shirts and knuckleduster whistles. He'd had some entertaining correspondence, and took pride in the way people around the world still considered England to be the home, if not of good football, then of civilised refereeing.

Tommy burned inside to be invited to referee an African Nations Cup game, to see the game played with flair and passion and no weight of history, and to be where he couldn't hear the commentary of the British pundits. Without wanting to arouse suspicion, he had even dropped hints whenever he was around the FIFA suits. So far, nothing like that had come his way.

Nowadays, if he was getting any letters, which he doubted, they weren't being forwarded by Lancaster Gate. As he sat twiddling his thumbs on the bed, he didn't even have the stomach to fish out his rule book and test himself on exact wordings, as he had done every few nights for the last six years. It all seemed so what's-the-fuckin'-point, as Rebecca would say.

As for his almost-sister-in-law's abortion problem, Tommy kept out of it. He exercised his man's right to choose to keep well out of the way at abortion time. After all, it wasn't his white stuff that had gone darting up her cervix. *Thank God.* To Tommy there was no need for her to get on a bus going the other way. He could have shown her a place just three streets away where she could have got sorted out, same day service, counselling, good doctors, modern equipment, and reasonably priced too. Not one of these Harley Street clinics for Catholic schoolgirls, nor a crumbling NHS annexe. They even had good magazines – current *Vogues* and *Cosmopolitans*, and *Loaded* and *Mojo* for the odd man. Tommy knew one of the doctors there, Linda Cheek, from medical school. She was OK. He liked her name.

But he kept out of it, not probing Melissa, not even asking her if she wanted to talk about it. There was a small fissure between the two of them, and this was one of those things that fell into it. And she ignored his hard-on as it lay against her coccyx that night.

After the turkey and baked stuffing, which Tommy was proud came out perfectly but which the other two didn't finish because they were hung over, snacked out, stoned, and pissed again, all at once, on Christmas Day; and after the evening Red Stripes and whisky in front of the hour-long unfunny comedy special set in a retirement community and the crappy film which they could have got any night of the year for a pound from the video shop; and after the Boxing Day breakfast out, which was horrible – garbled eggs benedict and lukewarm cappuccino served by a smartarse with a goatee – and the hours of baths and make-up and swapping clothes, the two women took off for Bristol to see their parents, whom they didn't really like. Tommy didn't like them much either, but he liked Bristol even less. It was a shithole.

"" He remembered seeing the crappy Rovers ground from the motorway, supposedly the harder of the two teams, and the cider-drinking tossers at Ashton Gate, with their farmhand accents and lack of songs. He remembered trading obscenities with some bowl-headed City fans across the double fence, years back when their team was good enough to play in the old First. They were the home team but they had no presence, no volume, no vocabulary. *The wankers.* A month from now Tommy would see a trip to Ashton Gate like a trip to Disneyland for a leukaemia tot. But in the dying days of December, when the shortest day had just passed but there were a lot more short ones to go, disgust held sway. Tommy had spent a good half-hour before that Burr-istol City game with another mate, mocking a pair of poorly kempt mods in parkas with bright red cheeks from the cold wind. Mark had just stood there, giving the evil eye to another lad until he had practically burned a hole in his soul and the lad moved away from the fence and concealed himself behind a couple of yards of bodies.

Tommy was glad the sisters were gone. If he was going to mope around the flat while everyone else refereed important football matches, he didn't want anyone watching him. The goons were constantly telling him how tough the Christmas and New Year programme was, and in his blackest hour Tommy even considered calling Mark, just to talk to him, just to check that everything that had ever happened to them had really happened. But he stopped himself. Quite apart from being in the midst of his own busy Christmas campaign, he wasn't sure Mark would want to talk to him, after his recent disastrous visit down south.

Two weeks before Christmas Mark had come down on the National Express on a Wednesday morning and strode over to the cathedral at Westminster. He sat in the rear pew and waited, until a tall man with silver hair and a kind smile greeted him. He wore a cassock with red piping, and had a silver cross around his neck. They went to his study, which looked like a university professor's, lined on four sides with old books. They had tea and talked.

Father Mark emerged smiling, and spent the rest of the morning looking around the cathedral. From the top of the striped brick tower he could see across the river to Vauxhall, while behind him were redbrick apartments and grand houses of the wealthy. Then he walked down Victoria Street and looked around the Army & Navy store. The bishop had told him he got all his black shirts there, cheaper than through the Catholic Suppliers. It was just inside his budget to get one.

The priest walked in good cheer down towards Westminster. He was amazed at the hurry everyone seemed to be in — office bods, van drivers, bicycle messengers. Some nuns smiled at him as they strolled by, and he nodded back. It always felt nice to see some of your own in strange territory, even if you didn't know them. His mate Tommy always used to say that, when they were walking round some strange city on a Saturday morning, but now he could really see it. The Houses of Parliament looked good, all cleaned up, and St James's Park was pleasant in the sunshine. He stopped at a bench and had his corned beef sandwich, which Mrs O had made him, and chatted with an old blind guy. He seemed OK until he started going on about 'the blacks'. Mark told him that he disagreed with him, and that we were all equal in the eyes of the Lord, whereupon the old geezer looked surprised and went quiet. Mark was going to give him the full sermon, but decided against it. He had said enough already. They finished in silence.

With the afternoon killed and darkness falling rapidly, Father Mark stood at the top of the steps to the Tube at Victoria, straight-backed and impassive, in his neat black crombie, shiny shoes and dog-collar, watching the traffic struggle by. His black hair was thick on top but short at the back, where it faded into the nape of his neck in a natural curve. Tommy came up the stairs two at a time. The London thing, being late, had got him.

'Tommy.'

'Hey! Mark.' They shook hands warmly and Tommy led him back down the steps to the Tube. *Even dressed like that in the middle of London he looks good.*

'So how'd your day go? Business good? How was the top brass?'

'Great. I met the archbish. We had a good chat.'

'No shit? The archbishop? As in, "We pray for N., our archbishop, and for Bishop N.?"'

Mark just smiled.

'So,' said Tommy, suspiciously. 'What does the old Church have in store for you, then?'

'Ah, y'know, wanted to know about our parish, general stuff.'

'They keep close tabs on you, then?' Tommy handed him a ticket and they went through the turnstiles.

'No, not really.'

Since he didn't seem to want to talk about it, Tommy didn't push it. He launched into an update of his own dealings with the brass. The fucking bureaucrats. The wankers who kept them in power. The other refs who hadn't lifted a finger to help. Mark listened, sympathetically. Tommy kept going as they changed trains, piling up the woes.

The priest listened for several stops, but gradually an impatience began creeping over him. At last he interrupted. 'But what did you do that they stopped you reffing? Come on, you must have done something.'

'Nothing! I'm telling you. Nothing out of the ordinary. I kicked the ball once. Twice. Played around with it. I told you that. Bit controversial sometimes, but not enough to outweigh the good I do. I was still getting good marks from the observers. Y'know, controversy seems to have followed me around this season. I was late for a game, but not that late. The only thing I can think explains it is ...' He paused, looking a bit uncomfortable.

'What?'

'Well, that maybe I'm *too* good.'

Mark guffawed, sarcastically. 'I think maybe you've been down here too long.'

Tommy was surprised. This was the first sign of the old Mark nastiness. On the one hand he wanted to encourage it. On the other, it was aimed at himself.

'What do you mean?'

'Well, that's the attitude down here, isn't it? Everyone thinks they're so *great*.'

He had never seen a priest sneer before. Tommy found himself in the position of having to defend the very people he cursed daily.

'Well, not everyone.'

Mark tossed his head in disagreement. They were silent together for two whole stops, sitting side by side, nudged in unison by the jolting train, watching the people around them. Tommy was trying to put faces to his friend's comment. People who thought they were so great. Most people on the train just looked ill and boring to him. He had promised he would be a good host to Mark, however, so he changed the subject.

'Did you see the Leicester ground on telly last night? Well, anyway, they're shutting it down, they can't afford to play there any more. They're gonna move to a sports centre.' He paused. 'Remember when we went there? The fence posts flying through the air? Fighting with the pigs on the pitch?' He thought he caught a trace of a smile on the edge of Mark's mouth, and set about tending it like the shoot of a plant, or a wisp of flame. He summoned up a stream of details, many of which featured himself and Mark in a heroic light, singing and charging and fighting, inside the ground and outside, the football lost beneath the real excitement. Mark listened, grunting occasionally, but would not be drawn.

When they got out at the other end, the streets were shiny with rain. They put up their collars and walked into it without comment. *I must remember to hand over that umbrella.*

Tommy opened the flat door and welcomed his friend in. They were hit by the warm breath of air and the bright light after the cold staircase.

'Mel? Where are you?'

'I'm in here,' came a muffled voice from the bedroom.

'Here, siddown, siddown. Hang your coat over there.'

Tommy walked into the bedroom and found Melissa doing her face in the mirror. She looked great, and blew him a theatrical kiss.

'I've got Mark in there.' He looked down at her. She was wearing a sheer white blouse with a white lace bra, and an ankle-length black skirt with a split up the front. 'Where've you been?' he asked, a little worried.

'Nowhere. Shopping. School's out, remember.'

'Oh yeah. Are you gonna change?'

She spoke as she painted her lips, without moving a single facial muscle. 'No. This is it.'

'Mel! You can't wear that! He's a fucking priest!'

He could see the outline of her nipples through the cloth already. He knew exactly what it would be like if she got any attention.

She stood up and kissed his forehead. 'Watch me.' She marched into the lounge and extended her hand before her, like some society chick. As he watched her bottom swaying in the skirt, and her fine carriage, from the heels which she had chosen to wear in the house up to her slender neck with the hair pulled up above it, he marvelled at her. He loved the fact that she still got dressed up. *She looks like a business exec, a high-class hooker and an air hostess all at once.* He saw Mark rise from the couch and meet her gaze, and her handshake, with a firmness and a warmth he hadn't expected. *They make a nice couple together, the tall handsome beasts,* he thought admiringly.

And they got on handsomely for the first forty-five minutes. Father Mark even had a glass of wine. The conversation began at the shallow end, as Mark was asked to recount his day in the Smoke. By comparison the couple weren't interested in each other's day, so they plied Mark for more and more information. Tommy filled his and Melissa's glasses again and went to put on the dinner. He heard laughter, and felt mightily relieved. He went back in and they were talking about Tommy's trips to Birmingham. She was telling versions of what he had told her, about the kids and the depressing living room with the couch and covered telly, and the lack of a congregation. He tried to intervene but the wine made it difficult to be casual about it. He saw the same faint look of impatience coming over Mark as he had on the Tube. Mark stonewalled, the way he had earlier.

'Well, we don't have a budget for replacing worldly things.'

'Why not? Worldly things are useful too. Telly helps you learn about the world.'

'Well,' and Mark coughed, a little embarrassed, patronising cough, 'I think I know enough about the world not to have to study those sorts of details any more.'

Tommy was disappointed. He didn't like Mark's tone to his girlfriend, but he forced himself to forgive it instantly, as two against one on a guest seemed unfair. Besides, he knew Melissa could take care of herself. The priest clearly didn't have a clue what he was getting into with Melissa. Being surrounded by little kids all day, she jumped at any chance of a proper argument with an adult. And Mark was ripe for the picking.

'Oh, the kids I see every day care more about worldly things, and the world they see in the television, than anything. That's what they learn from. Animals, cartoons, pop videos, that's what they care about. God and Baby Jesus are just a story we trot out for them once a year. They don't know what Easter is. We don't even bother with it any more.'

'Well, maybe you should.'

'No. Because I don't think it's going to help them. They can learn it when they're older, when they can choose.'

'I think we should get them while they're young, and give them the bedrock to fall back on later in life. That's what worked for me.'

'Huh.' She snorted loudly.

Mark looked over at Tommy with a penetrating glare. Tommy realised the priest didn't know where he stood. Did she know about his Villa days? Did she know about chasing Leeds fans all over the market and kicking their heads in? About hurling dustbins through the windows of random terraced houses? He was stuck.

'Anyway, love, I need help with the vegetables.' It was a standard dinner party cop-out, and he cringed to pull it on Mark. Melissa obeyed it robotically. *He's probably never been to a dinner like this in his life*, thought Tommy in shame.

'Just go easy on him, eh, Mel?' he whispered to her, putting his head inside the fridge with hers.

'Tommy, you . . .' She halted her protest. 'Here. This broccoli, and this bag of salad. OK? No slimy stuff. I'm going back in.'

When Tommy rejoined them they were talking about the new Pope. Mark was defending him, even though Melissa was doing gymnastics to make it clear she wasn't attacking him for his race, just for being another 'bejewelled puppeteer', as she put it. Tommy hadn't heard that from her before. He was surprised. So they talked about black-and-white things for a while, and they seemed to live on two different planets, or in two very different cities, with Tommy as the go-between. Melissa was on the lookout for racism, Mark for lost souls.

The food interrupted all this for a moment. Melissa went to the toilet. Tommy tried to joke about what a feisty girl she was, but Mark just looked uncomfortable. It was eight o'clock, and he mentioned his bus for the first time, which was going at ten-thirty. Tommy said he thought he was staying the night, but Mark said he had a day return.

He wasn't sure whether the priest was lying. The old Mark didn't used to lie much. He'd nut people, or try to push them into traffic, but he never had much reason to lie. Depressed, Tommy let it go.

'I'll give you a lift.'

The food was a mistake too. For some reason he made Chicken Kiev, which seemed to surprise Mark when he cut into it and the garlic butter burst out, weeping like abscess fluid on his plate. The priest put on a brave face. Melissa didn't really like it either, but Tommy had wanted to make something nice, something he wouldn't get in Brum.

Melissa had her fourth glass of wine and the conversation came around to theology, about which she knew nothing, then church decor, vestments, church architecture, war damage, Birmingham City Council (that was Tommy's effort to steer it), King Kong, the Bull Ring, football, refereeing, school again, and then what makes little boys bad. All the while Mark looked increasingly uncomfortable, unused as he was to being probed and attacked in such a subtle and sustained way. She was tossing her lovely hair a lot. Mark sat, stiller and stiller, as though not wanting to be noticed. The dinner was going on for ever. Once, when he wasn't in the conversation, he let his gaze rest momentarily on Melissa's blouse, and at times he could make out the outline of her breasts, and caught the shadows of her nipples, and was caught looking by both of them.

There was no pudding. Melissa smoked a cigarette, to look sophisticated, Tommy finished off the wine. Mark had a cup of coffee that took ages to make. They were both so depressed by it all that Tommy was getting used to the idea that the bus was leaving with Mark on it in an hour. Then the conversation turned to abortion and they were off again.

Tommy put a record on, by the Au Pairs, to try to distract them, but Mark didn't recognise it and by the third track it was jumping all over the place. He was reluctantly drawn into the argument to give his expert medical opinion, while Mark leaned forward and gushed about fetuses sucking their thumbs and Melissa told about friends whose lives had been ruined by bringing up kids that everyone ended up hating.

Melissa was surprised to hear, at ten o'clock, that the guest was leaving.

'I can't give you a lift!' she blurted. 'I'm way over.'

'I know,' Tommy jumped in. 'I'm OK, though. I only had a couple of glasses. I can take your car, can't I?'

She was stuck. She agreed. And in her alcoholic haze she tried to make pretty with Father Mark, first imploring him to stay, then to come again, finally giving him a London hug that totally took him by surprise. The sensation of her breasts against his chest took his breath away. Their softness and their warmth was no surprise, but the fact that she was pressing them against him was. He started regretting the hostility he felt towards her, even if she did advocate infanticide. He didn't know someone could tear him apart like that and then still show him love. Confused, he got his coat on, Tommy grabbed the car keys, and the men left.

Driving through the West End in the rain, Tommy apologised several times for his girlfriend, until it was fully accepted and, of course, declined as unnecessary. Then Tommy hated himself for betraying her like this. And he hated his girlfriend for not making an effort to behave better, and not go on about screwing and abortions and freemasons all night. And he hated Mark for changing so much that he had to treat him with kid gloves all the time.

He dropped the priest off and watched him moving away under the streetlights in the rain, until he was just a silhouette hurrying forward into the night. Suddenly, some cockney cab driver behind Tommy bibbed his horn for him to move. Tommy pulled out, flicked the Vs to the cabbie just for being a cockney, and drove back across the empty city, wondering why everyone was such a bunch of cunts. No one would go out of their way for anyone any more. *Fuck! I forgot to give him the fucking umbrella. Bollocks.* 'BOLLOCKS!' he shouted, in the muffling confines of the car.

It was January, and Tommy was in Birmingham for the second local derby of the season with Blues, but he was there to watch, not to officiate. Nearer the kick-off on the day of a Villa home game the number seven bus would usually be crowded with fans heading to the ground — a few away fans downstairs keeping out of trouble, a lot of old men and sons crossing the city from nicer parts of town like Northfield, which was in the south, and Five Ways, which was named after a roundabout. There would be some lads at the back, getting harder and harder the nearer the ground they got, shedding their weekly identity, whatever it might be — Ladywood bank clerk, Warley shop assistant — and getting nasty for Aston. These days the holes were put in the washers abroad.

Tommy remembered the dedicated days when he and Mark and a few others would go into town on the day of a home game to see what was up, and to drink in a Villa pub like the Hole in the Wall, then get the bus all the way back to the ground for three o'clock. It seemed a bit stupid now, though he marvelled at his youthful dedication.

Most of the traffic was going the other way. The bus was practically empty, except for early shoppers who had done town, mum-and-daughter pairs, and pensioners with their market bargains. But Tommy could see atmosphere out of the window: a flash of claret and blue here, a Blues fan watching from the door of a pub there. His leg ached and his eyebrow smarted, and he longed to crack someone.

He was going to meet Mark and they'd go to the game together. Mark had been persuaded. He had the afternoon off. And Tommy was happy to be out of London, home of his wretched failure.

When he got to Aston, he saw there was a crowd around the church gable as he rounded the corner – a wedding. Remembering the state of his face, Tommy ducked into the Indian shop. A ten-year-old girl with two long plaits sat behind the counter watching cartoons on a portable TV. As soon as he entered she got up, and shouted, 'Mum? Mu-um! Customer!' Her mother came out, eyeing Tommy with a trace of suspicion.

'Morning. Have you got any plasters?'

'Just a moment. I used the last ones on her.

The woman disappeared into the back. Tommy stood waiting.

'I fell ov-a,' said the girl suddenly, pulling up her skirt. She showed Tommy the little pink plaster on her knee.

'Ooh. Did it hurt?'

She nodded her head, but said 'No', all the time staring into his eyes, reading his response.

'Worrappened to your eye?' she asked.

'Oh, I walked into a door. I'm so stupid,' he said, pulling a face.

She giggled. *Well, she fell for that one at least.*

Mother returned with a fresh pack. He put the plaster on in the reflection of the door and thanked her.

The bell dinged as he left, and he noticed the church bells ringing for the first time. *God, I never knew Catholics rang the bells. Where's that Mark scallywag . . .* The first thing he saw was the battered black Vespa parked on the street.

Mark was shaking hands, accepting thanks and bestowing congratulations on the newly-wed families. Milling around inside the railings were several thick-set men in suits, one hand in a pocket, smoking and looking at their shoes. A gaggle of chunky women, all different generations, all the same heft, squeezed into thin two-piece outfits, their thick ankles disappearing into pale stilettos, stood around cooing as the bride and groom, a lanky woman with a face like a hatchet and a short barrel of a man with red skin, posed for photos to one side. Dotted stiffly among the crowd was the odd string bean of a person, but they had their own huddle over to the other side, smoking and staring at the happy couple, making sarcastic comments. Mark looked up from the tiny woman who was talking to him, caught Tommy's eye and, smiling, gave a small toss of the head that could only mean 'see you at the house'. A slight wave went through him. *That was the same nod he used to use to get us to cross over, or turn up a side road.* Tommy didn't like it. It seemed like a waste.

Father Kelly scowled at him when he opened the door.

'O'Mally is next door,' was all he said.

'Oh. Yeah.' It was left up to him where to wait. He didn't fancy the parlour again, where he had slept before, so he sat at the kitchen table with the elder priest, who was engrossed in the form in the back of the newspaper. There was no one else around. No Mrs O to make him tea, and the pot felt lukewarm. Nothing to read, except a Bible and some other religious-looking stuff in a glass-fronted bookcase. There was a story about the Blues–Villa game on the back of the newspaper, but the page flopped down, obscuring most of it. Tommy drummed his fingers on the table. Father Kelly lowered his paper just enough for a dark eye to glare at him through his glasses, halting him in mid-paradiddle.

'I think I'll just use the toilet,' he said, and got up.

The bathroom slowly came back to him from the last time he was there, pissed out of his head. The scalding Heat Miser, the magnetic Virgin on the high, damp cistern, the sad old bathtub with the indelible ring of ancient priests. After zipping up and combing his hair, he stood on the landing and listened. *Not going down there with that old fart again. Hmmm . . .* Mark's door was wide open. He could see the foot of the narrow old bed. He listened again, then crept in.

The room was even more spartan than before. The modest clutter of the desk had been eliminated. The reference books were now over to the side on a shelf, and instead of the open exercise book and fountain pen, there was a flat black box with an electric lead coming from it.

*Fuck me. The Church has got computers. It really is the end of the millennium.*

The front door slammed. He heard Mark going into the kitchen and a muffled tenor grunt coming from the elder priest, then Mark's light step coming up the stairs two at a time.

*Fuck.* Tommy didn't know where to stand. He walked towards the doorway, which made him feel even more guilty, like he was trying to flee. But Mark came in beaming.

'Hey, Tommy lad! Sorry I was running late. You saw the wedding, didn't you? The groom's lot nearly didn't show – he just got out of Winson Green this morning, but the screws made him wait extra.'

*Screws?* It came out of his mouth as natural as anything, and was music to Tommy's ears. Mark didn't bat an eyelid – he seemed high and full of energy – pumping Tommy's hand and clapping him on the back. The misery of the dinner party seemed to have been erased. Sensing Tommy's embarrassment at being caught in his bedroom, Mark put him at his ease.

'Father Kelly likes his paper on a Saturday morning. You're better off up here. Anyway, look at this, mate, I'm dying to show it you.'

He went over to the computer, and pressed the catch on the front. The lid sprung open with a smooth movement, accompanied by an electronic fanfare and a three-syllable sample of a choir, revealing a luminous colour screen which stretched right to the edge of the lid, with no perceptible frame.

Tommy said nothing.

'It's an IBM ThinkPad 990 with five hundred and twelve megs of RAM, a two-gig chip, one teraflop hard drive, sixteen megs of VRAM, full wireless modem, T2 link, two-day battery, running Windows 2000 and fully Oracle-compliant.'

'What the fuck does all that mean?' Tommy didn't like hearing all this shit about megs and teraflops. He didn't know what any of it meant. He immediately thought of Marge and the computer at work, and how the screen always froze whenever he touched it. The ThinkPad was now showing clear, television-quality video. The camera-eye view swooped through a Norman arch and focused on an image of the Pontiff, who now seemed to be hovering above the high altar at St Peter's in Rome. The choir's hosanna swelled – Tommy was surprised that the sound from the little speakers wasn't at all tinny – and the background changed. First to heavenly blue with fluffy white clouds, then to an aerial shot of a Brazilian favela with children waving upwards and the shadow of a helicopter moving across them, then to what looked like a giant funfair, illuminated at night. It all reminded him of an expensive car advert.

'They gave us all one of them. Well, one per parish. Father K wasn't very interested, he told me to deal with it.' Mark was talking quickly, excitedly. Tommy hadn't seen him like this for years. It was just like when he was a normal kid, and he got his racer for Christmas. Long after everybody else got bikes, because his family were dirt poor, but still, he had been grateful, and enthusiastic, and rode it everywhere for years.

'Who? The . . . Catholic Church?'

'Yeah. It's not just at the archdiocese level, this is national. International, in fact. Listen. This is his Message for the Day.'

Mark zoomed in on the handsome face, which was managing both to smile and show deep concern in its dark brown eyes at the same time. In a heavy African accent, the Pope was going on about charity, and the need to reach out even further, not just with money but with charitable acts. 'Think of this, my children. Your words today are cast into the air, just as they always were, and vanish in an instant. And your money today is written in electrons, and can be lost or erased just as easily. But your deeds, your actions, are as solid and as worthwhile as ever. They are worth more, in fact, my children. Go therefore, and change the world with your body, with your behaviour. Stand tall, and show others the way.'

Mark was engrossed, but he sensed his friend shifting on his feet.

'I've seen it already today,' he said, closing the lid of the machine to turn it off. Tommy was relieved. It was bad enough having to listen to Church gobbledygook, let alone computer-talk. But more than that, he resented seeing his friend change yet again. As the lid closed it gave one last sound, a long, benedictive 'A-men'.

'Very quaint,' said Tommy, unable to contain his sarcasm.

'Yeah, it came set up like that. Some of it's good, but you can customise it to open however you want, go wherever you want. I'm gonna keep the Pope, though. I like the Wog Pontiff, as Father Kelly calls him. He's a very impressive guy.'

The word went through Tommy like an electric shock, then he laughed at the thought of the old priest downstairs.

'So let me get this straight. That thing dials up the Vatican and fetches you messages from his Holiness?'

'Absolutely!'

'The Pope is in the house!' shouted Tommy, gleefully. Mark just smiled back. 'It's rid . . . well, I s'pose you find it useful.'

'It's great. You can download sermon themes, you can look things up in the Vatican Library . . . Just think of that, Tommy, the Vatican Library! I've never even been abroad, but I can go to Rome from my desk!'

'You *have* been abroad!' Tommy exclaimed. 'What about Holland for the European Cup Final?'

'Oh yeah. I forgot about that,' he said sheepishly. 'How did I forget that?'

'Only the greatest night in our history, that's all.'

'Yeah. I s'pose it didn't feel like abroad, all those Villa fans everywhere. Getting on the plane at Elmdon and getting off forty-five minutes later in Rotterdam. Hmmm.' He fell into contemplation.

'That was a magic night, man. You know, I haven't met a single person for about ten years that was there too. Pretty boring game, though. And no aggro. But it was a good crack, wasn't it, taunting the Cloggies and the Germans. That was before they thought they were hard, eh?'

Mark wasn't listening.

'I couldn't believe you didn't end up in the cells that night.'

'Eh? Oh yeah.' He was back. 'I think I was watching the football for once. Man, I'd forgotten all about that.'

'I've still got the programme at home, I must bring it up some time.'

'Yeah, great.' He looked at his watch. It was one o'clock. 'We'd better get going if we're going to make it to this match.'

They went downstairs. Tommy was relieved that he wasn't trying to get out of it. He had a hunger to go to this game, he wanted to march through the streets all the way. And he wanted Mark right there with him. Mark changed his shirt for a plain black Fred Perry, over which he wore a cardigan, then a long black raincoat.

'Same coat as the old days, eh?' asked Tommy.

'Yeah. It's still in pretty good nick.'

Father Kelly grunted as they nodded goodbye and left, then got up to watch them go down the street from the front room window. It was bitterly cold outside.

'Got any colours?' asked the priest. He was being surprisingly cheerful today.

'Oh. No. I never thought of that. It's been so long, I don't know what people are doing any more. I mean, apart from all those cunts with the team shirts on,' said Tommy. They were both from the minimalist age, when big knotted scarves gave way to plain clothing – cords and a tight jumper with a tiny metal badge that invited the opposition to get right up close before they knew who you were. After that it had got weird, like undercover wear – you had to know people just by the style of their clothes if you didn't know their face. Mark never seemed to have any trouble. He could sniff out, say, a Stoke fan, or Bolton – the kind of clubs you didn't really get worked up about – from across six lanes of motorway. Tommy had never been so certain. Sure, he could spot a scouser a mile off, and the Mancunians, as they started dressing like scallies too. Cockneys always looked a bit different — a bit fatter, a bit flasher — but that was about it. If a load of Forest came round the corner incognito, he wouldn't really be sure till he heard their voices.

'You can't really see from the pitch, everything happens so quick. And as for Villa, I've never had any of their games, ever.' They were walking to the game, still in the purest of Villa territory, heading south by south-east. They went up Bevington Road to Upper Sutton Street, then left towards Rocky Lane.

They had to raise their voices above the loud white noise of the Aston Expressway. 'Mind you, I never could tell this one either.'

'What?' asked Mark, astonished. 'You can't tell a Blues fan from Villa?'

'Well, er, not on a day like this. I mean it's hard, innit? Everyone mixing round the ground. The voices are the same ...' He felt like one of his patients when he has just coaxed it out of them that they were colour blind, or dyslexic or, worst of all, illiterate. 'I always knew better in town, you know, when we weren't playing 'em. But this ... ah, maybe the beer helps. I dunno.'

To his relief, Mark was amused rather than scornful, so he went on.

'Like this morning. I could tell they were City. But by that time ...'

Mark raised his eyebrows and interrupted him. 'You got *that* this morning? From City fans?'

'Yeah,' said Tommy, thinking this would bring out the old Mark. 'Look out for a blond-haired fucker in a green jacket. If I see him again I'm gonna drop him.'

Mark swung round and stopped him in his tracks.

'Hold on. Let's get it straight from the start, Tommy. No trouble. OK? I'm not going anywhere near trouble. I'm a priest now, for Christ's ... yeah, for Christ's sake. I don't go for the knock any more. Is that clear? I'm just going to watch the game, that's all. So don't go dragging me into anything. Is that clear?'

His face was about a foot away from Tommy's, and the blue eyes were burning into him. He had an idea what it would be like to be on the end of some vintage Mark hassle. He could see the black hairs of his chin and upper lip flush with the surface of the pores from where he had shaved that morning for the wedding. Tommy had never had a fight with Mark — at least not since Mark had suddenly become very hard around the age of fifteen. It wasn't just that this was the sensible option. Tommy didn't go in for the real gratuitous violence, and Mark never got pissed. They were always on the same side, or one of them was absent.

He started to say something in his defence, then stopped.

'I'm sorry, mate. I forgot what's it's like for you.'

Mark squinted a little, trying to work out the exact meaning of this response, but then he let it drop. He sighed, continued walking, and went back to being pleasant again.

They didn't speak much until they got on to Rocky Lane. Tommy smoked two cigarettes, which tasted good in the cold air. He was now up to a pack a week. There were some Villa up ahead, but no one they recognised from that distance.

'Welcome to Heartlands. What the fuck is Heartlands?' he asked.

'It's . . . Heartlands, innit? New developments. High tech.'

'Huh.'

Partly from memory, partly from instinct, they carried on, over the canal. Most other people walking from the north were following the line of the Aston Expressway, up to Dartmouth Circus, the huge island with the pump in the middle, then down Dartmouth Street into Bordesley. Blues land. But they weren't interested in that way.

'Birmingham & Fazeley Canal,' read Tommy from a plaque. He hadn't been here for years. There was another industrial park, this one with a Mediterranean restaurant that overlooked the canal. He looked over the wall. There was a bit of ice left, on the shady side, with a tubular steel chair set in it. This was always the bit where it started to feel strange. They weren't yet halfway there, but there was something about going past the breaker's yard and under the next railway bridge that felt like Blues. He never liked grounds like that. The old Millwall Den was like that, a fucking mess of cobbled streets, railways and wily cockneys. He had only been there once, and that was enough. He looked over at Mark, who seemed cheerful enough. Every now and then he'd come out with something a bit unconnected to the matter at hand – something about his impression of London, or a piece of team news that was several weeks old. Tommy was feeling a bit too edgy to follow it all. The fags made him feel a bit loopy too. He fancied a drink. This was the bit he always found hard to calculate. Where were the tectonic plates that separated Blues territory from Villa? How could you calculate the gravity of a ground? Did you go by the number of fans? If so, with Blues having only about fifteen thousand to Villa's thirty thousand, you would draw the line two-thirds of the way between them, nearer St Andrews – their poxy hole.

So he asked Mark his opinion. Mark reckoned Blues didn't start until right down by Watery Lane, at least, beyond all the railway lines. He definitely knew they stretched right out east, beyond Stechford and Acock's Green, but he seemed to think that was the limit of their little wedge of the pie.

'But other factors must influence it,' Tommy replied, noticing he was sounding like a doctor again for a moment. 'Blues are shit. They always have been. I mean, where would their part-time supporters come from? You'd have to be some strange kind of glory-hunter to follow them only in their good days, when they're fighting for a place in the play-offs, or more likely when they're fighting for their fucking lives on the last day of the season. I don't get it.'

At the top of Rocky Lane they turned right and continued south, down towards Nechells Parkway. *Nechells. Now that's always sounded like Blues to me. But then I did meet a few Villa from there. Maybe 'cos we mixed mainly with people from the north of the city we never met any of these borderline cases?*

'What about Nechells, then?'

'Villa, definitely.'

'Yeah, but look at it. It's a shithole.' BCFC was spray-painted on to one of the maisonettes – from the inside. It looked like someone living there had just leaned out of the window and done their business.

Out of nowhere, they heard men's voices uplifted in song, and turned to look behind them. There were maybe ten blokes a hundred yards back, singing.

> *'Come to Birmingham you will see,*
> *Ansell's brewery, M&B,*
> *We don't drink whisky and we don't drink rum,*
> *We are the Villa boys, from Brum.'*

Tommy smiled. It was sweet music. And he was relieved. There were only the two of them after all. Mark smiled too – the sound seemed to make him happy. For a moment he debated whether to wait for them, but he decided to press on.

'Plus,' said Tommy, 'they are nearer the city centre, which being non-residential, means they have to get some of their fans from us.'

'No it doesn't. They just go without.'

Without saying a word, they jinked left and then right at Saltley Road, joining a flow of pedestrians.

'You know what I used to like about walking to a ground?' said Mark suddenly. 'Any ground, not just the Villa. Preferably somewhere away. That feeling that we'd all get there in the end. That even though we all set off at different times and took different routes, we'd all come to the same destination in the end.'

'Sounds like an idea for a sermon,' said Tommy, laughing at his friend.

The priest shrugged. 'Hey, you might be right.'

'You should stick it out there on the Net or whatever it's called, see if there are any takers.' Tommy was finding new ways to deal with the priest all the time. His nice side seemed always to be in control – he didn't wanted to step on Mark's holy toes. And he realised he had become a sarcastic bastard since moving to London. But he was still fucked off about Blondie and his pals jumping him in town – *me! A thirty-five-year-old bloke!* – and thought it would be nice if there was some trouble today. And to be involved in it. And to have Mark there alongside him, like the old days. For a few hours at least, he had forgotten his refereeing woes.

The way they were going, they wanted to cut through the middle of an area that was bounded by a busy road, Nechells Parkway, on the one side, and by the railway sidings on the other. Duddeston Station, a little local station, sat in the middle of it.

'This is definitely Blues round here,' said Tommy.

'No way! Look around you.'

There were now hundreds of people around them. The lean-looking youths with the cold eyes, and the beer-bellied elders, were all Villa. Some of them had claret-and-blue shirts on; one bloke had a flag around him, a cross of St George with 'A VFC Kingstanding' on it.

'Fuck it, anyway. I'm itching for a pint.'

The priest looked slightly disapproving. He knew what this meant. The later you left it the better the aggro. And the more you drank the better the aggro. And the more you associated with other fans, the better the aggro. He looked at his watch, but it was only ten minutes to two. He sighed.

'Oh, go on, then. Remember what I said, though.'

Tommy decided to ignore that remark. They squeezed into a little pub called the Rocket, which was hot from the press of bodies.

'We're the Vi-lla, we're the Vi-lla, we are the champions!' The beat was stamped out on the pub carpet. Tommy's hair stood up on his neck. He hadn't been in an atmosphere like this — so loving, so dangerous — for a decade. A kid of about twenty with a dozen studs through his nose, mouth and ears stood up on a table and shouted:

'Shit. On. The City!'

And the whole pub joined in as one, to the tune of 'Roll Out the Barrel'.

'Shit on the City tonight!' The pitch rose.

'Shit, on, the City, shit on the City tonight!' Then it became lower and jollier. 'Shit, on, the Cit-ay, shit on the City ton-ight.' Finishing almost euphorically:

'Everybody shit on the City, 'cos they're a lo-ad, of, shi-i-ite!'

It was beautiful. Tommy pushed his way to the bar and got four pints. You never knew when it might end. When he got back to Mark, he was talking to someone. It was old Bonce. Bonce with touches of grey hair at his temples now.

'Fuck me,' said Bonce. 'Look who else we're blessed with today. Doctor doctor . . .' He didn't hear the rest, because someone with a hard, resonant voice started in with an old song about an old Blues manager, to the tune of 'Tavern in the Town':

> *'There's a circus in this town,*
> *Barry Fry's a fucking clown . . .'*

Bonce helped himself to a pint, Mark took one and took a tiny sip, and Tommy shut his eyes and drank a third of each of the remaining two, to prevent spillage.

Bonce pointed over at the corner. 'Terry's over there, and Trevor.'

''Kin' hell,' said Tommy. He could see their faces, the same shape as ever, apart from a little sagging around the cheeks, and the skin just a little more weather-beaten.

The kid with the piercings suddenly started another song, to the tune of the Monkees' 'Daydream Believer', everyone else joining in on the second line . . .

> *'Cheer up Trevor Francis,*
> *Oh, what can it mean?*
> *To a sad blue-nosed bastard,*
> *And a shit football te-ee-eam . . .'*

Tommy finished his left pint, and started to feel very, very glad that he was there. After a moment's pause at the end of the song, while people were still laughing and chattering, the deep voice started in again with the 'Winter Wonderland' tune. 'Bir-ming-um . . .'

And the whole pub jumped in for the rest:

> '. . . are you listenin'?
> To the song we are singin'?
> We're walking along, singing a song,
> Shitting on the City as we go-o-oh.'

Tommy wasn't joining in yet, he was still in thrall, and he felt like too much of an outsider. This was everything he had left behind when he crossed over to refereeing, and it looked to him like the only other pure part of the sport remaining. The skin on his back and skull tightened each time a song began, and he shuddered as the hard punch of the voices came back off the yellowed ceiling mouldings and the floor shook under him. With the lager swirling round his brain, he hit euphoria.

The pasty faces, the bare arms and hands tattooed, the balding heads and the badly bleached heads in the waning sunshine slanting through the window – it all seemed to make a mockery of his silly project of healing people, and trying to persuade them to eat well and look after their bodies. Mark was talking to someone he didn't recognise, smiling and laughing his low-key laugh. Tommy was even more pleased. He had been worried the swearing and the aggression, the sheer unholiness of it all, would put the priest off. From what he could remember, priests didn't like all that. There was a limit to how close to the people they would get to save their souls. *What the fuck am I thinking of? This is in his bones, there's no getting round that. And here's me all worried.*

Another song started, and the words were coming out of Tommy's mouth before he knew it was happening. Once he realised what he was doing, his stomach tightened but the words still came out clear and loud. It was the 'Glory Glory Hallelujah' tune, a hymn he had never sung, or heard sung, except by Evangelical Protestants on television.

'My eyes have seen the glory of the Villa win the Cup . . .' Glancing round the room, he could see no one who could say that with any honesty. You'd have had to have been a small boy or older in 1957, well over forty years ago, to sing that. But that didn't matter. When they got to the end of the next line, though – 'Seven times we've won it, no one else can catch us up' – Tommy sang it as usual, but everyone else coughed into their sleeves and muttered theatrically – a few teams had caught Villa up since the glory days. But the rest was true:

> 'We are the boys in claret and blue, we are the chosen few
> And the Villa go marching ON! ON! ON!'

Other fuckers sang it too, Tommy knew, they always had. Several times he had heard it ringing in his ears at Old Trafford, when he collected the muddy ball from some losing player trudging off the pitch, but that wasn't any reason not to sing it. *If your self-esteem is dependent on the opinion of people more successful than you, you'd never do anything.* That was just the sort of thing he was always telling his patients, especially when he could see that in a few years they'd have medicated themselves into a corner. If they were next door with Dr Aktar, anyway.

'Spacing out, Tommy?' It was Mark.

'No, yeah . . . shit, this is great. I can't believe so little's changed.'

'Looks pretty different from where you stand, doesn't it?'

Then he blurted out, 'Hey, Mark, about Melissa. She didn't mean any harm. She was just a bit pissed. In fact she wasn't that pissed. She told me she was really glad to meet you. She wants you to come round again, next time you're down. Come and stay. She just gets . . . she just likes to argue a lot. A bit.'

'Has she got a sister?' said a voice in his other ear. ''Cuz if she has *I'll* fuck her.'

He turned to see Jimmy. 'Jimmy! What are you doing here?'

'What the fuck are *you* doing here, more like?'

Tommy laughed in agreement. He liked Jimmy. He was one of those funny blokes who was easily distracted at games: when he was a skinhead he'd moonstomp around the empty bits of terraces at away grounds. And the home fans, all the old women and fat businessmen, would stare at him in disgust, glad he was behind a high fence.

'Yes, she has actually.'

'Good!'

'So how the fuck are you?'

Jimmy, it turned out, was now a bookie. Which made sense, since he was always down the old dog track in Perry Barr, with his dad, when he wasn't looking for his dad in the Corals and Ladbrokes around the area. Jimmy's dad was a professional gambler – he made money betting, and it looked like one day he would merge seamlessly into the bookmaking world and become one, crossing over like a ghost passing from one room to another through the wall. He made money – at least until the kids left home, and then it all started going wrong. Now he was just a pissed old Paddy betting two fivers a day. But Jimmy had ended up marrying a bookie's daughter, and now ran a healthy operation a few miles from where he grew up. 'Villa for the Cup!' he joked with Tommy. 'I'll give you fifty to one.'

When Jimmy spotted Father Mark, who had made no attempt to come forward from behind Tommy's shoulder, they went through the whole thing again, although the handshake was noticeably more respectful. The drink had knocked the edges off everything now, though, it was all flowing for Tommy. He could forget things quickly. He let the two of them catch up, and fetched another three pints from the bar, which was mysteriously still serving.

He stared proudly around the room. It was like going to Wembley. People were standing on tables, singing and stamping their feet. There was a big flag across the window, and the sun was shining through it, showing up the stitching and the grease stains. At one table was a pretty girl in a Villa shirt. Her boyfriend had her arm around her. She had good hair and good skin – *she must be a student*, he thought. She had a nice pair of tits too. *But all tits look nice in a Villa shirt. Except Bonce's.* The air was blue with cigarette smoke. A bloke standing on a chair with a crumpled face – he looked like a Van Gogh peasant – had his jeans down and was mooning out of the window at the police.

There was a song Tommy loved to start, to the tune of 'My Old Man Said Follow the Van'. The bloke with the deep voice behind him started it.

> *'My old man said be a City fan,*
> *But I said bollocks, you old cunt!*
> *We hate the Blues and we fucking know it,*
> *We hate the Blues and we're gonna show it!'*

It got higher, and slower, and more deliberate, and Tommy felt his spirits soar – especially because they were still singing the names of the old players, who by now were probably all youth team coaches and minicab drivers and brewery reps:

> 'There's Spinksy and Birchy, an' Alan McInally,
> They're the boys who're gonna do us proud,
> So if you support the Blues you're a blue-nosed bastard,
> And you ain't no friend of mine.'

It was pure musical joy to Tommy, especially the way it ended on a happy, bouncy note. He felt a thump at his feet, then his ankle felt wet. He swung round. Some young kid, perhaps twenty, had dropped his pint.

'Soz, mate, sorr-oy. It jus' slipped!'

He said it like that, as if the glass had a life of its own. He was looking up at Tommy with startled eyes.

'Ah, fuck,' Tommy muttered, shaking the beer off his shoes. He felt his thigh hurt, and realised he hadn't thought about it for ages. Then something occurred to him. *Here I am, I'm going to be a big man and give this little kid my spare pint.*

'Here. Have this.'

The kid looked uncomprehending, then happy like it was his birthday.

'Ah, thanks, mate, thanks.'

Tommy soon found himself in conversation with the lad and his mates. They came from way out, past Sutton, but they went to every game. They had a special hatred for Walsall, by induction. And of Albion and Wolves, to a lesser degree. And of Blues, by birthright. Because they were fighting on all fronts at home, they didn't much care about Northerners and Southerners, though they hated scousers, of course, and all loud-mouthed cockney wankers. But that was about it. Tommy explained to them what it really meant to support the Villa, telling them about the old days when there'd always be a knock, wherever you went. They asked what ends he'd taken with Villa, and he had to give them a little history lesson, that all that stuff was nearly over by the time he was old enough, the coppers had worked out how to segregate the away fans, keep them in after the games, put up fences and all that.

One of them knowingly turned to the other. 'See, they used to have fences everywhere. Look at the old videos. Great big fooking fences down the front.'

*Oh God*, thought Tommy. *These lot can't have been born till the late seventies.* One of the kids had a Sid Vicious tattoo on his hand, with the dates of Sid's horrible life underneath. *He probably wasn't even born when Sid died.* He felt like pointing this out, but restrained himself. *I'm just getting old, that's all*, he thought.

Two of their little group were standing back, not saying much. Tommy addressed some of his remarks to them, to make them feel included, but they didn't say anything. Finally, one of them, dressed in a suit and wearing daft Michael Caine glasses, piped up: 'Aren't you that referee?'

His mates looked at him, then at Tommy.

'Er, yeah. But not any more, I don't do it any more. You might have seen me on telly.'

There was a murmur of assent. Suddenly they all remembered.

'Why d'ya stop, mate? Couldn't stand giving them Blues goals? I wouldn't fuckin' give 'em any if I was a fuckin' ref.' His mates laughed, so he went into a mime of blowing his whistle, and shouting 'offsoid', 'pushing' and 'sorry, I didn't see the whole of the ball go over the line'. They loved it.

'No, actually,' said Tommy, a little uncomfortable. 'I did the Premiership. For the last few years anyway. I never did City.'

'Warrabout the Villa, then?'

'No, I never did them either.'

'Oh.' They lost interest, and started talking among themselves. *Wankers.* Jimmy came over.

'So, Mark tells me you're a fucking ref now. I thought it was you – but, y'know, it seemed pretty unlikely.'

'*Was*, Jimmy, *was*. I'm not any more.'

'What happened?'

'Ah, you don't wanna know.'

Jimmy looked at him suspiciously, but with his smile still in place. His eyes had the same look as when they were totting up numbers, multiplying and long-dividing.

They were distracted by a thump at the window, and some cheering. Some people rushed out into the street, the rest strained on tiptoe to see out of the window. At first all Tommy could see was two blokes across the street urinating against the wall. They were looking over their shoulders in the direction of the pub. People started cheering – someone was on the pavement underneath the window. A Blues fan. A body came sprinting past – a short man in a denim jacket with a moustache, venom in his eyes. He started laying into the person under the window. Other faces appeared, with their teeth set and their breath coming in short gasps, their bodies shaking each time they launched a kick that connected. 'City bastard!' he thought he read on someone's lips. A couple of Villa fans broke away from the fight to let others in, and stood in the road, singing, punching their

arms in the air: 'Villa! Villa!' Suddenly, the faces scattered, except for the
determined one with the moustache, and a chestnut-brown police horse
with mad eyes hove into view. The rider, a copper in a yellow jacket, bit
his lower lip and swung his nightstick hard as he passed, bringing it down
across the back of the kicker in the denim jacket. His face contorted with
pain. The policeman then steered his horse around so its huge hindquarters
shoved the fan, toppling him over into the window. There was a thump as
his forehead hit the thick, squiggly pane of glass and he fell to the floor.
A police car then pulled up and two coppers got out and started hauling
bodies off. One of them came into the pub and started shouting.

'Right, you lot, out you go.' People hissed, and called out 'Pig' and
'Screw' at him as he barged his way up to the bar. *Arrogant cunt*, thought
Tommy. He wasn't afraid of him, of being arrested, since the copper was
on his own in the lion's den. But he didn't like the way he barged his way
through, with the cold outside air cascading off his uniform. He looked
around. Mark was there, watching, expressionless. The barmaid looked
terrified as the policeman drew his finger across his throat, telling them
to close.

'It was your gaffer told us to stay open!' she protested, but her fat
little husband shushed her, and rang the bell to try to clear everyone out.

Tommy looked at his watch. 'Twenty to three,' he shouted to Mark
over the din. 'Timing.' Everyone was now drinking up, or just throwing
their glasses on the floor, trampling over chairs and tables, singing in one
deafening voice:

> 'Shit, on, the City, shit on the City tonight!
> Shit, on, the City, shit on the City tonight!
> Shit, on, the City, shit on the City ton-ight,
> Everybody shit on the City, 'cos they're a lo-ad, of, shite!'

It was his favourite time – his favourite place too. If they walked quickly
they'd run into the maximum amount of Blues fans. They'd get in just as
the game started. And they'd still be pissed at half-time. The only trouble
was they'd run into the maximum amount of police too – if they went the
wrong way.

Out in the street the cold and the brightness hit Tommy at first, but
he was insulated by the beer. He felt a firm hand on his shoulder. It was
just Mark.

'Remember what I said, Tommy. No aggro. If it kicks off ... I'm nowhere around.'

'Kicks off? Now you're talking, Father.'

'I'm serious, Tommy,' he said. For the first time, he was genuinely menacing.

Tommy shrugged himself out of his grip, scowling, and marched on up the street. The pilot light was still burning, for him at least. If Mark was going to shit out now, he could, it didn't matter to him. There was a kid with one of those gallon whisky bottles full of small change, with a chain around its neck, which pubs collect for charity in. He was trying to smash it open on the kerb. Tommy heard the pop of the glass, and several little kids dug their hands in at the money. Then they stood back as the kid in charge kicked it, scattering the coins in a line along the gutter.

The road was full of fans on the march, maybe two hundred in all, counting the ones who had been waiting outside the pub, and those who had heard the cheering and caught up with them. The van was gone, but a few police and the horse were bringing up the rear. Tommy thought it was best to get to the front, but when they came to the next chance to turn off, a line of coppers in yellow jackets steered them on down Great Francis Street and Vauxhall Road, towards the main road they wanted them on, Lawley Street, which led straight to the ground.

As they passed the street sign, it was the 'O Mammy' tune again:

> 'O-o-oh Francis, Francis,
> I'd walk a mile and a bit,
> To rub your face in some shit,
> Oh Fra-a-ancis!'

The road was filled with sound and bodies, and Tommy loved it. He was marching down the middle of the street. He looked back. Mark was about fifteen yards behind, on the pavement, inconspicuous. *Shit, that's where I used to walk.* Tommy crossed over to the other pavement, on the left side of the road. *The main mob must be somewhere else ... at least, I don't recognise many of these kids. Maybe they are the main mob now? But this can't be the main escort. Twenty coppers? We can turn off soon. I know this place. Fuckin' what's it called? Percy Street? North Street?*

Northumberland Street appeared up on the left, a tiny street with flats and maisonettes on one side. He saw a few lads break away and head down it, so he followed them. They looked at him approvingly. They all walked with their heads up and their nostrils flaring, ready to see what came next, exactly the way he had seen Mark hundreds of times. There were more Villa up ahead. No police had followed them. At the end of this short street was another name that leapt out of the past at Tommy: Viaduct Street. Now that really was Blues. It was a narrow strip totally hemmed in on one side by railway arches that had garages and businesses in them, and on the other by the blank wall of the goods yard. It was the sort of closed-off street where bad things might happen. Tommy checked behind again. More Villa were coming after them, clumps of five and six, walking quickly. Then he spotted a figure in a long black coat on the move. It was Mark, jogging to catch up.

Tommy laughed to himself, and carried on. A young man a few steps ahead of him in a puffa jacket and ski hat started chanting, 'The Brummies are here! The Brummies are here!' A thrill ran through him, then another when he heard a muffled chant from the parallel street, 'The Villa! The Villa!' The atmosphere was ripe, and on cue someone did the fitting thing: there weren't many windows on the street but there were some parked cars. Tommy heard the soft 'pfff' of a windscreen being put through, and turned to see two lads standing triumphantly next to a black Jag, one of them about to launch a lump of concrete through the passenger window, the other now vainly kicking at a headlight in his soft shoes. *It's gonna kick off.*

Then they heard another sound. The front-runners were about halfway down the street when it happened, but everyone heard it at once, a muffled 'Keep Right On to the End of the Road'. It was the Blues anthem, and it always stirred something in Tommy when he heard it: loathing, and a little fear. It meant they were around. No one knew where it was coming from, but it sounded substantial. The Villa fans in the lead slowed down dramatically, and the pantomime began.

'Stand! Stand!' they hissed at each other, and at the people coming up behind then. The default leader at the time, in the puffa jacket, defaulted. He went very quiet and melted away to the side, leaving his little posse of younger kids not knowing what to do. 'Stand!' Tommy shouted at him, and the young man looked at him with scared eyes, but continued slinking along the wall.

'They're up ahead! Fockin' Blues!' shouted someone on his other side. *How the fuck do you know?* thought Tommy. But then he realised, he used to do the same thing himself – give out speculative directions. It calmed the crowd, or at least kept them from falling apart. The others at the back were catching up – there must have been forty or fifty Villa now,

compressing themselves into a mob in Viaduct Street. Tommy hoped there
were a few more coming up behind, but he couldn't see very far back. He
expected to see Mark near by too, but he couldn't. Then he caught sight
of him: he was on the side, keeping close to the long goods yard wall so
he could see clear to either end of the street.

'C'mon, Villa,' shouted Tommy. He wasn't a leader by nature, but this
power vacuum troubled him. To his relief, a big skinhead in a sheepskin
coat, still breathless from having just reached the front, took up the cry,
and the mob started moving forward again.

There was another turning on the right, from which Tommy knew
anyone could come: the Blues mob they could hear, the rest of the Villa
from the road parallel to them, or a load of police. He didn't have long
to think about it. Right at the end of the street ahead of them, where the
sound had seemed to be coming from, appeared some bodies. Five at once.
Then another five. Then they doubled. He could see the pale blue line of
their denim jeans, and their darker tops, with tiny but telltale flashes of
royal blue.

'Blues! Fucking Blues!' people around him were whispering. 'Get the
bastards!' 'Stand!' 'Let's gerrem!'

Everyone's eyes were wide as saucers and their fists clenched. Tommy
looked around for Mark again. He was up close behind him now.

'Tommy!' he called. 'Let's go.'

He meant it. It used to mean 'Let's get 'em', but now it meant let's go
home. Let's get to safety. *Let's shit out.*

Tommy scowled at him. 'Fuck off!' he said, with real contempt.

The blue line was growing at the other end of the street, much more
quickly than he expected. It was orderly, stretching right across the street,
leaving no gaps. This was an unpleasant surprise for Tommy. He wasn't
feeling as brave as he had been five seconds earlier. A word popped into
his mind. *Zulu.* That was what they reminded him of, the film *Zulu*, where
a wave of bodies came at you, but you had no idea how far back it went.
Then he realised that was what they were chanting now, 'Zulus, Zulus,'
and he remembered, that's what their mob was called. They were a bunch
of fleabag schoolkids fifteen years ago. They appeared to have grown
up a bit.

'Tom!' He heard Mark shouting his name, but he ignored it. He marched
on. Picking up the pace from the skinhead. 'Let's get these *wankers*,' he
shouted. But there were more of them with every second. He could see
their heads bobbing up and down – they were jogging right at them. They

were up for it. Tommy felt a shiver of fear, but he knew it was too late to show it. He never had much of a battle plan at this stage. You never knew what could happen. His highest hopes were usually to find one of them, preferably someone who thought he was hard or was mouthing off, and get him to the ground; make sure Mark was OK; make sure you didn't get stranded in the middle of them and get kicked unconscious or killed; keep away from coppers, or anyone with a knife; try and enjoy it.

That was the old days, though. Looking around him, in the last seconds before the two sides met, he saw young faces and strange faces. Only the blood-coloured claret of the Villa shirts tied him to these people, and he could only hope it would be enough. He couldn't see Mark anywhere.

Given that they were outnumbered, and that they were in strange territory (even though they were only three miles from Villa Park, and a mile from the centre of town), and that they were being met, most of the Villa had an instinct to run. But the big skinhead turned and faced everyone, screaming, 'Stand, Villa, stand!', and you couldn't really argue with that. So the urgent murmuring and hissing, to 'Stay!' and 'Don't run!' and 'Don't shit out!', became more urgent, and more persuasive, and when the skinhead turned and started running right at the Blues, into the rapidly closing space between them, everyone else followed suit.

The roar went up all over the street, the hate-filled growl that was meant to make the other side scatter. Tommy liked the growl, but he was never one for going in first. There was something too mental, too suicidal, about the first people in, who were invariably swallowed by the opposition. He liked to be just after them, find someone he liked, and work on them. Kung fu kicks, or leaping into the air like two footballers going for the same ball, had never appealed to him. He wanted to trip someone and get them on the ground.

The first person that came at him, dodging round the Villa in front, was a scrawny git in jeans, boots and a Blues T-shirt. Tommy absorbed the whole impact of him with his forearms and with one knee raised in front of him. The fan bounced off him, looking shocked, and, feeling his heart about to burst, Tommy cracked him hard on the cheek with his fist. The kid put his head down and started flailing his fists, but Tommy grabbed the T-shirt on his back and swung him round and round, trying to get him to fall. Out of the corner of his eye, though, he saw a flash of golden hair. It was Blondie, from the ramp that morning. Tommy let the other kid loose suddenly, sending him spinning into someone's back. All around him there was chaos: twos and threes of fans on to one; people banging heads against walls and the ground; the panicked gestures and cries of people trying to tell who was who.

Blondie was stamping on the head of a Villa fan when Tommy got up to him and launched the sole of his shoe into his back. As the City fan rolled over and looked up, with the same nasty grimace on his face as if he were still winning, Tommy drove his foot into the kid's thigh as hard as he could.

'Uuurgh!' he screamed. He had forgotten about his bad leg, and the shock wave travelled right up his femur and deep into the muscles of his thigh, making his eyes water. As he hobbled and tried to hop away, Blondie got up and came after him, taunting him, 'Norrad enough, then, yer Villa bastid?', and kicked him hard up the arse, sending him stumbling forward to his knees. Suddenly Tommy was feeling very sore and angry, and very small. *Where's Mark?* was his first thought. *Oof!* was his second, as a familiar training shoe came in at his cheek with a thump.

They were exactly level with a small road that turned off to the right, St James's Place, and which led back down to the rest of the Villa escort. As he tried to get up using his one good leg, he looked up and saw the coppers arriving, coming straight at him. *Ahh, shite.* Their yellow jackets were approaching, the swishing of the plastic coming into earshot. People all round him were shouting 'Old Bill!' and 'Filth' and starting to scatter. He could hear dogs barking and horse hooves clip-clopping on the asphalt.

Thanks to the sort of good fortune that Tommy recognised but never expected, the first six coppers ran straight past him and into the thick of the scrum. There was still no pattern to how they worked, all these years later. Some of them fearlessly launched themselves between fighting fans, others went for someone trying to look innocent, punched them in the face and marched them away, arm pulled up behind the back until the tendons creaked and cartilage crackled. As Tommy was still limping out of the way, a horse came clattering past on the pavement, the rider grinning even more madly than his slobbering animal, swinging his nightstick like a windmill. To Tommy's delight, he brought it down square on the top of Blondie's head, and the City fan crumpled like a paper cup, holding his scalp in both hands.

The T-junction was a mass of bodies. The fight had moved into its final phase, where the arrival of the police caused an almost instant backing down of both sides, but a lot of singing and lunging. There were now three horses, stamping and shuffling in the midst of the crowd, and a white van screamed up, disgorging another six police. There were no black marias around, so there was no great danger of being arrested just yet. But almost in observance of the law, both sides settled back behind the two thin cordons of police, and settled for cursing each other.

'Shit on the City tonight!' went the one song, and the Zulus replied with their own. There was a sudden escalation, and the roar began, and the Blues fans looked like they were about to break through and attack the claret-and-blue mob opposite, who were flicking the Vs and singing with their arms up and their palms facing forward. But the coppers quelled it with shouts and lunges of their own, and the fans stumbled backward against each other, and kept up their curses. The coppers were now twenty strong, plus horses and now a dog.

As Tommy stood trying to rub some life back into his leg, he saw a policewoman running straight at him. She was late, but she wasn't going to be left short. Although the little bit of her face that was visible beneath her helmet was quite pretty, he could see in her beady eyes that she was coming in for the kill.

'Aww, fuck,' he muttered, and tried to rejoin the Villa ranks, who were already being forced back behind him. He felt her arms around his waist, and her eight stone dragging him to the ground. *Shit. I'm being rugby-tackled by a woman.*

They spilled to the ground together, Tommy landing on his back, she on top of him. A few fans noticed and jeered their loud innuendos, and even one of the coppers smirked and made a mental note to come and help, in a minute.

Tommy thought he knew what would happen next: some other copper would come over and help her, standing on his chest or grabbing his feet. But looking up, what he saw was the upside-down face of the priest.

'That's enough, love,' Mark said, and gently, but irresistibly, picked her up by the back of her jacket and held her, suspended, while Tommy rolled over, got up and limped for his life. Once his friend was clear, Mark apologised, dropped her face down on the pavement, and followed Tommy. He was fast. He dodged one lunging officer, and burst through the cordon between two others who were facing the other way. With his long black coat floating behind him, he dodged back through the Villa and disappeared.

All it took was one Alsatian to get the Blues fans moving, back down Viaduct Street in the direction they had come. They started diverting Villa down the side road to where they should have been in the first place. Tommy and Mark, separately, made their own way back, dodged the last few coppers bringing up the rear, and retraced their steps back to Vauxhall Road. Tommy caught up with Mark on the corner and nodded, and the two stood there, leaning forward, trying to get their breath back.

'Thanks,' said Tommy, in between gasps.

Mark looked over at him, still too out of breath to speak, and shook his head.

Tommy was still high as a kite from the adrenalin when he remembered all the beer he'd had. His face felt hot, like all the blood was rushing to it. The skin on his cheeks and round his eyes was pounding, so he stood up straight. *Not getting any younger*, was his first thought. *Wonder if I'm in any trouble with the priest? He nearly got nicked there. So did I, come to think of it.*

'Better keep out the coppers' way from now on,' he said out loud to Mark, who was still trying to catch his breath. *Hmm, not as fit as you look . . .*

Mark started laughing through his heaving breaths, which made it harder for him to speak.

'You fuckin' div! What did I tell you back there?'

*Ooh, fuck.* Tommy didn't really know how to handle a priest swearing at him. Especially not one as hard and mad as Mark. He started to protest: 'It was that bleached blond bastard who jumped me in town this morning, I couldn't just let him get away with it. And he was twatting one of us right in front of me.' Tommy heard himself getting plaintive. He had never been up before a beak before, but he had rehearsed his excuses a thousand times. They were never any good. Or rather, they never worked. The sequence always ended with the magistrate banging his gavel and telling him to shut up. He didn't even know if they had gavels, magistrates.

'Yeah, well . . .' Mark cut himself off. He didn't want to go down that path. He was showing the sort of holy self-restraint that Tommy had only ever read about. Now here it was in the flesh, in front of him.

They looked at their watches. It was almost three o'clock.

'Come on, we can still make it,' said Tommy, keen to change the subject. He set off walking as quickly as his bad leg would allow, Father Mark at his side, still trying to catch his breath.

Most of the Villa mob were being escorted just ahead of them, so to avoid the WPC and her friends they went the long way round, right up Watery Lane and cut the corner on to Coventry Road. They heard the players come out, the big 'booo' for Villa, and the game begin. With no colours, wearing their neutral clothes, they could have passed for any two thirty-five-year-olds going to the boxes, or maybe the press box. They walked straight through the remnants of the Blues crowd, those still queuing to get in. No one was going to touch them – Tommy and Mark didn't have the gleam of hate in their eyes. Life, and the Holy Spirit, had taught them other ways to be, and this was the mode they were in now.

As they walked behind the Blues' main side, the Spion Kop, which had been all done up with a fancy new roof, Tommy had a tiny flashback. He'd done this before. If he concentrated, for a fraction of a second he could see in his mind's eye silhouettes of young fans at the very back of the old Spion, when it was terracing. They were between the roof and the corrugated iron that formed the back wall of the stand, and they seemed to be hanging from the rafters, or sitting on ledges, sharp against the white sky. Other faces appeared over the metal sheeting looking out to the road. The back of the Spion Kop looked horrible enough at that time – it was a steep grassy bank with a few dangerous, narrow flights of stairs with ugly blue railings. These kids just made it look even worse, like they were looking for people like him.

Of course, that didn't matter any more. Tommy and Mark were invincible, and invisible too. He tried to remember if Mark had been with him that day, years ago. *Probably.*

They got in the Villa end – the Tilton – at 3.20 p.m.

'It's packed!' said Mark, the only thing he had said for ages.

'Yeah, as packed as seats can be,' Tommy replied. 'It's full up to the corners anyway. Sold out. FA Cup, you know, Blues always think they're gonna win it.'

It wasn't just today – Mark wasn't one for banter any more. For conversation even. Tommy wondered if maybe it was because he prayed all the time, like some holy people. Like priests were always telling you to do.

It didn't matter much – Tommy became absorbed in the game. The referee was good, and Villa were good too. When they went one–nil up on the stroke of half-time Tommy missed it because he was in the gents. Apparently it was a hilarious tap-in that made the City fans hang their heads and groan.

Melissa: ... So. Craig tells me you finally made it down the gym. What did you think?

Fiona: Of him?

M: The gym. Both.

F: He's awful. He gave me the total creeps.

M: Oh, come on, he's not that bad!

F: He's revolting, Melissa! He's bright orange, for a start. And he wears those skimpy little shorts . . . I bet he's gay.

M: He's not gay! You really didn't like him? That's interesting.

F: Oh God, Mel, where's your taste gone, he's a slimeball. And he comes close to me and he goes, 'You should check out the free weights. I'll spot for you if you want.' Aw, puke!

M: What's wrong with that? I've started on the free weights. He says I could be really ripped by summer. I need to move on.

F: Bleugh! Pass the sick bag! Are you sure you're not spending too much time down the gym? Where's Tommy these days anyway?

M: Oh, please. I don't want to talk about him.

F: It's all right now, hon. I don't hold anything against him. We all say stupid things when we're pissed.

M: I was *so* embarrassed. I don't know how I'll ever face Nick again.

F: Yeah, well, don't worry about him. He's got plenty of people feeling sorry for him already . . . like his bloomin' mother. I feel like sending him back there sometimes. Let her buy his milk and cook his dinners and get him off to interviews.

M: Yeah, I could do with a break myself. He's off up in Birmingham again today. I don't know why he bothers coming home sometimes. I'm just waiting for him to say he wants to move up there . . . Ever since he stopped doing the refereeing he's been a real pain in the arse. I said to him, 'If it's so unfair why don't you just go in there and tell them? Or talk to the media.' And all I get is this wimpy crap, 'Oh, I've written letters, I've told people in the media and they're not interested, it's all a big conspiracy . . .' And then he says he's giving it up anyway. So what's the point? Anyway, he's always moping around, I'm quite glad he's out of my hair for the day.

F: Is he with that priest again?

M: Yeah. Mark.

F: The one you told me about? The gorgeous one?

M: Yeah.

F: Phwoar. Get *him* down here. I've got a few things I'd like to confess to *him*. Beats steroid man with his beta carotene pills any day.

M: Don't let your imagination run away with you, girl.

F: Sometimes that's all I've got.

M: Did I tell you he propositioned me?

F: No! NO! The priest? You must be joking!

M: No, dopey, Craig at the gym.

F: Him? Get away! What did he say, what did he say?

M: He said to me in this really deep voice, like, obviously looking at my boobs, 'You know, I'm *also* a personal trainer. And I have a special offer for first-timers right now.' And then he winks at me.

F: Bleugh! Oh God! Show me the way to the vomitorium! What did you say?

M: I didn't say anything.

F: Oh, man, this I've gotta hear ...

The second half was more even, but Villa stuck it to them again in the seventieth minute, and then it was non-stop singing and dancing all the way. That was it for Blues' season, they were well and truly fucked. Villa were marching on to Wembley, though.

Mark seemed to enjoy the game. As the Villa fans poured out of the back of the Tilton and down the bleak hill of Garrison Lane, there were big grins on every face, even Mark's. The coppers did a good job of diverting them away from the Blues, giving them the Digbeth High Street way into town, and sending Villa up to Curzon Street, if they wanted, or on up north and home. A tight line of police kept the two sets of fans apart: policemen with their chinstraps on tightly, beating their gloved hands together against the cold. In the dark, the reflective socks of the horses gleamed every few paces, and the warm breath vapours of men and animals alike rose through the bright light of the floodlights. There were motorbike cops, nudging their way through the foot traffic, and tall black marias, white transit vans with tinted windows that people said were for the Special Patrol Group, and jam sandwiches with their lights spinning.

'I fuckin' love it, Mark, I really do.'

'What?'

'All this. All this. I miss it. Don't you miss it? I bet you do.'

'No. Not really. There are better things in life.'

'Like what?'

'Like ... Easter Monday Mass at St Chad's Cathedral. Being there. Saying it.'

Tommy was about to suck his teeth and say something disbelieving, but he stopped himself. *I wouldn't be so rude to any of my patients, and I listen to some strange crap from them. So why am I so hard on Mark?*

'Hey, Mark,' he blurted out. 'Thanks for saving me earlier. You took a fucking big risk for me. You needn't have, but I'm so fucking glad you did.'

The priest sniffed. 'Ah, don't mention it.'

As they walked down the hill, the escort loosened – there was no real way of keeping so many people apart, when several thousand were just normal middle-aged blokes or kids from across town who wanted to get home to their dinner. Some quiet, cross-looking fans started working their way into the Villa column.

'Aye-aye,' said Tommy, giving them a quick glance.

'Huh,' replied Mark.

That was enough for them – they were both still feeling invincible, and invisible. Tommy had a sore leg and an escalating alcohol debt. Father Mark was thinking about his sermon for tomorrow. January could be a pretty lean month once the crib was away and forgotten. There might be a pastoral letter to read out, but he'd probably be on his own for the six weeks leading up to Lent. He wasn't a great speaker – he couldn't riff off a headline or a phrase from the gospel yet. For Father Mark, thanks to his potholed education, pretty much every word had to be planned out beforehand.

The City fans worked their way into the middle of the column. There were only about twenty of them, and there were coppers every ten yards, so it didn't seem to be going anywhere. But the younger Villa fans were up for it, and started organising themselves behind and abreast of them, easily outnumbering them. They were still hungry.

Instinctively, the two men dropped back a little and crossed over to the other side, to get out of the way. It started with a song, Villa taunting them – 'Shit on the City, tonight!' *Well, this is tonight. The night was made for these kids,* thought Tommy. *They've waited for it all year, or since the last time.* The murmuring grew. There was some hissing and mumbling, then finally the City fans went for it. Their chant, 'City! City!', started with a growl and lasted just a few seconds as they spread themselves and started laying into whoever was near – jostling girls and old men alike. The young Villa mob came straight back at them, and the roar went up, for a few seconds, alerting the police.

The fighting lasted only about ten seconds. It was just another skirmish about pride. Mark and Tommy both stiffened, clenched their fists, and tried to just watch. Right in front of them, on the peaceful side of the street, they saw a Blues fan in a faded denim jacket facing the flow, offering out allcomers. A fat guy of about forty-five who was carrying his small son, maybe three years old, on his shoulders, came up to him, without changing pace, and smashed him in the face with one hard punch, a long thick arm in a donkey jacket that followed right through.

'Learn some fuckin' manners, Bluenose,' he shouted as he stepped over his body, and carried on walking. His son swivelled round as far as he could to see the prostrate figure, his eyes wide, his tiny hands hanging on to his dad's ears for life.

It was all over in a few seconds. The police came charging in. Two burly coppers grabbed Mark and started hauling him off, back against the flow of people.

'Hey, what the f . . . Get off me! Get off me! What did I do?'

Tommy's heart was in his mouth. He ran back alongside them, trying to pry their arms off his friend. 'What's he done? Leave him alone! He hasn't done a thing. Oi, copper, you got the wrong bloke. What's he done?'

One of the police officers had Mark's arm up behind his back, the other had him in a headlock. The priest struggled to try to look up and speak. His hair was messed up, and he looked totally helpless, like a rag doll, as he was dragged along. Tommy kept up his running vigil. He was getting angry because he was getting nowhere. And yet, the sense of doom in his stomach from the first second was familiar. You rarely got away from one arresting copper – no one ever did it from two, even if you fought like an animal. Reinforcements were always on the way. And then they'd subdue you properly in the back of the van, with a concert of flying Doc Martens while you rolled up into a ball.

'Fucking gerrof 'im! He's done nothing!' The rest of the fans flowing home against them just watched. Their eyes were wide with love of the spectacle, but they kept their hands in their pockets. Tommy didn't recognise anyone anyway. It had been so long.

'Oi, he's innocent! What'd he do?' He felt like a girlfriend for a second. One of the coppers twisted his head and snarled at him.

'You're next if you don't fuck off.' He was still struggling to keep Mark's face pointed to the floor. The black maria was parked about twenty yards away. 'Hey, Lisa!' he called out. 'Get this one behind me, will ya?'

*Shite!* Tommy recognised the pretty face with the pixie nose, and the eyes becoming beady. It was the WPC who nearly nicked him two hours before. *Oh fuck.* Tommy stopped in his tracks. Then he turned and he ran.

As he ran through the crowd, skipping and dodging the pedestrians, people heard his urgent footsteps and half turned to see. Some assumed he was a Blues fan on the run. He reminded others of a handbag-snatcher in the market, only even in the dark he looked too well heeled. Some Blues fans, still mingling, thought he was a Villa fan and that they should bring him down, but after a feeble chase realised he was far too quick for them. He was moving like a hunted man. He fucked Curzon Street off, he fucked Jennens Road off – he didn't want to go into town. He was heading north. He had to get home.

Looking back, he couldn't see the policewoman. *I must have lost her. She was probably tempted by Mark anyway.* Tommy imagined her little hand pulling Mark's hair to get his face in the right place while the two other burly bastards held him, so she could say something really spiteful to him. He felt sick.

He knew he had to get off the main road. Even at a jog he was attracting too much attention. There were coppers everywhere. The main road was leading him north-west, so at the first chance he could he turned off to the right, looking for something quiet. At last he could stop. He stood in a darkened doorway in a little road he'd never been up in his life, Heneage Street. His breath came back to him after two minutes, and the film of sweat on his brow chilled him nicely in the frosty air. *God, I'm fit,* he thought admiringly. *Still fit, after all this lay-up. But Mark . . .*

He began to walk on. He wasn't sure where he was going. Who would be back at the house? Where else could he go? He couldn't just fuck off and leave him. *Like I just did. Oh, shit!* 'SHIT!' he shouted out loud. There weren't many people around to hear him, just some women who had been shopping, who hurriedly got in their car. One of them nearly broke her nails trying to get her door open. *Where will Mark be now, then? It's not Queen's Road Station.* That was for Villa arrests. He couldn't remember where they put the bad boys from Blues. *In town? Digbeth?* He'd have to do some phoning.

He was worried about Mark, because he'd been arrested for trouble twice before. The first time he was laying into an Everton fan right by Witton Station, which was stupid, in retrospect. His mum got him a cheap lawyer and he got a hundred-quid fine. Which was a lot then. The second time was a total injustice – about a hundred of them were charging down a residential street in Norwich. Things were flying everywhere – dustbins through front-room windows, gates were being ripped off their hinges, old men pushed over and cars booted. There was one copper, and out of a hundred he picked Mark — mainly because Mark ran straight into him. They ended up on the floor together. Tommy hadn't even seen it, he was up ahead, shouting and laughing. They were still only young then too — maybe eighteen. Mark got three hundred quid and a three-month suspended sentence, because he got a better lawyer this time, one who specialised in aggro merchants, but it did mean having to go all the way back to Norwich on a Tuesday with his mum. That was punishment enough.

Tommy had never been arrested. He would never have got into medical school if he had. So he wouldn't be the posh doctor, living in London with his hard-bodied bird, with their weird food and their folded Harvey Nichols bags in the kitchen drawer. He wondered if he had planned this all along. That was the kind of thing he suggested to his patients. That, whatever it was, they probably meant it.

In the dark, surrounded by the cooling towers and railway tracks, with their patterned brick walls, strange workmen's cabins and metal staircases, Tommy felt his way back to Rocky Lane.

Father Mark let himself in at 10 p.m. Tommy, who was sitting alone in the freezing front room of the priests' house, jumped up off the sofa. He had been alone in there with his thoughts for three hours, and he didn't like them.

He was feeling guilty as hell. Guilty for being the one not selected by fate for tragedy. Guilty for not tearing the coppers off him single-handedly and whisking him away to safety, as Mark had done for him. And guilty for dragging him out to a football match in the first place, when he would obviously have rather stayed in and worked on his sermon, or sent e-mail to the Pope, or whatever it was he did up there.

He leapt out of the front room as Father Mark was hanging up his coat. The priest looked mildly surprised but didn't interrupt his actions.

'The old fellah let me in. How'd it go, how'd it go? You all right?'

Mark's eyes narrowed nastily at this last show of concern, but he controlled himself and managed a sweet, sarcastic smile.

'I got off. No charges.'

'What?' Tommy was incredulous. And incredibly happy. Relieved as a fuck. 'They let you off? How'd you manage it?'

'I think it was a combination of things,' he said, dryly. There was no emotion in his face now. His skin was yellow under the old glass lampshade in the hall. 'Both of the arresting officers were Villa fans — they thought I supported Blues.'

'Ha!'

'That WPC who chased after you was in the station too. She walked straight past me while I was handcuffed to a chair in the waiting room, without noticing me.'

'HA!' Tommy couldn't believe it.

'And the desk sergeant was a Catholic. A serious Catholic. The coppers didn't know what do with me once they saw my name and address, but the desk sergeant explained to them that they must have made a mistake.'

'Oh, man, this is perfect!' Tommy tried to clap him on the shoulder, but Mark pulled away. 'So no charges, nothing?'

'Nothing. I explained what happened . . . the bit after the game anyway. I told them I did nothing.'

'So you're in the clear, then? They won't tell the newspapers, like they usually do?'

'No, it won't be in the papers. They won't tell.' Then his face became hard like a china mask, and dark rings showed beneath his eyes as he jumped forward and grabbed Tommy by the lapels. 'But Father Kelly will find out. You FUCKING IDIOT!'

He slammed Tommy back against the wall, so that his head made a clunking noise on the plaster.

'I told you no trouble, and what do you do?' He slammed him again against the wall. 'You get pissed.' Slam. 'You go for the knock.' Slam. 'I save you from getting nicked and then you just watch as I'm carted off.' SLAM!

The last blow to Tommy's head was too much. He wrestled with the priest's grip and tried to speak, but it all came out sounding lame.

'There was two of 'em! If I'd stayed that bird copper would have got me and all, she was after me. Anyway, I never asked you to follow me on the way to the ground. I'm the one who got jumped this morning!' Tommy knew that if you looked at the facts from the right angle, right was on his side. Mark wasn't interested in lining up facts. There were far more important things in the world. There were invisible ties that bound. He lived by them, day in, day out. Tommy could keep his fucking facts, and his angles.

Mark was glaring at him, still holding him hard, burning him up with the hatred in his face. He had obviously tidied himself up since getting out of the station — maybe one of the coppers had even lent him a comb — but now a kiss-curl of black hair fell down on his forehead. After listening to Tommy, his face was screwed up with disgust, and he slammed him back against the wall one more time, then walked away, and mounted the stairs.

Tommy was speechless. He thought he was going to throw up. He looked around – *should I go?* There was a noise upstairs, a door opening. Father Kelly's voice – 'What's all this noise?' He heard Mark's subvocal murmur, then his door slam. Father Kelly leaned over the banister and looked down at him. He pulled a face and tut-tutted, then went back to his own room.

Still panting, Tommy let himself out, shutting the front door quietly. He began stumbling up the street, looking for a bus. *Maybe a minicab.* He felt sick. He had an instant headache from the blows to his head. *Maybe I'll be found dead in the street of brain shear? What will Mel think? She'll scratch his eyes out. She'll break his fucking neck.* He began to feel weepy. He tried to cross the main road and was almost hit by a motorcycle. He was already on the right side for going into town. He got on the first bus that came, and sat downstairs near the driver. His head ached.

He was still in shock from his friend's reaction. He deserved it, and yet he didn't deserve it. *There's no justice. Maybe he's not my friend after all? Maybe I've just been kidding myself? Maybe I should just get back to London, where I belong. Have Nick and Fiona over for dinner.* That thought repulsed him. He made the driver stop the bus between stops, by pointing to his mouth. He leapt off and threw up on the pavement in front of some teenagers, who started taunting him. The bus drove off without him. The girls were disgusted, so one of the boys wanted to fight him. He backed off, and started limping down the street towards town. He flagged down a minicab, which took him to New Street. He gave the driver a fifty and got change from a twenty, he later realised as he went through his pockets on the train, waiting for it to depart. He saw some football fans on the platform, three young blokes, a bit gawky, harmless-looking. He remembered that afternoon's match. It seemed like yesterday morning.

The heating on the train was bust so he kept his coat up round his chin all the way. Nothing helped. He saw his reflection against the dark glass. *Judas,* was all he could think. *Judas hung himself from a tree in Gethsemene, didn't he? Or am I making that up? Maybe it was just some other little park. Some municipal park in Jerusalem. Or wherever the fuck they were.*

They passed through somewhere depressing. He thought it might be Kettering. Or Rugby. He didn't fancy going back to London at all. The thought of the whole city laid out before him at Euston made him want to turn back. All the wankers round Euston selling crack, the squeegee tossers who thought they were in New York, all the pissed men with nicotine stains in their beards. *Stripy-shirted bastards. Young bastards all dressed up for going out. When was that Nick bastard from the BBC ever going to get in touch?* Which reminded him of his other misery. Refereeing. He sank further into despondency. *Maybe I should get off here and find myself a tree right now? Ughh.* He wondered if you could hear your own neck snap as you reached the end of your tether. The thought of coming in his trousers and being found by a stranger didn't appeal. *What a dumb fucking way to go. Maybe a bridge, though.* He remembered med school, physiology. *Drowning.* He had squeezed all his physiology notes on to a deck of plain postcards. Drowning was in the bottom left-hand corner of Respiration, under Aviation, Space and Deep-Sea Diving. There were three ways to go:

*i) Dry. Thirty per cent of all drowners inhale no water, due to powerful laryngeal reflex that causes spastic closure of the vocal cords. ii) Freshwater inhalation: water absorbed through alveolar membrane into the blood by extremely rapid osmosis. Blood electrolytes diluted, haemolysis of red cells, massive potassium spillage into plasma, anoxia, heart fibrillation, death three mins after inhalation. iii) Salt water: osmosis reversed. Loss of water from blood gives haemoconcentration, no haemolysis or cardiac fibrillation. Death by asphyxia in five to eight minutes. What a way to go. Ugh. Fuck that.*

It was all just play. Tommy wouldn't top himself. There probably weren't any rivers in this featureless plain anyway. The Pope was probably right, no sane person ought to kill themselves. It was a brink he liked to approach every now and then, to study, to play on, and to retreat from intact. He was really in it for the fantasy funeral – the lavish display of suffering, guilt, regret and remorse on a gigantic group-hysterical scale. *He just popped out to a football match and never came back ... That's what they'd say. Body never recovered. Memorial service at 3 p.m. on a weekday.* But he wasn't in the mood for that tonight, sitting on the chilly train. He just wanted to hide in the darkness.

# 7

## Letters; death comes quickly, funeral; Daytona 595; first of Scotland, rumbles in church

On picking up the letter he had written the night before, Tommy frowned. He recognised the handwriting immediately – the generous curves, the sudden spikes, the constant drift upwards. It was pub-inspired.

He read it with disdain:

'I don't know what to do at this point, or what came over me when I was in Birmingham, or how I feel about your treatment of me. It pains me to see you so angry with me, and yet I actually really wanted to see you the way you used to be again.'

*Oh God*, he groaned to himself. 'Perhaps we can bury the proverbial old Stanley knife and try again? I want to come back to Brum soon, but I can't see it happening. You are more than welcome ...' And so it went on. He even managed to blame Melissa for a couple of things. The élan with which he thought he was writing had vanished.

He stood at the desk in his white dressing gown. It was two weeks after the Blues game. Melissa was out. Saturday lunch-time with the girls. Melissa had been out the night before too. Friday night with the girls. Instead of eating ethnic with him. Having found a terse note on the empty fridge, Tommy had wandered around the neighbourhood hoping to discover a new pub. He fantasised about something warm and cosy, with horse brasses and exposed beams, a hard trivia machine, and maybe even a few students. Or at least something without strip lights hanging from chains. Tufnell Park had not lived up to the estate agent's promise –

having never been on the way up, it was now definitely on the way down. Just the amount of rubbish in the street was enough to tell him that.

So he went to the Usual, as he had taken to calling the Local where he was not a Regular. And he sat at the bar on his own and had a few pints (four), but they didn't do much for him. They felt more like three pints, without the chemical joy. For two weeks he had been thinking about Mark. How he, Tommy, had personally driven this young priest to effing and blinding and wanting to kick his head in. This was the old Mark he knew, but clearly, it wasn't right any more. He pondered this, then his mind hit lager-induced warp speed. It was clear he had to act. Stopping only for some revolting fried chicken, most of which ended up in someone's hedge, Tommy hurried home. He had decided to put his thoughts on paper for Mark.

There was even a grease stain at the bottom of the page. Tommy folded the letter in four and tossed it into the wire wastepaper basket in disgust.

'Fuck!' he muttered. His hangover wasn't too bad. He just felt a crushing loneliness. He had driven Mark away, and now Melissa. In the two weeks since Blues he had barely been able to mention it to her. All he said was the bus lurched as he was going down the stairs and that was how he grazed his brow. And the big bruise on his thigh? He and Mark had been mucking about on the Vespa, they skidded on some oil and he whacked his thigh against the bumper of a parked lorry. He was practically healed now – just a fine pink mark, and a sickly yellow splotch – on the outside. *I'm still a good healer, at least,* he told himself.

Two miserable weeks he had spent, trudging into work to see his patients, most of whom were dealing with the results of ritual excess. The old woman with concrete stools snaking halfway up her innards. The happy-go-lucky yobbo with the broken ankle from skiing: getting pissed one night and stepping heavily off the kerb hadn't helped. This time it would need pins. 'Or you could try not drinking for a few weeks,' he told him. *You fucking piss artist.* Two more cases of SAD, within an hour of one another. *Why do you live in fucking Britain, then? Why don't you fuck off to Spain or somewhere? Florida?* There was a new drug for this – *Lux Interior.* A rep had brought him a huge box of samples so he decided to get rid of a few. A man came in wanting diet pills for his love handles. Tommy sent him next door to the Speed King. Amitriptylene Carol came in. Instead of sitting down heavily in the chair, she smiled and was bitterly polite. She said she had just come by to say she had found a new doctor who gave her all the 'Ami' she wanted, that she was feeling much better, and that she was considering a malpractice suit against him. Tommy made no reply, except for whistling 'You Are My Sunshine, My Only Sunshine' as she left, slamming the door after her. *The fucking jokers.*

Pierced Man came in. He still had the yellow in his eye whites from a bout of Hepatitis B that Tommy had dealt with in the autumn. Pierced Man practically clinked when he walked, such was the amount of metal he carried around in his boxers: a coronet of studs through the prepuce; a bolt through the glans; and two rows of six silver hoops through his scrotum.

'Drop your trousers, please, and have a seat up here,' said Tommy. Although he was often bored, his professional cool rarely left him, and he performed better when his work was challenging. Pierced Man complained of a burning sensation when he urinated. Tommy snapped on some latex gloves, which he kept in a box by the couch like Kleenex, and delicately inspected the man's penis. The end of it was greyish-green.

'Hmm. Bowel OK?'

'Well, you know ...' said the patient.

'And you *are* keeping him clean?'

'Oh yes, every day.'

'Hmm. OK. Pop your clothes back on.'

He pulled the gloves off in two swift movements, bundling them in upon each other so that not a single stray virion or bacillus could make contact with the room, not even with the inside of his waste disposal unit. Then he sat behind the desk, pulled the top off his fountain pen and began writing on his prescription pad. He spoke at first without looking up.

'I could send you to the STD clinic at the university for some expensive tests, but I'll let you get a head start, because you need to act fast. You have a touch of gangrene in the penis.'

Pierced Man looked dismayed, but remained silent.

'It's complicated by the residual Hep B – your defences are very low down there. I strongly recommend no penetrative sex for a month or until all the discoloration has gone. Otherwise you could lose it.'

Tommy looked up and gave a reassuring smile. 'And not just the tip.' Pierced Man looked at the floor. The giant ball-bearing in his nose glittered under the fluorescent light.

'Oh, and lose the metalwork. You're not doing yourself any favours with all those holes, they collect bacteria.'

Pierced Man opened his mouth to protest. Tommy overruled him as if he were a recalcitrant defender, and handed him the prescription.

'Clean the whole area three times a day with rubbing alcohol until all the holes are totally healed. Thank you.' And he waved him out of the door.

Such highlights were few. The ill were not having a very generous February. He even found himself looking forward to the hayfever season, or a visit from a rep.

Still in his dressing gown, he made himself a cup of coffee with sugar and cream and sat down at the desk to have another go at the letter to Mark. He went through Melissa's pile of postcards that she used for quick notes to her friends. The Barbican Theatre. *What's she doing with that?* Harrods with its Christmas lights on. *Hmm, too materialistic.* Little stone cherub boy pissing. *Too blasphemous, he might think.* Hampstead Heath, taken in about 1971. *Too boring.* In the end he settled on Harrods, because from the angle it was shot at, he reckoned you could see a slice of the Brompton Oratory in the corner. *He might like that.*

He wrote:

14th Feb

Dear Mark,
     Sorry about Blues. Give me a call.

*Love? What do I put now? Love?*
'Oh, shit! It's Valentine's Day!' He said it out loud as if he were not alone. 'Jesus fucking Christ!'

The shock went through his stomach like a sword, and his arms felt weak and uncontrollable. *I completely forgot! It's never on a Saturday!* Then he remembered the last time it was on a Saturday. He had just met Melissa and was still snowing her – fascinated and desperate to get into her pants. Valentine's Day was a heaven-sent opportunity to flatter and he made the most of it, sending her a long letter detailing every last drop of pleasure he had got from their most recent date – a trip to the National Motorcycle Museum in Coventry. They went in her car but he paid the petrol and bought lunch. She said she liked to get out of London at the weekend, so this seemed perfect. The letter was folded inside a small card that purported to be anonymous (so she could stick it on the mantelpiece of the flat in Balham which she shared with two other girls and not have to answer too many questions) and a tiny box of hand-made chocolates, by some company called Godiva. Just the remote possibility of being with her then had him whacking off twice a day. He didn't put that in the letter, but he reckoned she knew it. She was a master of intimacy. *God, I bet if*

*I rummaged around the flat now I'd find that letter somewhere.* It gave him the creeps — he saw he had drifted further away from his old self in the last few months than in all the years preceding it. That Valentine's Day he had had to referee a non-league game in the morning which gave him the lustre of heroism when he returned to London, got spruced up and met her under the clock at Waterloo. She too was free for the day, free to go out with her friends and wonder about the coming evening, and what restaurant they were having dinner at, and whether she'd spread 'em or hang on a bit longer. So when they met under the clock they were very glad to see each other.

He scrawled 'Tommy' across the bottom of Mark's postcard, and added his phone number, then leapt out of the chair, pulled on some trousers, a T-shirt, socks and the first shoes that came to hand, and raced out of the flat, putting on his coat as he ran down the stairs. In the street he thought he saw her little hatchback turn in at the end of the road, so he turned the other way and fled, taking the side roads until he came out at Parkhurst Road.

An unshaven man, his hair awry, wearing running shoes with slacks, he cut a sad figure, pacing down the street, entering shops and bursting out again empty-handed. It was all shit round there, unless she wanted a blender or a bowie knife. He got on the bus to Camden Town, took one look out of the window and stayed on it into the West End. Remembering the postcard, he just caught Postie as he scraped the contents of a pillar box into a sack.

'I expect you got a lot of this yesterday?' said Tommy, playing for time while he addressed the card.

'Oh gawd,' said the postman, straightening up to chat. 'There's one at every box, I swear — 'Can I just get me letter back? I've changed me mind!' Still, we've all been there, 'aven't we?'

Tommy agreed whole-heartedly. *What a nice fucking postie*, he thought, and he set off into the shoppers.

Valentine's Day was a spectacular success. Tommy got laid, for one thing — *before* they went out. So they went out feeling all weak and warm, with their desires reconfigured: they were hungry, they wanted to be close, to talk. He bought her some angora undies, the price of which was staggering, but it was either that or the blender. She liked them a lot. He didn't even watch the football scores — she liked that too. He got a shave and a haircut in Covent Garden, and looked swell in his crombie, which he picked up from the cleaners on the way home.

They were still sufficiently distant that they had to tap-dance around the subject of his bad behaviour, his recent blues, and his deteriorating life. Tommy tried valiantly near the end of the evening.

'I think I've had it with football, Mel,' he said later, as she leaned against him in their booth in the emptying restaurant. 'The FA can kiss my arse after what they've done to me.'

'Don't let's talk about that now, Thomas.'

'I might just go back to the Sunday leagues. Damn, I forgot about Fat Paul . . .'

She went quiet. He looked at her. She was pissed off. He shut up.

Fat Paul's brother Phil left a couple more intimidating messages on the answering machine over the next week. Either he was too thick to realise there was no one home during the day or he didn't really want to speak to a human. In any case, his thing was he was going to avenge his brother and give Tommy 'a lesson in etiquette, viz and to wit, a good facking kickin'.' Both times he got to the message before Melissa and erased it. But it meant he had to check his messages every few hours from work, which was a pain in the arse.

English February was in full swing, as friendly as a lump of dry ice. The trees were as black as fire-irons against the sky. For all the wobble of the earth, the evenings didn't seem to be getting any lighter, and it was now two whole months since the shortest day. Sometimes it rained a cold rain, designed specifically to wet the cheeks and to go down the back of the neck, but most of the time it was just cold, cold enough to hurt the ears. As often as not there was frost on the ground when Tommy left for work. He began keeping an ice scraper in the front garden, behind the wall, and he'd go over to Melissa's car and clear her windows, and sometimes inscribe a tiny heart or a word in a little corner of the frost. He wanted to hang on to her. He had been thinking lately that soon she might be all he had left.

His patients still made him miserable. He had a man with depression, John, who was sixty-five. John had read somewhere that he had always been depressed, but that he had never realised it until his life fell apart. He was a school janitor, and he was let go at fifty-seven. His wife of twenty-seven years ran off with a younger man, the bar manager at the club they went to. So he couldn't go there any more. His kids had all left home, and were living messy lives of their own out in Staines and Esher. He didn't like going all the way out there and they didn't seem to want him round much. Tommy talked to him for a while and explained a bit about the condition, and wrote him out a prescription for some downers. He lent him a copy of a book about depression called *Darkness Visible*, and warned him that although it would make him even more miserable at first, and extremely frightened, it'd do him good in the end. John promised to read it before he started on the new tablets. He said he used to read a lot of books when he was a janitor, as the previous janitor had died and left a huge box of old Louis L'Amour westerns, so this wouldn't be too difficult. And he shuffled off back into the city.

There was a girl in, age seventeen, who thought she had the flesh-eating virus and wanted breast reduction. Tommy explained to her as patiently as he could that these were unlikely and unnecessary. The red marks on her arms looked like psoriasis, and he would have added that her ample breasts were fine, and, in fact, might turn out to be her two best friends in life, at least until she was about his age. But the doctor-patient relationship wouldn't have allowed it. So he asked her to wait a bit, at least until she was eighteen and wouldn't have to drag her parents into it.

These people sapped Tommy's energy, but none so much as the little boy with the caliper foot who sat obediently on the bench while his mother did all the talking. The little boy, no more than about seven, looked up at him through spectacles that were like the kind of glass bricks that architects built restaurants out of. Tommy tapped the kid's back, marvelling silently at how pigeon-chested he was, as concave as his super-powered lenses.

'So what do you want to be when you grow up, Scott?'

'I wanna play for Spurs,' he said shyly.

His mother sighed heavily, and Tommy tried to add something that the kid would remember, even as his stomach churned with sadness.

'Well, you keep practising, and maybe you will.'

The child looked up at him, smiling a huge smile. Tommy had to hide his face in a cabinet for a moment while the wetness in his eyes subsided and the tightness in his throat went away.

He sent them packing with an asthma inhaler. *Another one*, he groaned, and held his head.

And then one day he checked his messages and heard this:

'Tom. It's Mark. How's things? Give me a call tonight.'

His heart and mind raced: *What did he sound like? Is he still pissed off? Is he over it? He sounded normal.* He listened to the short message seven times, then erased it. *I still have his fucking umbrella.*

At five o'clock he raced home from work, as fast as the bus would carry him. He called, and got Father Kelly. He sounded fucked off, as usual, and wanted to know who it was.

'Ah, it's *you*,' he said, disapprovingly. 'Well, you left in a fine state last time, didn't ye. We don't really want any trouble from your sort up here ...'

Tommy interrupted him. 'Could you just put him on? I'm returning his call.' He heard Mark's measured step coming down the stairs and along the hall, and the rustle of the elder priest relinquishing his grip on the phone.

'Mark, how's it going? You get my card?' He gulped. 'I'm really sorry about Blues and all that, I was thinking I could come up ...'

The young priest interrupted him. His voice was flat, affectless.

'Oh. No worries, Tom. Everything's OK. I should have got back to you sooner.' He sighed. 'I've just had some bad news, Tom. In the last hour.'

'What? What?' Tommy was terrified. He knew nothing about this man's life, was attached to nothing that surrounded him, and yet he was terrified that something bad had happened. Surely someone had died. His mind spun crazily as he tried to think who.

'I don't believe it. Darren's dead. Killed on his motorbike last night.'

'Darren? What, Our Darren?'

'No, no, a different one. You don't know him. He's a local lad. Goes to church ... he used to be an altar server here. He was nineteen. Now he's ... dead.' He spoke slowly, and sounded like he was spacing out.

'Mark? You OK?' *Fuck, it's just another death after all. He should be used to it by now. I bet it happens all the time. What's up with him? What's so special about this one?* 'Mark?' It had gone very quiet at his end.

'Yeah, I'm still here. I can't believe it. The coppers ... the police just rang. They spoke to the hospital. The hospital said he died of massive internal injuries ... what does that mean?'

'Could be anything. Ruptured spleen, punctured lungs, liver knocked around, massive shock to the nervous system ... there's this thing called brain shear, where the brain shakes around so hard inside the skull that it comes away from its moorings — there's, like, little rubbery handles that hold it in place, stop it spinning around too much in the skull. Could be that. But that normally just leaves you like a vegetable. It was probably a combination of things.'

There was a short pause while Mark took this in.

'What kind of bike was it?' *Oops, wish I hadn't said that.*

'Triumph. Daytona T595. One of those new jobs.'

*Nice. What year?* he wondered.

'So ...' Tommy tried to think of something else to ask. He realised how much he took death for granted, from his time in casualty at the teaching hospital where there was a mushed corpse being brought in every day (always followed by bewildered parents or kids), and from his everyday life as a GP, where everyone was shuffling towards their end. No one ever came to him when they were well. No one came and said, 'Doctor, I feel fucking fantastic – my head is clear, my dick is hard, I can taste my dinner and everybody wants a piece of me ...' Death seemed like natural punctuation to him, even when it occurred a bit early.

Mark roused himself from his daydream.

'I have to tell his mum. I don't know what to say.'

'Did you volunteer? I thought it was the coppers' job. They're paid a lot more than you are to do that sort of thing.'

'Yeah, I volunteered. What am I going to say?'

Tommy leapt at his cue and grabbed it.

'Just stick to the facts. Hold the commentary. In your case, the religious stuff. Start with "He's had a bad accident – in fact he's dead", then work backwards. Tell her what the coppers told you, and what the hospital told them. Motorbike, internal injuries, that's it. She'll have the picture by then. Believe me, they can't take much in after the death bit ... well, they can take some things in, and it sticks with them for ever. So if you get too abstract with them – telling them that he's probably up there on God's right hand right now, or that the doctor said he held on for half an hour – you'll just spook her and she'll hate you for ever. Let the hospital deal with the ugly stuff. And save the right hand of God for the funeral.'

Mark was silent for a few moments. 'I see what you mean.' It was as though his voice was thawing around the edges, there was some warmth in it again. 'Thanks, Tommy. I probably would have mentioned heaven, just to cheer her up. Right now I s'pose she won't take it. It's just that he was such a good kid ...'

'Yeah, I know,' said Mark softly. 'You sound like you were close.'

'We were,' he replied. He was choked.

'Listen, man, you have to remember, just do your job. It's his mum you're talking to. I don't know her but I doubt if she'll want anyone else competing in the grief stakes for the first few minutes. You have to be very strong, and very calm. It gets easier after that. You'll thank me for this, Mark. I know what I'm on about.'

'Yes. Thanks.'

'Give me a call ... tomorrow night.'

'OK. 'Bye. Thanks, Tom.'

'No problem, man. Good luck.' He hung up. 'Fuck, it feels good to be useful,' he declared. Melissa had just come in from school and heard the last part of the call.

'What was all that?' she asked, suitably reverent. She hadn't heard that tone of voice from him in years. Or seen that shine in his eyes for months.

'One of Mark's mates ... one of his congregation, actually, just wiped out on his bike. He's dead. Nineteen.'

She was aghast, dropping her bag and sitting down next to him on the sofa, her coat still on. Tommy often wondered about that: why other people's deaths, which had nothing to do with some people, could make such an impact on them. *She didn't even know he existed until ten seconds ago. Strange.* He had no intention of saying anything about that, though. That was one for the vault.

'What happened?' she asked.

What happened was Tommy got a bit of leverage back in his relationship with Mark. He had made some impact, and in a way he never thought possible – with his worldly London way, with his doctorliness, with his bedside manner. He felt OK. He felt a bit sorry for the kid's mother, and for Mark having to deal with it. But mainly he felt better in himself.

He explained the facts as he knew them. Then he filled her in on the relationship front. Then he threw in a description of the bike – its full sport fairing, its racing bars, its 128 horses, d.o.h.c. – and his understanding of the injuries that might have killed him. He knew she loved his adventures in physiology, his X-ray eyes and his Latin name for each separate thing.

This death seemed to cast a pall over her evening. Tommy didn't mind – they sat in and talked for a bit, then they watched telly together, quietly, disengaged and unimpressed. It became clear to him that it took more than a TV tube pumping bad news into the living room to stir up their feelings. If it was on the news, it would have meant nothing to anyone in England. You'd have to make an hour-long documentary about this kid, including footage of his corpse, if not his actual crash, to bring the tragedy home to a stranger. On the other hand, all you needed was a tenuous human link and it went straight to the heart ... to Melissa, a friend of a friend of a friend had just died, and that was enough to send her spinning off into melancholy for the rest of the evening.

So when Tommy floated the idea of his going up for the funeral, she readily assented.

*I'm an old hand at this, I'm a fuckin' old hand at this, oh yes I am, getting off the train, finding my way through this other city,* he thought cheerfully to himself as the train pulled into New Street at lunch-time that Saturday. Every link in the chain was familiar again to him. The buying of the ticket, the magazine and the sandwich at Euston. The locomotive's *glissando* departure. The thinning out of the cockneys on the train, being replaced by green-belters and finally, at Rugby, the genre-defying mutants with accents half Midlands, half southern. The pretty woman going north. The students, who smelt of kitchens, damp and cigarettes. The white sun hanging low in the winter sky. The bit where you rolled into Brum through Small Heath's blasted landscape ... *Hmm, I never noticed all those new houses before,* he thought this time. They had built new back-to-back houses there for the poor, a bit like the ones they pulled down in the seventies, and called it Bordesley Village. As in Bordesley Green. Only these were made of that stuff you can punch a hole in with your fist, instead of brick. *New slums for a new millennium. I wonder if they need a slogan?* And so they rolled into the heart of town, going into the darkness at the last minute.

Flourishing the umbrella like a gentleman, Tommy strode up the stairs, through the ticket barrier, and out by the taxi rank. Mark was meeting him at the Odeon again. The funeral was that afternoon at Witton Cemetery. Only Mark would do a funeral on a Saturday. The mother of the kid – Biker Darren, as people in the area called him – couldn't get him buried by Friday, and refused to wait till the Monday. First it was delayed because the paperwork wasn't in order. Then she hadn't paid for his plot. Then the jobsworth at the cemetery said he hadn't time to dig a grave. And he didn't encourage Saturday funerals anyway. Mark had gone down there personally, at six o'clock on the Friday night, and pleaded with them to dig the hole.

The old bastard was having none of it, but the goofy-looking work-experience kid with a mask of acne came up to him. The boss packed his things away and walked out, calling to the kid to make sure he locked up.

'Hang on a minute, Father.'

They waited in silence till he had gone down the path. Mark was edgy, pacing around. He saw a shovel in the corner of the office and grabbed it. He was up for it.

'No need for that,' said the kid, looking very determined and serious. 'I know where the digger is.'

He led Mark outside to a shed and opened the door. There was a yellow mini-JCB inside that was used for digging graves.

'Just cleaned it up for the weekend, but ...'

'You're a good man,' said Mark, looking him in the eye, and the boy blushed. He started it and drove them out to the plot.

'It was that young kid, wasn't it? I know where he is,' he shouted. They bumped along together down the grassy aisles. 'You 'ave to be careful of the arm, keep it down as much as you can. First time he let me out on this I knocked the 'ead off an angel. He went fuckin' spare at me! We spent hours trying to glue it back on.'

They found the plot and laboured together under the feeble headlights, taking turns at operating the machine and calling out directions. The teeth cut through the frozen soil with ease. Mark got hot, throwing off his coat, then his jacket, then rolling up his shirt-sleeves. The boy was impressed as he watched the cleric's big forearms and hands mastering the controls with ease.

Because of the dark, it took them an hour to get the grave dug, but they did it. When they got back to the office, Mark looked in his wallet for something to give him. There was just one tenner, his pocket money for a week, but he gave it to the kid, forcing it into his hand and thanking him profusely.

'God bless you, son, you've done a great thing tonight.'

Tommy sat on his haunches outside the Odeon. While he was waiting for the battered old Vespa to come round the corner, he watched the people idly. There seemed to be more well-heeled old people around than he was used to, not just the normal moth-eaten pensioners existing on 1940s diets. A splendid motorbike pulled up, catching his eye. It was black, sporty-looking and with a showroom sheen. The rider looked like a space alien – he wore a well-fitting black leather one-piece, with cream stripes coming from the shoulders, right down the sleeves to the cuffs, and on up the gloves to the little finger. The helmet, which was pointy like an egg, was all black, with an impenetrable black visor.

Tommy stayed where he was – impressed, interested, but unaware that it was anything to do with him. After waiting a few seconds, the rider kicked down the side stand and opened his visor. He saw the cool blue eyes of Mark.

'Fucking hell, what's all this?' shouted Tommy, getting to his feet and marching over.

Mark grinned at him. 'I'll explain later. Hop on. Schedule's tight today.'

Tommy recognised the scabby old helmet tied down on the passenger seat with an elastic octopus. He put it on and hopped on to the pegs.

With a flick of his wrist, Mark flew out into the traffic, threw it down the long gap between two buses, and headed off up New Street. They approached the turn into Corporation Street at thirty.

'WHOA! Look out!' Tommy shouted. He already thought they'd had it. At first he assumed they'd slow down. Then he assumed he'd be wrapped around a traffic light in the next half-second. Mark leaned in viciously to the curve, like an animal on all fours, leaving his passenger high and dry, his torso waving under the Gs. They took the corner without losing speed, and once on the straight, Mark popped it into second and they hared up Corporation Street.

'Hang on to me, not the seat,' he heard Mark shout. 'And lean!'

He rearranged his grip just in time, as they flew up the humpback by Rackhams at sixty. Tommy's stomach dangled in the air. He was sure they had left the road for a second. He was trying to keep the umbrella jammed tight under his armpit, and every few seconds imagined how nasty it would be if they crashed. The noise in his ears was frightening – the smooth howl of the three-cylinder engine and the streak of black had all the shoppers turning to gape.

Round the big island they went again, up the James Watt Queensway to Lancaster Circus – Tommy leaning hard by now – then on to the Aston Expressway. Tommy's life was flashing before his eyes – what took minutes before was being accomplished in seconds.

'Slow down, you mad fucker,' he shouted.

If Mark replied, he didn't make himself heard above the noise of rushing air and the hammering 955cc engine. Tommy leaned forward against the tornado wind and tried to get a look at the speedo. He felt a clunk as Mark kicked it into fourth gear, and saw to his horror the needle moving smoothly round the dial, like the second hand of a school clock: 80 . . . 90 . . . 100 . . . and settling at 110. Villa Park went by like a cartoon backdrop, fast parallaxes gobbling up the edges and angles of the new stands.

*Oh, Jesus. Let me off this thing alive,* he prayed, *and I'll go to Mass again, I promise. I'll do good deeds. I'll be nicer to my patients . . .*

They were coming to the turn-off – Tommy noticed because he surged forward until he was glued to his friend's back, and the speedo needle dropped like a stone back to forty. A few wiggles later they were pulling up outside the priests' house.

Tommy pulled his helmet off. His ears were ringing from the noise of the wind and the hammering triple. All he could do was stare at his friend. Mark locked the steering and began walking in.

'I've got fucking frostbite, I swear,' Tommy muttered, banging his hands together.

They sat at the kitchen table, and Mark told him about the motorcycle.

'Darren's mother said I could have the bike. She insisted on it. She said she never wanted to see it again, or have anything to do with it. I told her someone should try and sell it ... must be worth a few thousand pounds. But she wouldn't have anything to do with it.'

'What, so she wants you to break *your* neck on it?'

'No, no! She just wants to get it out of the way. That bike was his passion, in the few months he had it. He had a paper round at school, then he saved from his job like mad until he had enough. He was barmy about it. She wants it out of the way, but I expect in a few months she'll be back for it.'

'What year is it?' asked Tommy, relieved that it was OK now to talk about the motorbike, to which he had a strong attraction already. Melissa had made him sell his old 350 Suzuki when they moved in together. She claimed it was 'too dangerous', even though she'd never ridden it herself, or even been on the back for very long. She wouldn't let him have a bike. He could read bike magazines, but that was it. As a protest, he refused to buy himself a car.

'Ninety-six. Three thousand on the clock when he got it. Five and a half now. Well, I've ridden it a bit since he ... died.' He sighed. 'I just wanted to ...'

'What?'

'Oh ...' Mark had suddenly run out of steam. He was having trouble with his words. There was a look of immense sadness on his face, and he wasn't used to going heart to heart with anyone. The sun was coming in through the kitchen window, adding an inappropriate jollity to the atmosphere. Over his shoulder Tommy saw a robin skipping around on the window sill.

'Did you go out to where it happened?' he asked quietly.

Mark nodded. After a few seconds he got up the strength to speak.

'It was out past Monkspath, Solihull, that way, heading out into the country. He used to go for these long rides after work, in the dark, because it was the only time he had. His insurance was something silly, you know – mad young kid, probably a hundred quid a month. He just wanted to ride. Someone saw him on the M42 earlier in the evening.'

'Going mad?'

'No. Seventies, eighties. I talked to him about this before. I don't think he was a speed freak. He just loved his bike. And it killed him.' Mark stared at the ground, his face dark as thunderclouds.

'Did they find out what happened?'

'Well, it's pretty mysterious. It looks like he just missed his turn. It was a sharp bend, but open fields on both sides, just a bit of a hedge. I suppose he must have taken it too quickly, because he went into a field of grass and just slid. Police measured it, forty yards. They reckon he was doing about sixty-five. I went down there. It looked like the most ordinary place in the world. The corner was a bit sharp, but not a right angle. He must have totally missed it. It was cold and dry, but there was no frost. Those bikes corner really well ...' He was choked up again, and paused. 'Anyway, the hospital reckon he was *shaken* to death. You were right. The bike was absolutely fine, just a bit of mud in the air intake on one side. The only thing was ... no one saw it happen, and his lights went out, so he was lying in this field all night, all on his tod, till he was found by a postman in the morning.'

Mark was leaning forward, shaking his head as he stared at the ground. 'All night on his own. In the cold. And the dark.' The thought brought tears to his eyes. One of them dropped from his downturned face and landed on the gear-changing toecap of his boot.

Tommy waited. There was nothing to be said.

After a few minutes, he moved in his chair and said in a cheerful voice, to reel his friend back in, 'Nice gear.'

The priest flicked the gloves on the quilted leather of his knee, and sighed, and looked up with a watery smile. 'Yeah. He had all the stuff. Boots, everything fits. I really should get it off the street, though, before she comes round for the funeral. They'll be here in an hour or so. I shouldn't be wearing this stuff either, but it makes sense, doesn't it? Better than trainers. And a cassock. Hah!' And he laughed bitterly at himself.

Tommy had never seen a bitter, sad priest before. He had never seen Mark like this before either. He had seen him angry, and violent, and fucked off, and proud, and pleased. He'd never seen him really happy either. Or bored, now that he thought about it. His mind was always ticking over. Mark held his head up at all times – going into a strange pub, when Villa were slinking back from a day of shame somewhere; even when he was being nicked the coppers had to struggle to hold his head down. Tommy found the change a lot to handle. But he decided to handle it.

'Hey, this is for you,' he said, handing him the umbrella. 'Merry Christmas.'

Mark unfurled it and put it straight up. Neither of them was superstitious. When women came to him with chain letters, Mark made a point of tearing them up for them during Mass, just before the sermon. Just to show you couldn't get bad luck in the post. It always sent a thrill through the congregation. It seemed to make them listen harder and trust him more, for the next ten minutes.

It was big and broad, and had an elegant curve to it. 'Smart!' he said. He was touched.

'See, no rattling, and no weedy stitching. And if it ever breaks they say they'll fix it for free.'

'This is great, Tom, thank you.' He furled it up again with some pride. 'Better bring it with us today.'

They were both on their feet. There was still the bike to deal with.

'Here, I'll stick the Triumph round the back for you.'

'Thanks.' He threw him the keys, and Tommy went out into the cold again and wheeled it round the back of the house, hiding it behind the bins.

When he got back in, the priest was upstairs shaving and getting ready, so Tommy fished in his coat pocket and spent a productive hour at the kitchen table with Old Moore's Almanac. Apparently, it would piss with rain all March and the pound would sink. But it didn't say who was going to win the FA Cup.

An hour later, Tommy stood at the back of the Sacred Heart Church as the mourners began to file in, traipsing confetti bells and horseshoes up the aisle. He didn't fancy everyone looking at him wondering who the fuck he was. Up the front was the coffin, the usual cheap ash veneer and hollow brass fixtures. He could just make out the crucifix attached to the lid.

There was not a great crowd by kick-off time. There was the mother – ashen-faced and deadly grim, dressed in total black, including a black lace mantilla. The two sisters – a sixteen-year-old with some puppy fat around her face and a barrel shape through her coat, looking by turns bored and cross, and a twelve-year-old who tried to hang on to her mother's hand as much as the adult would allow it. There were several uncle-looking blokes, and a few of their kids, a granny type on the other side, and some spotty teenagers who stuck together. There were some work people, a mixed bag. Most had made an effort to wear black, except for the elder sister, whose coat was red and turquoise. But there was a lot of grey showing – grey ties, grey shoes, badly washed whites.

Mark came out. There was no altar server, as obsequies were not a Holy Communion event. He had always thought this was a wasted opportunity when he was younger – get some of those heathens and lapsers back on track. Feed 'em. But now he saw the rationale: people couldn't stomach too much Jesus at a time like this. He needed no help sprinkling the long box with holy water. One of the kids had suggested they put his helmet on the coffin, but Mark and the mother were both against it. She was grief-stricken at the mere thought of the object; Mark didn't want to glorify the way he died.

Instead of going behind the altar, the priest stayed on the steps and conducted the short service from there, within yards of the coffin and the mourners. He dispensed with the standard opening – 'In the name of the Father', etc. – simply beginning, in a loud clear voice, 'Friends and family of Darren Coates. I welcome you today into the house of the Lord, to say goodbye to His son. The service will be followed by a burial at Witton Cemetery. I ask you now to pray for the soul of Darren ...'

Mark looked good with his neatly combed hair and his vestments. He wore the *feria* green, the nothing-important-about-today colour. Tommy tried to imagine him in the white of Easter Sunday, or the gold of benediction ... It would suit him.

Suddenly he heard a voice at his side with a thick Brummie accent.

'Well, look what the fuggin cat dragged in!' A few people turned to see what the noise was. Mark paused a moment. Tommy turned to see who it was. It was Kevin in his wheelchair, and he was addressing his remarks to Tommy, who shushed him, out of reverence rather than fear of embarrassment.

Kevin wheeled himself around a pillar and then reversed, so that he could be as near to Tommy as possible.

'The fuggin doctor is in the house, is he? I tellya, mate, yow's a bit late now, eh?' Kevin had on a zip-up nylon jacket and jeans, and his chicken legs were lashed together with a rainbow luggage strap. His hair was down, and looked like it had been washed. But nothing could wash the leering smile off his face, or straighten the mouth that was preparing for its next sarcastic remark.

Tommy nodded, and looked back at the sanctuary.

'So what the fuck brings yer up to Brummagem?' he asked, still in a disturbingly loud voice. Then, accusingly: 'Ambulance chaser!'

Tommy was forced to move down to the end of the row to keep him quiet.

'Knock it off, Kevin, people can hear you,' he hissed.

'Oh, foine, *foine*, be like that. Just deaf me out, then. Send me to fuggin Coventroy,' he went on in a theatrical whisper.

He waited a few minutes, rustling in his chair, trying to settle. Then he whispered again. 'So 'ow long did yow know Darren, then?'

'I didn't know him. What's it to you anyway?' whispered Tommy coolly. *Something about this fucker always rattles me. I never know what he's gonna say next.*

'Nuffink! Nuffink!' he said, with exaggerated innocence. He waited another minute. Then: 'Hey, yow ain't one of those weirdos who looks through the paper and goes to random funerals, are ya?'

'Shut up and listen.'

'Oooh, we're very hoigh an' moighty, aren't we?'

'Please be seated,' the priest said.

'Fanks, oi already am,' said Kevin loudly, but his voice was masked by scuffling of feet and creaking of wood. Tommy sat and crossed his left leg over his right, then put his chin on his hand. He wanted to hear what Mark was going to say. He wanted to know why he was so upset. But Kevin was getting on his tits. After he had been quiet for the duration of the reading, Tommy looked around and saw Kevin mimicking his pose, only without the crossed leg. *Twat*, he thought. Kevin grinned back. Tommy slid down the bench a couple of feet to get away from him again.

Mark was speaking slowly and carefully, almost as if he were avoiding the subject of the dead young man. He was speaking of scripture, finding examples of where death had opened up on to life. This was small comfort to the grieving, however. The sixteen-year-old twisted in her seat every few minutes and looked around at the boys behind her. The twelve-year-old rested her head on her mother's shoulder. Everybody else seemed agitated and bored, scratching and picking, and flicking through the missals. Mark then began running through some of Darren's attributes. Again Tommy was surprised at how many he managed to come up with, given that the kid was only nineteen. He was selfless, he was hard-working, he had a vision and he stuck to it. He didn't drink (the boys rapidly put their heads together on this one, but Tommy couldn't tell from the backs of their necks whether they were disagreeing or just checking what the others knew). *I hope Mark's right*, he found himself thinking. *I hope he's not just making a prat out of himself.*

'Darren was, and I hope will always be remembered as, a product of this environment. He was born a few hundred yards from here, he grew up here, he was an altar server long before I ever came along.' Mark was now walking around as he spoke, very slowly, coming close to the coffin and the six lit candles, but never looking directly at it. 'I remember once, when he was about fifteen, he gave me a mini-lecture on how to shave three and a half minutes off the Mass time. His technique was to walk quickly, bring up the chalice and the missal and everything I needed before I asked for it, and to avoid long pauses. I thanked him, and I said Mass. When we came into the sacristy afterwards, he looked at his watch and said we had taken exactly the same time as before. He wanted to know why that was, since, as he put it, "It felt faster to me." So I had to explain to him that all the hurrying had left us with more time to pray and be alone with God, together, at the end, after the communion, which is the most important time of the Mass. He said he hadn't noticed. That was when I realised what a special person he was, and thought he was destined for great things. Because it takes a truly holy person to be able to commune with the Lord and be so absorbed in it, and not feel restless. That is the goal we always aim for as priests. Good deeds are not enough unless they are accompanied by good words, and the best words we can speak are in the privacy of our own head, to the Creator.'

Suddenly it came to Tommy. *He had him down as a vocation, that was it! Poor bastard. He was looking for just one kid he could help become a priest like himself. Now he's fucked. Look at this lot. There's no chance after this.*

Mark continued, never mentioning the bike by name, just briefly referring to 'his hobby', and 'his tragedy'. Tommy instinctively looked over at Kevin, who had grown very quiet. Kevin turned and glared back at him. When he remained unmoved, Kevin used his best muscles and pulled a stupid face at him, then turned away.

After the sermon came the hymn. A few days before, Mark had asked the mother if the boy had had a favourite hymn. Sheryl, the little sister, said he had, it was the Christmas carol 'Good King Wenceslas', but her mother overruled her harshly. She went instead for 'Lead Heavenly Light, Amid th' Encircling Gloom'.

'Why don't you just play one of his Slayer tapes?' said the surly sixteen-year-old, for which she got a whack round the back of the head. Mother scowled at her, and looked to the priest for forgiveness – for herself and her daughter. She was devout. And there weren't many like her left.

As the last verse ended, and the sobs grew louder, Mark nodded to the boys, and then to Tommy. He wanted bodies to help carry out the coffin. *Fuck, right,* thought Tommy. *Here we go, then. Four should do it.*

As he slid past Kevin's wheelchair he said to him, 'You coming up to help, Kev? You can strap him on and we'll push.' He didn't wait for a reply, but within a few seconds his annoyance had turned to self-loathing. *Why did I have to say that? What a sick bastard I am.* For a second he tried to justify it, as he often tried to justify his whole life, by saying that he was around disease and decline and death all day, and that humour was his coping mechanism. But he knew it wasn't true. He was beginning to realise – sometimes he was just very bad, by choice. Arguing about it, with others or himself, was just window-dressing.

Outside, they manhandled the coffin on to Killingworth & Son's chrome trolley and it was slid into the back of the hearse. Then came the awkward hiatus. The lucky few got into a Daimler, which was part of the Economy Package – three live passengers, two cars, one box. The other people stood around saying in strange accents, 'Where did he say it was?', and replying, 'Follow the hearse, you fooking idiot, before it gets away from us!' Then they scurried off to their own cars, their Datsuns and their Granadas.

They all set off, and that left Mark, Tommy and Kevin on the pavement.

'Well, I've got a minicab coming,' said Kevin. 'But I'd rather be alone at this point. If you don't mind.'

*You scheming little bastard. 'Fraid we won't split the cost?*

Mark heard it differently. 'Of course, Kev,' he said gently, 'I understand.'

Kevin's face betrayed nothing. One could even imagine he was feeling upset.

'Looks like the scooter for us, Tommy boy,' Mark said, marching off. He seemed suddenly excited about getting everyone there, like he was organising a family day out.

'Yeah, well, watch how you drive. I want to do this trip again some day, but in style.'

They wove through the traffic at Witton Island, went over the snot-green

River Tame and past IMI, past the flower-seller under the M6, then left, to run alongside the high brick wall of the cemetery until they got to the gates. Tommy had the umbrella square across his lap this time. Inside Mark thrashed the two-stroke engine to get them both up the hill. He had to search a little for the plot, as he hadn't yet seen it in daylight. When he found it, he parked the scooter on the asphalt and walked across the grass to the spot.

'I've got a deal with Killingworth, he's a good bloke. When Father Kelly's got the car and I'm on the scooter, so that the relatives don't see me turning up on "that piece of junk", as I heard one of them refer to it once, I give him my gear and have him take them round the long way, right under Spaghetti and down the side of Brookvale Park. That way I get here before everyone else.'

'Apart from him, of course,' said Tommy, drawing his friend's attention to the figure in the wheelchair struggling across the frozen ruts to get to the hole. The three of them arrived at it at the same time.

'Ah,' went Kevin, acknowledging them. Clearly he didn't take the piss so much in Father Mark's presence. They all stared at the grave. 'This is a bit wonky, innit? That's what it'd look like if I dug it.'

The grave was perfectly shaped at grass level, a slender seven-by-three rectangle. And it was nice and deep, the requisite six foot – in the middle. Unfortunately at each end there were sloping ledges, and at different heights, caused by the earth not being fully cleared. It was obvious the coffin would perch unevenly in the hole, halfway down instead of at the bottom.

'Oh no.'

'Who did this? It's crap,' said Tommy.

'Hang on,' said Mark, and he went sprinting away across the grass to the gravediggers' HQ.

Tommy hadn't been in this cemetery for years. He had forgotten how good the view of the city was. The air was grey, slightly misty, and through the haze you could see Villa Park clearly, and the city centre faintly. The constant drone of traffic was a comforting white noise that went perfectly with the bad air.

Tommy and Kevin looked at each other. 'I bet you a fiver he comes back with two shovels,' said Kevin.

Mark came sprinting back with three shovels. He threw one to Tommy, laid one across Kevin's lap, and set to work himself, jumping into the grave and chipping away at the web of soil.

'I can't reach that!' said Kevin, incredulously.

'Just do your best, Kevin. They'll be here any moment.'

Tommy set to work too, smirking. Kevin inched forward to the abyss and leaned as far as he could, dangling the shovel with one hand, trying to make an impact on the frozen earth. He didn't say a word.

They got it clear, and the hearse arrived, right on time. Mark got changed under a stripped elm, slightly away from the crowd, and with everyone ringed around the hole the interment began. Even though it was bitterly cold, it started to spit with rain.

Tommy and Kevin had placed themselves back a little, away from the crowd. When he felt the rain, Tommy remembered the brolly, meaning to hand it over to the priest. But Killingworth sprang forward and protected Mark with his own umbrella – giant and black and just as impressive as his own. A few more went up – five-pound jobbies with one-foot stems, in paisley and flowers. Some of the men without merely hunched their shoulders against the cold water and squinted. The rain pitter-pattered on the plastic sheeting around the grave.

Mark's voice was mostly lost on the wind, as he spoke the words to the service. 'Ashes to ashes, dust to dust,' he intoned bravely, and then a bit would be lost. He looked freezing too. The mother's shoulders shook as the tears flowed again. He was her only son. He had been the man of the house ever since the father had run off. In fact, he had kicked him out when he tried to come back one time, pissed and broke and looking more for a place to sleep and people to look up to him than simply for a shag. Darren had kicked him down the stairs and dragged him into the street by his leg.

Tommy and Kevin suspended hostilities as they sheltered together. The words, the tears, the whole business of standing round and waiting for the box to be lowered ... it depressed the hell out of both of them. When it came to the shaking of the holy water on to the coffin and the priest's was the only voice fighting against the wind, and the priest was the only one with anything to say, and all that he had to say was ancient ritual, lines long ago written down that spoke of returning to the soil, from where we all came, Tommy was gutted. It was wretched. *Is he trying to console us any more? Or is he going off on his own trip about heaven and how great it's gonna be? Look at the mad determination on his face ...*

He glanced down at Kevin. His ears were scarlet from the cold, poking out through his long hair, but his face was as white as if he'd just staggered off the hovercraft from Calais.

Then the coffin was lowered in on canvas belts by Killingworth and his son, and the relatives were invited to throw in a handful of dirt. Mark had to step across and help the mother, whose hand shook so violently that at first she couldn't pick any up, and then she couldn't let any go.

Kevin was staring steely-faced, straight ahead. He was barely breathing. Tommy sighed. Just before death, he could handle. Just after death was a lot more troubling. *Nineteen-year-old kid going to his grave so soon. Never even got to ride his bike anywhere interesting. Never got to ride through St Tropez in shorts and flips-flops, or sit on it backwards eating cassis sorbet and watching the girls go by. Wonder if he was an organ donor?*

Tommy imagined the boy's clean liver curled up like a young cat in his ribcage. He had found people didn't really appreciate the liver – how huge it was, where it sat, how important it was. Everything was important in the body, of course, but the liver did loads of things, not just cleansing the blood. You couldn't go out and get pissed and go into work the next day without your liver. He used to get people to point to it. Most of them went for the kidneys or the appendix. Melissa knew where everything was. She could even point to his prostate gland. *She hasn't done that for a while. God, we really are getting less intimate.*

The service was over. The next awkward phase was everyone heading back to Darren's mum's house, where the family had prepared a buffet. Kevin even let Tommy help him through the muddy ruts. The cabbie folded up his *Mirror* and got out to help the cripple into the car.

'I hope you had the fuggin meter off this time,' said Kevin once he was in. He was scowling again.

Soon everyone was gone, trailing exhaust smoke in the cold air. Mark looked drained. He was back in his black raincoat, wearing the old helmet. They got on the scooter and made their way back into Aston, doing less than thirty all the way. *He must be bad,* thought Tommy. *So much for the heavenly host and the choir of angels.*

Mrs Coates wasn't such a hot host either. Her daughters made sure everyone had four fingers of Irish whiskey, but she just sat in her chair like a zombie. It was an hour before she even took her coat off. Everyone sat around, in silence at first, in the tiny parlour, spilling over into the hall and the kitchen. As the booze and the sausage rolls went down, the conversation started and gained momentum. The little sister put on some Metallica, so quiet that it could only be heard in the gaps. Mark floated around as best he could, consoling those who cared, encouraging the rest to reminisce. Even the few work people who felt nothing more than their own guilt at not really knowing the boy very well came under Mark's spell, and relaxed.

Kevin parked himself next to Tommy, who had found a spot on the floor and was tucking into his whiskey. He didn't much like whiskey, but after the first few gulps it began to appeal. It had to. There were no good stories about Darren – he had been too young and wasn't very funny. He didn't have a girlfriend. His mother could have told a few toddler tales, but her mouth was pursed shut, her drink untouched.

So the conversation came round to football, since that was the one thing everyone had in common. The few relatives from up north were Sheffield Wednesday fans, which caused Tommy's ears to prick up. He had respect for Wednesday. They used to be hard. He had done a Wednesday game earlier in the year, versus Sunderland. He was impressed by how much they hated each other. That was the only advantage of being stuck up in the north of the country, as far as he could see – you were more prepared to go out on a limb and make a local rival out of someone. It wasn't the same in Brum. Tommy had never really loathed people like Coventry and Leicester, he just pitied them. Notts Forest maybe. *They were bastards.*

The Northerners talked about their team, and their city. It sounded like a decent place. Tommy wished he had stayed overnight there when he had the chance. Things were going well, there was a hubbub in the room. It died down for a moment when Mother got up and left to go upstairs. The little girl followed her but soon came back. The noise started up again. Kevin was arguing with one of Darren's mates about bikes. They were young kids and as far as he was concerned, they knew fuck all. One of them had a 125, that was it. He bragged about his old De Luxe, as he called it – his CX 500 – and also the Gold Wing he'd ridden for a summer once, but they didn't really know what he was on about. He started sounding off about the Yamaha YZF600R and how it compared to the Honda CBR600F3. He talked as though he still rode, as though he were thinking ahead to his next part-exchange. The kids were mystified, but politely did not mention his rubbery legs.

Time was zipping by. Tommy was feeling very pissed. The little girl kept topping him up. He wanted so badly to talk to her. She hadn't said a word but he could read her: she and her sister didn't miss their brother much – who would? – but they missed their mum right now. They were in agonies of loneliness.

Someone suggested putting the scores on – it was twenty to five. They sat through some rugby league until finally it came up. Villa were away at Chelsea. They drew one–one. *Boring. But a relief. At least we didn't lose. Cockney bastards.*

'Good draw,' said Tommy, and then he made a remark about the referee, Danson, who he knew was intent on lowering his disciplinary output. 'You watch – for the rest of the season he'll hardly book anyone, and he won't send anyone off. The press have been on at him. They've got their man and they're sticking with him.' The others in the room listened to him reverently. The tables flashed by. Villa were in the bottom half of the league. Wednesday were in the drop zone. It was humiliating for everyone. Someone switched it off, Tommy had another two fingers of whiskey, and found himself holding court. He was explaining the area to the Northerners.

'Hey, Mark! Stick BRMB on! Stick the sport on.'

Mark just laughed. 'It's not my house, Tom.'

The sixteen-year-old and her sister both jumped up to do it, the older one yanking her sister's hand off the radio so she could tune it. A typically transparent local radio voice came on.

'See,' slurred Tommy, 'this used to be a great show. The phone-ins after the matches. There was a bloke on called Tony Butler ... Butlah! – that's how he used to say it. He was great. Knew his football inside out. Never talked about London teams, or Liverpool or any of that lot much. It was all West Midlands. Kids ringing in after the game with nothing to say and he'd put 'em down, hang up on 'em, or they'd tell him to eff off and he'd mask it with a jingle. He'd have a decent conversation with someone, some bloke, say "Terry from Ward End" then at the end they'd say, "Oh, one more thing, Tone ..." *BRMB Ra-di-oooooo!* And you know they're on the other end going, "Fook off, ya tosser" ... 'Scuse me, kids. You didn't hear that.' The little girl just giggled, and her sister made eyes at him.

'I think I've heard of him,' said one of the Northerners helpfully.

'Oh, he was great. When we were in Europe, away, and desperate for a goal, he used to say he was getting the prayer mat out, and point it towards Villa Park, and tell everyone to get down on their knees at home, and pray to Allah for a goal. And it worked! It worked, I swear!' More and more people in the room were tuning in to Tommy now. 'Mark, what happened to him?'

'He got the sack.'

'What for?' asked Tommy, grinning.

'Er, well, I think he overran.'

'Eh?'

One of Darren's local uncles jumped in. 'No, no, he didn't overrun. He left after he had a go at someone in a wheelchair. The bloke before him did a programme about the handicapped, and he ran over into Butler's show. Two minutes – which is a lot in radio. Our kid used to work at Radio WM in the post room.'

Mark shook his head. 'I can't believe that.'

'What!' said Tommy, flabbergasted. And then he laughed like a drain ... 'A-ha, ha, HA! A-ha, ha, HA!' His eyes started to water. 'You can't be serious ...' He thought it was the funniest thing, and the fact that the bloke had told him it in front of Kevin without being bothered made it even better. A few in the room started laughing too, the ones with high alcohol content and low immunity to laughter.

Tommy laughed and laughed. The alcohol had cut him loose. Pretty soon everyone was chuckling, especially the two girls. Finally he turned to look up at Kevin in the wheelchair next to him. He realised it didn't really matter how Kevin reacted. He'd have to live with it.

Kevin was trying to laugh, but it hurt too much. His face felt frozen with a new grief, made up of pain and embarrassment. He was trying to push the corners of his mouth up and look like he got the joke, but it wasn't very convincing. Tommy smiled at this too, and slapped his lifeless leg. And then laughed some more. Slowly, Kevin thawed, and finally he managed a chuckle. No one had touched him for years, except his mom, when she wiped his bum and strapped his legs in.

'Come on, Kev, have a drink.' So far he had stuck to cola.

'I can't, I can't,' he said.

Tommy was pissed, though, and went on and on at him. 'Come o-o-on! Sheryl?' he said to the twelve-year-old. 'Get this man a drink. Stick some of that fine whiskey in his Coke.'

'I can't drink,' pleaded Kevin, like a kid being tickled. 'I'll piss meself.'

Tommy was briefly taken aback. He thought they taught these people how to control these things. 'Well ... piss yourself, then!'

Everyone laughed and the girls fought to remake his beverage. Kevin grinned inanely. He hadn't been in a situation like this before. All this attention. He didn't quite know what the fuck was going on, but he knew it wasn't that bad.

Mark stood up, looking immensely tall to the merry figures seated and sprawled about the room. 'I'm off. I'm on for the vigil tonight. Goodbye, everyone. See you later, Tommy.'

'Yeah, mate, seeya.' He tried to get to his knees but wobbled back against the wall.

'Man, you're fucked up,' said Kevin.

'Yeah, I'm legless,' said Tommy, and exploded with laughter again.

Mark shook his head, and walked out. 'Let's go and find your mum,' he said to the girls, and one scampered, the other slunk, after him.

From then on the girls only brought Tommy Coke. Then water. Then coffee. He moved to the sofa and watched a bit of telly, but couldn't really follow it. The radio show was off, but he couldn't recall a thing he'd heard. Most of the guests were drifting off. The Northerners went, shaking his hand warmly. Kevin went, saying goodbye just as Tommy turned to ask someone a question, so he never heard. Gradually, the evening turned into a puzzle, of trying to remember who was who and when they'd gone, and then it started to straighten out again. His mouth felt woolly. He started to feel a bit low. He was starving. The girls brought him the last of the ham sandwiches, and when he'd finished them, they made him some bacon baps and a pot of tea.

'Thanks, girls,' he said, feeble with self-pity. He was the last one there. Mother was still upstairs. Just the two girls remained, waiting on him.

'And listen, girls,' he said. It was time for a bit of paternal advice. 'Watch out for boys. They're only after one thing.' *Ooh, I wish I hadn't said that.* The elder one blushed crimson. The younger just looked curious.

'What?'

'Shurrup!' said her sister, and shoved her hip into her. He didn't answer. He looked at his watch. It was gone eight o'clock. 'Jesus!' he said, bolting forward. 'Me train! I have to get the train by nine.'

The elder girl's expression changed when she realised he was trying to leave. Glad to change the subject, she said, 'Father Mark said to tell you not to get the train. He wants you to take the bike to London.'

'The bike?' he said, amazed. 'Your ... brother's bike?'

'Yeah,' said the little one. 'Mum wants it out of the way, but no one's supposed to tell her you've got it. And he said we had to ... you're too pissed to drive.'

'Sober me up?'

'Yeah.'

'Right. OK. Right, girls, I'd better be going, see what he's on about.' He looked at them suspiciously. 'Sheryl? You're not making any of this up, are you?' He quite enjoyed saying that. There was a protocol for dealing with the kids who came into his surgery — you couldn't accuse them of lying, in case it skewed the results, so it was nice to get away and say whatever you wanted.

'No-o!' she said, amazed.

'Well, OK. See me out, then.'

They got his stuff. He had a bad headache already. He bade them goodbye and stumbled through the wet streets back to the church, where Mark was waiting for him.

There was no bollocking, but Mark was cool with him.

'Will you take the bike? Just say yes or no.'

'Well, why? Yeah, OK, if you want. But I still think I'm way over the limit. And it's freezing. I'll freeze.'

'You can wear the gear. Just keep everything down there for a few months. If it's here, I know I'll ride it, and I don't want to, it doesn't look good.'

'Yeah, fuck, OK, if you're sure.'

'Sure I'm sure.'

'But hang on ...' Tommy had to sit down and think. He didn't mind losing thirty quid on his train ticket, it was just that he didn't feel very steady. 'I dunno, Mark, strange bike, goes like a rocket, in the dark, in the rain ...' Mark seemed impatient. 'Tell you what — I'll get it towed! That's it! Melissa stuck me on her RAC membership, they'll put it in a van for free and take me back to London.'

'Are you sure?'

'Yeah, no sweat. I'll just fuck up one of the plugs or something, so they can't fix it.'

'You can't get to the plugs in those things very easily. Just, I dunno ... loosen the chain. Disconnect the light. And speed up the idle.'

'Right. They won't bother with all that.'

'And say you just bought it,' said Mark.

'Off a scouser. Yes! They'll go for that.'

They called the RAC, who said they'd send someone.

Mark got the leathers and the boots together, bringing them downstairs in his suitcase. 'Here, you can borrow my suitcase. I'm not going anywhere.'

'Great.'

The van came. The two of them explained the situation to the RAC guy, who was dressed like Field Marshal Montgomery — beret, ribbed sweater, handlebar moustache. He wasn't really interested in their story, though. It was all the same to him whether he sat in a room in West Brom playing cards all night, or took a ride to the Smoke and back.

'That's it, then,' said Tommy cheerfully, trying to leave on a high note. Mark was still not being very indulgent.

'Yeah, right, thanks for coming. Take care.' He shut the door.

Tommy walked down the path with the suitcase and the crash helmet and got in the front of the van. The RAC man was just finishing off the elaborate bondage procedure with his straps and his chocks, to secure the Triumph.

Pretty soon, they were bowling along the M6 past Fort Dunlop and off towards the capital.

He was home by eleven. Montgomery made liberal use of his flashing lights to clear the fast lane for them. Tommy remembered him talking about racing at the real Daytona, in south Florida, but the booze was so draining that he nodded off and only awoke as they careened down the Finchley Road. The RAC man turned out to be quite a gentleman. He would accept no help getting the bike out. He handled it with care, setting it on the centre stand right outside the house, in the spot where Melissa usually put her hatchback.

The flat was empty. There were three messages on the machine: Fiona, organising some night out for the girls. Quite politely, she said that she knew Tommy was out for the day and that Melissa wasn't sure what time he'd be back, but that if she wanted to come to meet at the Sublime Bar in Chelsea. *Fucking Chelsea.* Fat Paul was next. He said, in the roundest of terms, that his 'lickul bravver' had been 'righ' ou' o' order to leave vem disrespeckful messages', and he wanted to talk to Tommy as soon as possible, preferably this weekend. *Hello, cockneys are back.* It felt like he had been away for months, not hearing those tones. The last one was a Scot with an almost impenetrable accent. 'Helloo, Mister Burrens, this is Jim Mitchell of the Scottish Football Association, on behalf of the Referees' Committee. I was wondering if we could have a chat. Give me a phone on 0141 332 3217. Mah home phone is 0141 942 8076, an' mah mobile is 0831 882611. 'Bye now.'

After several listens Tommy managed to transcribe the numbers into his notebook, which he now used as a pad for such fleeting things: thoughts about patients, references to look up, phone numbers and train times. *Fucking Jocks, what do they want?* He had had enough of FAs by now. The English had dicked him around enough, but he couldn't see what the Jocks with their Cowdenbeaths and their Alloas had to offer. 'Scrofula.

King's balm. Herbs: ?' he read in the notebook. *Maybe I'll start taking things a bit more seriously. Set up my own little clinic? Specialise. Maybe dermatology. I could take my final year again. I could probably teach it too, as soon as I've done it. Maybe go to California. I wonder how Mel would like that? She looks great all brown. Gorgeous. If she'd come, the cow. She's probably out fucking some stripy-shirted knobhead right now. On his water bed. Fuck. Where the hell is she? She has such beautiful skin.* He started getting ready for bed, hanging up the contents of the suitcase, brushing his teeth and flossing. *Maybe I should have done dentistry? That's a piece of piss. Money for old rope. Everyone needs dental work. Especially the English. Nah, I couldn't stand the bad breath all day, and the whingeing. And everyone hating me. Jeez, I really fucked up.*

Every year Tommy convinced himself that he had messed up his specialisation at medical school. He shouldn't have gone so general. 'Doctor' or 'General Practitioner' – both sounded good at the time. Where he came from they were both like Olympic gold medals. Meanwhile all his peers were staking out their futures, balancing cash return against pleasure and cocktail party kudos. He thought of the three people he used to hang out with. Linda Cheek had gone into the abortion field and now had her nice little earner a few streets away. He had run into her again at a dinner the year before, where she had stood up for herself and what she did. She was really good at doing abortions – that was her thing. If people were going to do it, they might as well come to the best. She knew her way around the inside of a uterus as well as any man; she had never freaked anyone out, punctured a wall or left anything dangerous behind. And her tissue room staff were the best. Tommy was impressed, especially when he heard how important she had become in the abortion hierarchy. Then there were Simon Carlisle and Dave Brewer.

Simon had gone into plastics – which to him meant button noses, pouty lips and eminently grabbable breasts. Same-day service in most cases. He used to fuck about half of the single women who went under his knife. 'When they're awake, of course,' he used to joke. He said that when they came round from the anaesthetic they were like ducklings coming out of the egg and quacking 'Mama!' at the first thing they saw, whether it was a duck or a human. He reckoned it was half gratitude, half road test. He loved it. And he was a charming bastard too, which didn't hurt.

Brewer was a psychiatrist to the children of the absurdly rich – children who often as not recommended him to their parents. So his scheme had paid off double handsome. He now had a brass plaque next to the doorbell at his clinic in World's End, Chelsea. He was minting it. Half his patients lived in the same tower, although he rarely ran into them in the corridor. He just kept doling out the downers and the slimming pills, flattering them and fixing up their egos. *Anyone could fucking do that*, thought Tommy. The bitter man got into bed. Then he remembered what *he* had been really good at until quite recently. Youngest ref in the Premiership. Fastest rise to the top in the modern era – only six years. Youngest FIFA ref in Europe at that moment. Strongly tipped for duty at the World Cup ... and who knew, if it wasn't a European affair, maybe for the World Cup Final itself? With a groan, he rolled over and tried to sleep.

Fat Paul had an annoying habit of telephoning early on a Sunday morning. Tommy was in the shower at the time, so he didn't hear it, so it was left to Melissa, who was woken up by the emptiness of the bed, to answer it. She staggered, bleary-eyed and naked, along the hall to the lounge, her breasts swinging each time she hit the wall, her one millimetre of fat shivering on her thighs.

'Hello.'

''Allo, sorry to bovver you this early, is Tommy there?'

'Ugh. Yeah. Who is this?' She remembered the nastiness associated with Fat Paul, and didn't want to encourage him to bring it near her home.

'Vis is Paul, Tommy's friend.'

'Uh. Hang on.' She staggered back, banging on the bathroom door as she passed it. The shower went off. 'It's Fat Paul,' she shouted, throwing herself back into bed.

Tommy came out, rubbing his hair with a towel. *Hmm, Fat Paul. We meet again. I wonder what the fat bastard really wants?* He was feeling particularly fearless this morning.

'Paul. Tommy. Got your message. What's up?' He wasn't going to fuck around – it was better to seize the moral high ground from the start with these types. Paul he had down as a fat, pseudo-gentleman yob with a very slow fuse. Better to stamp on it from the start.

'Well, well, Mr Burns, what a long time it's been.'

Tommy remained silent.

'You and I have a few things talk about,' he continued, his Peter Sellers accent fading quickly from lack of attention.

Tommy still said nothing, but breathed audibly.

'I'm feeling a lickul better now, Tommy. But I was surprised, to say ver least, that you didn't visit me in hospital.'

'So your brother Phil implied. But I've seen rather a lot of hospitals in my time. I've developed an aversion to them.'

'Well. P'raps we could meet and talk about this, and avver things, today?'

Paul's effort at being enigmatic was barely holding up. Tommy let him wriggle a bit longer.

'Only, I fink you owe me an apology, Tommy.'

Tommy replied as mildly and as quietly as he could, 'I think I do too, Paul.'

Paul's piggy smile leapt out of the mouthpiece at him.

'Well, well!' was all he could say.

'What do you say we meet at the World's End pub in Camden at eleven and bury the old hatchet?' said Tommy quickly, skipping to the bottom line.

No sooner had the fat man tentatively agreed than Tommy had hung up the phone. He dived back into bed so he could come inside Melissa while she was still half asleep. Then he took the new bike for a spin.

Eschewing the leathers, Tommy put on his jeans, and the basketball boots that Melissa had bought him but he never wore, and went outside to the bike. He felt warm and good after the sex. *This is probably as good as it gets for me, and for anyone,* he thought. *A girlfriend I love moaning under me, a black bomber of a bike to ride, and a fat enemy I'm unafraid of.* He put the key in the ignition and pressed the START button. The starter motor whirred and the engine burst into life with a chuckle, idling into a creamy purr that sent a thrill through him. *One hundred and twenty-eight brake horsepower.* He twisted the throttle a little with his fingertips. The engine noise climbed and settled, a cross between a metallic whine and a fast-thumping heartbeat.

*Oh man, this is too good for me,* he thought. He was alone in the street, grinning. The drive chain was tight and clean. *That poor little bastard Darren must have been out there every week cleaning it with his toothbrush.* It had a big, wide petrol tank like a Fireblade, which it competed with. The only one he'd seen before was parked in a street in Soho, and that was a luminous, egg-yolk yellow. This one was called Diablo Black, he'd read somewhere. An inky, glossy black that nonetheless showcased the oval curves and scoops of the fairing. It wasn't as flash as the Ducati 916, but he didn't care about that. This wasn't Italy. The big word, Triumph, was on the tank in silver capitals. 'Daytona' was scribbled at an angle between two air intakes. *That sucks a bit, that horrible handwriting style.* Still, there was a British elegance about the whole bike that separated it from the Italians and the Japanese.

Tommy got on. *Jesus, it feels wide.* The handlebars were wide apart and angled forward. The seat was a deep square notch in the bike's profile, and as with all sports bikes, the natural riding position seemed to be with your nose pressed against the tank. He rolled it forward off the centre stand and pointed it down the street. *Suspension feels a bit soft.* Then with the sole of his foot he stepped it into first gear.

'Whooooaaaahh!' he yelled into the sealed space of the helmet. The bike shot forward with the minimum of gas, sending him streaking down the middle of the road, head thrown back, hands straining to hold on to the bars. Even without throttle he was still doing thirty when he reached the main road. He hit the brake and was thrown forward, his face lashing down towards the rev meter, which plummeted to zero. A lorry rumbled past where he would have been.

'Jesus H. CHRIST!' he shouted. The engine stalled. He wheeled it to the side of the road and waited for his heart to stop banging and his jelly legs to become strong again.

The second time he took off it was better. He lurched forward, applied the brakes, lurched forward, applied the brakes again, and so on, until he achieved an average speed of about fifteen miles an hour. Gradually, as he went up the hill in the slow lane, he began to find his footing. The engine seemed happiest in second gear, its soft whirring almost silent from inside the tight-fitting helmet.

Slowly it all came back to him from his Suzuki days: how to do lights, how to overtake, how to stop safely. At one point a Honda Blackbird pulled up alongside him. The rider nodded to him with cool appreciation, and Tommy checked out his girlfriend, who was riding on the back. She had her tight jeans on, ankles exposed even though it was February. He nodded back at the man. He had forgotten about the companionship of the road, and just how many great bikes there were in London. You just didn't see them from a car.

He took it to the North Circular, thinking he might open it up a bit there, but even on a Sunday morning it was too crowded. So he brought it up to the MI. He was up the ramp in a second and a half, shooting ahead effortlessly against gravity. *This thing eats hills.* He got it into third at seventy, but was too cautious to go for fourth. He was still too nervous to throw it around. Trying to hold his line and stay away from all nutty drivers, dozers and lane-hoppers, he became paranoid. When he saw the police video cameras mounted on a bridge, he had had enough. He got off at the next junction and turned around. The cold air was beginning to bother him, so he rode back to Camden from the North Circular slowly and carefully.

Still cranked from the ride, he waited for Fat Paul at a table near the window. The possibility of a cruel and merciless beating came back to him. An hour ago, he had a vague plan of action in case Fat Paul, his brother and a few dangerous cockneys they played football with jumped out of the white van and came for him with planks and pipes. Now he had a vague sense of acceptance. He would take the risk, but it now felt like a minor risk.

Fat Paul came up behind him, alone.

'Tommy Burns, I presume.'

'Hey, good to see you, Paul,' said Tommy, standing up and pumping his hand. Paul looked cautious. The warmth of the greeting had taken him aback. Something in Tommy had said 'Fuck it, let's be good to one another', and it was catching. Within seconds, Paul warmed to him.

Tommy had a pint of shandy, which he sipped with impressive restraint over the next hour. He didn't want to lose his balance and go sliding under the wheels of an artic. It turned out that Fat Paul didn't want to kick the shit out of him, nor even much of an apology. He would settle for an explanation as to why Tommy left him in the crumpled cab of the van with his ribs caved in.

'Well,' said Tommy, keeping so straight a face that he began to believe what he was saying, 'same reason we were wrapped round a Belisha beacon in the first place — *pissed*. I was out of it. And you didn't look *that* bad. I suppose,' he said, deepening his voice and looking grave, 'I forgot I was a doctor for a moment. Haven't you ever drunk so much you've forgotten who you are, Paul?'

'Er ...' Paul looked confused. The answer had to be yes, he guessed. 'Yeah, but ...'

'Exactly!' said Tommy with a sudden grin. A waitress walked by. 'Here, have another pint.'

Paul took solace in another pint, Tommy nursed his shandy. Once the relationship work was done, Paul had to ask his main question: would Tommy referee a game for them. Two weeks' time. It was a friendly against a touring French side. He didn't have to be registered.

Now Tommy was a little taken aback. Refereeing? He ummed and aaahed. 'No more reffing' had been his battle cry just an hour ago, his firm new position.

'Caam on, Tommy! We gotta show these Froggies a good time. Naffink but ver best. Pitches, food, entertainment ... we really want to show 'em.'

He was deeply touched by Paul's spirit of European union. The first thing he had imagined was that the French, with their long hair, bottled water and *slip* underwear, would get stamped and studded and kicked all over the pitch, still win, and then get ambushed in the carpark by their opponents, have their coach bricked and their wallets nicked and be forced to return home penniless on Le Shuttle under police escort and in the care of the French consul. But Paul actually planned to welcome them.

'Well ... you might not know this, Paul, but I've retired from big-league reffing.'

Paul was flabbergasted, grunting and exhaling and raising his eyebrows until Tommy interrupted him.

'But I'll do this one, just for you. You're a good man, Paul.'

Fat Paul was still puzzling it all out when Tommy stood up and took his leave. He watched him hop on the motorcycle and sweep out into the traffic.

'He's one 'ell of a cool geezer, 'e is,' said Fat Paul to the watching waitress. 'And a real gentleman to boot.' She looked at him, wondering what his boots had to do with anything. 'Navver pint please, doll.'

After the pleasant way the morning had gone, he returned to the flat hoping Melissa was out, because he didn't fancy explaining the bike to her. She was in, and she went a lot madder than he anticipated. Her main points were 1) You don't tell me anything and 2) It's too dangerous, with an addendum about how he didn't know what he was doing any more or where he was going, and that he was in danger of becoming a miserable, twisted has-been. And why didn't he do something about those prats at the FA if that was the cause of all this behaviour?

Tommy was very fucked off at her bringing the FA up again, and worse, at her talking about *behaviour*. He had already explained that he was only looking after it for a few months and that he didn't see that he'd be using it much, especially as it was winter, but instead of going over all that again he told her to shut up and that he'd go to work on it every day if he wanted. And that he was reffing a game for Fat Paul in a few weeks and he'd be taking it there. Especially as it was east London and tricky to get around.

They didn't speak to each other for six hours.

He tried to watch a bit of the live Sunday afternoon game, but the sight of referee Miller, and the ridiculous comments about him by all the panel (how young he was, how firmly in control), made him sick with disgust and envy, so he turned it off. He thought about reading up on the Epidermis, which was to be his New Subject, but he couldn't be arsed. Getting a New Subject seemed to be rooted too much in self-loathing, he thought, in not being happy with his lot. He would put it on hold till he understood himself better.

He looked out of the window at the city in the dusk for a while, at the lights coming on and the trees disappearing. It was really pretty horrible, London. Melissa gently pushed him away when he tried to touch her. So he went and did the dinner. All she said was 'Thank you'. Afterwards he read the Sunday paper, avoiding the sport, although in the big coloured section he ran across a new poem by Nick Plumage. It was called 'O Referee'.

> '"Offside!" my father shouted.
> "Off bloody side!"
> Then he looked at me with shame.'

Bored, Tommy started to skim . . .

'. . . His ink-black shirt, his pencil stub . . . unsung hero . . . He's never won, he's never lost . . . His wine-dark shirt, his wife at home . . . No position . . . no parking spot . . . Dad's matches . . . unacknowledged legislator . . . red card.'

*Hmmph*, went Tommy. It was ten-thirty. Melissa had marked books all day, then sewn defiantly in the living room all evening. 'That reminds me, Mel. Has a bloke from the BBC phoned? Nick Felcher?'

'No. You always ask me that. Not that I know of.' Her voice was still cold, but at least she had spoken. She was thawing. Things might be back to normal in twelve more hours.

'Oh.' *The bastard.* 'Fuck it. I'm going to bed.'

''Night.'

*Let's see what this Scottish bloke wants. What's his name? Jim Mitchell.*

Tommy was sitting in his clinic with his feet up, taking a break.

'Hello. Tommy Burns here. Returning your call.'

Mr Mitchell had answered in person.

'Ah, Tommy Burrens! So glad you called back. Heh heh heh.'

*Sounds like a jolly bastard for a Monday morning. Maybe he's been at the Glenlivet or whatever it is they go in for up there. Injecting shampoo between the toes.*

'What can I do for you?'

'Well, I have a little proposition for you.'

*Uh-oh,* thought Tommy.

'Now I understand you haven't been refereeing for a while in your own country, have you not?'

'That's right.'

'Well, in that case I'd very much like to meet with you and discuss how we can help each other. Do ye have any Scottish relatives?'

'Eh? *No,*' he said emphatically, then realising he may have sounded a little too pleased to not be Scottish, he added, 'My lot are all Irish. Catholics.'

'Aye, well, never mind that. Perhaps I could meet with you, Mr Burns?'

'Doctor.'

'Sorry, Doctor. I really think we have an interesting proposition for you.'

'Well ... I'm not feeling so great about the refereeing business at the moment, if that's all you want to talk about ...'

'Of course not, of course not. Let me make it easy for you. Do you play golf?'

'Golf? Never. When would I have time for golf?'

'Aye, no. Er, we have some excellent facilities up here and ...'

'Look ...' Tommy had had enough. *Pissed Scots git.*

'Perhaps you'd like to visit, that's all I was suggesting. I can sort you out with accommodation, plane ticket, et cetera. To discuss my offer.'

'Well, why can't you come down here?' Tommy could feel himself beginning to ask questions instead of hanging up. *Maybe this is why I'm not working for myself. I don't have the killer instinct on the telephone. Linda scoops, Dave shrinks, Simon sells saline, all with a bit of hard phone work ...*

'Oh, no, nooo. This must all be handled discreetly for the time being. Trust me, Mr Burns, we have an excellent proposal for you. But I must discuss it in person with you.'

And now Tommy could smell the bait. He knew what they wanted, but he wouldn't admit it to anyone yet, including himself.

'When would all this take place?'

'Well, as soon as you get here we can talk.'

'Well, I'll think about it.' He got off the phone as fast as he could.

He didn't know much about the Scottish FA, nor did he know Mitchell, the Chief Executive. He knew that Scottish football wasn't very good, that Scotland was the land of gambling goalkeepers, and that the Rangers and Celtic balls were warmed before they were put in the bag for the FA Cup draw, to keep them apart. At first he thought it might be something shady. *Come up where you have no ties and help us fix a game. We know you're down on your luck. We know you're all washed up in England. We know you hate your job and need some instant cash* ... He wondered how they could think he was so stupid. Tommy hated the idiots that were taking over the game, the millionaires and the stock-floaters, the super-agents and the cross-media owners. He fell into a daydream about deep cover. Going in there, agreeing to all their crooked demands, then blowing the whistle on them at the last minute. Purging the system of corruption and parasites. He'd be the double agent. He'd be hidden in the most obvious place, visible and invisible at the same time. *I'd take it right up to the day of the game, then tell the press about the rigging and the pools men and the chairmen. Fuck them all, right down to the last crooked ballboy. I'd have tape recordings, blurry video, names and addresses. I'd set an example for the world. FIFA would be licking my boots by the end of it. The English would welcome me back on to their precious soil ... Jesus, I'm getting carried away. I don't even know what they want. Probably just some dinner they want me to speak at.*

He buzzed in the next patient. One look at Mrs Bacon the Talker's old, tired face and he knew her story from beginning to end. The wheezy chest, the neglectful children, the prescription rises. It was then that he realised he should call back as soon as was decent. Simon Carlisle wasn't going to have all the fun.

He called at 3 p.m., telling Mr Mitchell that he would come up and talk to him. He sounded pleased. *Maybe I could make it on the after-dinner speech circuit. I could tell them about the fox that ran on the pitch at Wimbledon that one time. How I carried it off by the scruff of the neck. It would be nice to get applause. Then I could stick in a bit at the end about how fucked up everything is nowadays.*

Mitchell's secretary got back to him within ten minutes, saying she had booked him on to a British Airways shuttle the next day. Everything was sorted. She reckoned he'd be home again in time for his tea.

Like a fired man, Tommy said nothing to Melissa. He dressed as though for work the next day, cleaned the ice off her windscreen, called Marge from a pay-phone to say he was ill, and set off on the Tube to Heathrow. There was just enough time for him to get through an article in *High Life* magazine about the scandal of Prince Harry's bodyguard when the plane began to descend. Mr Mitchell picked him up in person and they drove out to the Cawdor Golf Club in Bishopbriggs.

They sat by a window in the restaurant. He was a tall, broad-shouldered man with a wind-chapped old face that Tommy instantly trusted. His corruption fantasy evaporated as Mr Mitchell got the drinks in and began to speak of Tommy's predicament. He knew a football scout who knew a chairman who knew Proctor the linesman, and so word had come to him about Tommy's being dropped from the referees' list and the way the English authorities were dragging their feet with the investigation. It was like an apocryphal reel of his life being unspooled before his eyes. He knew Lockhart too, by reputation. He was known to be a bitter man, his refereeing career curtailed by a ligament injury.

'You know, we're a bit more, shall we say, *progressive* in Scottish football than you may be used to in England,' continued Mitchell. 'The fact of the matter is, we're moving towards professional referees a lot more quickly than the English. It could be that in the next two years referees will be paid a flat fee, a lot more than they are now, for each game they cover, and we want to attract the best. Plus expenses. To make our point, we'd like to offer you a Scottish match to referee ...'

Tommy interrupted him. They clearly had the wrong man. 'First, I don't believe in that sort of professional refereeing. Second, I can't take a Scottish game because I'm a member of the English FA. There's no crossover allowed.' Tommy leaned back and took a sip of his Bloody Mary. When Mr Mitchell looked embarrassed, a cold, dark horror crept over him.

'You mean you don't know? I'm sorry nobody's seen fit to tell you this. Perhaps it's indicative of the English system. I'm afraid you were officially deselected from the English FA's refereeing list two weeks ago.'

Tommy's throat began to tighten. He sat up straight. 'WHAT? You mean no one told me? No letter? No phone call? They kicked me off the list and no one fucking told me?' He laughed. 'No way! Who told *you*, then?'

'Well, initially I heard about your predicament indirectly through your friend Proctor, as I said. But as for your being, er, deselected, well, I keep an eye on things in England, and when someone is not refereeing at any level for more than two months they're technically no longer registered with the FA. You have to reapply. I think it's a new ruling down there. The new man in charge is strict, I'll say that for him. Surely somebody told you?'

'The bastards,' said Tommy. 'The fucking BASTARDS!' he said loudly, pounding the table with his fist. 'They can't do this! They can't do this to me.'

He was huffing and puffing, and instinctively looking around the room for a pay-phone.

'Calm down, lad,' said the older man. 'They can do what they want, and they just did. Now *I* know you're a quality referee – perhaps the best,' he added, hoping to reattract his attention. 'That's why we want to give you a taste of Scottish football. You could flourish up here.'

Tommy looked at him like he was mad. *Flourish up here? I don't want to live in fucking Scotland! Fucking shithole.* He was still so shocked he was unable to speak, and his mind was thinking ahead to what he'd like to do to the man behind the desk at Lancaster Gate.

'Look at all this,' said Mitchell, gesturing out of the window at the green curves of the golf course, the creamy bunkers and the powdery blue sky. 'This sort of lifestyle could be yours.'

Tommy could barely think straight, but he restrained himself from pointing out that he had no intention of hobnobbing at a bar with professional golfers, spoiled, pissed footballers and Scotland's meagre handful of flash managers. He was not tempted. He sighed heavily, unable to believe his misfortune.

'So what's this game? Aidrie versus Heart of Midlothian?' *Whoever the fuck they are.*

'Old Firm,' said Mitchell.

Tommy's expression changed to surprise, and he stared at the man.

'Rangers–Celtic? Are you joking? I thought that was the big honour up here, refereeing that.'

'It is. I told you, we're prepared to stick our necks out for you. We like you up here, Tommy.'

*Fuck it, I'll do it,* he thought. He pretended to think about it for a whole minute. 'Can I have a night to think about it?'

'Well, OK, if you must,' Mitchell replied, a little put out.

'My status, you see. I don't know where I'll stand with the English FA if I do this game.' Tommy was stalling for time. He had a pretty good idea the English FA would fuck him off completely and for good if he did this game.

'Aye, well, they may not be too happy. But nor are they now,' said the Scotsman, chuckling. He seemed to know he had his man at last. Tommy was pleasantly surprised at his frankness.

'I think I'd better get back to London now. Can we go?' They stood up.

'Of course. I'm sure you have lots to do,' he said, and tapped Tommy's belly with the back of his hand. 'Got to keep up your fitness. Old Firm games are no pushover.'

*Yeah, fucking right.* Tommy laughed indulgently. *Scottish git. I can handle it.* 'I'm sure I can handle it,' he said.

On the plane home, Tommy pressed his belly against his seat belt to see if there really was any flab that the old man could have been indicating. He skipped the peanuts and had a diet Pepsi instead of wine. He went for a long run that night, circling Hampstead Heath in its entirety. Every time his breath ran short on a hill or the cold hurt his flesh, he thought of his hatred, and pressed on, warmed within.

Fiona: ... Calm down, calm down!

Melissa: I've just about had it, Fi, he's making me so cross. Does Nick ever make you this cross?

F: Sometimes. Yes. Well, not the way you are now, but that's you.

M: Is it? D'you think it's just me?

F: What's he done this time?

M: What hasn't he done! He's off on that bloody bike every chance he gets. I just caught him, going to the shops on it – all we needed was milk! I've told him how dangerous it is, but he never listens. Then there's this bloody referee thing – one day he's given it up and is all mopey and under my feet, and getting disgustingly fat, I might add, and the next he's jogging his arse off again, training for some game in Scotland ...

F: Calm down, will you? You're chewing my ear off here. Well, do you think he's seeing someone on the side?

M: *Tommy?* To be quite honest I don't think he's got the balls to do that. Anyway, if he was I'd know soon enough.

F: So what does he do up in Birminum, then?

M: Oh, he doesn't go up there much. I think that little episode's all over. I found a letter in the bin that he wrote to his friend up there, Mark the priest, but it was just some garbage ... I think Tommy upset him. Mind you, that's where the bike came from, the priest told him to look after it.

F: Well, I'm buggered if I understand him. Don't you two talk any more?

M: To be honest I avoid him when he's like this. I spend half my life down the gym now. If I'm not out with friends that's where I am.

F: Aha! Heard any more from the muscle man? The bloke with the ponytail? Craig.

M: Maybe.

F: Come on, spit it out — for once in your life.

M: Stop, you dirty cow. Well, he's just always around when I'm there. Actually he can be quite helpful sometimes. He knows his stuff.

F: Hon, *trust* me when I say, I've *seen* him. I *know* his sort and all he wants to do is help himself. To the goods. You know what I mean?

M: Yeah, well, I was down there tonight and he asked me out again. About two hours ago.

F: You're kidding!

M: He just said he's got a loft in Docklands, and it was a cool place to go out for a drink.

F: The dirty sod! I can't believe it.

M: Hang on, I can hear Tommy coming in.

F: So what did you say?

M: I'll tell you later. All I said was I've heard about that area, it sounds good. Better than Tufnell Park anyway. He's OK. At least he knows what he's doing. Oops, gotta go, here comes Motorcycle Boy. See you Friday, right? I'll call you tomorrow.

F: Mel? Wait! Mel ...?

Since his trip to Scotland two weeks before, Tommy's life had hit a plateau. He was training hard for the Old Firm game, convinced his career as a top-class referee in England was over. He was running every weeknight, and testing himself on his rules again. He even caught himself watching golf in a shop window.

He enjoyed refereeing Fat Paul's game against the French. They had lost six–three, which was a respectable score for a shower of underemployed labourers and salesmen against a team of dashing Mediterraneans and Black Africans, whose skills Fat Paul praised afterwards in the highest terms known to him: 'silky'.

Tommy had been an instant hit with the foreigners as he rode up on the Triumph. He had recently bought the manual and had been working out how to alter the suspension, and how the air intake system functioned, to see if he had to modify it for hot weather, and he wanted to put on some nasty aftermarket cans. He fancied taking Melissa down to Nice in the summer. And he had started buying bike magazines again. For the articles.

Paul was puffed up with pride after the game as he made a solemn invitation in pidgin English to the opposing captain to come for a 'drink' and 'sam food' at their local pub. He had alerted the strippers in advance that he would be bringing in some classy Europeans. Even the fact that he had been sent off didn't spoil his anticipation. The big defender, as he liked to refer to himself in his fantasies, had clipped the heel of their gypsy centre-forward as he broke clear with only the 'keeper to beat. Tommy reached for the red card automatically, and after slamming the floor with his hands once, Fat Paul had lumbered off, disappointed, but increasingly impressed that he had witnessed the actual professional foul ruling in the flesh.

His relations with Melissa had reached a plateau too – or rather, the floor of a U-shaped valley. She let him fuck her only when she really wanted it. She repaid his vagueness with indifference, and his affection too.

'You know what? There's a term for people like you,' he snapped at her one night. 'You're passive aggressive.'

She didn't answer. He toyed with tracking down Simon Carlisle, Plastics Man, to see if he wanted to go for a drink.

Many times he considered calling Mark, but he could never justify it. And since he wasn't getting pissed very often, he never acted on it. Mark probably didn't want to see him anyway. He'd pestered him enough – making an arse of himself at Blues and after the funeral. *Fuck.* He was thinking that maybe he could get him into the Rangers–Celtic game ... but then he probably had plenty of other things to do. He was getting used to the idea that he and Mark had outlived their meaning to one another.

Mark had been a great mate, and would have risked any danger for him. And now he didn't have any mates. And not much of anything else either. He thought about getting some lager from the corner shop to cheer himself up, but then remembered the Old Firm game. He was determined to have a stomach like a slab of marble by the time that came around. *Fucking Jocks.* He was gonna show 'em how you take control.

Coming home from work one night he saw Melissa going up the steps as he rounded the corner, so he started to run. It didn't seem right to enter the house separately. He managed a good sprint and got to the house just as the door was closing itself.

'Mel!' he shouted, and ran up the steps. She was in her black leggings, with her gym bag over her shoulder. She looked down from the stairs and registered his smile, and knew what was up. He ran the few yards down the hall and up the first few stairs and called her again. *God, I love her bum.* She said nothing but speeded up, then laughed and started to run up the stairs two at a time. Tommy marvelled at their ability to make their own entertainment. This was better than telly. He could see her hard bottom racing up the stairs now, just half a flight ahead of him. She was shrieking, he was shouting. Like a toddler, she loved being chased, and he loved being right behind her. She got the key in the door and burst in just before him, dropping everything as he tackled her and sent her sprawling on the couch, face down. He bit her on the bum and buried his face in the crack while she shrieked and giggled. Love was coursing through his veins, he felt horny as hell, and his head was dizzy with the comfort of being home – home in her affections again. She was still giggling as he rolled her over and kissed her passionately on the mouth.

He was loving it – it was like getting his hands on her for the first time again, only this time he knew exactly how she handled. He had a glorious feeling of not knowing where to start, since she was all laid out before him and each part of her looked ripe. He knew where he wanted to end up, though, and he let his greed lead him, tearing open her sheepskin jacket and pulling up her T-shirt so that it sat on the shelf of her breasts. She had on a gym bra which was black with a white logo in the centre of her bosom. He stuck his nose and mouth in the gap at the bottom of the bra, where it was taut and did not rest against her skin, and pushed and kissed until it rode up, snagging her breasts on the way. They tasted of sweat. *I wonder how clean my hands are? She's always saying they're too clean. Doctor clean.* He stuck his finger in her mouth for her to suck, then he pulled the bra up completely to expose her nipples. He thought of Simon Carlisle, Plastics Man. *I wonder if you can tug on them when they've been repositioned?* It seemed an odd thing to him, repositioning nipples. *Where does the milk go?* He made a mental note to definitely call him. All the time he was murmuring how much he loved her, and how much she turned him on, and what he wanted to do to her. She liked that stuff too. The thought of milk reminded him of a story she had told him once, something that happened before they met. She was jogging along the street one day, in her sports gear – leggings, clingy bra and T-shirt – her breasts bouncing obviously, when she approached a young man – 'a squat little bastard with a moustache', as she put it. She didn't like moustaches. Instead of doing the decent thing and waiting till she had passed before making his remark, he said, cheerfully and within a yard of her, 'Making butter?'

Tommy thought it was a good line, though with rather a high risk factor. The way she told it, she passed him, grew incensed when she got the joke, and instead of letting the moment and an apt reply pass for ever, turned around and ran after him. When he turned to defend himself, as any man would, she socked him once in the jaw, so hard that he fell backwards over a garden wall wailing in agony. Then she turned and legged it. Tommy had always wanted to meet the man who thought up 'making butter', but even more he loved imagining Melissa charging off up the street with her sore hand and her pumping heart. That was when he fell in love with her.

The only sounds were the rustle of the cushions beneath them and their heavy breathing. They had got their breath back from the sprint home, but were losing it again to each other, with every new sensation. The man upstairs walked by on his hardwood floor in his boots, but it didn't register. They screened out the ambient street sounds – engines advancing and fading, car doors closing – submerging themselves in each other instead, like bathers slipping under the water for peace.

Ribcage. Abdomen. Navel . . . Tommy knew the way, and he savoured each step. She arched her back while he pulled down her leggings, using his nails to get under the edge of the tight fabric. Melissa Ebensgaard's pudenda, as Tommy liked to refer to them in casual conversation with her, were gloriously, obscenely hairy. Whichever way you looked – frontways, underneath, from behind, even from her angle up above – all you saw was a bush of jet-black hair that spilled over on to her belly, her thighs and her perineum. It always took him a moment to get used to it. He would never tell anyone (because he didn't have the men friends, and because he couldn't think of a woman who deserved to hear it), but he reckoned it looked like she had a black Scottie dog sitting on her lap. When he first met her, she was, in the fashion of the day, shaved. As bald and clean as a baby on the beach. That was when he fell in love with her again. Then one day, two years ago, she decided to let it all go – 'grow it the hell out,' she said, laughing. Tommy loved it both ways. Now it was like knowing her before he had ever met her – a considerable bonus. He fell in love with her one more time.

But just as he buried his face in the soft black hair the fucking phone went, causing them both to freeze. Now they had to decide what to do. It wasn't like their young days, when they would fuck for hours, whenever and wherever they wanted, and the phone never mattered enough to answer.

Now they were older. Now they were in their mid-thirties, and the phone's insistent trings meant far more. They knew the answering machine volume was up. They weren't going to answer it, but these days it put them off their stride as they waited to see who it was. Each of the four double trills went through them like the chimes at midnight. It could be just a friend (for Melissa). Since they both had proper jobs and were responsible for other people, it could be work-related (mostly for Melissa – Tommy had long ago given up being on call). It could be some chore thing they were waiting for – the bank, the garage, or the bloke to fix the bath. It could be her parents – Tommy always stopped, Melissa carried on. It could be her sister Rebecca – vice versa. It could be someone embarrassing. It could be someone embarrassing who was going to leave a message. Tommy's conscience was clear. He wondered if hers was.

They heard Tommy's curt outgoing message. Then the beep. Then the voice. It was Mark.

'Fuck!' muttered Tommy, and looked up at her. This was embarrassing as hell – as though they had been caught at it by their parents. Tommy felt very guilty for letting Mark's voice into the room.

He stopped dead still when he registered the tone of voice. Mark sounded terrified.

'Tommy, uh, Tommy? Are you there? Where are you? Melissa? If you get this message, call me back. I'm in a call-box. I . . . I . . .' Tommy stiffened, and they listened with rapt attention, looking in each other's eyes. Melissa knew trouble when she heard it. She seemed to sense that Mark never got scared. 'There's a lot of mad shit happening up here, Tommy, I don't know what to do. I can't go home. And I've got nowhere to go, except you. I don't know what the fuck I'm gonna do, Tommy . . .'

He rolled off the couch and struggled to the phone, interrupting Mark in mid-sigh.

'Mark. It's me. What's wrong?'

Mark's voice was heavy with relief. He told Tommy about the coppers coming to the house and taking Father Kelly away. Then about the crowd that had begun gathering at the gates.

Tommy merely muttered 'Oh' and 'God' and asked him to repeat a few things. Melissa lay watching him, wide-eyed, her sex forgotten.

'What is it?' she hissed.

He covered the mouthpiece and whispered, 'The other priest's been arrested. Interfering with minors. Mark's on the run.'

She looked horrified.

'What are you going to do?' asked Tommy. Melissa tried to read his face as he listened to a long, long speech.

'You know what? If all that's true you'd be better off out of there,' he said, ignoring Melissa's frown. He looked at his watch. 'It's a fucking squeaker, but I think I can make it. Just go and stand outside the Holte End. Or walk around, keep moving, go through the park a few times. Just look normal. Blend in. I'll be there by kick-off. Dump the scooter, but keep the lid.' He paused while Mark said something.

'Hey, no worries, Mark, all right? Count on me. 'Bye.'

Tommy sat down on the couch next to Melissa. She was still half naked, and dying to know what was going on. As he recounted Mark's tale, he idly stroked her hair.

'The coppers hauled Father Kelly in this morning, the old bloke, right out of the blue. Apparently some kids have been saying he's been touching them up. Altar boys. Anyway, Mark didn't know what to do. Some mums started coming round to the house and asking him what was going on. So he went off to the station to find out, and they wouldn't tell him anything. When he got back there were loads of people outside the church, a lot of big blokes too. He was shitting himself. He went inside and the housekeeper had fucked off. So he tried to get through to the bishop's office, but got nowhere. He went back out and they were really getting nasty, so he got on his scooter and told them he was going to St Chad's Cathedral in town to find out what was going on. As soon as he got a few streets away he stopped and phoned me. He's fucked, Melissa. There's a lynch mob after him.'

'So where's he going to go?'

'He's coming here. There's a night game at Villa. Liverpool. I just told him to hang around the ground, stay in the crowd, just blend in until I get there. I'm gonna bring him back here on the bike.'

'What? And what'll he do here?' She was sitting up now, her eyes burning into Tommy. Unconsciously she put her bra straight. She didn't want him bringing home any trouble, much less a child molester. God, she spent half her working day teaching her kids how to spot them.

'I dunno. Lie low till the Church brings him in. I don't know what they do. All I know is, I'm not leaving him up there to get torn to pieces by that lot, or hauled in by the coppers and the social services. I'm not.'

There was a fire of determination blazing in his eyes. She didn't answer. They looked at each other for a solid minute. He wondered if he would get home and find her gone. He was still stroking her. She gestured to him to lean forward. When he did, she pulled him down with her arms and kissed him on the mouth.

'I love you, Tommy Burns. You're a mad bastard but I love you.'

He felt a giant breaker of joy come over him and submerge him, and he hugged her hard. Leaning on her, he could feel her breasts against him. The hunger to make love began to creep back. He knew the game started at seven-thirty so he'd have to get to Brum in less than two hours. He tried to remember how far round the speedo went on the bike – *160? 180?* That was fantasy land, but it meant he could thrash 140 out of it if he had to. The way he felt right then, he would do anything for Mark. And anything for Melissa too.

'I'll go right after this,' he said, squeezing her beneath the ribcage, which she loved. She assented.

Twenty minutes later she watched as Tommy struggled into the leathers of the dead boy.

'You mean you don't wear anything under those things?' she asked from her spot on the couch. She raised an eyebrow suggestively. 'You'll freeze.'

He thought for a second. They had a thin fleecy lining. 'You're right,' he said, and put her leggings on as thermal underwear.

'Hey!' she shouted.

Tommy was feeling very pleased with himself: his loyalty, his dirty girlfriend, and his bad-boy motorcycle waiting outside. He was radiating pride, though he tried to disguise it. He started talking motorbike mag talk, in the deepest voice he could muster. 'I pulled on my leathers, easing them over my slim hips and zipping them three-quarters up, leaving exposed the pure white of my silk undershirt. Donning my three-hundred-quid Shoei, I kicked the Bonneville into action. She hummed gratefully beneath me while I warmed her engine. The sun broke over the hilltops, I pulled out on to the A64 and like a bat out of hell I was gone ...'

His girlfriend was laughing and egging him on with catcalls.

'Then it was time to get serious ...' He went back to his normal voice, as he leaned over to kiss her forehead. 'I'll be back in a few hours. Wait up for me, eh, love?'

'OK. 'Bye. Be *careful*. I love you.'

He knew the first bit of London was going to be slow, but he went as fast as was safe up the Finchley Road to the MI, nipping between cars, overtaking others in sweet curving motions. He felt the familiar ramp rising up beneath him as he hit the motorway, then took it up to eighty mph until he had passed the last of the police cameras. The sound of the wind was tolerable, as the helmet fitted well, its soft pads pushing up on his cheekbones. The view was tough, because the tinted visor and the darkness of the night reduced everything to points of light. The road surface he just had to pray for. One dead cat or a plank of wood and he would be fucked, Barry Sheeneing down the asphalt on his knees and elbows till he met a concrete kerb.

In twenty minutes the lights of London faded away, and without any pylon lighting it was just himself and the red and white dots of the road. The clock on the instrument panel hit 6.30 p.m. He had an hour to make it to the ground. At eighty mph, he felt worried for a while, but gradually eased into it. The road was fairly safe – just the usual selection of grinding lorries, boy racers and struggling hatchbacks. The boy racers were annoying him, either going too fast and constantly coming up behind him flashing their lights, or hanging back at eighty themselves and constantly leapfrogging him. *Fucking idiots. No respect for bikes.* He decided to take it up to a hundred, but no sooner had he been there for a few minutes than he came upon the cones and yellow lights of some contraflow, and had to brake hard, coming almost to a halt and then rolling through it at fifty.

Time was ticking away – *6.40 p.m. and nowhere near.* He had got it into his head that he would ride up and snatch Mark away at the last moment, just as the coppers began to close in. *He has to prove his innocence first. I have to help him. With his record he hasn't got a chance if they get him. Nicked twice, and hauled in again just a month ago.* Tommy felt flooded with guilt as he considered his part in Mark's downfall. The cold was starting to gather in his knee joints, and the noise was giving him a headache. As he came out of the contraflow, which had wasted so much time, he pulled away hard, making the engine sing and the horses pull with all their might, back to eighty, then ninety. *Fuck that.* He shot off into the dark. *And fuck the police too. It's too late to worry about them now.*

He twisted the throttle further than he ever had before. The revs were at five thousand, but the bike wasn't doing much. *This is a bit flat,* he thought, and kept going. Suddenly he hit the power band – the engine accelerated effortlessly, with decreased sound and vibration, as if it had just been waiting for him to take it seriously. The ton came up. Then 110, his wrist twisted so far that he had to readjust his grip. The road was taking over, flashing towards him, a short strip of asphalt in a tiny cone of light. There was less traffic now but he began coming up behind cars so fast that they didn't see him. *Hurry up, hurry up, Mr Slow, you bastard!* The cold hurt his arms. At this speed steering had become a matter of twitching a buttock or a shoulder. He glanced down at the road rushing by in a blur, and thought of his skin being spread along it like a pat of butter on a summer's day. *How long would it last?* He knew the stainless-steel studs in the palm of the gloves would be red hot from friction in seconds and start burning into his flesh. If the gloves didn't just disintegrate completely. Maybe he would flail like a rag doll until disappearing under the three pairs of wheels of a lorry behind him?

*This is so slow. I need to get up there.* The traffic was light. He pushed the bike even harder. People were getting out of his way now, with worried looks on their faces. Landmarks were coming up strangely soon – the Granada services. The cars in the slow lane looked like they were parked.

'Fucking hell,' he gasped as he passed within inches of a giant strip of exploded truck tyre in his lane. He moved over slightly, but found he was then too close to the cars he was passing. There was a madness rising in him, the mad cackling terror of someone on an adventure park ride who voluntarily lets go of the safety rail. Tommy was hanging on to the bars for his life, his body bent forward like a hairpin against the force. His helmet was taking a hammering from the wind, but the tiny fairing and windshield were doing a surprisingly good job of keeping the rest of him clear. He knew that if he sat up now he'd be torn from the bike by the wind and thrown clear. He kept his head down and tried to hide totally behind the windscreen, and gripped the sides of the bike with his thighs. The white line between the lanes now appeared continuous. Although he had to look further ahead than ever – at least a mile – he reduced his observations to small glances every two seconds.

The radio masts at Rugby shot into view and the curve on to the M6 was suddenly upon him. Under the lights he could see the faces of other drivers, shocked to see him racing by, all out of synch with their journey. He braked coming into the bend and leaned hard, scaring himself in the process, as the steering felt hard. Leaning harder, he put all his trust in the tyres. For a moment it was all out of his control. He was leaning over like the page of a book – any further and he'd be sparking his pegs. He could only hope his sideways momentum would run out before he hit the crash barrier.

The tyres held. *Thank God for that lad Darren.* They were hardly used. He wondered what the dead boy would have thought of him, in his boots, in his leathers, on his bike, slashing through the winter air at mental speeds. But it was impossible to think straight any more. He was feeling his way through the dark.

He came out of the bend feeling weak with fear. His extremities were chilled but adrenalin kept the rest of him functioning. Slotting into the new flow of traffic, he worked his way through the ranks until he found a blank spot, then raced forward for a mile or so until he had filled it. Twisting the throttle hard, he took it up to 120 and pressed himself to the tank again. He was amazed at the way traffic seemed to move in clumps several miles long, like insects that do not know the boundaries of their group but know how to fit in. Then 120 started seeming ordinary. He still didn't feel near Birmingham. Mark would be waiting for him. He *had* to up his average speed. He pushed it again: 125, 127, 129, 130 . . . the engine seemed to be screaming hysterically now. His mind was focused totally on the road half a mile ahead, which was eerily clear in his lane. For a second he thought maybe the fast lane had been closed and he'd be coming to an abrupt stop against a digger or a concrete wall. But he couldn't hold any thought for more than a few seconds. All he could entertain was the fear of death, and the thrill of pure speed. All traffic was flashing by like a time-lapse film. He saw the service station near Coventry, a patch of light and a bridge over the road. It was gone in an instant. He let himself stop thinking about the police for a few minutes. They couldn't react to him fast enough anyway. The roar was unbelievable. The road was a blur. He cranked it one last time, until the throttle came to rest. The engine whinnied and climbed, one mph each time he glanced, until it hit 142 and stopped. He had reached his terminal velocity. Nothing could touch him. Except death, which could have him any time. He screamed inside his helmet. And that was it.

The lights of Birmingham were upon him. He killed the gas until the bike fell to a manageable 100 mph. The traffic seemed to spread and come to greet him. The fast lane had traffic in it again. He dropped it down to eighty, which felt like a walk. Fort Dunlop. Bromford. Spaghetti Junction. The engine sighed and moaned as he geared down, and took the island at a dawdling thirty. His ears were ringing. He thrashed it for the last clear hundred yards, then ran into a stream of late cars and police vans heading for the match. *Scousers*. They barely mattered. He had to find Mark.

He pulled up outside the Holte End on Trinity Road at 7.35 p.m. *A hundred and ten miles in one and a half hours*, he thought. He felt like he had just emerged from an aeroplane, when you end up in some distant place and feel you don't deserve to be there yet, that you've only just left home. He had never felt that in Birmingham before. He got a glimpse of the pitch through the corner gap, vivid green under the halogen floodlights.

The crowd roared at some unseen action, then went 'Oooh', and a rash of applause broke out.

With the air noise gone, and the pressure on his bones gone, Tommy felt loose. For a moment he thought he might have the bends. He saw Mark leaning against the wall. The stragglers were squeezing into the turnstiles. Tommy came to a halt across the road from him and tried to flip his visor. It crackled as the ice gave.

'Mark! Get on.'

He did, putting on his helmet as they swept through the crowd, regardless of what the police might say. Suddenly, for both of them, life was a lot more serious than whatever some spotty young cop could get them for.

8

London together; being cold; hiding
& Soccer Museum; bringing Mark in;
Double Suspension; Old Firm

When they got back to Tommy's flat just after ten that night, Melissa served up hot soup and thick roast beef sandwiches that she had heated in the oven. Mark barely spoke, except to give thanks. Tommy was still cranked from his ride up. He had felt life accelerated, and never had it seemed more thrilling, and yet so precarious. For a start it made him wonder what he was doing pussyfooting around with the FA, letting them walk all over him when he could pick up the phone and tell his story to the papers. The proper papers, not some kid off the radio who wouldn't know a story if it pissed in the hood of his anorak. He kicked himself for not having resigned, instead of waiting around while his membership lapsed. Melissa had been exceedingly pissed off when she heard what he had done. Or rather, what he had let happen.

Like Mark, Tommy was too cold to do much talking. They sat at the table together eating their soup and staring into the bowls between bites of sandwich. Melissa couldn't get any sense out of them. She worried about making up a bed for Mark. Where do you put a man who loves boys? was the burning question in her mind.

So far, Tommy hadn't even explained to her what was now going on. As he began to thaw out, he looked askance at Mark, his coat still buttoned up to the neck, his shoes still on. He looked like he had just spent a night in a Polish prisoner-of-war camp. His hair was all flipped up from the bad helmet. He had a sock on one hand.

'Tommy? Can I have a word with you, please?' Melissa said.

He got up and followed her to the bedroom, where they shut themselves in.

She looked fierce, and whispered urgently, close to his face. 'I'm sorry, I
can *not* have that man staying under the same roof as me,' she said. 'You'll
have to find him a hotel. Not after what he's done.'

'What's he done?' asked Tommy, incredulously. 'You think *he's* the child
molester?'

'Well ... Why's he on the run?'

'Melissa. He's done nothing wrong. It's the other bloke, the *old* bloke.
I just got him out of there because I know what happens next. I didn't
want to see the mob get their hands on him.'

'Well, how do you know he's innocent?'

''Cos he fuckin' told me on the way down, that's why.' Tommy was
getting worked up. Melissa's doubt was worrying him.

'Because he told you. OK. Fine. Now *fucking* get him out of here.'

'Yeah, he told me. And I believe him.' Tommy squared up to her.

'Oh, please,' she said, getting sarcastic.

'He said he had nothing to do with it. I don't think he even believes
the old fellow did anything either.'

'Denial,' chimed Melissa.

He hated her for a moment. It sounded like she was bringing home
a bit of her lunch-with-the-girls vocabulary, and he didn't like it. He
imagined them all sitting round dissecting each other's feelings and shouting
'Deni-al!' at each other like in a parlour game.

But he couldn't wallow in his hate. He had to convince her they were
protecting someone innocent, who really needed help, not sheltering some
bad-boy criminal.

'Melissa,' he said, forcing himself to sound gentle, 'Mark is not a liar.
He's not the type. And he's not a nonce either. I doubt he's ever had sex
with anyone.'

'He's the one who runs the altar boys, though, isn't he? He's the one
who looks after the football team.'

'Altar *servers*. They have girls too, now, you know. And the team is all
handicappers ...' This explanation wasn't going very well for Tommy. He
could see her processing the data and coming to the wrong conclusions. He
still believed Mark was innocent, but he began to see how fishy everything
she knew about him looked.

'Huh. That could just be a matter of taste!'

Trying to be gentle again, he took her hand and sat beside her on the bed. He described to her what had just happened on the way back to London.

Mark had put on his helmet as they sped through the stragglers going into the Villa–Liverpool game. Within a few minutes they were racing up the ramp on to the M6 southbound at Spaghetti, leaving the lit-up stadium behind them, and the little church that sat almost in its shadow. Mark felt like a sack of potatoes on the back. He wasn't holding on very tightly, and with every corner they made, his body acted like a gyroscope, pulling in the wrong direction. Tommy was still high from the ride up. His body wanted to go fast again, at least cruise at a ton. But he decided to keep his speed down below the power band. He had another life on board and had to be responsible. Plus he didn't believe his luck at having no coppers around would last much longer.

They were beetling along at seventy when Mark spotted the first service station just before Coventry. He tugged Tommy's arm and jabbed his finger at it. Sweeping across three lanes, they just made it into the turn-off, and decelerated rapidly into a parking spot.

'What's up?' asked Tommy as he kicked down the side stand. Mark could barely speak. He gestured to the café, then began walking towards it, keeping the chipped old helmet on his head.

Tommy got them coffees. He wasn't sure what was up. Mark sat opposite him, shivering.

'Fucking hell, man, you're freezing!' He felt his hands – they were like ice blocks, and his face was red from the visorless helmet.

'What about the rest of you?' He looked over the side of the table at Mark's legs. 'Jesus! Ordinary trousers. Those shoes!' He could see his ankle exposed where his plain black socks ended. 'Hang on a minute, right? Stay there.'

Tommy got up and marched over to the gift shop, where they sold sweets and souvenirs and leisurewear. *Fucking nutter. He'll be dead of exposure soon.* Rummaging through the racks of clothes, he grabbed some tracksuit legs, and the thickest sweatshirt he could find. It said 'NEC. In the Big Heart of England' on it. He found a packet of tube socks too, and threw them on the counter, and paid for them with two fifties.

'Here, stick this lot on,' he said when he got back to the table.

Mark went off to the gents' and came back a few minutes later, looking a bit more comfortable. He looked bulkier.

'So tell me what the fuck happened,' he said.

Mark sighed. 'I don't know. It all blew up this morning. One of the
kids' mums came knocking on the door saying she wanted to see Father
Kelly. He came down. I went back up to my room, 'cos I was answering
my e-mail. I heard them barneying, but when I went out to see what was
happening he told me to mind my own business. I did the lunch-time Mass
– the usual three people – and when I came back there were coppers in the
doorway talking to him. They got him his coat and stuck him in the back
of the car. And drove off. After that it all went mental.'

'So what's he supposed to have done?'

'I dunno,' said Mark. 'I can't imagine. I just can't imagine. Touching
little kids? I can't imagine it. He's an old bloke, look at him. He never
hurt a fly.'

Tommy cocked his head on one side. 'Hey, come on, Mark. There's
a lot of it about. And it doesn't discriminate. I see it all the time. All
the time.'

This seemed to confuse Mark even more. His handsome face was a map
of emotions. And his hair was still a mess. Even his eyebrows were tangled.
He dropped his eyes and looked at the table-top. Then he looked up. 'I
didn't do anything, Tommy!' he exclaimed. He wasn't begging his friend
to believe him, he was begging everyone else. 'They were standing outside
shouting to the coppers "Get the nonces!" and "Bring out the other one!"
Some bloke shoved me and called me a paedophile. He said it right in my
ear. It was getting really ugly. And then the bishop's office were useless, no
one got back to me. I even sent an e-mail to the cardinal. That was just
before they started hammering on the door again. I mean, these were people
I see every week. I look after their kids for them! I hear their confessions.
Then they turn on me.'

'That's the thing, Mark. You have contact with their kids. If they
suspect it's inappropriate, one, they'll never trust you again, even if you
can prove you did nothing, and two, they'll try and jump you. But didn't
you even suspect anything?'

Mark looked ashamed, and hung his head again. 'Suspect? Suspect what?
I don't even think about things like that. And he seemed such a nice old
bloke . . .'

'Nice? I would never describe him as nice.'

'OK, not nice. But decent. He kept himself to himself.'

'Mark,' said Tommy after a moment. 'You're really a clueless git
sometimes, you know that? I believe you. But you're going to have to
make your case a lot better than that if you don't want to end up in

Section Forty-Three, if you know what I mean. Where the nonces go. But don't worry, I'm with you, OK? I know how these people talk.'

His friend looked sick. He shook his head. They finished their coffees. On the way out Tommy remembered the fucked-up helmet. He went to the grill counter and tried to get someone's attention. They all ignored him.

*Fuck it,* he thought, *I'll help myself.* He went into the kitchen and found the industrial-size roll of clingfilm on the counter, and pulled himself off a yard. A manager spotted him and came across, shouting.

'Oi! Wharra you doing back here? This is staff!'

Tommy had what he wanted, but feeling pissed off, he turned and shouted, 'Just fuck off, OK? Just *fuck* off!' It worked a treat. The manager raised his hands and backed off. He didn't want any trouble.

He plastered the clingfilm double across the place where Mark's visor should have been. 'Here. And stick some socks on each hand too. These gloves are too thin. Keep your hands balled up.' He stopped short of telling him to put one round his exposed neck too. There was a limit to how much he could look after him.

They rode back at a crawl, doing sixty and seventy to keep the wind chill down, but it was still bad. Tommy was cold in his leathers. He could imagine what it was like for Mark.

After hearing him out, Melissa pulled her hand away and asked Tommy a question.

'So you really think he's OK?'

'Yeah.'

'And even though you can't move these days without hearing about this stuff, you think he wouldn't know the signs even if he saw them?'

'Yes. He's very cut off up there.'

'And you understand what this all means to me? You know that if he isn't OK, and this gets out, it'll be the end of my career? No more kiddies. No more teaching. You know all that, don't you?'

'Well, yeah. This time you just have to trust me.'

'I normally have no trouble trusting you. Well, at least until recently. Recently you've been a nightmare.'

'Well, just go back to the way we were. Trust me again.'

She thought about it. She was stuck. What was trust, like love itself, if not a verb as well as a noun?

She sighed. 'OK.'

He smiled and hugged her.

'But you know the risks too,' she added, getting up and heading for the bathroom.

Back in the lounge, Mark was warming himself in front of the radiator. He was grimacing from the pain in his feet as the circulation returned.

They sat up for another hour, Tommy trying to talk to him. He tried to keep off the subject, but he kept looking for clues in the way Mark spoke – clues that might suggest that Old Man Kelly had been playing with the kids. As a doctor, Tommy had seen the results of such 'playing', as the kids often referred to it. He had seen the evasive response to questioning. He had heard the strange parental explanations for behaviour that seemed to be a re-enactment of sexual acts. And he had touched the ruined body parts and their infections. The health authority sent him to hear lectures by psychiatrists, psychotherapists and social workers about abuse, and he had read books and newspaper articles and scientific papers about hoaxes and hysteria. Having seen all that evidence, and ploughed through the studies and their methodologies, he could only conclude: there was a lot of it about.

And it was hard to know who was telling the truth. Mark, though, he instinctively trusted. He was just wondering about the other fellow. He wondered what the coppers would make of Father Kelly. *Maybe he'll get the Catholic desk sergeant and get off?* Tommy had to laugh. Mark looked at him, curious.

'Ah, it's nothing. Anyway, tomorrow we'll sort out some help for you from the Church. There must be some sort of representation available. Some sort of brainy priest-lawyer.'

Mark slumped lower at the thought that he needed another lawyer. It was a sure sign that his life had gone off the rails again. He wondered what his old mother would make of all this, from her perch in the heavenly host.

He showed him into the spare room, clearing Melissa's sewing stuff out of the way and pulling out the narrow camp-bed.

'Er, this is a bit of a rack. Switch to the floor if it gets too much.' He gave him some extra blankets and bade him goodnight.

Melissa was pretending to be asleep, so he lay there with the side light on, having a cigarette and thinking. *Wonder what it'll be like when the law come for him? Will the Church fuck him off? No, they always seem to look after their own. They'll pull something out of the bag. Not like the fucking FA, anyway. Ooh, Old Firm. Missed my run. No rules tonight either.*

If he had slept at all, Father Mark appeared to have slept in his clothes.

The black shirt and dog-collar. The NEC sweatshirt. The black trousers, tracksuit legs and multiple pairs of socks. When Tommy went to rouse him at eight in the morning he was sitting up on the floor on his pile of blankets, deep in thought. His clothes had picked up balls of wool and acrylic in the night, and his hair was still flipped. He didn't seem talkative.

'Cup of tea?' asked Tommy.

'Thanks. Are you going to work?'

'Nope. I only do a three-day week these days,' he lied. 'Cuts.'

'Oh.'

'We can get going on the lawyer business,' said Tommy.

Mark seemed hesitant. 'I'd rather talk to Father Kelly first. I want to find out what's going on.'

'I don't think it'll help.' He paused. 'Well, whatever.' Tommy was a bit miffed that his plan wasn't getting the response he expected. Mark was supposed to sleep on it and then agree.

He was glad to see Melissa in the bathroom getting ready for school. He gave her a squeeze as she was putting her lipstick on. She was good at it. She didn't elbow him out of the way. 'So what's the plan? What do fugitives from justice do on weekdays?'

'Fugitive from the *law*, love. Slight difference. I dunno. When he makes his fuckin' mind up, we'll go and see some Church types. Other than that, it's just hanging out.'

'Just like the old days, eh?' she said, turning in his arms and planting a red smacker on his forehead. 'Just don't do anything stupid, that's all.'

*Yeah, just like the old days.* He knew he couldn't talk to Melissa about this. *If it was like the old days we'd ... well, what would we do? We were always running one way or the other. Settle things with aggro ... no, we didn't really settle things with aggro. Aggro was the thing. Mark had the right attitude — it was just about protecting territory, and wherever you went, you were either protecting your own or attacking others'. And upholding the good name of the club, of course. Funny how useless all that is now.* For a moment, Tommy was glad he had become so bourgeois — he finally had a use for it. He knew a bit about lawyers, the social services, the police, even the way the Church worked. He could get Mark out of this.

'No breakfast for me, love,' she said. 'I'm getting in early. What about you?'

'Er, I thought I'd take the morning off. Just to see he's OK.'

'OK. 'Bye.' She kissed him again.

After breakfast and some morning TV, and while Mark was in the

shower, Tommy got on to the office at Westminster Cathedral. Pretty
soon he got hold of a friendly secretary, a middle-aged English woman
who bought his line about wanting to trace a priest from his youth, whom
he heard had run off with his housekeeper to Ireland just a few years ago.
When he mentioned the name – Father Sean Tucker – she recognised it.
Tommy said his mother had died and left something in her will for Father
Tucker, since he had been a good priest, and now had a child to support
and clearly would need some help as he obviously wasn't trained to do
anything else. The lady was fascinated with Tommy's story, and he kept
her talking until she had given him her unofficial version of the Church's
internal disciplinary procedures for such cases. Like a university, they tried
to deal with these things internally. They had ecclesiastical courts, which
kept the state at arm's length for a while. 'And these cases are not as rare
as you think!' she whispered. He got the name of the person he wanted – an
SJ – and decided to give him a call right there, before Mark emerged.

He got through to him straight away. *Ah, these holy people. In the office early.
That's what I like.*

Tommy introduced himself with a false name, as a parishioner, and asked
if he could find out what was going on at his local church, the Sacred Heart
in Aston, since the priests seemed to have all disappeared and no one at
St Chad's Cathedral knew anything. Father Ignatius was cordial, at first,
but not helpful. Once he found out what Tommy was really getting at,
he became hostile and cut to the chase in a very unpriestly manner.

'If you have information about the whereabouts of Father O'Mally I
suggest you co-operate with us now. We know that young man and we
know about his past. We want to help him.'

*Jesus,* thought Tommy. *They're on to it, all right.* 'OK. Why don't you just
tell me the best thing to do?'

'Tell him to come and see me immediately. And . . .'

He had heard enough, and hung up. *I'm not gonna let the bastards tell me
what to do.*

Mark appeared in the lounge looking clean and with wet hair, but still
miserable. He had on some jeans and a T-shirt Tommy lent him, and the
NEC sweatshirt. In the Big Heart of England.

'You know what, Mark? I think you're right. We'll leave it a day or
so. Let's just keep calling home until Father Kelly turns up. So what you
wanna do today? This is the Big Smoke, lots to do.'

'Oh yeah,' said Mark. The one place he knew – Westminster – was off
the agenda. They both locked on to the TV. The first wave of daytime

trash was starting, for housewives, invalids, the terminally unemployed and the chronically ironic. 'Next on Ricki Lake,' said a pompous English voice. 'My Handicapped Lover is Da Bomb!' The voice had a hint of distaste, as though it were above such foreign vulgarity. Tommy and Mark settled down to watch.

Tommy was unable to pull himself away. He hadn't had a day in front of the box like this for years. He was beginning to see where his patients got their vocabulary from. It was me, me, me, all the way, with a lot of effort going into feeling 'comfortable' and 'empowered', and sustaining a strange state of collective guilt, whereby admitting things guaranteed instant absolution. He looked at Mark. Mark looked blank, like it didn't mean anything to him.

Next was the Wheelchair Romeo, as the graphic dubbed him, a full-on quadriplegic whose whole life, he declared, was dedicated to 'eating —'. He was bleeped out.

Tommy had an idea.

'Hey, what about Kevin? You could send him down the church to see what's happening.'

Mark had been thinking just this thing. He wanted someone unconnected with the trouble to see what was going on. Someone neutral but loyal.

They got Kevin's mum's phone number from Directory Enquiries, and soon had him fighting his way up the cramped dark hall to take the phone off his mum. He didn't get many calls.

Mark dealt with it. Kevin agreed that if the lifts were working, and his ride to the community centre turned up, he would look in there later, if the driver allowed. But he didn't really fancy his chances. Tommy detected a grudging obedience in the way he dealt with the young priest. He either didn't know about the trouble yet, or he didn't give a fuck.

They watched the news, half expecting to be on it. Then they watched some more TV. Tommy dragged him to the pub for lunch, but he didn't really want to go. He was no fun. Tommy just had a pint. Back home, they watched telly all afternoon, Tommy nodding off in his armchair.

*Well, that was a wasted fucking day*, he thought, when he awoke at half four and realised where he was. No messages on the machine. Mark had gone to his room, and was reading. *Hmmph. Reading now.* He still couldn't get over the idea of Mark reading anything. A train timetable, maybe. Or a *Sports Argus*. But that was about it.

He tidied up and got the dinner on, just as Melissa came home.

He was glad to see her. They whispered about his nothing day in the kitchen.

Dinner was a sober affair. Melissa was polite and avoided asking Mark anything embarrassing. Mark was miserable. Tommy tried to keep everybody happy. 'Let's get a video,' he suggested afterwards.

They all trooped down to the store and began shuffling around the aisles. Melissa's usual choice was adaptations of European novels, but she couldn't find one without any sex. Tommy thought a good old comedy would be fun, but everything that was in – all the Abbott & Costello and the Marx Brothers – didn't look that funny. He ended up in the family section, shaking his head. It was either *It's a Wonderful Life* (and it wasn't, so that ruled that out) or shit like *Beethoven*, about a fucking dog. Mark didn't have a clue. He didn't have a video, he didn't watch telly, and he hadn't been to the pictures for eight years. Tommy caught him fondling a documentary on dolphins.

'You want that?' It went in the basket. At the end, that was all there was in the basket, so it was what they got. They trudged home.

When they got in, there was a message from Kevin.

'Hallo? Hallo? I 'ope this is fuggin workin'. 'Allo? This is that referee's 'ouse in London, innit? Anyway, I went down the church this after, and I'm tellinya it wasn't fuggin easy gettin' the driver to stop. Anyway, it was fuggin all locked up. There was a police car outside and the pigs was talking to some people who seemed to be jus' standin' around. Anyway, when I gorrin I was readin me mum's *Evening Mail* – she gets it delivered – and there was this bit on the inside about a priest going missing, i.e. you, Father Mark, but nothing about the ol' fellah. So anyway, that's all I fuggin know. Wish you would tell me what's gooin' on. Here's me numbah: 0121 444 3816. Tarra.'

Melissa didn't look very impressed, but Tommy glared at her before she could comment. He put the tape in and poured drinks for everyone. They sat in silence watching the creatures swimming round in the blue light. Tommy hated dolphins. They were so overrated. They looked like they wanted slashing with a Stanley knife, coming up to the side of the pool like that. Of course, *he* couldn't do it because of who he was. And he knew that as soon as some yobbo got round to doing it, as they inevitably would, he would take it as a sign that the country was going down the toilet. It was a no-win situation.

'What do they talk about to each other anyway?' he asked. No one answered.

'No work tomorrow, love,' he said as they got into bed. He expected her to give him hell, but instead she rolled over and hugged him.

'I know it's hard for you, Tommy. I just hope you're doing the right thing.'

'Thank you, Mel.' He felt a surge of gratitude at her response, and a wave of little-boy comfort. 'I know I'm doing the right thing.'

He didn't know for sure, but it was nice to have her on his side.

The phone didn't ring again all next morning, and there was no answer when they tried the house. Fearing another day in front of the TV with an increasingly apathetic Mark, now looking rather dodgy and unshaven in his Big Heart of England top, Tommy decided to take him to the West End.

'Come on, Mark. It'll do you good.'

He obeyed.

In the very heart of London, just a few streets from the base of the Post Office tower, Tommy couldn't resist asking. 'Remember this pub?' he said, as they passed a cruel box of a boozer where they had drunk once before a Tottenham game. Their coach had left so early they were in London by ten o'clock, and the mob spent the morning wandering all the usual streets: Carnaby Street, Oxford Street and Regent Street, jostling people and embarrassing girls. Some kids went on a looting spree in a tourist shop but everything they brought back to the pub – bowler hats, Union Jacks, stupid toys that crawled around for ever – was soon smashed to pieces. They marched to King's Cross to get a bus, and met up with some more Villa on the way, then piled into a pub near the ground. Mark had been on good form that day, full of abuse and quick on his feet. He was permanently up for it.

They peered in the window to see if it was the same, but passed by. It was too early for drinking. They drifted on down until they reached Piccadilly Circus and Tommy had a brainwave: 'Ah, the Soccer Museum! Come on, Mark, you'll love this.'

He paid them both in, which came to eighteen pounds, plus five pounds for the 'programme'. Tommy hated it from the start, because you had to enter through a turnstile. 'How fucking corny,' he said loudly, so that the man behind the counter and his manager could hear.

Inside they could see the people who had already been through filing through the gift shop, which was full of Man United shirts, to the exit. Signs guided them to the right, so in they went, shoulder to shoulder with Dutch and German tourists, and some schoolboys. There was a big panel with a long essay about the origin and purpose of the museum, who helped set it up and who ran it. After the first few lines they skimmed it, and finding nothing of interest, moved on at exactly the same moment.

The first chamber was dedicated to the Origins of the Game. The walls were covered in etchings of public schoolboys and daguerreotypes of teams like Notts County and Newcastle. In tiny writing there were mini-essays on the early running of the League, and the formation of the Football Association. There was a bit about Rugby School, where rugby was invented. In a darkened alcove with room to seat twelve people there was a wobbly old film loop of Manchester City winning the FA Cup in 1904. Mark and Tommy stood at the back. *So where's the bit about Villa having the FA Cup stolen while it was on display in a shop window in Newtown Row in 1895?* Two young women in denim jackets came in and sat down in front of them, and began talking loudly. One was a platinum blonde with some acne scars in the centre of her cheeks and calves like sandbags. The other was a redhead, who looked a bit more classy in her well-cut trousers. She sounded southern.

'Ooh, what's this? What's this?' said the blonde in a northern accent.

'Look at 'im, phwoar!'

'Must be the Fifties.'

'Hey, Ref, put your glasses on!' And they laughed loudly.

Mark and Tommy left and went on to the next room, which was devoted to the Twenties and Thirties.

'Eh?' said Tommy. 'Did we miss a room?' They retraced their steps.

'Looks like this is it,' said Mark, bemused. 'The Twenties and Thirties.'

The Twenties and Thirties section was all about giant crowds of men in flat caps waving their hankies and standing on uncovered terraces. There was a chart of attendance growth, and a list of League and FA Cup winners ran all around the wall, leading into the next room. There was a video showing a policeman on a white horse helping to clear the pitch at the first FA Cup Final held at Wembley. 'April 28th 1923, and over two hundred thousand men crowded into the new stadium. Constable George Scorey on his white mount Billy was the hero of the hour in front of the King ...' went the soundtrack.

It was looped so that it repeated every forty-five seconds.

'C'mon.' They moved on, following the line on the wall.

'Hey, whaddya know – it's the Fifties!' said Tommy. 'OK, don't look. What's it gonna be?'

Mark laughed and shut his eyes: 'Man United win the FA Cup. England get thrashed by Hungary. Uruguay win the first proper World Cup. And something about a foreign club ... er ... Juventus!'

They looked around. 'Here it is! Man United! The Busby Babes!'

'Yep, here it is,' said Tommy. '"... And the Jules Rimet Trophy was awarded to Uruguay."' There was a plastic replica of it in a perspex case.

The girls came in and went straight for the Busby Babes. They stopped talking while they read the text, and then looked at each other in disbelief. The blonde hung her head and started to weep, silently at first, then in great heaving sobs. Her friend comforted her with an arm round her shoulder.

Tommy was standing a few yards away and began to sing, just loud enough for them to hear: 'Who's that crying on the runway, who's that dying in the snow ... ?' Then he cackled. The girls glared at him, one with pure hatred in her eyes, the other with a solution of tears and mascara.

The Sixties room was slightly bigger. There was a lot of Arsenal stuff on the walls, and a lot of Tottenham. They watched a video of Jimmy Greaves dribbling round four defenders and scoring, which was pleasant. Several panels of text made the point that football was entering its 'pop' period, and backed it up with a video of George Best making his debut at sixteen, and the Beatles meeting Harold Wilson. This left Tommy scratching his head.

There was a sign saying 'World Champions '66' on the wall, and a giant blow-up picture of the England squad in the white shirts they didn't wear. There was another small chamber under the sign. As they lingered, the girls tried to squeeze past them. Tommy stood back and, smiling, said, 'Excuse me, ladies!'

In the gloom they stood at the back and watched familiar black-and-white newsreel of the 1966 World Cup Final. An actor doing a plummy Pathé voice added extra information, explaining the controversy over the ball bouncing on the line in terms of the rules, with a cutaway to a computer animation explaining it all visually – presumably for the foreigners. It was always a thrill to see the goals going in, even though to Mark and Tommy it seemed like the game had taken place in another century, and on another planet.

The girls cheered every time a goal went in, and booed the Germans. Just before Geoff Hurst lashed in the killer fourth goal they shrieked in unison with the commentator: 'They think it's all over ... it is now!' They had it down. The film of the goal was repeated several times, and each time they provided their own soundtrack. The two men stayed long enough to see Bobby Moore collecting the trophy – 'Watch 'im wipe 'is 'ands! There!' crowed the southerner – and then hurried out.

'Ah, the Seventies. George Best's boutique, Jeff Astle's sideburns, and the Kop,' he said as they moved on, trying to get ahead.

There was indeed a huge photo mural of the Kop at Liverpool, packed to capacity. You could see every bony scouse face, every bad haircut and cheap jacket.

Tommy was comforted by an old tune that came into his head:

> '... They look in the dustbin for something to eat,
> They find a dead dog and they think it's a treat,
> In the Liverpool slums.'

They had Toshack's boots and Shankly's wedding ring.

'Come on, I can't wait to see the Eighties.' They walked through. The final room was huge, at least eight times the size of the biggest previous room. Down one side was a bank of eighteen computer terminals, and a banner saying 'Microsoft Premier League'.

As the nostalgia industry hadn't got a handle yet on the Nineties, they had been lumped in with the Eighties in one hi-tech environment. There were interactive displays everywhere, allowing you to touch screens and wade through video clips and statistics, and print out your favourite team's kit from when records began. All four divisions and the Scottish League and Welsh League were covered, with all the information residing on a central server. Round the side there were tributes to ex-England managers: Bobby Robson, in his rumpled tracksuit, and a large cartoon from the *Sun* showing Graham Taylor with his head as a turnip. A few yards down, Tommy spotted a large fake oil painting of Nick Plumage with the England manager and Graham Kelly.

'This place is a fucking mess,' said Tommy, as they moved on to the End of Hooliganism display. They skimmed the text silently, looking for familiar names. It was all Chelsea and Leeds, and the mobs invented by Millwall fans for an old TV documentary, 'F-Troop' and 'Treatment', still in circulation. You could scroll through the Taylor Report in full.

'Pah. Let's get out of here,' said Tommy. He saw the girls at the automatic autograph machine, putting in their pound coins to get personalised print-outs of their favourite players' scrawls.

'Hang on . . .' Mark was looking at the people playing on the computers. They were all wired to the internet. People were looking at all sorts of things, checking their e-mail, video conferencing, watching television . . .

'Give me a pound,' he demanded urgently. Tommy handed it over. They waited their turn and Mark got on-line, entered his password and began connecting to his mail server.

'What are you doing?' He didn't like watching people play with computers, but Mark's face was animated and determined, and his fingers were flying.

'Checking my mail. Damn. Give me another pound. This thing eats them. Come on, server.'

Tommy obliged. The screen read: 'Searching for mail for marko@sh.bham.vat'.

'Still searching. I don't know what's up. Damn . . . have you got another pound, Tom?'

'This is my last,' he said. He was glad it was, he didn't like seeing cash go down the drain like this. *Into a fucking computer.*

'Hey, you can't do that,' piped a little voice. Tommy turned. It was a boy of about ten wearing a tiny Man United shirt and scarf. He was a solid little kid, with a thick neck and big hands. 'There's a limit, one pound each. It's my turn.'

Tommy gave him a cold stare, but the kid went on. 'It's my turn! It's my turn!'

Tommy crouched down and said very softly to the little boy, so that he sounded like a gentle teacher, 'If you don't shut up and clear off right now, I'll wring your little neck and hang you by that fucking red rag. Have you got that, son? OK. Now *fuck* off.'

The little boy looked horrified, stepped back, and then bleated, 'I'm gonna tell my daddy what you said.'

Tommy watched as he disappeared into the crowd. *Fuck, I hope he's not some big bastard. Still, I've got Mark here.* Then for a second he doubted whether Mark would do anything to help if they did get into any trouble. Especially after last time, what he said to him after the Blues game. *Nah. 'Course he will. Mark's sound.*

'Shit!' he heard him mutter behind his back. He was still glued to the monitor.

The little boy came back, leading his father and pointing. 'That's him! Tell 'im, Dad.'

Tommy smiled inwardly. Not because the boy's father was a seven-stone weakling – he could still have been a dangerous bastard at that size – but because he was well dressed and wearing glasses. *He's going to reason me into a corner. Come on, mate.*

'What's all this, then?' he said. He was talking to Tommy like he was a kid, which rankled. *Perhaps it's just a habit.*

'What do you mean?'

'My son tells me you pushed in front of him.'

*Eh?* thought Tommy. That's odd. He saw his chance and ran with it.

'Excuse me, but I did not. I'm just waiting for my friend' – he nodded towards the priest – 'to check his electronic mail. I don't know what your son has told you.'

'He said he'd beat me up!' piped up the little boy.

'Is this true?' asked the dad, looking cross.

'What do you think?'

The man looked down at his son. Then he looked back at Tommy. He found it hard to believe that this well-dressed man, with his rolled umbrella and his crombie overcoat, could have said such a thing. He liked Tommy. He could see something of himself in him. He appeared to be *one of us.*

'Well, Nick's teachers are always telling me he has quite a vivid imagination. I'm sure it was all a misunderstanding.'

'Da-ad!' wailed the boy.

'No buts!' said the man. 'Say you're sorry to the man.'

'No!'

'Apologise!' he barked, and shook him by the shoulder.

'Sorry,' mumbled the kid.

His father gave Tommy a gracious smile, part 'Terribly sorry', part 'Didn't I do a good job of bringing him up?', and led him away. The kid dawdled, staring back at Tommy, who winked at him. The boy stuck out his tongue, just as he was dragged away.

'Access denied! I can't believe it! They must have taken my computer.'

'Oh, shit,' said Tommy sympathetically. He paused. 'Was there anything ... anything on it you need?'

Mark was in a huff, and marched out of the museum without another word or glance. Tommy caught sight of a book about refereeing in the gift shop, which they had to pass through to reach the street, but hurried on.

'What's wrong?'

'It means the police are in the house. They must have gone through all my stuff. They must think I'm a suspect.'

'Stuff? You don't have any stuff. Anyway, you've always been a suspect.'

Mark looked shocked. 'What do you mean? You think I'm in on all this now? Oh, great. Thanks a lot, mate.'

Tommy was impressed that he had called him mate again, for the first time in years. But he rushed to calm his fears. 'No, not a *suspect* suspect. Just a suspect in that you were in the area, you know. A police suspect. Coppers suspect everyone, that's their job. "Wanted for questioning" is more your line at the moment.'

The priest looked mightily fucked off and confused. Tommy dragged him into a pub on Glasshouse Street where they could sit and talk. They nursed their Cokes. Mark wasn't saying much. He did say he wished he hadn't come to London, what was he doing down here, and he should have stayed and faced his people. Much as he hated London, Tommy was disappointed to hear it being slagged off in this way. He swallowed his pride, however, and said they should wait and see. 'Give it another twenty-four hours. Call the cathedral again.'

Seeing someone with a *Standard*, he got up and went outside to get one for himself. On his way back he couldn't help noticing Miller's picture on the back, and a small heading: 'Top English Refs Vie For World Cup Positions'. *Bastard! Fucking bastard!* He stopped dead in the street to read it. It was about 150 words long and would surely vanish by the evening edition, but it still fucked him off no end. Miller was up for a place. The only other Englishmen mentioned were a couple of no-marks who had never done anything. *Bollocks!*

As he entered the pub, he turned to the front and flipped through until the story he had been looking for caught his eye. 'Police Quiz Sex Priest And Search For One Other.'

Without reading more, he passed it to Mark. 'You're in,' he said, still cut up from his own omission. Mark fell on the paper, his eyes nearly popping out of his head. He read out: 'Police in the quiet suburb of Aston, Birmingham ...'

*Suburb? It's not a suburb*, thought Tommy ...

'... were today questioning a Roman Catholic priest concerning allegations of misconduct with several young boys. Oh, Lord save us,' he groaned. 'A detective with the West Midlands Police Vice Unit said that Father Michael Kelly, sixty-six, had been detained overnight. Several parents in the parish have come forward since Tuesday saying their children, many of whom were altar boys at the Sacred Heart Church, spoke of being touched in an inappropriate manner.' Mark turned white. Tommy noticed it was beginning to sink in at last. He said nothing. 'Police are requesting information about the whereabouts of the curate at the church ...'

'Curate? You're not a curate, are you? I thought that was a Proddo thing?'

Mark carried on reading: '... Mark O'Mally, thirty-five, who was last seen on Wednesday afternoon, heading off on his moped ..'

'That's not a fucking moped! How can they call it a moped? It's a one-two-five, isn't it? At least!'

'... in the direction of the city centre. The moped was found abandoned half a mile away. "He said he was going to see the bishop," said Mrs Dolores O'Connor, fifty-seven, the church housekeeper. "I never ..."' He gagged and read again. '"I never trusted that boy."'

Mark was crushed. Tommy leaned over and placed his arm on his shoulder. 'Come on, mate, you know it's all bollocks. What does she fucking know anyway? She's just dazzled by the media. She'll say anything.'

'How could she say that?' He seemed lost. It took him a minute to get himself back together and continue.

'Crowds gathered at the church, whose gates were padlocked shut, for the third day running to demand an explanation, many parents holding on to their children. Flowers and soft toys were placed on the railings. "I think it's shocking," said Tom O'Grady, fifty-five, as he stood with his wife in the rain. "They should string 'em up. I don't care if they are priests."'

'D'you know him?' asked Tommy.

Mark answered feebly. 'Yes, he's a lay reader.' He read the last bit.

'Kevin Brownlow, twenty-seven, said, "It's a f—ing disgrace. I can't f—ing believe it. Who would have f—ing thought it?" Mr Brownlow was in a wheelchair.'

'Hey-hey, Kevin!' said Tommy. 'Good to see you doing your job. You little git. Next time I see you you're going off the balcony.'

'That's it, Tom, I'm going home. I'm not going to let this calumny continue behind my back.' He got up to go. Tommy was keen to temper the situation. He caught up with him outside.

'Well, let's go back to my place and make a few calls first.'

'Calls! What good have they done? I should have stayed and faced the music from the start.'

The ingratitude rankled Tommy, and he began shouting. 'If you remember, *you* phoned *me*. All I did was save you from getting kicked to fuck, or from getting hauled in by the coppers before you knew how to defend yourself.' He squared up to Mark, blocking his path. He was on the verge of whacking him. One more provocation and he wouldn't give a fuck any more.

Mark stared back at him, straight in the eyes. It was as though his brain took a moment to process the data. The old Mark would have been up for it, but this one had learned to reason. Slowly, but religiously.

Mark stepped aside, then carried on walking. When his friend remained behind, he turned, shrugged, then waved him to come. 'OK. Come on. You're right.'

Slowly, Tommy rejoined him. 'So?'

'Let's go back to your place. I'm still going back to Brum, though. I can take the bike.'

This too stung Tommy for a moment. He had been hoping to keep the bike at least until the summer. He had plans: two-up with Melissa on the Riviera, the Maritime Alps, Provence, all that stuff she loved. Top off. Pernod. Running into acquaintances. And then back for the World Cup, of course. *I suppose it is his bike, technically*, he thought, *but . . .*

'Yeah, but you know how bastard cold it is this time of year. Get the train.'

They were going down the steps into the Tube station now. 'It's fifty quid. I don't have that sort of money. I've barely got the bus fare out of town.'

'Don't mind the money, I'll sort you out. The train's fast anyway,' he said, crossing his fingers. 'I'll drop you at Euston. You know how mad you ride anyway. You'll be paste by Watford on that mother.'

Mark appreciated his care, and eventually agreed to everything. The Tube ride home was strange and thrilling to them both, as they watched the Friday passengers reading the *Standard*, seeing which stories they read and if they looked up. None of them did.

As they rounded the corner into Tommy's road, he leapt back, pulling Mark with him.

'There's a police car outside my house.' He was all prepared to hide behind a wall and watch what happened, but Mark was having none of it. He strode out, shrugging him off. 'I told you, I'm not running from this lot any more.' Tommy raced up behind him. *This is it, then, this is it. God, look at that pig standing on my steps ...*

They strode down the street together. It appeared they were interviewing Mrs Thorpe outside her basement, but when they saw the two young men, the two officers, one a middle-aged male, one a young female, turned all their attention to them. Tommy could see their pig ears pricking up. He had seen it hundreds of times. He got the first word in:

'Good afternoon, Officers. Dr Thomas Burns. Can I help you?'

They moved a bit closer, ready to pounce.

'It's all right, Officers,' said Mark, very quietly. 'I'm on my way back to Birmingham right now. If I can just get my things ...'

The WPC reached out and grabbed his wrist. She was almost a foot shorter than Mark, and half his weight. He could have flicked her off with one hand but he partially submitted. She wanted to crank his arm up behind his back like a common yob, but he resisted that, keeping his arm rock solid without showing the strain.

'Officer!' said Tommy.

'OK, easy now, that'll do.' The older man touched her hand to persuade her to let go.

Mark thanked them both, and asked again if he could get his things. The first copper led them up their own stairs, while the WPC remained in the street by the car. Tommy was relieved to see that Melissa was out.

The older copper didn't read him his rights, but said that they were from the Metropolitan Police, and that they had to take Mark back to Birmingham. 'No lights, no sirens. You'll be there in a couple of hours,' he said, with a neutrality that, in the circumstances, seemed to Tommy like warmth.

Back in the street the WPC was standing by the car with the back door open. She had her baton ready, and stood in a kung fu crouch, ready for anything. The old man looked slightly embarrassed. 'At ease, Constable,' he said, and she obeyed, but kept her warlike expression.

Just before Mark dipped his head into the car, he looked back at Tommy.

'Thanks,' he said, and tried to smile.

Tommy didn't know what to say, with the coppers looking. *Help the police, beat yourself up* — that's what they used to shout as someone was being carted away at games. You couldn't get done for a joke, for some reason. The door shut and he stood back, then he shouted, 'Don't worry, Mark, you'll be all right.' *I'll be praying for you. Sort of.*

There was a message on the machine from Wheelchair Kevin in Birmingham. "'Allo? 'Allo? We had coppers round our flat today. I think they're after you ... er ... Father Mark. Anyway, I don't know what's gooin' on down there but there's a lorra people wand'rin' around. Central News was there. I think I'm gonna be on telly tonight. Anyway, keep ya posted. Cheers. This is Kevin.'

*Little chicken-leg fucker*, thought Tommy. *The things this does to people. One sniff of the cameras and they turn somersaults. One whiff of child abuse and everyone's ready with the first stone. The British love a queue, but the whole world loves a crowd. I should write to the* Evening Mail. He sat down in the flat. It was afternoon and grey outside, but surprisingly, not getting dark. He tried to remember how to pray. He was rusty. *Dear God ... no, that sounds too much like a letter. God — what are you playing at? I mean, WHAT are you playing at? You know what I mean. Could you sort this out, please? Mark hasn't done anything. Call off the Gestapo, eh? Thank you.* He had that sinking feeling, that this was not going to get answered. He remembered it from times past, and other prayers unanswered. '*Knock and the door shall open, ask and you'll receive.*' *That's what those American nuns used to sing on the records in school assembly.* Unanswered prayers were a big reason he had lapsed. That and the shops being open all Sunday. He always had a PS, too — maybe that was why it sometimes didn't work. One came to him now. *Oh yeah, PS. Rangers–Celtic this weekend: make sure I don't make any big goofs. And make sure Celtic spank them. You're a Catholic, after all, aren't you? Amen.*

There was nothing on ITN or the BBC about the case. Tommy wasn't surprised; the lag in coverage by the news media, while they waited for a critical mass of interest to occur, had dogged him for the last few months. *A critical mass of teddy bears on the railings, that's what it'll take.*

Melissa was home at 7 p.m., fresh from the gym. Tommy explained the evening's events to her. She was upset.

'So the police took him away, and you still think he's innocent?'

'Yes.'

She crossed her arms in front of her. 'I think you're just doing all this because you haven't got any friends. You just want someone to look after.'

Tommy tried to laugh mockingly. 'Look after? I'm a doctor, for Chrissakes. What do you think I do all day?'

'And what do you think *I* do all day? Listen to little kids and try and work out what they're on about.'

'Yeah, well, maybe you should hold off on the amateur psychology and just teach 'em how to read and write?' He realised he had gone too far as soon as he said it.

'You *bar*-stard,' she said.

It was bar-stard time. He hadn't heard this for ages. Not for a couple of years. Three choices: apologise; ignore and continue; outdo her in anger. He chose the rare middle path.

'The coppers just want to question him. They were very nice about it.'

'So what about the Catholic cavalry? Did they come and help?' He had got her back on subject, but she was still fighting.

'No,' he said limply.

'And the media will be round here in no time, I bet. That old lady in the basement ...'

'The media know fuck all, they're always a day late and a dollar short. We can go away for the weekend if that's what you're worried about, love.' Then he remembered Glasgow. 'You can come up to Glasgow with me! I've got that Old Firm game. It's a big deal up there.'

'Old firm? What old firm?' She liked the sound of Scotland, but it was still sinking in.

'No,' he laughed. 'That's what the Jocks call it, Rangers v. Celtic, the Old Firm. The two old enemies.' He sighed through a smile, the way he knew could turn a row around. 'We'll go up tonight on the shuttle, get a hotel in the city centre, have dinner ... I hear they have a lot of ethnic places up there ...'

After a little cajoling she was sold. It was such a relief to be getting away from their troubled home. It took her twenty minutes to fill the wheelie bag with nice clothes, bathroom stuff, shoes and a book. He took a little bit longer, folding his refereeing kit meticulously, checking he had a spare shirt, and shorts, and bootlaces. He decided to bring his shirt with the FIFA crest, not the English lions. He packed his notebooks and second watch, his rule book to read on the plane, and his address book containing the details of his contact in the Scottish FA, given to him by Jim Mitchell. He considered bringing his regulation FIFA line flags, since one never knew what it was like up there, how wrong things could go. *One of the linesmen could be pissed and sleep in, then we'd be fucked. Hmm. Unlikely, though.* He threw them into his Adidas bag anyway, along with fresh underwear and a couple of shirts. Everything else he would have to wear.

'Don't, whatever you do, look back at Mrs Thorpe's, OK?' he ordered Melissa as they went down the stairs. As he closed the door behind him and they got into the car, he felt a pang of guilt at leaving his house when Mark might be calling for help. But he reminded himself that life had to go on.

Glasgow on a Friday night was a thrill for Melissa. She had curiosity written all over her face as she walked the streets in her new silver trousers and her short leather coat, Tommy looking swell in his suit on her arm. She was surprised they had all the good shops up there – Armani, Muji, Daniel Poole, Silicone Valley – and at how well dressed everyone seemed to be when they came out to play. After checking into their hotel and getting changed, they went to a couple of bars before dinner and then out to eat. Tommy was watching his booze intake, because of the game the next day at Ibrox Stadium, but he was happy to see Melissa having a good time. After dinner (Abyssinian, a first for them both), they ran into Sandra, an old friend of Melissa's from college whom she'd lost touch with in her twenties. They were delighted to see each other. They decided Melissa should go with her and her friends to a nightclub, right there and then. Tommy half wanted to go too, but he knew he had to be up early for the game. Besides, he had been warned that all the players would be out drinking tonight and that he would be better off if none of them recognised him on the pitch from some club. It was OK, though, walking home alone, through the quaint Victorian streets, back to their hotel. It was business as usual for him, like doing a FIFA game, a European Cup game where he had to get to the country twenty-four hours before the kick-off. Anywhere in Europe they were always good to him – after the pitch inspection they'd take him on a tour of the city and out for dinner. He and Proctor had seen a lot of cathedrals together, and a lot of shopping malls. It was like that now, only nicer knowing that Melissa was in town and would be creeping into bed with him later. But he was bitter that the refereeing was practically all over for him.

Her hair smelt of smoke and her breath of whisky when he awoke in the morning. He was stone cold sober, and felt well for it. He put on the TV very softly as he was getting ready. Even the breakfast news had stuff about the game on it. All the presenters seemed to have ants in their pants about it, all nudging and winking. Tommy was puzzled. *Maybe it's a lean news day?*

Mr Mitchell had arranged for one of his henchmen, the Referees' Development Director, a bloke called George Lynne, to meet him in the lobby and take him to Ibrox for the pre-match formalities. He took his time over breakfast in the restaurant, read the paper – which was also bloated with Old Firm coverage – and finally strolled out to meet him at ten o'clock.

'We'll get a taxi to the ground,' he announced rather excitedly, and proceeded to point out the sights on the way, the main one being a large armadillo-like structure down by the defunct riverside. Tommy had always thought Birmingham needed something like that. In terms of joules of idle curiosity generated, the fifty-foot King Kong in the Bull Ring had been well worth it.

The ground looked at first glance to Tommy like Villa Park. He had only one true impression of Rangers, and that was the day they came to Villa for a friendly and took the Holte End. He and Mark had been slightly too young to understand the extent of what was going on, right up until the time they paid into the Holte and were confronted with a mob of at least five thousand pissed Scots singing, waving flags, burning scarves and throwing sparklers. Right up the back of the Holte End, where no invaders ever stayed for long.

They might have known better, given the reports on the telly as early as Friday night of the hordes wandering round town and taking over. But they didn't quite believe it. They might have known better when they saw away fans – the same tartan mobs – wandering down quiet roads near the ground like the Broadway. And they should definitely have known better as they stood outside the Holte in Aston Park with a handful of other confused kids, looking up at the mob inside and hearing the strange songs.

> *'Fuck the Pope, and the IRA,*
> *UDA, all the way,*
> *Fuck the Pope, and the IRA.'*

That was sung to the tune of 'Sailing'.

Inside, a Billy Connolly lookalike (long hair, moustache and beard, flared jeans and a Wrangler jacket) draped in a yellow Scotland flag gathered round the pair of them with his mates and chatted to them down the front. His conclusion was, get on the pitch and get down the other end, or you'll be killed by this lot. 'Ahm doin' it for ye and yer friend's sake, wee man,' he said to Tommy. 'Get yer fockin' scarves off and get oot o' here noo! Ahm just thinkin' of yer safety.' And he was the nicest one among them.

Mark and Tommy did as he said and joined the small but growing Villa mob in the old Witton End, an exposed hump of concrete that held fifteen thousand. It was all a bit of a blur after that. The sound from the Holte was pretty loud. A lot of the Villa mob were smarting down in the corner, and there was a photo in the paper of someone being stabbed in a heaving mass of bodies. A Rangers fan, fortunately. No one had expected them to bring so many fans for a nondescript friendly designed just to fill an empty Saturday in the calendar.

Nobody expected Villa to beat the team that had just done the Scottish League and Cup treble either, but Dennis Mortimer scored the goal that put Villa two up. After that Tommy and Mark had had enough. The Holte was a boiling mass of humanity that was moving down towards the pitch. There were no big fences then. There were hardly any stewards or coppers on duty that day either. Someone had fucked up big-time. Tommy and Mark got out and jogged home just at the right time, as a strange roar went up shortly after and the warriors went at it. The pitch was invaded, and the rest was in the papers. A lot of arrests. A lot of kickings. The referee abandoned the game. *I wonder where that ref is now?* thought Tommy. Rangers hadn't been popular down the Villa for a long time after that, not until a new wave of youngsters with no memory had come through and started chanting their name as an alternative to Celtic. It had even taken the city a few days to round them all up and send them back to Glasgow. Tommy disliked them.

Everyone inside the ground was extremely hospitable. He had imagined at least someone would hate him, for being English, or for having the same name as an old Celtic manager, but he was totally wrong. They treated him with an almost European respect. The assessor had come early to welcome him – the man who was to observe his performance from the stands – as had the top referee in Scotland, Jim Alloway, whose position he had usurped for the day. Tommy was a bit embarrassed on finding this out, but Alloway was a gentleman, and assured him that it was OK, and said that he respected Tommy's work, and couldn't understand what was going on in England since Colin Marsh had been forced into retirement. He himself had been prevented from doing the big FIFA games when the world body reduced the maximum age for refs covering internationals from fifty to forty-five, catching him in the middle. So he wasn't the only one struggling with the powers that be.

As Tommy went about his business, accompanied by his new entourage, inspecting the pitch and checking the team colours, Alloway explained a bit about what to expect. He had done eleven Old Firm games. 'Your linesman cannae hear your whistle, the crowd are so loud, so use gestures. And you'll find Scots players are used to refs who try not to give fouls or cautions if they can.'

'That's how I like to play it too,' said Tommy. It was nice to find a place where people didn't take too seriously FIFA's rigid directive that every bookable offence be accompanied by a card.

'My philosophy is the players are there to cheat me, so I have to stamp my authority on the game early on or it gets out of control,' said Mr Alloway.

Tommy raised a polite eyebrow. He had heard it all before. He had lived it. And he was starting to get a bit tired of being followed around.

'Excuse me, please, gentlemen.'

He called the hotel and told Melissa about the two match tickets the club had given him. She could pick them up at the club reception if she wanted. She was hung over, and while she wanted to go to the game with her friend from last night, she wasn't in the mood for traipsing across town.

'But you're coming here anyway, aren't you?' he laughed. She hadn't been to see him referee for years. Suddenly he wanted to be sure she came.

'Aw, can't you just bring them over? We're meeting in some place called the Nile, a pub, at half eleven. Sandra and some more friends. Can't you bring them there?'

She sounded all fuzzy and vague. He sighed. 'Yeah, OK. I could do with getting out of here for a bit.'

He announced that he had to go into town for an hour. Mr Lynne, Mr Alloway, the assessor, Mitchell, the club chairman, and the linesmen and the reserve official, who had now turned up, all looked at their watches and muttered to each other. It was decided that Mr Burns, being their guest, could do what he wanted. They arranged for a taxi, and Alloway was to go with him into town.

In the cab, Jim Alloway had another warning for him. 'Aye, there's a lot o' selly bigotry still, ye'll nae see the like of it in England.' Tommy grunted. He had heard all this before. It sounded like bollocks.

The Nile bar was thronged with dark blue and white shirts and hats, and a roar greeted him as he entered. They were watching a tape on the big-screen TV. It was footage of a dog running on the pitch at the last Old Firm game. It had bitten a Celtic substitute warming up, lapped the pitch and disappeared into the tunnel. The Rangers fans were in ecstasy. He spotted Melissa at a table with about eight other people. There was a bloke on each side of her talking in each ear. They were chain-smoking Hamlets and had several empty Becks bottles lined up on the table.

'Hey, Tommy, over here!' she called, waving.

'Oi, Referee,' said one of them, a carrot-top, jumping to his feet. 'Good to see ya! What the fuck are ye doing in here on a match day? What are ye havin'? Becks, is it?'

'Aye, get him a pint!' said the other one, a large young man. He extended a meaty hand. 'Kenny Godsman. But ma friends call me Sumo. Welcome to Scotland. You have a beautiful girlfriend.' He was beaming.

'Sumo, you daft get, he cannae drink. Can ye drink? And wha' aboot your friend?' He meant Alloway.

Alloway spoke for himself, in Scottish dialect that Tommy didn't catch but which seemed to satisfy everyone else.

'No, I'm just here to drop off these tickets. Three o'clock, directors' box,' said Tommy.

The two men fell on the tickets. 'Aye, these are magic. You're a lucky lass, y'know that?' Melissa smiled into her Bloody Mary.

'Oh, stay a while, Tommy. It's early yet.'

He looked at his watch. Then at Alloway, who shrugged. The decision was clearly up to him. He felt the conflict of interest that had been raging in him for years. On the one hand he wanted to stay in the boozer where the action was, get pissed, talk bullshit, meet new people and rub up against Melissa, and on the other his professionalism told him to stay sober and alone in a quiet spot and build up his concentration for the game.

'Och, sit doon,' said the carrot-top. 'Tommo's the name, by the way. What'll ye have? A Coke?'

Tommo stepped aside and Melissa pulled him next to her. Alloway sat round the table from them.

'OK, soda and lime juice.'

The bar was getting more packed by the moment, and another great roar went up. The local news was interviewing the new Rangers signing, a black striker from Milan. Then a song started and went round the room in an instant:

> 'Oh, no Pope of Rome,
> No chapels to sadden my eyes,
> No nuns and no priests, fuck yer rosary beads
> Every day is the Twelfth of July!'

There was a merry savagery about the song which spoke to Tommy. He loved it. He tried not to smile, and to concentrate on what Godsman was saying, leaning towards him across Melissa. Tommo came back from the bar with an armful of drinks and a new pack of Hamlet.

'... Y'see, Rangers have to win this one to show those Cath'lic bastards. Ten in a row, it's never been done. I hoop you'll be fair today. I want a penalty for Rangers in the last five minutes if you're not!'

Tommy laughed. They definitely weren't as tight-arsed and reverential as the English. The redhead sat down and was now leaning over his back, chatting up Melissa. Something about a wee discothèque where they were all going after the match. Godsman was relating a story of papal treachery, and asking had he heard about the latest goings-on in England with the bent priests. He said no. Godsman told him about the old Rangers player who had been suspected of – or was it arrested for, or was it charged with? – child molestation. The next time he played in an Old Firm game the Celtic fans unfurled a giant banner with his name on it, in huge letters, followed by SIMPLY THE BEAST. He chuckled at how cruel the world could be.

Tommy's drink tasted fine, the hard bubbles biting his tongue and the lime giving his palate the creeps. He suddenly felt very strong, being the sober one in this den of drunken indulgence. Melissa was assenting to something over his shoulder. She was hoovering up the attention. He knew that tone of voice: sometimes cool, sometimes giggly, sometimes encouraging. She could modulate it from sentence to sentence and run rings round a guy. In the nicest possible way. Godsman was on about King Billy's Day in Belfast. There were several other friends of his around the table, respectable-looking men, executive types, management, white-collar, some of them even in their office clothes, all knocking back beers from the bottle and discussing the game with serious faces.

> 'Hello! Hello! We are the Billy Boys.
> Hello! Hello! You'll know us by our noise.
> We're up to our knees in Fenian blood,
> Surrender or you'll die,
> We will follow the Rangers!
> Hello-o! Hello-o!' etc.

All the conversation was suspended or drowned out for a minute while they ran through the song. Tommy had always thought it was a Villa song. *We must have started it, though.* Alloway seemed to be having an amicable chat with Melissa's friend, Sandra, who wore a cream scooped-neck top and a bra that pushed her breasts up like a bowl of fruit. She had on a tiny pair of shorts, and her hair was fine and long. Her mouth was broad and scarlet and had a life of its own. That was something he loved about Melissa and her friends, they all looked like grown women, even when they dressed like teenagers again. Even groups of pissed men went silent and stood out of the way as respectfully as they could when they passed. *Respeckful*, as Fat Paul would say.

Melissa: Fi? Fiona? Are you screening? Pick up, pick up ... Fi? Ah, sugar. Listen, soon as you get this message, do me a favour. Call the gym and get that Craig bloke on the phone – don't leave a message with anyone – and tell him I won't be able to make it tonight. Just tell him that. I'm calling from a pub in Glasgow, that's what the racket is. Why's your mobile off? Me and Tommy are up here 'cos he's refereeing a football match, I just decided to come at the last minute, to get away from it all for the weekend. It's pretty good up here, I'm having a nice time, and Tommy's being OK for once. We ran into this old friend of mine last night and we all went out to this really cool club, it was really cool, you'da loved it. And the shops are really amazing up here ... shit, I've got twenty seconds ... don't forget, call the gym, get the number from Directories, I can't really do it from up here, you know what it's like, just tell him I'm sorry I had to rush home to my mum's, and I'll call him whenever. No, don't say that, say I'll call him when I get back. And I didn't have his number. Or ... well, just make something up ... but something sensible, OK? I know you'll do the right thing. Thanks, love, 'bye, 'bye ...

Tommy turned his attention back to Sumo. A mobile phone went, and everyone reached into their jackets, even the tiny kid on the end who looked about eighteen.

'Hey, Fat Cat, it's for you!' said Sumo. 'What ye doing getting calls on ma phone? Use your own number. Is it some burrd?'

Tommo exhaled a large clump of smoke and laughed. 'Fuck orf, Sumo. Fat cats like me need four lines, not two. Hello? Oh, hi, dear. Aye. Yes. We're in toon. Yes. Aye. Yes.' Everyone began jeering at him. 'Aye. Yes. Noo.'

As he was getting off the phone his words were drowned out by another song, to the tune of 'She'll Be Coming Round the Mountain'.

*'Could ye go a chicken supper, Bobby Sands?*
*Could ye go a chicken supper, Bobby Sands?*
*Could ye go a chicken supper, ya dorty Fenian fucker,*
*Could ye go a chicken supper, Bobby Sands!'*

Tommy was impressed. 'Who's Bobby Sands?' he heard the young one
ask. 'Dunno. Some Fenian bastard,' replied his friend, and they took
synchronised swigs of their drinks.

Fat Cat Sumo commandeered a barmaid and made her bring a double
round for everyone, plus single-malt chasers and two more packets of
Hamlet. Tommy felt the whole room lifting off like a rocket around
him, as the alcohol went to the group nervous system. His mind felt
clear as a bell-jar, yet part of the excitement made him feel drunk. *This
is intoxication by induction.* He reached for his notepad, thinking it might be
a research topic, but then he realised his notebook was at the ground with
his refereeing kit. Alloway was keeping an eye on him, and everyone else
around the table. He praised this refereeing skill, circumspection, quietly to
himself, with a prayer that was a strange combination of self-love and thanks
to some outside force. Only it wasn't a prayer, it was just a feeling sweeping
through him in a pub. He nodded at Alloway, just to acknowledge that
everything was OK.

Time was shooting by. As if on a drunken night in a pub he suddenly
found himself at the bar chatting by turns to Sandra and her cleavage. He
was fascinated to know all about her, where she had been for the last few
years. Turned out she was brainy as fuck and had done a doctorate at
Glasgow University in communications. She helped carry the drinks back
to the table, where Melissa was like a tennis umpire fielding conversational
gambits from Sumo and Tommo. Someone else had got a round in at
the same time, which meant everyone had to drink a little bit faster.
Tommy was on his fourth soda and lime already. He loved the feeling
of it flushing out his liver, even though he knew it was a myth. His liver
would be sparkling clean. Like a drunk man, he put his hand inside his
shirt to feel his stomach while he was talking to Sandra. It was rock hard
and fatless, just as he had planned.

She broke off, laughing and curious. 'What are you doing?'

'Oh. Y'know.' He wasn't really embarrassed. He didn't have space for
that in his head. 'Shit, y'know, I can't wait to get out on that pitch today.
I haven't reffed in so long, 'cos of all these wankers in England, and I'm
fuckin' ready for it. You know what I mean? I'm fuckin' ...'

He never finished his sentence. Another roar went up, followed by another song.

> 'Cheer up, Tommy Burns, O what can it mean,
> To a sad Fenian bastard and a shite football team!'

Sumo was on his feet as he sang this one, pointing at Tommy and grinning. When his name spread round the table, people stared at him and wiped imaginary sweat off their brows, but it was all in good fun. To Tommy this was sheer alchemy, seeing hatred turned into fun.

Melissa smiled at him. She had never realised what his name might mean elsewhere. She thought refereeing was pretty dull on the whole, the preserve of middle-aged bank managers and professionals. But here was her Tommy at the table having a grand time, the centre of attention.

It was nearing one o'clock. Sumo and Tommo had been in the pub since the doors opened. They were now on their sixteenth and seventeenth bottles of Becks respectively, and were talking to each other across the table on their mobiles. They were planning how to get to the ground, how to make sure the girls got in the ground — each of them had a taxi company on the other line and was co-ordinating their movements for the next twelve hours. There was no aggro brewing — this was all about getting *pished*. Tommy signalled to Alloway that it was time. He pecked Melissa on the cheek and fended off a lot of last-minute ribbing about how they expected a penalty in the last five minutes, or in the last two, or a direct free kick on the edge of the box for the new striker who was a specialist ... each had his own preferred scenario.

The pair of them struggled out into the daylight and straight into a black cab. Tommy's head was spinning, though he tried not to show it. Alloway chuckled.

'Aye, the bigotry's still there, but it's no as bad as it used to be. Not until the kick-off, anyway. Are ye OK?'

Tommy had his head out of the window, trying to get some air. He was thrilled — with the welcome, with the knee-deep hatred, with the wide motorway and the old factories, with everything.

'Have to get the smell of smoke off, y'know.'

'Aye.'

Everything was immaculate. His FIFA shirt. The respectful way the managers presented the team sheets. The way the linesmen digested his instructions without any query.

'You can flag for fouls, but I'll only consult you if I feel I was very poorly sighted.' This was his way of centralising power, which experience had taught him was completely necessary for taking control of the game. Like a good partner in parenting, sometimes they had to defer to him whether he was right or wrong. He also said that in the event of a penalty he would take up position on the goal line and would watch for early movement by the goalie, Law 14 'trickery' or ungentlemanly conduct by the kicker, the ball crossing the line, and rebound complications. The linesman would watch the edge of the box for encroachment.

As he led the teams out, Tommy was staggered by the noise level. It was like a permanent goal. It was like Wembley. The capacity was now up to fifty-five thousand. *This is what the Theatre of Silence could sound like in Manchester if they got rid of all the moaning wankers and glory-hunters*, he thought. But he could barely hear himself think.

The game got under way. In the second minute a Celtic player, an Italian striker, was judged offside by Tommy. He ran on, the flag stayed down, and he hammered the ball past the goalie. The Celtic end went mad, erupting into a sea of green and white, while Tommy frowned and blew furiously on his whistle. In seconds he was surrounded by players who were pointing at the linesman, whose flag remained stubbornly down.

'*Porca Madonna!*' said the player in his face. '*Stronzo!*' Tommy was swamped. His heart was hammering inside him, and he could barely hear for the noise from both sets of fans. He ran over to the linesman.

'What did you see?'

'He was just onside,' said the linesman.

'I whistled, why didn't you flag? You support my decisions, remember.'

The linesman looked stoic. He wasn't used to being dressed down, let alone by an Englishman. But this was Tommy Burns, the supposedly great English ref, so he controlled himself. 'I didn't hear you whistle.'

'What do you mean? Are you deaf or something?' Tommy could feel the pressure building. He knew the fans thought he was debating whether to give a goal or not, but he had no intention of doing that.

'Your whistle must be too low. You need a higher frequency. A higher pitch,' the man said helpfully.

'What?'

He shouted, 'They all have them for this game, because of the noise. It's something about the noise at Old Firm games.'

Tommy was astonished, and deeply embarrassed as the clock ticked away and he stood on the sideline. He stopped his watch. That was step one. And he gazed into the main stand. He was looking for Alloway. He caught sight of Melissa and, mortified, looked away. After a moment one of the managers sent a substitute into the dressing room and brought back a couple of whistles from the training bag. The linesman showed him which one had the higher pitch and, cringing with shame, Tommy accepted it, thanked everyone, marched over to where the offside took place and raised his arm for an indirect free kick. All four sides of the stadium exploded again. Tommy saw the Celtic manager on the cinder track shaking his head in disbelief, and he remembered what Alloway had said, that Sky TV had twenty-six cameras at a game like this. They dissected everything.

In his shame, though, he clung to one belief, that adversity was there to be overcome. He was *not* going to lose control of the game. If the players thought he was an idiot, and if Jim Mitchell was in the stand rubbing his chin and wondering at what a fool he'd been, he was not going to let it stay that way.

Turning twenty-two players around that quickly wasn't going to be easy, but Tommy pledged himself to it. The next few minutes were hell. The Italian brushed past him, accidentally on purpose, which was a sending-off offence, but Tommy controlled himself and ignored it. Several players muttered behind his back that he was a wanker, and even the Rangers captain mocked him, asking him if he was OK. He let it all wash over him. He knew the hatred had to come off him like water off a duck's back. He wanted to be like a stealth bomber with its mysterious black coating, protecting itself with a cloak of invisibility, soaking up enemy radar, giving nothing back.

Several players thought they could get in nasty fouls while he was still rattled, daring him to not book them. He dealt with each according to its severity, and according to the mood of the men and the fans. The Celtic centre-half made a perfect tackle from behind in the area, and the player flew through the air like an Olympian. Tommy waved play on, and the Rangers fans erupted into abuse.

He was concentrating so hard he couldn't tell whether it was one or ten minutes later that he heard the 'Daydream Believer' tune from the Copeland Road end:

> 'Cheer up, Tommy Burns, O what can it mean,
> To a sad Feeeenian bastard an' a shite football tee-e-am!'

He was sure they couldn't all know his name, or care enough to look it up. *Must be a favourite old song.*

He forced himself not to listen. He booked someone for a vicious sliding tackle that sent the Celtic centre-forward rolling into the advertising hoardings. Sweat was starting to build on his forehead and there were only twelve minutes on the clock. *God, I'm not fit enough. Who is this little Rangers bastard, and what is he saying? Time for a new ball.* Some Rangers fans had kept the ball, so he ordered a new one from the dugout. *Fuck 'em if they want to be like that,* he thought, testing the pressure with his thumbs. He threw it to the player and ran upfield. *I'm gonna break these kids if it takes me all day.*

He shared no jokes with anyone for the next ten minutes, but plugged away with his decisions. He penalised for pushing and shirt-pulling, but he gave the advantage when it was due. He spoke back to a couple of players who were speaking back to him, and he saw the fear in their eyes when he did. He booked another player for accidental handball. Gradually, things settled down. The niggling stopped. The teams started to concentrate on the ball, not on their sense of injustice, and the game started to flow. Racing from end to end, Tommy felt it all coming together, all coming back. The spring of the turf under his feet. The strange double vision necessary at set pieces and in the box – part tunnel vision, part ESP. He concentrated on the white ball like a monk with his mantra, his gaze followed it like a kitten with a ping-pong ball.

If either team had scored before the thirtieth minute he would have been selfishly relieved by the distraction. But by the fortieth minute, when Celtic scored, he had attained the necessary state of selflessness. He was like a machine, able to run at full tilt and position himself for the perfect view, take in the line of the offside trap, see that the player controlled the ball with his thigh without using the hand that was very close by, see the foot go back and the goalkeeper sprawl, and the ball lash the back of the net. No controversy. *Name, number, forty minutes, nil–one, back to the centre.*

The embarrassment at the beginning of the game had been like a huge flesh wound from a shotgun, but now Tommy knew he had healed it, through sheer faith in himself.

Celtic were twirling their scarves all the way to half-time, in a way that Tommy knew, as he walked off the pitch, would be making the Rangers fans' stomachs turn. He wondered if Kenny Godsman was chundering in the aisle right at that moment, green and white from too many Hamlets and Becks. He caught Melissa's eye as he came off. She was standing up in the directors' box applauding like royalty. She looked good.

At half-time Tommy sat in his dressing room and tried to maintain his concentration without ignoring the others. He apologised to the linesman about the whistle fiasco. In everything else both linesmen had been spectacularly good. Tommy loved good linesmen. In one way they had a harder job than him – they had to concentrate so hard on so little. They had totally become Two-Dimensional Man, running up and down their slot like the old arcade game with the electric players in grooves. They had to watch the line of defence and the foremost attacker, and translate all his movements, his circling, his dummies and his turns, into simple vectors. He was either forward or aft, onside or off, that was it. And the linesman got more customised abuse from the fans than Tommy.

In the second half the game didn't need a referee, it needed a conductor. Both sides went at it and the football blossomed. *Maybe it is a beautiful game after all,* thought Tommy afterwards. But he suspected he only felt that because the hate factor was also satisfyingly high. The game became so easy for Tommy to ref that he began to tune in to the crowd again. The hatred coming off them was sustained and intense – all the songs he heard in the pub were blasted out time and again at a thousand times the volume. They taunted each other mercilessly – Celtic brandished their old European Cup, Rangers their Scottish title wins. The football didn't matter so much when you had something to beat the other side over the head with. Although his disinterestedness was never in doubt, Tommy actually began to develop a soft spot for Rangers.

They poked in two goals in the last ten minutes to win the game two–one. Nothing controversial. The Celtic players cursed each other, ignoring him completely. The three-quarters of the stadium in blue boiled with ecstatic, dancing fans, bear-hugging each other and rolling on the ground. The green end was like a graveyard. He blew the final whistle.

Of everyone that came in to congratulate Tommy on his performance, not one was ungentlemanly. Even the Italian striker shook his hand and smiled in the tunnel afterwards. All the officials told him how good he was – then mentioned his wobbly start, and remarked how well he had overcome it. Jim Mitchell declared himself pleased. He wanted to have a private word with Tommy, but Tommy excused himself. He was drained. The Sky guy gave him a videotape of the game, as they did. He left the stadium with his hair wet from the shower, his Adidas bag tucked under his arm, his coat, the tape and the programme in his hands. He never drank in the players' lounges – it was unprofessional to hobnob like that.

He met Melissa and her friend Sandra outside, who both kissed him on the cheek and made him feel like a hero, and ushered him into another taxi. He relaxed in the back and let it take him off into the night, to whatever fun was arranged for them all.

# 9

## Back from Glasgow; school day; FA warm to Tommy again; priest death; Fat Paul in snow; Ultimate Crime, Villa semi; graveyard

'Do not forsake me, O my darling ...' wrote Tommy on a piece of hotel stationery. He propped it up against the mirror for Melissa to see when she woke up. The whole thing read:

Melissa, love,

I was up half the night thinking about Mark, wondering what the police are doing with him. There is still no answer on his phone, and then on the six o'clock news on the radio this morning there was a mention of the old fellow being charged. I've booked myself on to the first plane I could get from here to Birmingham. I have to do something to help him.

I know we had planned stuff for today but I really can't stay. I'm sure you'll have a good enough time here with Sandra and friends. Thanks for a lovely time last night. You were sleeping like an angel through all this, I didn't want to wake you. I'll phone you at home this afternoon.

Then he signed it 'Love Tommy', and as a postscript added 'Do not forsake me, O my darling ...'

That was the lyric to a tune he had hummed for years. Melissa had never asked him what it was, which at first seemed odd, but in time he came to accept and then enjoy it. He liked her independence. He cultivated such gaps between the two of them. And he knew she liked to hear him humming the tune, the way a child is comforted to hear a parent going about their usual business around the house.

He propped the paper up against the mirror, took up his Adidas bag and slipped soundlessly out of the room. Out on the street he began walking quickly, looking for a taxi. He stood on the kerb, waving as a black cab went by. A minute later another passed with its light off. *Balls. Come on.* He looked at his watch, but before he registered the time he was struck by a question. *What the fuck am I doing out here, trying to get to Birmingham a few hours early when I could stay in bed with Melissa? I can get the next plane. And maybe I shouldn't be getting any plane, other than straight home? Fuck!* The pain came to him like heartburn to an after-dinner speaker. He knew he had come too far to turn back. He could feel the organisational momentum behind him, pushing him into a cab, whisking him through check-in, lifting him above the clouds and dropping him again on the edge of another city. He never usually gave himself a chance to turn back in such circumstances, when his bag was packed and his ticket was waiting for him. Spontaneity was a luxury he rarely allowed, unless he was very pissed.

He thought about Melissa, how cross she'd be. How *disappointed.* Then he thought about Mark, sweating in his cell somewhere, trying to answer questions he didn't really understand. He dithered on the spot, feeling paralysed. *If I go back he'll suffer. If I go on, she'll suffer and make me suffer too.* Both ways seemed bad, and all his planning began to collapse. A taxi bore down on him with a dramatic squeaking of brakes, and the driver leaned over. Normally, this would have been enough to push him on – things would have been decided for him. Barely aware of what he was doing, he took his doubt as a sign that he should go back and be with Melissa.

'Er, sorry, mate, changed my . . .'

'Ah, away an' shite ye!' said the cabbie, a respectable-looking middle-aged man. Tommy was too ashamed to get him back. He began walking back to the hotel, and in his excitement began to trot and then run. He raced into the lobby and talked the girl on the desk into giving him his room key again, and then hurried to the lift.

The silent pastel corridor, with its identical doors, seemed brand new to him, like he had never been there before. For a second he wondered whether he had the right floor or not. Then he was hit by a fear – suppose he burst in on his girlfriend making love to another man? Or suppose she was just up and reading his note? He held his breath and let himself in.

The room was silent. She was still asleep in bed. The note had not been moved. He put it in his pocket. He looked at Melissa, who had not sensed his presence, or his absence. She looked beautiful as she lay there sleeping, her face devoid of emotion, save what he projected on to it. He gently sat on his side of the bed and took off his shoes and lay down, very sober and straight, clasping his hands on his stomach. After a minute or two she must have smelt him, or felt his warmth, or the beating of his pulse through the mattress, because she rolled slightly and reached out to him and put her arm across him.

*Thank you. Thank you, for letting me do the right thing.* He lay there for another hour, in a blissful state of alertness and worthwhile mental activity. Everything he thought seemed to be right. And decisive. Not a moment or a word was wasted − it was as though he were refereeing in his head, or writing inside a dream. Everything went into the mental notebook, and everything was good. *Must look up that J.L. bloke, what was his name, John Lewis? What a dream. I couldn't have imagined such greatness, unless it was already in me. I could be good at something else too. I could be the best.* He thought about the game the day before, how well it had gone, once he had got a handle on the Scottish and their peculiar passion. He thought about his motorbike ride to Birmingham, how mental he must have been, and how close to his own death, and felt happy to have stumbled across that double helix of fear and physical pleasure. He was already planning what he would do now that he had blown his chances for good with the English FA. He would go back to medical school and retrain, respecialise. *Plastics, or maybe psychiatry − I fancy both. They're both a doddle, and they pay shitloads of money. That's the way to go now, make enough money to forget about football and all its stupidity, all the moronic chairmen and fucking bureaucrats, the coppers and the pug-faced fans. Maybe Mel can have a kid. We'll settle down, I'll be home weekends, play with it, look after it. I know she wants one really.* He looked over at her sleeping form, a sine wave of flesh beneath the solitary hotel sheet in the overheated room, from head to hips to ankles. He put his hand on her belly. She opened her eyes, smiled a smile of pure love, and took a moment to register that he was fully dressed.

'Mmm,' she murmured. 'What are you dressed for?' She closed her eyes after this effort, preferring to await his answer in the soft world of semi-sleep.

'Nothing, love. What do you want for breakfast? Want some tea? Toast?'

'Mmmm,' she approved.

Tommy used the sad tea-making equipment provided by the hotel.

It tasted stale from the start, but he didn't care. Life suddenly had a sweetness that such minor things could not touch. He let her wake up slowly, watching her all the way, pleased with his choice. He sat through the whole process – rousing, showering, make-up, hair, striding around in towel, shimmying into clothes, packing – until they had checked out and were walking along the street. They passed a newspaper stand and Melissa bought a Sunday paper. She soon found it – on the back page was a report on the Rangers–Celtic game, which included the sentence 'After a shaky start in which he threatened to deal all his cards in one go, referee Thomas Burns of London took control of the game and slowly faded from sight, until all that remained, like the Cheshire Cat's smile, was Justice itself'.

Trying to hide his pride, Tommy took the front section as they settled down to brunch in a café. It didn't take him long to find what he wanted. On page five in the home news was a small piece about the arrests, entitled 'Police Swoop On Suspected Paedophile Priests'. His stomach turned. This was the first time the word 'paedophile' had come up. And 'priests', that plural, made his heart sink. It meant that things were getting heavy, fast. He turned white.

'What is it, Tommy, love?' she asked softly and urgently.

He read out the headline, then every word of the article as he himself encountered it for the first time. His voice was quiet, as he was still conscious of being overheard by the doubtless normal people around them. '"Authorities are questioning Father Michael Kelly and his colleague Father Mark O'Mally, who was remanded in custody Friday night after police swooped on an unknown London address where he was thought to be in hiding. A neighbour is reported to have told the media that 'several young men' lived in the building. A spokesman for the Roman Catholic church said the men were expected to be granted bail. Police are now considering widening their investigations." 'Oh, fuck,' said Tommy. 'That's us. That's me.'

It was Melissa's turn to blanch. Her skin remained olive, but it was as though the fire in her eyes had been put out.

'Several men? You mean they're coming for you too now? Tommy . . . !'

'Look, I know what you're saying. But Scout's honour, they've got nothing on me. Or Mark. Honest.' He laughed as he said it.

And then Melissa burst into tears. She didn't know whether he was being weird or just knew more than he ought to, but she couldn't stand not knowing. It wiped the smile right off Tommy's face and he darted around to her side of the table to hold her and assure her it was all right. The rest of the room stared at them. The waitress avoided them. Tommy tried to reassure his girlfriend, but he ignored the stares of the diners around them.

Eventually she calmed down. He told her that everything was OK, but he insisted on going to Birmingham to see Mark. She bit her lip and accepted it, all her Amazon fire and bronze gone, nothing left but the soft mouth and the damp eyes.

'Melissa, you'll be OK. If you don't want to hang around here all day, come with me to the airport. You go to London, I'll go to Brum. I'll see you again in a few hours.'

She sniffled, then looked up at him with an innocent appeal in her eyes. 'Can't I come to Birmingham with you?'

Tommy was speechless. It was as if she had asked to follow him into the gents. In fact, he would have found that much easier to deal with. He could see no way around it. 'I . . . I . . .' and he shrugged, and snorted, raising his eyebrows and opening his palms. 'Yeah. OK. I don't know whether you'll like it, though . . .'

'I'm not going there to see the . . . as a *tourist*.'

'I suppose not.' He knew she had never been to Birmingham. He had no family there any more. Like most British people, she had a vague idea of what it was like from slipping through it, or rather over it, on the elevated sections of the M6. She had been to the NEC, once, to a concert, but never into Birmingham proper. There was an increased danger of this happening since they opened the Symphony Hall and more convention space off Broad Street, and then some new bars and clubs, right in the city centre, but it hadn't quite filtered down to the lifestyle of the busy Southerner yet. Besides, by the time she or Fiona or any of her circle heard of anything fashionable enough to be worth trekking the 110 miles north by north-west for, it had moved on.

Of course, Tommy had resented all this heartily, for years, but had made a conscious decision to put a cap on this particular branch of his hatred. Birmingham and Melissa, never the twain should meet. He would rather she left it all to her imagination. *What if she thinks it's a shithole? I think it's a shithole, sort of. How am I gonna defend it? Balls.* Then a consoling thought arrived. *I've still got the cab ride to talk her out of it.*

So they stepped out into the streets of Glasgow once more, and a black cab came to a halt at their feet in fifteen seconds, and Tommy began talking as they headed to the airport. He quite liked Glasgow – the flats and the motorways and the industrial relics. It reminded him of Brum a little. He told her about Elmdon, the little airport out in the grassy fields of Solihull, which he hadn't been to for years, and about the Bull Ring and the obsolete optimism of the early sixties. He confused her by telling her about the big model of King Kong that had stood there for a while, and he tried to put her off by talking about all the chain stores that populated the city centre, and the market where she'd find cheap, crumbly crockery, clothing for the very poor and bad imitations of well-known sweets. There'd be bad kids hanging round the Midland Red bus station, and skinheads everywhere (he was going back a few decades here, but they were nearing the airport and she still hadn't wavered). It would be colder than London ('Is it any colder than here?' she asked, innocently, to which he had to say no), it'd be uglier than London, it'd be a concrete jungle with clearings of municipal grassland with damaged trees and unusable bus shelters.

'Sounds like parts of Bristol,' she mused.

'Don't you have any marking to do?' he asked.

'It's half-term.'

'Oh, so it is.' He fell silent. The cab driver opened her door for her with his right hand, conspicuously checking her tits and arse as she got out. Tommy gave him an extra five, because it was the airport. As he was getting out, the driver stopped him with a question.

'Are ye a football referee?'

'Yes,' said Tommy. He was instantly alert for trouble.

'Ye no did the Rangers game yestadee?'

'Yes.'

The man beamed broadly. 'Thanks for the win, an' all. Great game.'

Tommy eyed his fiver, which was firmly in the man's hand. He would have lunged over and grabbed it if it had looked possible. As it was, he scowled and got out of the car without acknowledging him. *Thanks for the fucking win. Who does he think I am? Scottish twat.* Then he said it out loud so Melissa would hear it as they walked into the terminal.

'What's wrong?' she asked.

'Ah, fucking cab driver was a Rangers fan. Thanked me for the win. Like I fucking influenced the score. Cheeky bastard. I fucking hate that.'

'It's all right, Tommy, calm down,' she said softly.

They headed for the British Airways desk. It was his last chance to get rid of her.

'Excuse me,' he said to the young man behind the desk. 'We have open tickets back to London. Well, we had, but I changed mine on the phone this morning to a British Midland flight to Birmingham. Can she get on that flight with me? Oh yeah, and I missed the flight but I thought I could just get on the next one.'

The man looked very doubtful, which pleased Tommy. Then, in his retrofitted Glasgow accent, he said he'd see what he could do, and started tapping away at his computer. Tommy tapped the edge of his ticket on the counter agitatedly. After a minute, the man looked up and smiled at Melissa.

'You're in luck, miss. There's one seat left. If I can just have your ticket I'll send you over to the British Midland desk and they'll give you your boarding pass.'

She looked at Tommy, who was looking like thunder. 'Mmmm ... Oh, it doesn't matter, I've changed my mind. Just make mine the next plane to London. I have to get back.'

The young man looked puzzled, then sighed theatrically and began tapping again. He civilly handed over her ticket to London. The computer decreed that she could get on a London flight that was boarding right at that moment, whereas Tommy had an hour to wait.

He smiled at her. 'I love you, Melissa,' he said.

She said nothing, but smiled, stuffing her boarding pass into her coat pocket and grabbing the wheelie bag. They began running together, flying past the pensioners creeping their way to Miami and Orlando, past the nuclear families and their mutant kids, past the Sunday businessmen and foreign tourists. She was a good runner, upright and light on her feet. She raised her bag off the floor because she didn't like the roar of the wheels and, passing it to the other hand without stopping, caught it by the side handle. Tommy watched, proudly, from a step behind and to the side. They made it just as the stragglers were getting on.

'Whew!' she said. She got her breath back in a few seconds. 'This is it, then.'

'Bye-bye, love,' he said, holding her gaze hard.

'What do you want for dinner?' she asked with a cheeky smile.

'You're gonna cook?' he asked, with exaggerated amazement. 'Cook me *dinner*?'

'Hey, I cook. Leave it to me. Just don't be *late*.' And with that she turned and breezed down the tunnel to her plane.

Tommy's plane barely got through the clouds when it began its descent into 'Birmingham International Airport', as the pilot put it. He wondered what sort of pilot got that run – Glasgow to Birmingham. It didn't seem to be going anywhere interesting next – Ibiza or Turkey. *Must have done something wrong. Missed his eye appointment by a day. Forgotten what airport he was going to. Fellatio at thirty thousand feet.* The thought wearied him: whether it was better to suffer, carry on and work your way back up to the glamour gigs, the Cape Towns and Los Angeles, or just say 'Fuck 'em' and find a new life, a new hobby. What would an ex-pilot do anyway? *Air traffic control? Drive a coach?*

Then for the first time he saw Birmingham from the air. They broke through the lid of clouds and suddenly there it was, a great grey crust of humanity. It was like any other city on earth, a mass of people huddled together avoiding the emptiness of the fields beyond, enjoying a mutual closeness. The plane curved anticlockwise, revealing the city to him in all its aspects, a mile every few seconds. He saw the modest muddle of the city centre, the black tops of office towers, the scab of brickwork around the canals, grey ribbons of concrete marked down their middles with engine oil drops, the golf courses and tennis courts of Edgbaston and the cramped streets of Small Heath and Spark Hill. There was the green patch and L-shaped roof of the Blues ground, and then he could see the green rectangle of Villa Park, its grass mown into neat chequers, its goalmouths faintly muddy. Goalmouths where, at last, he knew for certain he belonged.

They were only in the air twenty-five minutes. Compared to this, waiting for trains and buses seemed an obscenity, so Tommy got another cab, pointing the man in the direction of Aston. As they swept up the M42, Tommy tried to see the field in which the young motorcyclist died, and to tell the driver about it, but it made no sense to him. He didn't know him, he hadn't heard it on the news, it happened all the time. 'Some of them bloomin' bikers are pests, harin' up and down here, I'm not surproised, I'm norra bit surproised.'

Then on to the M6, and it was Spaghetti again, the beige concrete pillars, the expansion gaps between sections of road. It spooked Tommy how close it all was. Only an hour ago he had been in Scotland, and now *this*.

'Oh. Yow a reporter, then?' asked the cabbie as they pulled up outside the church. There were two TV vans, several reporters' cars and a police car. Late afternoon on a Sunday, and the area had never seen so much activity.

'Yes I am, as a matter of fact,' he said, using the plummy voice he had heard on Nick Felcher's answermachine. 'BBC, Radio Four.' And he stiffed him. After walking a few paces he looked back to catch the driver's expression, but the man was too busy gawping at the

satellite dishes and the mums being interviewed to care about Tommy.

The gates were still chained up, but the number of people had grown
since the first television coverage, and the number of toys jammed in
the railings seemed to have increased fourfold. The first few teddy bears
and soft pandas had been outnumbered by other things: Action Men and
plastic dinosaurs, and a pair of tiny football boots meant to be hung from
a rear-view mirror. Only that morning someone had brought along a Villa
scarf, and soon everyone was doing it. Every few minutes an innocent tot
was shoved forward by its parents and made to lay a claret-and-blue bobble
hat or a player's picture on the railings. One kid had a stuffed lion in a Villa
shirt with its foot on a ball. His parents had happened upon the symbol of
the hour and were trying to line their five-year-old up for the cameras, but
they were having trouble persuading him to let go of the toy.

People turned and looked at Tommy as he approached the crowd, which
was now around fifty people in all. They whispered to each other, because
he looked London. And he'd just got out of a taxi. The reporters all knew
he wasn't one of them, because he was dressed too smartly. The coppers
thought he might be a detective, only he had that Adidas bag. Other people
in the crowd murmured that he might be another priest, and got ready to
move forward. No one knew what to make of him, and as he merely stared
at the buildings and said nothing to anyone, they eventually ignored him.
Tommy walked around the back. There was a lone snapper perched on a
nearby wall drinking tea from a flask.

'All right,' Tommy called to him.

The photographer nodded.

'Been here long?'

'Since six.'

'Double time, eh?'

'Freelance,' replied the man on the wall, smiling for the first time and
gesturing with his mug, a faint hint of a 'Cheers'.

Tommy couldn't see much over the back wall, which was topped with
carefully placed shards of glass, and the house was dark.

'Is he in there, then?' he asked.

'Who?' asked the snapper, warily.

'That young priest.'

'Nah. 'E's gone.'

'Oh,' said Tommy. He was confused. *What are all the people hanging around
for?* he wondered.

'Well, what about the other one, the old boy?'

'Dunno, mate. 'Spect so.'

'When did the young one leave?' Tommy asked.

The man looked annoyed. 'Look, who are you wiv? Do your *own* fackin' research.' He put down his mug and picked up his camera, with its telescopic lens, as though he were considering using it against Tommy.

'I'm not *wiv* anyone,' he replied, trying to keep cool. *Cockney wanker*, he thought. He looked at the strong legs dangling over the wall. He wanted to rush up to him and heave them upwards so he fell over backwards on to God knew what was behind there — hopefully a kennel of Rottweilers — but he knew he risked a cowboy boot in the mouth if he tried.

'So, you up from London, then?' he ventured.

''Ere, I fink I know you,' said the photographer suddenly. 'You're a footballer, aren't you? I never forget a face. Who are you?'

Tommy felt a silent pulse of panic. 'No, I'm a doctor. I've come to see ... well, anyway. Seeya.'

He turned and began to walk away, and as he did he heard the shutter and motor music of the camera. He kept his back squarely to the camera as he went, determined to show nothing more then the back of his head and the dark slab of his coat. Even as he rounded the corner he turned his head slightly to keep his face hidden. *Cockney bastard. What does he mean, Mark's gone? Where's the fuckin' old man, then?* He turned the corner and headed away from the church, picking up his pace just in case the photographer was after him. As he walked, the school that was attached to the church was on his right-hand side. They shared the same depressing brick architecture, and the same style of railings ran along the road. The school was dark and quiet. He saw a navy blue skip in the playground, and two sets of doors with instructions written in the brickwork above them: 'BOYS' and 'GIRLS'. The playground sloped awkwardly, and there was a drain in the middle of the netball court. This was just the sort of school he found most depressing, one where you couldn't play football because of the windows, and if you did and the ball went over the fence, it was lost to the traffic.

The windows had children's drawings blu-tacked to them, clouds and moons and suns. As he walked along, looking into each classroom and waiting for another corner to turn, he saw a pale object in the gloom. It was near six in the evening, and almost dusk. Spring was working her slow magic. He took another look. It looked like a face. Then he realised he was staring, through the railings and deepening gloom and the grimy glass, at the man of the moment. Mark. He stopped dead in his tracks.

*Jesus! Am I hallucinating?* That thought more than any other terrified him. He prized his sanity and good judgment. He treasured it and cared for it and constantly looked out for it. He looked behind him, thinking this would be the time he was being followed, this would be the thing to get him caught.

When he looked back, two seconds later, the face was still there, wan and faded, a few yards back from the window. He pressed his face between the bars to see better, and called out.

'Mark! Mark!' He didn't know what else to shout, not wanting to commit himself to an apparition.

Very slowly, the face moved forward. The black hair, the pale eyes, the slightly Roman nose and the strong jawline all fell into place. It *was* Mark. He moved forward and opened the window. 'Tom!' he shouted.

'Mark! What the fuck ...? Hang on, I'm coming in.'

Mark looked nervously around and jabbed his finger in the direction of something further on. Tommy began running forward until he came to a gate. He climbed it easily, standing on the padlock and leaping clear of the spikes. He landed cleanly on both feet. The shock wave that ran through his body reminded him that he hadn't jumped like this since he was a little kid. Only a real criminal would need that sort of skill beyond the age of about sixteen. He was impressed that his body – his skeleton, sinews, cartilages and muscles – was in such good shape that he put nothing out.

He grabbed his bag and ran for the doors. Mark had opened the one marked 'GIRLS' and hurried him in.

'What the fuck are you doing *here*?' Tommy asked, astounded. 'There's coppers all over the shop back there ... well, media anyway. And people just milling around. What happened? It looks like there's been a slaughter, all that cuddly-toy shit. What happened?'

'C'mon.'

They were standing in a small corridor that led from the girls' toilets through their cloakroom to the main corridor. Tommy was almost overcome by the smells of carbolic soap, toilet cleaner, and the oily odour of gloss paint. He caught a glimpse of the tiny girls' cubicles, three in a row. Mark led him inside, past the rows of pegs that had the odd sad pump bag or puffa jacket abandoned on them. There the smell was of floor wax and more disinfectant, which flooded Tommy with the feelings of confinement and powerlessness of the child at junior school. They went past the corridor artwork and the headmistress's office and into the classroom in which Mark had been hiding. He looked shabby, and gaunt, as if he had tried to sleep in his clothes and failed. His dog-collar lay curled on the teacher's desk, which he seemed to have made his base. Underneath it was a PE mat on which he must have made his bed.

'How long have you been here?' Tommy demanded. Mark was looking out of the windows nervously.

'Since yesterday. The coppers had me in for questioning up town Friday night, didn't get anywhere, then my lawyer came and bailed me out yesterday afternoon. We got as far as the end of the road in his car, saw the mob had got bigger, and turned round.' Mark's voice was hard and scornful, the way Tommy knew it from days gone by, from dissections of away days and discussions of who shat out and who stayed. 'This lawyer bloke – the Church sent him but I think he was just an ordinary lawyer – he tried to stick me in a hotel. He just wanted to fuck off back to London. So I said, "Here's one, the Aston Hotel."' They both knew this was just a pub, a big football pub only a hundred yards from the ground at Witton Island. Tommy tutted and shook his head.

'So I went in, waited till he'd gone, then walked out and headed home. When I got nearer I saw a telly van shooting up the road and thought, Fuckin' hell, I'm in the wrong place here. So I went over the fence and got in here through a window.' He scowled and then shook his head. 'School – best days of your life, Tommy boy!'

Tommy tried to keep him on the subject, thinking it could only be one of three things: he was in shock, he was very cross at him personally, or he had lost his faith entirely, overnight. He sincerely hoped it was the first.

'So you've been hiding here all night? What happened to your hand?' He had been holding his hand close to his stomach, out of the way of trouble.

'Fucking coppers, surprise surprise. They were all right till Watford Gap, then they switched me over to the West Midlands, and they were a hard lot. Bastard had a go at me in the back of the van, calling me a perve and a nonce and a child molester ... Hey, so I found out what a nonce is! People can shout it at me now, I know what it means.'

He sounded harsh and more disturbed. Tommy again tried to steer him. 'What, they beat you up?'

'Ah, y'know, the usual. Hit me with their truncheons across the arms, so no one can see. Only now they have batons instead of truncheons. Hurt like fuck.'

'Let's have a look.'

Mark rolled his sleeve up on his left arm, exposing red marks and thunder-blue bruises. Tommy moved to examine them, but he pulled away, then said, in a gentler tone, 'It's all right, they're just bruises.'

'Nothing . . .'

'Nothing broken? Nah.' They sat down on the floor opposite each other, Tommy on the mat, Mark on the bare tiles.

'So where'd you sleep?'

'Friday? In a cell, next door to some nutty Scots bastard, pished out of his head, he kept saying. Singing too. He kept rambling on about the time he'd done in Barlinnie, and the nonces he'd battered. Normally . . . well, you know what I mean. Normally I wouldn't be afraid of someone like that, but if they think it's you, when you're *it*, you're shittin' it. I know the coppers wouldn't have done fuck all. It's just lucky they had a lot of empty cells that night. I asked them what they'd done with Father Kelly . . .'

'What was the questioning like?'

'They just said they'd dealt with him. "The Ringleader," they kept calling him. Like there was a lot more to come. You were right, Tom, you were so fucking right. They come for you with a fury and nothing can save you from them.'

'Except a decent lawyer,' he interjected. He wanted Mark to acknowledge just how right he had been. But along with that came the task of explaining where he was the night before. Why *he* hadn't been kicking down the doors to help.

Mark snorted. 'Yeah, the one I had was a dickhead.' Every time he swore it was like a tiny dart going into Tommy's skin. Seeing his friend shedding his grace like this was making him nervous.

'So anyway, I got in here and I didn't know what to do next. I didn't wanna get pulled to bits by that lot outside the house, and I didn't have anywhere to go. I thought about hitching down to yours, but I s'pose everyone's looking for me now. And I haven't done anything wrong! Why the fuck aren't they out catching the real criminals?'

'I just spoke to a press photographer hanging around the back of the house. He reckons the old boy is inside.'

'In the house?' asked Mark, surprised. 'I don't think so. Well, if he is, he's on his own. The housekeeper's long gone. They really said that?'

Tommy nodded. He could see that despite all the trouble he was in, Mark still felt something for the older priest. He still had some hold over him.

'The police came out with all sorts of bollocks, saying the kids had said

I was all part of it, and that Father Michael had said I was involved. I found it hard to believe anything had happened at all till then. I mean, I was right there after all. But when they said that, that he had blamed me, I knew they were lying, of course, but I realised they were on to something with him. That's the sickener. That he could do such sick things. The coppers told me there's about ten kids, all altar servers, who've come forward and said the priests had been sexually abusing them. But you can't trust anything a copper says, can you? Especially when they've just been beating you up.' He shook his head again, and looked at the ground. He looked to Tommy like he was fighting back nausea.

'Did they do the good cop, bad cop routine?'

'No. Bad cop, bad cop. Not even a cup of tea in twelve hours. They treated me like I was pure evil. Then they dug up my football record.'

'Shit.' Tommy was stabbed with guilt.

The light outside was fading fast, giving the classroom an eerie atmosphere of abandonment. With each chair sitting upside down on its desk they could see right across the room to the back wall, to the lemon-coloured radiators on which kids doubtless leaned during boring lessons, and the large noticeboard where their paintings were displayed. It all reminded Tommy of the rare times when, as a kid, he had seen his classroom at night, on the occasion of a school play or some such excitement, when he had to go back in to get something from his desk. He would have been happy if his classroom had stayed dark for the rest of his life. Tommy had always wanted to be outside, where the adults were parking their cars and striding up the school path, their kids skipping feverishly ahead of them, pulling their hands and trying to show them everything.

'I really don't like kids,' said Tommy, provoked by the memory.

'Don't say that. Kids are great, I love them!' Then Mark stopped himself, bitterly aware. 'I s'pose I can't say that any more! Fuck! Look what's happened to my life, Tommy. I'm fucked. Everything's fallen apart in a week. Why did this happen to me?'

'Take it easy, mate. I know it looks bad . . . and it may *always* look a bit bad too, but just keep reminding yourself you're innocent.' He paused. He was finding it so hard to help. 'Think of it as a test. Isn't that the idea? Like the Book of Job? I mean, that's the problem I always had with the Church, and God, and all that. If the world contains such fucked-up things, as well as beauty, what's He playing at? He might as well not be there. That's how I live my life. He might as well not be there.'

Mark groaned. He was leaning back against the sharp steel leg of a desk. The normal speech he gave when confronted by an agnostic was, well, pretend there's a New Testament God out there and things will pretty much fall into place. Live like Jesus and you won't go far wrong. And don't *worry* so much! But now he didn't feel much like rising to the challenge. He wasn't feeling very holy.

'I've never had any doubts before, Tommy, since my calling. Can you imagine what that's like? To find your place in the world, to start doing something, and do it day in and day out, something that takes up your whole life, so you're never off duty, and never have any doubts about it? I mean, one day you're on the dole, or working in some dump of a factory full of borstal boys, and the next minute you're on your belly in a white robe being blessed by the bishop and told to go out and do your business. But maybe you're right. I haven't been doing much praying in here. Just worrying. I'm tellin' you ... I'm thinking of chucking it all in. Going off to be normal somewhere.'

'Oh no, don't do that! You're good at it. You're good with the old ladies and the small kids and the pissed old men.'

Mark shrugged, by way of a thank-you. They sat quietly for many minutes.

'You got anything to eat? I haven't eaten for a day. Not that I was hungry until a few minutes ago.' Tommy looked in his coat pocket. He had four tiny bags of peanuts from his flights and handed them over. Mark devoured them while Tommy told him about the Rangers game, how well it went, and how fucked off he was that he wasn't refereeing any more.

'I fucking blew it, I really did. I had it all set up nicely, and someone kicked the stool away from under me. And I just let it happen. I don't think Melissa's very impressed with me either.'

'I thought that,' replied Mark, when he had finished. Even though he looked like a homeless man, he still ate nicely. 'She looks like the sort who wouldn't put up with much nonsense.'

'Does she?' Tommy was impressed. That his friend had any insight, and that his girlfriend was so admirable.

They fell into a long silence again. It was dark except for the streetlight.

'Don't pack it in just yet, Mark. Like I said, you're good with people. And your sermons are good ...' He trailed off.

'What, you looked in my book?' He shrugged. 'Well, thanks. I never knew what to think of them. You don't get a lot of feedback once you leave the seminary, you know.' Then his face clouded over. 'The coppers said they had seized my computer. They were in there straight away. That's why I couldn't get my e-mail when we were at that poxy Soccer Museum. This fat copper leans over me and says he has "computer experts" working on it. Ha! I nearly laughed in his face! Computer experts. I think he meant someone who knew where the ON button is.'

'So what was on it?'

'That's the thing – nothing. I mean, it opens straight on to the Vatican home page, like it's supposed to. The only thing I did was customise a few of the sounds. I just had my sermons on there, and my correspondence.'

'What about all the filth I keep reading about in the papers? The kiddie porn.'

'That's it. You're never more than two clicks away from "adult triple X" sites and all that, live shows from Amsterdam, they're always sending out their messages telling you to click on this link and you'll be transported there. I think they mail it out just as a wind-up half the time. But I don't go near that stuff. Just like I don't go near the cookery pages, or the car pages. I don't even look up the football results, for Christ's sake!'

'Can you get the football results on there? What about the match reports?' asked Tommy, suddenly understanding something of what was going on. He was seized by the idea that people – obscure reporters, fans, even other referees – might be writing about his performance yesterday, even as he sat there on the floor. He had to rein himself back in to keep his attention on Mark. *He's the one going round the S-bend, after all.*

Mark didn't answer.

'You reckon they can hold that against you, then?'

'I dunno. And now that I think about it, who's to say Kelly wasn't in there when I was out, chatting up little boys on-line?'

They both became gloomy at the thought. The feeling that their worlds could suddenly slip out of their control, and that the far-fetched could be taken as gospel by everyone around them, depressed the hell out of them both, and silence descended again.

Eventually, Mark spoke. 'Fuck knows what I'll do when Monday morning comes. Hide in the toilets, I s'pose.' He gave another bitter snort and then looked at the ground.

'I think it's half-term, mate, you'll be all right,' said Tommy. He wished at once that he hadn't said it, but Mark looked up, and laughed for the first time. He laughed a black, bitter laugh like the cawing of an old crow, which celebrated his own misery and mocked himself. Tommy couldn't help chuckling either, out of nervousness, the way he imagined doctors humoured mental patients, but then, catching sight of Mark's eyes, he began to laugh properly. It was nice to laugh. And Mark began laughing properly too, revealing another side of himself Tommy had never seen. He laughed so much he rolled over on his side to laugh harder, and hurt his arm with his own weight. He yelped and cursed, and laughed some more, which made Tommy laugh louder.

'You can tell the headmistress you're here to say Mass,' Tommy said between gasps. He reached up and got the dog-collar and put it on, and sang: '*Credo in unum De-o ...*' Then paused. '*De-o, de-e-o,* daylight come an' I wanna go home.'

This started them off again.

'And I'll say I'm here to teach sex education to the five-year-olds. How to tell when your sister's on the blob, et cetera.' Tommy laughed some more, and felt better. He stood up because his bum was numb from the floor and walked around the room. He laughed and he kicked a cardboard box of skipping ropes out of the way. He looked at a painting on the wall of a family, complete with cat and dog with stick legs. He took out his pen and wrote in the corner: 'Little Liar'. He found some exercise books, and started marking them: 'See me!', 'Very Poor', and 'Stay Back a Year'. He tossed them on the floor. He was getting angry. Mark had finished laughing, and was on his feet too.

'You really think Melissa thinks I caved on the referee thing? Did she tell you that?'

'Eh? No, she didn't say anything, it was just obvious the way she looked at you when you talked about it. Personally, I think you blew it, though.'

This bred even more anger in Tommy.

'Fuck this,' he said suddenly. 'You're right! You're absolutely right! I let them walk all over me. And *you're* not gonna sit back and let all this happen to you. *Carpe diem!* he shouted. 'Didn't they teach you that in Latin class at priest school? Seize the day! Or seize something. Get ahold of yourself!' Mark looked at him with a hopeful expression. He was reading Tommy's face for the first time as if at last it held something useful for him. 'You can't sit around here hiding! You've ... we've gotta go out and face the fuckers! Walk right up to them.'

'What ... ?'

'Face them! Like you wanted to.'

'But it's worse now than I thought two days ago.'

'Yeah, well, it's not gonna get better if you sit around here. Let's fucking get out there and put them straight. The lot of them – coppers, telly and the lynch mob!'

'But we'll get fucking hammered out there. What are we gonna do?'

'We'll tell 'em we're going to the house. You haven't been convicted yet. Fuckin' hold your head up and show 'em you're innocent! I've fucking let them walk all over me and look where I am. I'm a fucking mess. You're not going the same way.'

Tommy put on his coat and marched to the classroom door. Mark went after him, calling 'Hang on!' He turned back and got his dog-collar and stuffed it in his pocket.

Tommy was way ahead – through the cloakroom, through the girls' bogs, out into the playground before Mark could catch up.

'Just get right in there, then?' the young priest asked. 'Just steam in?'

'Just steam in, that's right.'

They crossed the asphalt together. Tommy ran three steps with the elegant spring of a high jumper, leapt up on the railings and pulled himself over the top. Mark threw the Adidas bag over after him, and followed. They hit the ground with similar thuds, rose up, dusted themselves off and began walking. There was a hundred yards to go before they would turn the corner into the crowd.

'Maybe they'll have all gone home by now,' said Mark. 'It's dark.'

'Forget it,' said Tommy, not looking around. He was half a pace ahead of his friend. 'They love a crowd. They love a queue and they love a crowd. So right, when we get round, keep walking, straight into the middle of it. If anyone touches you, I'll get 'em off. If one of us gets nicked, the other carries on. You've gotta get the coppers to open the gates. Or we could go over them,' mused Tommy, suddenly ready for anything. His heart was banging in its cage.

'I've got the keys,' said Mark.

Tommy looked round at him in surprise but kept on walking. 'You? So ...'

'Father Kelly's got his own set. It was me who locked up the church in the first place, the day all this blew up. I locked myself out. Sounds like he locked himself in.'

'Yeah, that photographer said he was inside. He must have got bail. How weird.' There were twenty-five yards to go. 'This is it, man,' said Tommy through his teeth.

Mark looked across at him and composed himself.

They turned the corner. The crowd had since grown to around a hundred. They counted four TV vans, each with floodlights on their roofs. Their roving camera crews also had white lights, which shone in the faces of whoever they were interviewing in the crowd. There were two police vans, two police cars, a black taxi and an ice-cream van that doubled as a burger and hot-dog stand. The street was full of people and the pavement was covered in vehicles. There was a murmur in the air, the likes of which Tommy had hardly ever experienced. Like when the Villa ticket office opened after they queued all night for League Cup Final tickets when they were young lads at school. Or when the doors open for the Harrods Christmas sale.

All eyes turned to the two men, the newest arrivals, and then the word went up: 'It's him! Nonce! Get the bastard!'

Two angry men, three angry women, a camera crew and two burly policemen were the first to reach them. The crowd swarmed in front of them, but Tommy and Mark kept pushing through. One of the men was huge, he looked like a coalminer. He was shouting at them, like someone heckling a politician who knows they can shout all they like but can't touch their prey, 'You bastard! You are the Devil! You'll go to hell for this!'

'Evil! Evil! Evil!' one of the old ladies screamed in Tommy's ear. She pushed up against him. He gave her a hard dig in the breastbone with the point of his elbow. His other arm was busy shielding Mark's back. They were being jostled all around now. The coppers seemed to be helping.

'Get off me, you fucker!' shouted Tommy at someone who had their hand on his arm. 'Oi! Leave him alone! He's innocent!'

'Hang the bastards!'

'String 'em up'

'Nonces! Fuckin' nonces!'

The policemen protecting them had their own comments: 'Oof' and 'This way'.

A news bimbo in a jacket with a fur-trimmed hood had her microphone pushed into Mark's face, which was deathly white under the lights. 'Mr O'Mally, are these allegations true?' She repeated it over and over.

'No,' he said, without meeting her gaze.

''Course they're not fucking true,' shouted Tommy at her. He felt a small glow of satisfaction at knowing how to handle the media for his friend.

Another man had Mark by the scruff of the neck and was screaming 'Babby-fucker, babby-fucker' in his face. One of the policemen swatted him off with his giant arm. They were getting near the chained gates which led to the church and the priest's house. Mark was almost up against the railings. A two-pence piece pinged off his shoulder. Tommy could see a policeman with a flat helmet silhouetted by a floodlight, speaking into a megaphone.

'Please stand back! Do not obstruct the way! Please stand back!' He repeated this over and over, but the nasal electronic tones only added to the crowd's exhilaration. Tommy felt something soft underfoot, which horrified him, but he looked down and saw it was only a teddy bear. They were trampling all over the flowers and toys now in trying to get to the gate. Mark was right up against the wall, surrounded by police, while Tommy, whom no one recognised, had to fight to stay near, and was attracting more and more of the hostility. A teenage boy in a baseball cap with an evil expression pulled a small penknife on him, not two feet away, and not three feet from the nearest copper. The blade was like a silver dot in the dark crush of clothing around him. Tommy lunged to the side and drove his body through the police scrum like a prop forward to avoid the blade. All the time people were shouting, over and over, 'Ponces!', 'Queers!', 'Paedophiles!', 'Murderers!' and 'I'll fuckin' kill you!'

As Mark fumbled with the padlock and chain, Tommy fought off the kicks and blows for both of them. The police officer next to him received a large stringy deposit of phlegm on the smooth navy pelt of his helmet. 'Gerrin there, you bastards,' screamed a young woman as the gates opened. 'You're going to hell!'

Finally they got through the gates.

Two of the police came in with them, the rest had to pull the gate shut and try to secure the padlock before the crowd pushed them through. Once they had done this the coppers began fighting their way back, lashing out at the crowd, kicking and heave-ho-ing until they were back in the street. They would leave the people up against the fence to do what they wanted.

Inside what now felt like a compound, Mark and Tommy were dusting themselves down. Tommy felt a wet greenie in his hair. 'Eugh! Fuck! Those fucking animals! I'm gonna ...' He wanted to go back out there in the middle of them and tear them apart, but it was hopeless. His next-best option was to heave a dustbin over the railings on to their heads, but that was absurd. The two coppers with them were panting and watching Mark's every move as he fumbled with his house key. Tommy got out his white handkerchief and tried to mop up the moisture and drag out the rubbery slime. Under the streetlight he could make out the colour of the phlegm, and shuddered at the thought of what might be breeding in it.

At last they got inside, into the familiar hall. Tommy had never been so glad to see it. The first thing Mark saw was Father Kelly's coat on the hook. He touched it gently with his fingertips, then hurried up the stairs. Tommy looked outside again.

'Copper!' he yelled at the youngest one. 'Stand on guard here!' The boy looked shocked and did as he said. The other police officer followed Tommy up the stairs.

They found Mark in Father Kelly's bedroom, standing over his body as he lay on the bed.

'Is he dead?' asked the policeman, his chinstrap pulling hard on his jaw as he spoke. Tommy moved forward and looked at the old man in bed. He was dressed in his normal clothing – plain black suit, black shirt, dog-collar, polished shoes. His eyes were open. Tommy felt his pulse. He was warm, and the pulse was there.

'Can you hear me?' he said. 'Blink if you can.'

The old priest winked.

'He's had a stroke. Get him an ambulance.'

The other two stood there doing nothing. It suddenly occurred to him that Mark might actually want him dead, and that the keeper of the law might also want him dead. *Come to think of it, Father Kelly knows he hasn't got much of a future here on earth either. Maybe he wishes he was checking out too.* Tommy felt like the only person who would take any responsibility. He couldn't say he *cared* on a personal level for the old reptile, but his training taught him to save him before the stroke finished him off. 'Get an ambulance, copper, now!' he shouted in the officer's face. He loved ordering them around. This one stooped to his radio and spoke to his sergeant in the van outside. The boss said he'd sort it out.

The three of them stood there in silence around the speechless old man. Tommy was in professional mode, his mind buzzing with equations and estimates, assessing the man's mortality. Mark hung back, partly to be out of his way, partly to avoid the old man's fixed gaze. The police officer stood around, picking his nose unnoticed, monitoring the fuzz on his radio for instructions.

Ten minutes later the ambulance arrived. The copper took the keys and opened the gates to let it back right up to the door. The crowd was still howling and shouting. A chant would have been quite effective, but for all their time spent together on the pavement, nothing had evolved.

The ambulance neatly blocked the gateway and reached almost to the front door, so the paramedics were only in shot for a few seconds as they loaded the patient in. Mark and Tommy got in the back too. As Melissa watched at home on the television, she thought she recognised the half-second glimpse of Mark's white face, but when she saw the familiar sleeve of Tommy's coat steadying the saline drip and his silhouette clearing a way for the stretcher, a pang of pride swept through. Compared to all the strangers around him he looked real. He looked like home, encountered far away.

The ambulance pulled through the crowd, which was still shouting 'Bastards!' and slamming the thin metal sides, and raced off to Dudley Road Hospital with bike cops on BMWs front and rear.

'What do you want to do, Mark? Come back with me, or wait with him? I've gotta go soon as I can.'

Mark didn't know. He had nowhere to go, and couldn't think of anywhere he really wanted to go. All he could think was that if his old mother had been alive he would have gone straight to her.

Tommy waited.

'I'll stay with him.'

As they got out and the casualty staff ran towards them, unaware of their cargo, Tommy had a word with one of the nurses, then took out two twenty-pound notes and pressed them on Mark. 'Get something to eat. Call me tomorrow. Please?'

Mark looked shrunken. His presence was gone, and his confidence. He took the money. 'Thanks, Tommy. I will. 'Bye.'

It was chaos around them – more police pulling up, then a TV van. Tommy turned away. He had seen enough, and he had to get home to Melissa as promised. There was a queue of minicabs just over a low wall, waiting for fares. He jumped into one.

'New Street Station, please.'

'OK, mate,' said the driver. It was a young Asian with a Brummie accent. He turned down the radio and they set off. As they cruised down Summer Hill Road, Tommy changed his mind. He leaned forward and said to the driver, 'Hey, how much do you earn in five hours?'

'Depends, mate.' He checked the mirror. 'Fifty quid, sometimes more. But I have to pay petrol out of that. And ...'

'I'll give you seventy-five if you take me to north London, fast.'

'Ah ... I dunno, mate ... it's not really worth it. I've got a wife and kids, I'm supposed to be home in an hour. She won't like it.'

'Me too,' he lied. 'But she'll be happy when she sees the money, won't she?'

'Ah, I dunno, mate.' He seemed very uncomfortable.

'OK,' he sighed, feeling more money bleeding away from him. 'A hundred quid.'

The driver thought about it, stroking his chin and glancing in the mirror a lot. When he got to Paradise Circus, though, he seemed to decide with his body, swinging the car towards the Queensway tunnel and off in the direction of the motorway.

Tommy smiled. 'I said fast, though.'

The lad complied. Once past Fort Dunlop, he slowly increased his speed until they were nudging eighty, eight-five, all the way down. Tommy counted his money. It had been an expensive weekend. *Have to go into work tomorrow, then.*

He dozed in the car until the driver woke him at Junction 1, Brent Cross. *London,* he thought, as the large houses of the Finchley Road loomed through the window. *It's not so bad.*

Melissa had just finished watching him on the news when he got in. It was 9.15 p.m., which in his book counted as practically eight or eight-thirty, as promised. He was exhausted, but pleased with himself.

'I saw it all on telly!' she exclaimed when she saw him. She helped him off with the big black coat. 'What happened? Is it true he committed suicide?'

'Eh?' he asked. 'No, that's bollocks. God, they can't get anything right. He had a stroke. He's still alive. Or was.'

Melissa was excited about the meal she had cooked him. She made him sit down on the settee and take off his shoes while she served it up in the kitchen.

'Meat casserole,' she declared. She didn't want to talk about child abuse or bail bonds or even what would become of the young priest with the handsome face and no parish. And nor did he.

'That was delicious,' he concluded. 'And now I've got to lie down.' The food felt heavy in his belly. He had eaten far too much. Melissa found him snoring a few minutes later, undressed him and put him to bed properly.

Tommy was in mid-yawn when Marge buzzed him in his consulting room the next morning.

'Call for you, Dr Burns.'

'Mark!' he said, without waiting to hear who it was.

'Er, no, this is Ian,' said the grey voice on the other end.

'Ian who?' he asked, peeved. *Not another patient?*

'Ian Lockhart, English Football Association.'

'Oh. What do *you* want?' *Fucker wants his badge back, I suppose.*

'Good morning, Dr Burns. I saw you on television over the weekend. I was very impressed.'

Tommy snorted derisively. 'Thanks. But it's a bit late now to get involved with all that. The man's innocent, I'm innocent, he's just a friend, that's all. I was just doing someone a favour.'

'What do you mean? Isn't innocence rather a peculiar term, under the circumstances? Everything was in plain view, after all. I simply called to congratulate you ...'

'Look, I don't need your comments, I've got enough on my plate as it is.'

'So I see. I just wanted to touch base with you, that's all.'

'Yeah. Thanks. Great. Now fuck off!'

He hung up. 'Pervert,' he muttered. *Fucking freaks coming out of the woodwork.*

Just as he buzzed in the next patient, the penny dropped. *He's talking about the Old Firm. Shit! Where's his number?* He stood up and searched his desk for his personal phone book.

The patient was Veronica, a deaf girl, twenty and a Prozac fan. She'd been turned on to it in America while teaching at deaf camp for a summer, and now couldn't get enough. Tommy waved her over to the examining couch. He mimed to her, *two minutes, two minutes,* and she smiled and sat back.

He found the number and got straight through to the Referees' Secretary's secretary. She sniffed at him, then slowly put him through.

'Mr Lockhart. What were you talking about just now? I'm sorry, I was distracted by a patient.'

'Yes. Well. I simply called to congratulate you on your performance in Scotland on Saturday.'

Tommy sighed so heavily it made an electronic rasp in both their ears. He gave the thumbs-up to the girl on the couch.

'Oh. How did you hear about it?'

'It was live on Sky Television. I'm interested to hear how you made contact with the Scottish Football Association. I spoke to Mr Mitchell this morning and all he said was he couldn't discuss it with me yet.' He paused, expecting Tommy to fill the gap. Tommy let him hang.

'You see, Mr Burns ...'

'Doctor.'

'Doctor, do forgive me. You see, we've almost reached a settlement in your case and if all went well and the final report was satisfactory, I was going to contact you again this week.'

'Ahhhh no you don't,' said Tommy bitterly. 'You don't think you can just phone me now because you've seen me on the telly and I'll come running back to your league, do you? The Scots were very good to me over the weekend, very good indeed. We had talks.'

'Yes, but . . .'

'The future is in Scotland,' he said, trying to sound proud. 'Things are moving swiftly up there.'

'Well, things are moving swiftly down here too. I've been in meetings discussing your case all morning. There is considerable interest, if I may say so,' and he lowered his voice as if he were whispering to a twelve-year-old about an upcoming birthday treat, 'in seeing you return to the Premiership scene. The wheels are in motion, Mr Burns.'

Tommy sighed. He didn't know where to begin. He still had his patient on the bench. She waved at him, a coy fingery wave from deafworld. 'Can you hold for a minute, please?'

He put the FA on hold and went to attend to the patient. He could do a bit of signing, and together they managed to establish that her prescription had run out, that she still loved Prozac, in fact, felt great about it, and had met a young man and was going away for a weekend with him. Tommy took his time. He asked her if she thought her finding the lad had anything to do with the drug (no), and in that case, why would she need it (she couldn't answer that, but looked like she was thinking about it). He asked her if her general health had been good (yes), and finally he broached the subject of shagging, asking her if she was fully equipped to protect herself from diseases and unwanted pregnancies. She said she was. All the time she answered with a light in her eyes that impressed him. *It must be love*, he mouthed, and renewed her prescription. She beamed, and scampered out of the room.

'Mr Lockhart. I've been thinking.'

'Yes, I was going to suggest you come in for a little, er, meeting.'

'I don't think so. Once was enough for me. But explain to me one thing. I heard that my membership of the Association had lapsed, and that put me back to square one, as it were. Why wasn't I warned about this, and why did I have to hear it second-hand and too late?'

'Er . . .' Lockhart cleared his throat. 'In answer to your first question, all I can really say is ignorance of the law is no defence. It was in the latest memorandum from the Association. You should have received a copy.'

'Well, I didn't.'

'Oh dear. Er, anyway, as for the second, well, allow me to humbly apologise. You should indeed have been informed about this by my office. Anyway, it has been agreed by all that your membership should be restored, and the interruption be struck from the record. You will be, Mr Burns, fully eligible to referee English Association Football matches at the Class One level once again, and your FIFA Grade One status remains intact. We are all ready to welcome you back. All we have to do is dot the i's and cross the t's and you could be back in action by the end of the month.'

Tommy was incredulous. He had a volley of abuse all ready for this little worm of a man, five months of abuse in fact, which he wanted to let out, clearly and loudly, preferably to his face. And here he was dangling the Premiership before him. Out of the blue. He thought of his dream of umpire J.L., strapped in the confessional chair and taking no shit. He thought of the view from the plane, the chequered grass of Villa Park, and how he had known he belonged on the pitch. And he recalled the Rangers game, the blowtorch of hatred coming from all sides of the ground, and how he had missed it, the passion and its acting out, and promised himself he would be back.

He was stuck. He didn't want to give him the satisfaction of luring him in, but he wanted to say yes. It was a clear yes/go fuck yourself situation. So Tommy spoke up. He said he needed more time, and more of a commitment, and that perhaps if he was sent the next Referees List – plus all those he had missed through *suspension*, as he put it – he might consider it.

Both men replaced their telephone receivers, leaned back in their chairs and sighed. *I'm still gonna have the bastard, though. His head will roll*, Tommy promised himself.

He tried to settle into his Monday routine, but was distracted by his need to check up on Mark. Eventually he got Dudley Road to put him through to the secure room where the younger priest was keeping a vigil over the elder, with a police officer on the door. Mark could only speak for a minute, because, according to the copper's understanding of nonces on bail, you had to make sure they didn't make contact with the rest of the ring. The copper listened carefully to everything Mark said, then sat on his chair out in the corridor and made notes.

The message was Father Kelly was still stable, but still unable to communicate. Mark had spent the night in the chair. No one had been in touch.

Not long after Mark hung up there was a noise at the door of the hospital room, and in walked another priest, this one middle-aged and carrying a briefcase. He introduced himself to Mark without hesitation.

'Father Ignatius Johnson, from the archdiocese of Westminster. How are you, my son?'

Mark's eyes widened and he nearly fell to his knees. He knew the finely cut cloth of a Jesuit when he saw it.

'Pleased to meet you,' he said nervously.

It didn't take Father Ignatius long to take control of the situation. First he looked at the patient and felt his pulse, muttering to himself in Latin. Then he explained that he was there to help Mark. He wanted to hear the whole story, from Mark's point of view. He told Mark that his e-mail to the cardinal had been forwarded to him.

When he heard all this, Mark forgot how rough and stubbly he looked, and poured out his whole story, from his initial ignorance, through his hectic days on the run, to now, what he compared to life in limbo.

Father Ignatius looked at the poor man. This was just what he had expected to hear, a short travelogue of the soul. He was impressed with the young priest.

'And how did the Lord help you in these times?'

'The Lord ... well, the Lord ...'

'You had doubts, my son? We all doubt.'

Mark looked up. 'Yes, I had doubts. But in the end I saw it as a trial. Like the Book of Job.'

'You were right to do so,' said the priest. 'And now I will hear your confession.'

An hour later, Father Ignatius gathered his papers together and, taking Mark by the arm, led him from the hospital room. They got in his car, an old black Jaguar, and drove a couple of miles across town to St Chad's, where the Bishop of Birmingham's butler greeted him and showed him to the palace guest room. Mark was in awe of his surroundings. While he slept his clothes were washed and his suit was cleaned, and he awoke to find fresh razors and soap provided for him, next to a deep Victorian bath with giant taps and endless hot water.

When Tommy got home from work that night he passed the schoolteacher from upstairs, coming down. He had his park clothes on — woolly hat, leather bomber, Levi's, Docs — and stopped Tommy on the stairs.

*Oh, shit.*

'Hey, do you know anything about that old lady in the basement?'

'Er, no.'

'I don't know what she said, but she had me hauled in by the police for some outrageous questioning. What about you? Have the police been in contact with you?'

'No, no,' said Tommy.

The teacher looked at him, wondering how much he should say. 'Well, they made some pretty outrageous claims, totally spurious. I'm thinking of suing for defamation. I know where this can lead. If I hadn't had a friend who works down the station I don't know where I'd be right now. Probably in some awful remand prison somewhere,' he said, with a slight twinkle in his eye. The automatic stair light went off, to Tommy's relief. 'I'm just warning you,' said the man in the woolly hat, going down the stairs. 'Watch out. The first young officer who questioned me said he was "gonna get every single one of us in the building". Don't say you weren't warned.'

*Fucking hell*, thought Tommy, as he fumbled with his key trying to get in. *Better not tell Melissa about that.*

On Friday, Tommy got an envelope in the mail from the FA. It contained the appointment lists he had asked for, plus a grovelling personal letter from Lockhart, stating that he had been fully reinstated and that they hoped he would be available for action from next week, which was the beginning of April. He turned to the April list and saw that there had been some considerable rearrangement, in Biro, of who was to officiate where. Henry Miller was untouched, but several other names had been switched around to make way for Tommy, who was down to referee one game a week for the month, plus – and this made him warm inside – an FA Cup semifinal.

'Hmmph!' he said loudly. Justice had been done. *Almost.*

Life was sweet with Melissa. Lots of nice food, lots of sex, lots of lying around with each other. His appreciation of her was reaching a new peak. That Saturday morning, although he still hadn't informed the FA of his decision, he went for a long run in anticipation of the rest of the season. Hampstead Heath was bathed in the warm air and sunshine of Britain's annual false spring, when the temperature soared and everyone threw off their coats and was nice to each other, only for it to snow a week later and then piss down until June. Other runners nodded to him as he ran.

He came home and wrote to Jim Mitchell at the Scottish FA, thanking him for the game, but declining his offer of a move to the Scottish Premier League. Yes, it was attractive, the idea they would fly him up and down the country every week, and true, it wouldn't add anything to his travelling time, but he felt his heart lay in England, and with English football, at whatever level, and he was sure Mr Mitchell would understand that. Melissa even let him come out to tea with her in Knightsbridge, and on the way home they stopped in Harrods' electrical section to see the football results. It was the FA Cup quarterfinals. Villa were having a crappy season, mid-table, but they had crept their way through the FA Cup so far with a series of one–nil wins at poxy grounds. They had won again today, and were marching on to the semifinals. The draw was made minutes after the whistle went – owing to its spectacular incontinence, the FA couldn't wait for Sunday's games. 'We've got Newcastle. That'll be a Miller job,' he told Melissa. 'I'll get the other one, Leeds or Stockport versus Man United or Barnsley. Nice.'

'What are you on about, Miller job?' asked Melissa, wrinkling up her nose.

'Y'know, the semifinal. I never get Villa. I'll get the others. Man U– Leeds, though, nice.'

The last thing Mr Ian Lockhart, Referees' Secretary for the English Football Association, did before he resigned that Sunday afternoon, forced out after an extraordinary meeting of the Chief Executive and two of his close friends, was to assign Tommy the Newcastle v. Aston Villa cup tie. It was a last attempt to redeem and ingratiate himself.

Tommy's mind was swollen with excitement at the forthcoming games he had to referee. He was like a man who, when imprisoned, makes all sorts of promises to himself and the world, to savour beauty, to bless all people, and to make sure he never ends up back in prison; and then on being released, carries out every promise to the letter, and lives happily and humbly ever after. Only, Tommy hadn't made any promises in his darkest hour. Apart from at the end, when he vowed to have Lockhart's head on a plate.

Proctor the linesman phoned him with the good news shortly after the games on Sunday afternoon. Tommy was loafing around the flat, wondering where that extra hour of sleep had gone, then answering his own question, looking out of the window and seeing it was still light at nearly seven o'clock.

'That's it, he's history. Colin Marsh's coming back, temporarily, to do his old job,' said Proctor, rather excitedly. 'Goodness, some of the things I'm hearing ...'

'Like what?'

'Well, the state Lockhart left the smaller leagues in! He was just useless at his job.'

They both knew, from having worked their way up the ladder, that the Referees' Secretary had to appoint referees and linesmen not only for the Premiership, which was a piece of piss really, but for a slew of other cup games: all the FA Trophy games for the semi-professionals, and all the FA Vase games, for the amateurs. In September alone, in the first round, that meant 160 matches in one weekend – 480 officials. Not a job for the disorganised. Plus there were all the early rounds of the FA Cup. And the Women's FA Cup. Tommy had reffed a couple of them before, but he found it impossible to concentrate.

'Applications and schedules were going out late, people were being double-booked, it was a disaster. And he kept blaming his secretary and being off ill.'

'Yeah, I remember not getting some stuff. I thought it was odd. Fucking hypochondriac,' said Tommy. He was slightly disappointed that the sacking wasn't about his own mistreatment, though. 'So, Proctor, how come you know all this so quick? Two hours after it happens. Who do you know up there that you're not letting on about?'

'Internet, Tommy. It's all out there.'

'Oh.' *The fucking internet.* He felt its shadow coming over him. *Maybe I'll get a computer. Melissa knows how to work one, I think. Teaches it at school anyway. Perhaps we could borrow a child to teach us how to get on-line and all that bullshit? Hmm, perhaps not.*

He was reminded of Mark. He hadn't heard from him all week. When he had phoned the hospital they said since he wasn't a patient how should they know where he was? He came and went. At least the old boy was still in there, hooked up to his drip. He could try Westminster again, but it was Sunday, the office was probably closed. Then again, he didn't feel too worried. He had a feeling that Mark was being looked after somewhere. The media, who had lost interest in the story since the vigil outside the church had fizzled out during the week and had been reduced to filming each other, said Mark was in hiding, in custody, and in hospital. So it was clear none of them had a fucking clue.

Two days later, Tommy heard that under sustained cross-examination by their parents, two of the allegedly abused boys, who were not altar boys but had played in the football team, had made their stories up. They were taken before the police and the psychologists and social workers, and with their parents at their sides, withdrew their accusations against Mark. This caused a few more to come forward and do the same, but they still insisted the old priest had sexually molested them. They too admitted making up the bit about Father Mark being involved, and wanted to say sorry to him.

Fat Paul rang. Tommy said sure, he'd do a match. Love to. Good practice. Fat Paul was a happy man.

Father Kelly died the following Thursday, Holy Thursday, at approximately two in the afternoon, just as it was starting to snow over Birmingham. As he lay there alone, blinking his one eye and thinking about his life, and the afterlife, all the years of grease and potatoes took their toll and he suffered a cardiac arrest. He had a myocardial infarction, probably brought on in the short term by acute coronary occlusion, and in the long by ischaemic heart disease. That was what the doctor told Mark, who was called out of preparations for the big service that evening at the cathedral to come down to Dudley Road. He had been going in to see the old priest every morning. He still cared, even though the priest had tried to implicate him in his crimes. Or at least that was what the police had said. He still wasn't quite sure on that. But after a few days sitting there being angry with him, keeping a lone vigil since no one else in the world would have anything to do with Kelly (even, to Mark's surprise, Father Ignatius, who showed far more interest in Mark, the living, than in Kelly, the speechless and nearly dead), he forgave him. He found it gut-churningly sad that this man could have done the things he was alleged to have done. Some of the details were starting to come out in rumour. He could forgive pain inflicted on himself, but could he forgive, on behalf of God the Father, crimes against others? He had expected Father Kelly to recover enough to be able to speak, and to make a confession. But he died. He would be on his way to the cold desert right now. Maybe even the lake of fire.

Nobody had noticed he was dead for an hour or two. The copper outside the door looked into the room and, seeing the red old face, decided to wander in and check on him. The priest was dead as a doornail. Which was disappointing, because it meant there would be no trial, and no details, and no sentencing. On the other hand, it provided some small excitement for the next half-hour.

'Oh,' said Tommy when Mark telephoned him that evening. 'I'm sorry. You OK? How did it happen?'

Mark tried to remember what the doctor had told him.

'Oh yeah,' said Tommy casually. 'Ischaemic heart disease — commonest cause of death there is. It's caused by atherosclerosis, which is where cholesterol and other fats become deposited beneath the intima in many of the heart's arteries. Then a sort of fibrous tissue builds up, which usually becomes calcified, forming what you call atherosclerotic plaques – hardening of the arteries. Now, acute occlusion of the coronary artery usually comes when a *thrombus*, which is Latin for blood clot, grows when the plaque breaks through the intima and offers a rough surface for the blood to clot around. It grows and grows until the artery becomes blocked. Anyway, once the blood stops flowing you get infarction, which is where the heart muscle doesn't have enough blood to keep alive and pumping – it has to service itself too, after all. Then you get the downward spiral, all the oxygen gets used up, the haemoglobin goes to fuck, the cells die, and usually it takes a few days before it all seizes up, but I guess he was badly off.'

'So basically, the grease got him?' asked Mark.

'Yeah. So what's the plan?'

'I don't know. He gets buried. I don't know where. Someone has to claim him first, though. I think he has a sister in Ireland somewhere. But I've heard nothing about her for ages.' Mark really *had* had enough. He changed the subject. 'What happened with the refereeing, then?'

'Well, fuck, you know what happened? The tosser in charge got fired, I'm back, and I've got an FA Cup semifinal to do. The Villa one!'

'No kidding? I heard they got through. That's great. But is that allowed?'

'Search me. I don't know what's going on. Looks like they know less about me than I thought.'

'Don't they ask?'

'Yeah, they used to go "Can you do Wimbledon–Leeds this week, and do you have any connection to either club?" And I'd go, "Yes" and "You must be joking", and they'd give it to me. No one's asked me fuck-all about this one, though. I think they're all feeling too guilty, or else they're just disorganised.'

'Will you do it? Can you do it?'

''Course I can,' said Tommy, feeling insulted. 'Don't you trust my impartiality? F'fuck's sake ...'

'OK, OK, you're right. I'm sorry.'

'Ack, listen, I didn't mean to snap. I just get this all the time from fucking taxi drivers and fans. I'm sorry.'

They finished the conversation and hung up, neither making plans to call the other again, but perfectly assured that it would happen. Each had his own stuff to get on with, but each knew he'd report back to the other.

Because of the snow, which then froze, and then because of an England game, there was barely any football played over the next three weeks, save at a handful of grounds that had undersoil heating. Fat Paul, however, was determined that his game should go on. He conducted his own pitch inspection that Saturday at Hackney Marshes with his lickul bravver Phil, and declared that if they could see the pitch markings it would be OK. So the pair of them spent two hours shovelling snow off the lines. He called Tommy, assuring him that the pitch was OK, so Tommy got on his leathers and rode out on the Triumph. It was a sunny morning, and he quite enjoyed it – the crushed slush made the bike slide and swagger as though he were going over an endless section of resurfacing grooves. Every few seconds he felt like he was losing control, only to have it instantly restored. Riding across the snowy field was much harder, but he got there.

'You can't play on this,' he said to Paul, without even getting off the bike.

'Nah, mate, it's all sorted, the lines are clear. 'Snot as bad as i' looks. Iss only a few inches deep. We've got an orange ball an' all. Everyone's camming. I just phoned 'em all.' He had a way of begging while seeming to have a point, which Tommy had to admire. When he put the bike on the centre stand the snow still grazed the bottom of the fairing.

It was a beautiful game, all right – very like a ballet. The players ran with tiny steps like geishas, and anyone who took a swing at the orange ball – which seemed hard and bouncy like a Stanley Matthews-era caser – ended up on his arse. They pussyfooted about for ninety minutes until the frustration was complete. Everyone longed for normal conditions, fantasising how good they would be if only they could keep their balance. It ended nil–nil, which Fat Paul declared was 'a fair result'.

So although he ran every night and practised rule situations in his head, Tommy didn't referee again until the day he led the teams out, Newcastle and Aston Villa, at the neutral ground Old Trafford, to a thunderous roar from all sides. He got to the stadium very early – he was on the train out of Euston at 7.45 a.m., feeling sharp and sober and very, very nervous. A few fans got on at New Street, but nothing dangerous, just reasonable-looking men and boys in wool hats, with packed lunches in their backpacks. No one who would recognise him from the old days.

The Manchester United hospitality machine was in overdrive, especially since they had crucified Leeds the day before – crucified them, and offered them vinegar on a sponge. Tommy was fed and introduced to people and, as he was there so early, offered the tour, which for once he took.

He whiled his time away in the United Bistro, the United Media Centre, the United Museum (not much on Tommy Docherty, he noted), and the Eric Cantona Library. He spent twenty minutes staring at an artist's impression of the United Adventure Park to be built in Trafford Park. He was desperately trying to remain impartial, but every now and then he'd hear a fan hollering in the nearly empty stadium – 'The Brummies are 'ere!' or 'We're the Villa, we're the Villa, we are the champions!' – or a distant, slow chant from outside, 'Come on, ye Lions!' It made him shudder. When he checked the team colours, holding the claret-and-blue Villa shirt in his hand made his stomach tighten. He kept thinking someone from the FA would turn up and expose his duplicity.

He read the Laws of the Game again, and the Guide for Players and Referees, from cover to cover. He inspected the pitch twice. Finally the linesmen arrived, and the observer, and he had someone to talk to. The momentum of the rituals began to take him over – checking his gear, getting changed, instructing his linesmen. They were good men, they accepted everything he said without question, and they seemed pretty nervous themselves. When he saw the players lined up in the tunnel, his heart started racing. He felt unworthy to be leading out this team of Villa men, even though half of them were young pups who hadn't been born when he was going to away games and whipping up noise for their predecessors. He felt unworthy, he felt immense pride, which he immediately tried to suffocate, and he felt terrified that still, any second, the chief executive of the English Football League would come running across the pitch in his blazer and slacks and order him from the field for being a Villa fan.

*I'm not really a Villa fan. I'm a referee first, and an armchair supporter second. I don't even know all the players' names any more,* he told himself just before he blew his whistle for the kick-off. The familiar pre-match roar was reaching cacophony status, when all the hope and optimism and aggression of the fans is expressed in one ten-second burst, before anyone has had time to do anything wrong.

He took a glance at the Newcastle fans, lined up in their identical black-and-white striped shirts. They seemed to have fallen headlong for the myth that the fans were now part of the show. They had become a complete self-parody, always ready to pose for the roving camera. Tommy remembered the mob of hard men that had once walked down Witton

Lane from the coach park right past the Holte End, summoning up a cacophonous 'United! United!' They were defiant, and curious. They were raw fans, as raw as coal, and during the game they stood in the rain in a hefty mob, singing constantly even though they lost three–nil. In those days they even had a leader who wore a long white raincoat and sat on someone's shoulders for an hour, ostentatiously conducting the singing. *Now look at 'em*, he thought. *Bunch of students. Pity.*

He was racked with tension, unable to cultivate the disinterest that made for perfect concentration. Whenever Villa got the ball he felt warm and comforted, and hung back slightly, secretly urging them forward, but not wanting to be on the scene if they scored. Every time a Villa attack broke down in the familiar, pathetic manner, he felt the old frustration. And yet he could see the linesmen concentrating furiously. And the players were all too worried to give him any lip, knowing that winning that one match would make them a part of history, that a trip to Wembley would give them bragging rights for the rest of their lives. Everyone was ignoring him. Tommy became aware of his invisibility.

Although it made him feel like a traitor, Tommy was actually relieved for a few seconds when Newcastle, who were playing far better, swept up the pitch and scored, leaving the Villa defence staring miserably at the net. *At least no one can accuse me of being partial now.* The Newcastle section went mad, boiling over with glee. He allowed himself a look at the Stretford End for a few seconds, where the massed ranks of Villa stood in grief, silent and still, drowning in the inevitability of loss.

By half-time Tommy felt he had acquitted himself well. His linesmen grinned nervously and he reassured them he was happy with their work. They sat in the dressing room drinking lemon barley water and not talking much. Tommy stared at the floor. He could hear the fans still singing in the stand above him. *Strange being at a big Villa game without Mark. Wonder if he's watching? Nah. Probably doing something useful.*

Mark was now back at the Sacred Heart. Though the parents of the sexually abused kids had been in a mixed fury when the old priest had died without them being able to get their hands on him, Mark had been cleared of all the accusations. His advocate in all this, Father Ignatius, had done a sterling job of clearing his name. In his civilian clothes with just a tiny silver cross in his lapel, the Jesuit was calm and impeccably polite in a way that no one was used to. He never appeared to argue, and he seemed to have nothing to gain personally. He just kept reiterating the facts, as he saw them, accepting the guilt of Father Kelly, denying the guilt of Father Mark.

Going through each family in turn, Father Ignatius had persuaded the children to say what had really happened. He spent hours in the offices of social workers and with the police, examining their evidence, talking to them about their interviewing methods, every now and then stressing the damaging effect on the children of having to go to court, especially when it seemed the younger priest was wrongly implicated. He sat with the psychologists and listened to their elliptical storytelling, and came away smiling as they conceded his version of things.

Through all this, Mark remained in his room at the cathedral, reading religious works from the library, and beginning to pray again.

Father Kelly, with a tag round his toe, was still in the fridge at the hospital morgue, waiting for someone to bury him.

Fiona: ... I can't believe you did that! I just can't believe it! You slept with that greaseball?

Melissa: We didn't *sleep* together. We just, you know, did the business. Once. It was no big deal.

F: This is incredible. Why ... what was it like?

M: It was all right, actually. You know, I was round there having this drink and then he comes on to me, like 'This is the hall, this is the kitchen, this is the bedroom, nudge nudge', so I just thought, the hell with it. Let's give it a go. He was alright.

F: Blimey. I don't know what to say to you. What about Tommy?

M: Ah, well, I felt a bit bad afterwards, you know, for Tommy. These last few weeks he's been so sweet to me. But this guy, I'd promised I'd go for a drink with him, and there was no reason I couldn't. And he was always asking. I felt a bit sorry for him in the end. Like when we were finished I just wanted to get the hell out of there, and he wanted to talk. And I'm like, 'Er, no thanks. I'm not a great one for talking.'

F: When did you decide to do it?

M: Oh, when I got there. I just fancied it, you know what I mean? I just thought, 'Fuck it.' Me and Tom have been together so long, and he's been such a sod this last year, well, this last six months. You know how you get to thinking ...

F: Tommy's going to go spare.

M: No he's not. I'm not going to tell him, d'you think I'm mad? I'm not a masochist, you know. And you're not going to breathe a word of this to anyone. Right?

F: No, no, of course not. Who do you think I am? But . . . Oh, you
old slapper! My God, I want all the details. I still can't believe it.

M: I knew you'd have something to say about it. It was so funny, I
wish you could have seen him, he lets his hair down, all sensuous, then
he takes my hand and runs it through it, and says, 'Do you prefer it
up or down?' and I'm lying there thinking, 'Whatever, never mind
the scrunchy, get your kit off.' You'd have laughed. Anyway! What
are you doing tonight?

F: Nothing.

M: Why don't you come over? Come and have some dinner.

F: What, no gym?

M: Ha! What do you think? I think I'll give the gym a wide berth
for a few days. Come over and we'll have some drinks. Tommy's on
the telly, doing some game in Manchester, we can watch that. I'm
taping it for him. Come on, it'll make me feel less guilty.

F: I hate football. I'd rather hear about your adventures in
Docklands.

M: OK, we'll turn the sound down. I'll give you a special one-off
rendition, but after that it's in the vault for ever. Don't tell anyone.
Not even Nick.

F: I won't, I won't!

M: OK. See you later.

The Villa manager must have bollocked his team at half-time because they
came out in the second half and fought like the lions they were supposed
to be. It became a fast and attractive game, which suited Tommy, as his
brain was so occupied in tracking the ball and the various tricks of the
defenders that he had no room for troublesome feelings.

The fans hit a quiet patch between the fiftieth and seventy-fifth minutes
as they watched the game closely. Even the Newcastle fans were too busy to
taunt their opposites, since they were acutely conscious of having an expensive team, shares traded on the stock exchange, a fun image in the media but
fuck-all to show for it. They never won anything. They were nervous.

Once they could see the end in sight, both sets of fans picked up the
noise. For Villa it was a last-ditch bout of encouragement – they named
players, they commented on the play, they summoned up an old song:

> 'Yippee aye-ay, yippee aye-o,
> Holte Enders in the sky . . .'

Newcastle, however, just sang their old Blaydon Races song, over and over
again, like they were in a frenzy of fear.

The team were still playing well, defending everything that was thrown
at them. The clock ticked on. It was going down as a miserable loss for
Villa. The fans got louder, and Tommy started to feel their pain. Every
time the ball was hoofed out by a Newcastle defender, his heart sank a
little. He tried to fight it, telling himself to concentrate on the ball, not
on the colour of the shirts. But the lush claret and the pale blue kept on
at him. They still held the power to thrill — whether seeing those colours
outside a pub in a strange and dangerous city, or flapping from the window
of a Mercedes in Aston, he couldn't shake it off. He was so excited now
that, like everyone else in the stadium, he was bursting for a piss.

The ninety minutes were up on his analogue watch. He had two minutes
of injury time on his digital stopwatch. Villa kept up the pressure. He
could hear people screaming in agony as the ball neared the Newcastle
goal and was booted back upfield again. *C'mon, Villa! You can do better than
that.* Tommy was shocked at himself, and tried to lose the thought. But
Villa built another attack. Someone slotted a pass through from midfield
that set their number ten, who was known for being a carthorse, through
into the penalty area. He and the skilful Newcastle sweeper were running
diagonally towards the byline, away from the goal, chasing the ball. Tommy
streaked forward with them, not fifteen yards behind. The sweeper, who
had half a yard start on the attacker, timed his intervention. He stuck an
elegant toe out, right in front of the Stretford End packed with Villa fans
standing up in their seats, just as the attacker leaned into him and drew
back his foot. Their ankles were together, barely touching. The elegant toe
touched the ball forward, and the attacker crumpled and fell in a pile at
his feet, while the defender raised his arms in total innocence. The Villa
fans screamed hopefully for a penalty.

*Fuck it. Penalty.* Tommy blew his whistle and pointed to the spot. The
attacker sat back on his heels and looked bemused, then raised his arms in
triumph. All eleven of the Newcastle team surrounded him, screaming in
his face that it was a dive. And it was a dive. The linesman was flagging
for a corner. Tommy ignored it. He was closer, after all. Who was going
to call his bluff? Villa weren't going out just yet.

'You bastard, Ref, you fucking cheating bastard!'

'It was a dive! A fucking dive! Look, the linesman's given a corner!'

'Corner, Ref, look at yer linesman, fer Chrissake!'

'Get back, clear the area, ten yards!' shouted Tommy, over and over.

The Newcastle captain was trying to hold back the sweeper, who had more to say to Tommy. He got free and started screaming again, above the noise of the delirious Villa fans, 'You wanker, you fucking cheat! I never touched him. Are you fucking blind? Are you fucking blind?'

Tommy had to book him, but as he reached for the yellow card, realised he had booked him in the second half. *Oh dear.* 'You're off, sunshine. Don't come back.'

The player had to be dragged from the pitch by the trainer and the captain. The penalty was taken six minutes after the offence. It went in, and the Villa fans were in raptures. Tommy played another forty seconds after the kick-off, as his watch told him, but he was terrified of Newcastle scoring.

It went to extra time.

The abuses were rife, as the newspapers put it. The Sunday newspapers with the most money signed up several of the altar boys and their families to give their stories a few days after the elder priest was silenced for good by his heart attack. And as they had all week to transcribe what the kids said, they went big with it, an Easter treat.

*He used to make me take down my pants before Mass and he'd rub my w— with his hand. He used to put it in his mouth and then he'd make me put his in my mouth. I used to choke but he'd shout and make me do it. Then all white stuff would come out. Afterwards he'd want to hear my confession.*

*Father Kelly used to wear girls' clothes under his vestments and he'd make me and my friend [omitted] sit on his lap. Then we'd have to get undressed and bend over and he kissed us on the b——s with his tongue.*

*First he used to just make me stay behind after Mass and ask me questions about girls, and did I have a girlfriend and all that, and tell me it was wrong. Then he used to say I had to come over to the house, and we'd go up to his room. The other priest was always out. He'd take off all my clothes and slobber all over me, then take off all his except for his shoes and socks and get on the bed next to me and hold me, like a bear hug. It was horrible but he said I'd go to hell, to the Lake of Fire, if I told anyone. Then he made me do my confession.*

One paper printed a gruesome account of one of the boys who had been given a muscle relaxant and was then buggered by the old priest. It consisted

of long passages about small anuses being ruptured by leering old men in
frocks; children being beaten; more children being threatened with being
smothered with plastic bags; engorged erections and cock rings; and novel
uses of over-the-counter drugs and lubricants. 'This child is now under
psychiatric care,' it said at the end of the article.

Tommy pored over these accounts with mild nausea. He had heard it all
before, but every time it happened, it was as bad as before. He could never
get used to such evil, as the woman shouting in the street had called it.

Mark was back at the Sacred Heart, trying to conduct a reduced roster
of services, but it was proving very difficult. Many parishioners still couldn't
accept that he was innocent. Many more found him inextricably associated
with the old demon priest and even though they knew he was innocent,
they couldn't bring themselves to go near him. And many more had had
it with the Church for good. It was an impenetrable nest of vipers, traitors
and hypocrites, and its tentacles reached around the world, squeezing the
life out of innocent people everywhere it went.

In extra time, things went Villa's way. Newcastle were still chanting, to
the tune of the chorus of 'Bread of Heaven',

> 'Who's the bastard,
> Who's the bastard,
> Who's the bastard in the black?
> Who's the ba-stard in the black?'

when Villa came out and hit the post. That shut them up. Although
Tommy couldn't help feeling that they had a point. Still, this was no
time for idle sympathies. Five minutes later, Villa scored again, or rather,
a Newcastle player headed into his own goal, and from then on it was
plain sailing, a carnival of singing and standing and jumping up and down.
Tommy could hardly wait to blow the final whistle, and his heart was in
his mouth as he did so. As he walked off the pitch he got to shake hands
with a couple of Villa players, and felt he would be unable to wash that
hand for several days. None of the Newcastle players said a thing to him,
though the manager did call him a cheat on national TV, and the goons
in the studio puzzled over the video for many minutes.

Being a registered referee, though, Tommy was not allowed to comment
on the game to the media, on pain of expulsion from the FA. That was
the rule, and they were strict about it. The linesmen were also puzzled,

but they knew that everyone makes mistakes, and has to be given some leeway. Otherwise no one would do anything.

Tommy hung around in the library again after he had changed back into his civvies, on the advice of a steward who said there were a few Newcastle fans waiting for him. 'About two hundred,' he said. 'Not very friendly.'

'Well, if they *were* friendly, it'd be a first,' said Tommy, laughing, which gave the steward something to reflect upon.

Having escaped scrutiny by the police in the case against Mark, and having been sympathised with by the restored Referees' Secretary for having made a crucial mistake, and reassured that everybody makes them, Tommy settled into a long, luxurious week of self-congratulation. His upcoming fixtures were not threatened. He knew nothing could touch him. The Monday papers seemed to have the idea that he had been off with a knee injury for several months. He heard the same story repeated in a piece on the radio that morning by Nick Felcher, who mentioned in passing, and in his strange accent, that this disputed penalty was the exception that proved the referee had had a very good game. He had been 'largely invisible throughout'.

There were only four people in the cemetery the following Wednesday afternoon. Or six, if you counted Killingworth and Son. Mark was in his vestments, the white robe of the Paschal season, reading from the missal. Mrs O'Connor was sobbing into her hanky, looking quite good in black, like a Greek or Italian widow. Kevin was in his wheelchair. He was waiting for a lift to the community centre, since the bus driver had recently kicked him off for abusive language, but hadn't counted on having to go via the fuggin cemetery. As Mark had inherited the Morris Minor, he was the likeliest candidate to take him. 'If anyone sees me in that fuggin noncemobile I'll never live it down,' he said to Tommy as they waited by Father Kelly's grave.

No one had come to collect Father Kelly and he had lain a long time in the hospital fridge. The sister in Ireland told Mark to get lost. Mark argued at length with the board of the seminary, who were supposed to take care of these things and put him in their private little priests' plot, but they said no. They couldn't take him because they were 'running short of room'. So that was that. Mark said the priestly equivalent of 'Fuck it, I'll do it myself then', and after slipping the cemetery manager six hundred quid – the entire contents of the cigar box found under Father Kelly's bed

– he secured him a spot in the corner of Witton Cemetery, right up by the wall where the traffic was really loud. Digging the hole was a hundred extra. He had to pay that himself.

There was no funeral in the church. Mark merged the service with the burial, and read from the missal, an interesting passage about forgiveness and hope. He said a few words that stressed the good things about Father Kelly's life – that he was a priest, and was loved by many (Tommy cringed at this construction), and had a fine singing voice. But there wasn't much more to say.

Mrs O cried constantly from the moment she saw the hearse. She cried a wet, sneezing kind of cry that made everyone feel sad. She cried at the grave for the kids who had been abused, and for her son who had turned out so bad. She cried for Father Mark, whom she had wrongly suspected, and begged his forgiveness. She cried for Father Kelly, who had been so good to her for so many years. Then she cried a bit more at the horror he was capable of. She cried for herself, for her wretched self and all her woes. And she cried for all humankind, as only a mother can.

The sun was shining. There was a cherry tree in blossom behind Mark's head. It was quite a nice day, mild for once. You could see clear across the motorway to town. Killingworth and his pizza-faced son took the ends of one of the canvas straps, Tommy and Mark took the other, and they lowered him in. No one really wanted to sprinkle any dirt on to the coffin. They couldn't quite run to that.

It started to rain. Mark closed his book and everyone was relieved to hear 'In the Name of the Father ...' Everyone stood around for a second. It wasn't like you could go up to anyone and shake their hand and commiserate, and there was no piss-up planned.

'Well, I'm gooin' back to the fuggin car,' said Kevin loudly. 'I'm not sirrin round 'ere gerrin pissed on.' He scowled and wheeled himself off between the tombstones to the road. Mark quickly divested himself and put the bundle in his black bag. Mrs O, it was arranged, would get a lift back with the obliging Killingworth to her sister's house in Handsworth, where she had been staying since the scandal. All the soft toys and dead flowers had long since been gathered up by the bin men, and although the gates were no longer chained shut, the church was no longer a going concern.

'So that's the end of that, then,' said Tommy.

'Yeah,' said Mark. He seemed sad.

Tommy had been keeping Mark's big black umbrella for him, and now that the rain was starting to fall heavily, he raised it above their heads. It easily covered them both. They walked across the grass to where the cemetery's main path ran. It was a broad avenue of grey asphalt, lined with poplars, its elegance quite out of keeping with the neighbourhood, but perfect for a cemetery.

As they walked along, Mark sighed. He revealed that he would be leaving Birmingham soon for Rome. He had been given a place at the English College there, which was a bit like a classy Catholic university.

'Fuck, I've heard of that place,' said Tommy. 'How'd you get in there?'

'Oh, I used to have quite interesting Latin e-mail discussions with a fellow at the Oratory in London, and he put my name forward. I just heard I'd been accepted a few days ago. I just got my computer back from the police the other day, I had a stack of old electronic mail.'

'Fuck, that's great! Rome, wow! I did a Lazio game there once, great city. Beats this shithole anyway. What? What's wrong?'

'Ah, I never wanted to go away. This is my home, this is my place. I had my flock here.'

'Pretty mangy bunch, though. Your flock would not reach EU standards.'

Mark looked at him disapprovingly for a second, then relaxed. 'Yeah, well, now I feel I'm going 'cos I have to. Mud sticks, Tommy. I'll never be accepted round here again. Or at least not for a long time. But you know what the worst thing is? All the time I was there, me and Father Kelly would hear each other's confessions. And he never said a thing about, y'know ... *longings* or anything. Not a peep about those boys and all the stuff he did. Remember when I got nicked after the Blues game in January? You know why I was so mad? Because I knew I would have to tell him in my confession. Remember when I got cross with you?'

'Well, I think it's a bit naïve to think he'd implicate himself like that, even with the protection of the confessional. It's just not that kind of a world any more.'

Mark sighed. He knew he'd have a hard time coming to terms with that betrayal. 'Anyway, Father Ignatius says it's a good move. Fresh start.'

'Yeah, I reckon it is. Will you take the Morris?'

'Maybe. I fancied going down on the Triumph, though, you know, just me and my laptop. Motorbikes and laptops – the only way to go.'

'Oh.' *Shit. I'd better get used to the idea, though. Letting go of that bike.*

'Depends on the weather, of course,' said Tommy.

'Right,' said Mark.

They were the only people in the whole cemetery, the two old friends, tall figures in black walking together under the umbrella.

'What about here, though — can you walk the streets?'

'Oh, it's OK. Just very quiet. Mrs O's not coming back, we don't need a housekeeper now. But she wanted to apologise for something that was in the paper. She said she was "quoted out of context".'

Tommy smirked.

'Carol says she still loves me, though.'

'Carol? Oh, her! The girl with the language?' Tommy was profoundly touched. 'She was great, I loved listening to her. Her words were like ... little gifts.'

'Yeah.' They paused and walked on in silence for a bit, listening to the rain drumming.

'How's work?' asked Mark.

'Work's OK. Another afternoon off today, but what the hell. It's work.'

'And how's Melissa?'

'Oh, great, great. We've got her friend staying at the moment, Fiona. Mel's looking after her — she left her boyfriend. I thought she was a pain in the arse but it turns out she's quite nice. You never know with people, do you? Until you know people. I think Mel's enjoying it. She says hello.'

'So, what was all this stuff about you doing the Villa game? I never saw it but I kept hearing people say you made a big mistake or something. Sounds very suspicious, Tommy boy.'

'Yeah, well,' said Tommy. 'It was. Very dodgy. I gave a penalty that never was.'

Mark raised an eyebrow, but kept on walking. He'd heard worse.

'I just ... I just didn't want to see Villa go out. You know what they're like, always cocking it up. I just thought they deserved a second chance. And they took it! Won two—one in extra time. It was kind of a spontaneous thing, but no one's really said anything about it. No one who matters anyway. The FA don't quite know what to do with me. I think it was so soon after getting me back that they had to forgive me.'

Mark laughed. 'I take that back about mud sticking, then.'

They walked on. The tree-lined avenue stretched out before them and behind.

'So anyway,' said Father Mark, 'the FA Cup Final, eh? D'you reckon you can get me a ticket, then?'

Tommy laughed. 'Yeah, I don't see why not. Let me see what I can do.'

# Shoutouts and big thanks to:

Steve B, in on the ground floor, for transglobal encouragement, e-mail attention, big laughs and for being a cool critic – hope you got 90 minutes worth; ditto Simon P, editor, man-with-plan, and loot provider – double thanks for taking a chance, on this one and the next, you make it easy; Professor Boaz, for wading thru a script unpaid and comments – does it get any grander than ninety grand?; Agent Antony who got off his Hog and milked it, all power to the Yamaha machine; Natasha, Katie and Diana; Anna-Maria, Neil, Ian and Chainsaw Lynn; other helpers in my wanderings in the winter of 1996, Malcolm & Daire deep in Bloomsbury, Tim, John, Dan, Teresa & Bill in Brum, and the top-notch Jocks, especially Chris & Auds, nine-in-a-row champions of hospitality; real Tommo and real Sumo for tickets, lager on demand and plenty of abuse; Lisa and Evan Solley for the free tree-house; other readers and supporters – Adam, Damian at Lanigan Barrow Bobbins, FT Henry, Jon Smith the Happy Chappy, Michael Bahn on Maui, baalhead Sam in Africa, Coz Pete, Portland Ben, SW1 Gaby, for keeping the pressure on just right; top ref Jim McLuskey in Ayrshire and main man Colin Downey at Lancaster Gate; Holte Enders in the Sky, yippee-aye-o, and all villa@mcc.ac.uk; and last and most, Spring Rain, for the Love that always goes one louder.

# REFEREES WANTED

Throughout the country local football depends on the services of keen, dedicated people who make a vast contribution to the national game as referees, enabling players to more easily enjoy their matches.

## CAN YOU HELP?
Every year more clubs are registered with The Football Association. There are more and more matches to which referees must be appointed.

## CAN YOU HELP?
If you have played the game at any level you will know how important it is to have a qualified referee present.

## CAN YOU HELP?
If you are physically fit, with good eyesight and are at least fourteen years of age and willing to attend a local course of instruction, in preparation for a straight forward examination.

## WILL YOU HELP?
If you are interested in accepting the challenge of refereeing local football matches.

## PLEASE CONTACT:–

**THE FOOTBALL ASSOCIATION 16 LANCASTER GATE, LONDON W2 3LW.** (Tel.: 0171–262 4542) quoting referee recruitment or your local County Football Association. Don't forget that today's top referees all started at this level.
This is the first rung on the ladder.